Unbecoming

Unbecoming

Rebecca Scherm

Viking

VIKING
Published by the Penguin Group
Penguin Group (USA) LLC
375 Hudson Street
New York, New York 10014

USA | Canada | UK | Ireland | Australia | New Zealand | India | South Africa | China
penguin.com
A Penguin Random House Company

First published by Viking Penguin, a member of Penguin Group (USA) LLC, 2015

ISBN 978-0-525-42750-6

Printed in the United States of America
1 3 5 7 9 10 8 6 4 2

Designed by Nancy Resnick

For Jon, my love,
and
for Katie, my accomplice

1
Paris

1

The first lie Grace had told Hanna was her name. "Bonjour, je m'appelle Julie," Grace had said. She'd been in Paris for only a month, and her French was still new and stiff. She'd chosen the name Julie because it was sweet and easy on the French tongue—much more so than Grace was. The best lies were the simplest and made the most sense, in the mind and in the mouth. These lies were the easiest to swallow.

Jacqueline, the boss, had shown Grace to her worktable, abutting Hanna's, and where to store her tools in the jars along the center crack, what she could borrow and what she would need to procure herself. Hanna had reached out to cover a jar of picks and pliers. "I don't share these," she'd said with a taut smile, like someone forced to apologize.

When Grace sat down on her spinning stool a few minutes later, Hanna asked where she was from. Grace was so obviously American.

"California," Grace said, because most people already had ideas about California. They didn't ask you to explain it to them. Grace hated lying, got no joy from it, and this was how she knew she wasn't pathological. But California satisfied people so easily, even in Paris. Garland, Tennessee, where Grace was really from, was a confusing answer that only led to more questions. "Tennessee?" Hanna might have started. "Elvis? *Péquenauds?*" Hillbillies? When Grace had lived in New York, everyone who asked her where she was from followed her answer with the same question: "What's *that* like?"

As if her journey from somewhere as tiny and undistinguished as Garland had required a laborious transformation. As if getting from Garland to New York City had been some kind of pilgrimage to the first world.

Grace had been in Paris for two years now, and she had been Julie from

California since her arrival. Her life was conducted entirely in French, another kind of disguise. She and Hanna seldom discussed anything deep in the past, and when the conversation took an unwelcome turn, they quickly righted themselves. Facing each other across their tables, they hunched over their antiques and talked of busted hinges and gouged veneer, not sorrow or worry, not home.

The boys would be paroled tomorrow, released from Lacombe and sent home to Garland with their families. It was three o'clock in Paris now, morning in Tennessee. Riley and Alls would be eating their last breakfast of powdered eggs and sausage patties, doughy-faced guards planted behind them. Grace had always imagined them together, but she'd begun to imagine their lives without her so long ago that she often forgot how little she really knew. She didn't know a thing about their lives anymore. She hadn't spoken to them in more than three years, since before they were arrested for robbing the Wynne House: three years of imagined sausage breakfasts.

He wouldn't come for her, she told herself. It had been too long.

Grace had often felt like two people, always at odds, but when the boys had gone to prison, one Grace had stopped her life's clock. Now it had begun to tick again. She had no control of Riley now, what he would do and where he would go, and these unknowns bred in her a private, shapeless dread. She'd left lies unleashed in Garland and now she couldn't mind them.

Riley and Alls were twenty years old when they were sentenced to eight years each in Lacombe. This was the minimum: it was their first offense, they were unarmed, and, more important to Judge Meyer, they were "not your typical criminals," and Riley's family was a *nice* family. The Grahams had lived in Garland for seven generations, and Alls benefitted from the association—as had Grace, when she'd been associated. Grace often thought that if Alls alone had been charged with the crime, he would not have gotten off as easy, and that if only Riley had been charged, he probably would have gotten off altogether. Greg had pled guilty too, but his parents had won him a plea bargain for turning in his friends. He was released in a year.

Grace had robbed the Wynne House too, and she could not go home again.

She remembered the moment—maybe it had lasted minutes or maybe days; she didn't remember—after the judge had handed down the eight-year sentence, but before she'd learned that they could be paroled in only three. Eight years had seemed an incredible length of time. Eight years was longer than she had known Riley. Eight years seemed long enough for everyone to forget.

She gave the birdcage's latch a final swipe with the chamois and called for Jacqueline. The filigree onion dome alone had taken her nine days to clean. The wire metalwork was so fine that from a distance, it might have been human hair. On the first day, she'd held the vacuum hose in her left hand and the hair dryer in her right, blowing off dust and sucking it up before it could land again. Then she'd spent more than a week swabbing the curlicues with dental tools wrapped in cotton and paintbrushes dipped in mineral spirits. This morning she'd finished scraping off centuries of songbird guano from the cage's floor. It wasn't a birdcage anymore, but a gilded aviary, *orientaliste*, late nineteenth century, nearly as tall as Grace was. Jacqueline would return it to the dealer who had purchased it from the flea market, and he would sell it for at least five thousand, maybe much more. Perhaps it would be wired for electricity and made into a chandelier. Maybe an orchid collector would use it to shield his best specimens from human hovering.

When Jacqueline emerged from her skinny office beneath the stairs, Grace stood apart from her work. She waited as her boss pulled a pair of white cotton gloves from the bin next to the tables. Jacqueline ran her gloved index finger lightly along the wires. She gently turned the latch on the door and bent close to listen to its movement. She craned to see the underside of the onion dome.

"Ça suffit," she said.

That was as approving as Jacqueline got. She did little restoration herself, only the most basic things—regluing a horn handle to a letter opener, or cleaning larger metalwork—and only what she could do while on the phone. Now she clacked over to Amaury's dark alcove, where he was slumped over an open watch. After decades in exactly that position, his shoulders had slid into his belly. Jacqueline reached for the watch, but Amaury grunted and swatted her hand away. He'd been at Zanuso et Filles the longest. He'd even worked for the original Zanuso, back when

Jacqueline and her sister were the *filles*. Jacqueline had neither the head nor the hands for antiques restoration, but she was the senior Zanuso now. Grace supposed that made her and Hanna the *filles*.

Hanna cleared her throat, eager for their boss's attention. Last week she'd begun a new project, and now she wanted to show off her progress.

"C'est parti," Jacqueline said, squeezing the bridge of her nose. "Yes, Hanna?"

"My beaded centerpiece is Czech, 1750 to 1770," Hanna said, though they all knew by now. "I will have it to the decade by the end of the week."

Hanna was sitting in front of the shared computer, clicking through the hundreds of photographs she'd taken of her project. The centerpiece was the size of a card table and divided into four quadrants, each containing beaded miniatures of flora and fauna: spring blossoms, a summer peach orchard, an autumn crop harvest, and a snowy thicket with white wool sheep and shepherdesses. The centerpiece had clearly once been exquisite, if silly. Grace imagined it as a diorama that some young countess had hired palace artists to build for her. The trees, their leaves made of cut silk, were as detailed as real bonsai.

"The materials," Hanna continued, "are linen and pinewood, glass, mica, copper, brass, steel, lead, tin, aluminum, beeswax, shellac, white lead, paper, and plaster of Paris. I have disassembled and numbered it into 832 parts, each corresponding to this diagram. You will see how the glass beads have been discolored by oil, no doubt applied by someone with limited knowledge of the period."

Jacqueline rolled her eyes. "Julie will help you with this one. It's a very big job."

"I don't want any help."

Jacqueline put her finger to her lips. "Until something else comes in for her to do, she will assist you."

"You'll have to measure all the old wires," Hanna said to Grace. "The new ones will be steel, which won't be historically correct, of course, but my primary objective is to preserve the integrity of the object's intention."

"Which is to be a centerpiece," Grace said.

"Precisely."

Hanna was Polish, thirty-four, twelve years older than Grace, whom she treated like an unexpected and unwanted little sister. Hanna was small and as thin as a young boy, with closely cropped blond hair and blond skin and pale gray eyes. Her crisp androgyny was so thorough that it sometimes distracted older Parisians, who wanted to peg her as one sex or the other before selling her a sandwich. "Sans fromage," Hanna would say. "Pardon?" they would respond, still looking for clues. "Sans fromage, pas de fromage," she would repeat, blinking, her frame as straight and pert as a parking meter. She wore silver-rimmed glasses and clothes only in shades of beige.

When Grace had started at Zanuso, she'd hoped that her humble beginnings would appeal to Hanna's arrogance, which had been obvious from the start. She'd thought maybe Hanna would help her, out of either pity or some sense of big-sister altruism. But Hanna had no such inclinations. She was one of six daughters of a rural Polish grocer and she hadn't seen her family in more than a decade. No one, Grace gathered, had ever helped Hanna do a goddamn thing. Grace and Hanna's friendship was an often crabby by-product of professional respect: Grace had done well at Zanuso without asking for help, and *that* Hanna noticed. Grace envied Hanna's unfiltered confidence, her clipped and precise judgments. Grace struggled to calculate the probable reactions to nearly everything she said before she said it, looking for risk and reward and hidden pits she might trip in. She'd never met a woman who cared so little about causing offense.

Now Grace pulled her stool around to Hanna's table, where a long row of wires was arranged by size. She pulled a ruler from Hanna's cup and saw Hanna flinch a little. She would have preferred that Grace use her own tools. Grace took the first of the hundred wires, set it against the ruler, and recorded the measurement on the list Hanna had laid out on a sheet of graph paper. Nineteen centimeters. She placed the wire back in the row, just to the left so she wouldn't accidentally measure it again, and picked up another. Eighteen and three-quarters centimeters.

Grace had met Riley when she was in sixth grade, just turned twelve. He was a year older. At her first middle school dance, he had plucked her from a gaggle of girls she wanted badly to impress, and she and Riley had swayed, arm's length apart, to the ballad over the loudspeaker. He'd invited her to his house for dinner, where Mrs. Graham gently chatted to Grace about school while her husband and four sons stripped three roast chickens in ten minutes. Riley, the youngest, was the worst, lunging for the last of the potatoes while Grace was still figuring out how to cut her chicken breast with her fork and not make so much noise against the plate. Mrs. Graham reached to still Riley's hand and suggested he save seconds for his friend before he helped himself to thirds. "Some chivalry, please," she had said. Grace had read the word in books, but she'd never heard anyone say it out loud.

Grace tried not to stare at her, but Mrs. Graham pulled at her attention whenever Grace looked away. Mrs. Graham was thin and tan and freckled, with sleepy green eyes that turned down slightly at the outside. She had a slow blink; Grace thought she could feel it herself, as though a light had briefly dimmed. Her cool, feathery brown hair curled under where it hit her collar. Grace admired the light shimmer on her high cheekbones, her sea-glass earrings, her low and tender voice. Her fingers were long and delicate, nails polished with a milky, translucent pink, knuckles unfairly swollen from arthritis. That Grace's own nails were bitten to the quick had never bothered her before.

At the end of the week, Riley had kissed her in the school hallway between bells, so quickly that she wondered later if she had imagined it. Within a month he had bought her a necklace, a gold dolphin on a thin chain, and pledged his love. She felt as if she were in the movies.

What she wouldn't give to see herself and Riley like that, from above— to watch a flickering reel of Riley, his hair still victory red (it hadn't yet begun to fade), pulling her toward him on the sweaty, squeaking floor of the gym. Had she been scared, excited, smug? She'd been just a child, and then she had entered a *we*. An *us*-ness. She and Riley had seemed cute to his parents and their teachers, something from *Our Gang*, but Riley had three older brothers and the precocity that came with them, and Grace had no one else.

Tomorrow, Riley and Alls would be released.

She felt as if she had been standing in a road at night, watching a car's distant headlights approaching so slowly that she had forever to step out of the way. Now the car was upon her, and still she had not moved. She imagined what tomorrow would look like: Riley's parents, or maybe just his father, going to pick him up at the prison. Dr. Graham would bring him a change of clothes. Riley had worn a thirty-two-thirty-two. Did he still? He would look different. He would be paler, less freckled, from lack of sun. And he would be older, of course. Twenty-three. She kept thinking of them as boys, but they weren't boys anymore.

Dr. Graham would bring Riley's old clothes, a pair of worn khakis and one of his paint-stained button-downs with holes in the elbows. *Here,* the bundle of clothes would say, *this is who you were and will be again.* Grace imagined Riley riding home in the passenger seat of the Grahams' ancient blue Mercedes wagon, the diesel loud enough to bring the neighbors to the windows. Everyone would know today was the day. Mrs. Graham would have made barbecue, probably pork shoulder. And Riley's brothers would be there. Grace didn't know if all three still lived in Garland, but they probably did. The Grahams belonged to Garland as much as Garland belonged to them. She imagined Riley excusing himself from the cookout and going inside to sit on his bed in his old bedroom, which would be his room again, at least for a while. She wondered if he would go upstairs, to the attic bedroom Mrs. Graham had made up for when Grace stayed over.

Where would Alls go tomorrow? Did his father still live in Garland? He would have no welcome-home party. She imagined Alls and his dad driving through Burger King on the way home, unless he went home with Riley. He would have, before, but that meant nothing. The line between before and after couldn't be sharper.

When people had read about the Wynne robbery as a footnote in a national newspaper, small-town folly picked up on the wire, they'd probably laughed or shaken their heads. *Listen to this one,* millions of people would have said over the breakfast table. But those stupid boys had been Grace's. She used to think she knew Riley so well, she could peel off his skin and slip it over hers and no one would ever be the wiser.

They had gone to prison because of her, really. Grace longed to tell someone what she had done. She'd never had friends, just Riley and now Hanna. Grace could have only one friend at a time. Any more and it became harder to keep track of how they knew her, what she had told them, which pieces went where.

She had not been in Garland the day of the Wynne robbery. She was already in Prague then, at a summer study abroad program. Riley had paid for her tuition and ticket; Grace didn't have that kind of money.

Grace had read of the robbery online the night it happened, on the home page of the *Albemarle Record*'s website: A young white male had entered the main house of the Josephus Wynne Historic Estate, in Garland, Tennessee, on Tuesday, June 2, between eight and ten in the morning, and locked the docent in an upstairs bedroom. The groundskeeper was found unconscious in the foyer; he was at Albemarle Hospital in critical condition.

She had not heard from Riley since the day before, but she knew he had done it. Four days later, he, Alls, and Greg were arrested in Tennessee. Greg was first, alone at his parents' cabin on Norris Lake. Hours later Alls and Riley were arrested at the boys' rental house on Orange Street, where Grace also had lived, until she went to Prague at the end of May. She was sure that Greg had turned them in.

She received just one call from the police, after the arrest. The front desk matron sent her son, a dull-eyed boy of about eleven, to knock on the door of Grace's shared dorm room. She followed him downstairs, her heart beating so heavily that her chest cramped.

The American detective asked if she knew why he was calling. She said she did. He asked her to tell him. She said that her boyfriend had been accused of robbing the Wynne House.

"You mean your husband," he said.

"Yes," she said. She and Riley had never told anyone they had married.

He asked when she had last communicated with Riley. "A few days ago," she said. "Five days. He e-mailed me, very normal, nothing strange. He said he was going to his friend's house, on Norris Lake. He couldn't have robbed the Wynne House."

"How did you find out about the robbery?"

"I read it in the paper," she said. "Online."

"You're reading the local paper while you're in Prague?"

"I've been homesick."

"You didn't talk to your husband at all after you heard about the robbery?"

She had not. She told the detective that she knew Riley wouldn't e-mail her from the lake. They always started drinking before they unhitched the boat, and they only dried out when it was time to drive home. Grace herself had just taken a trip to Kutná Hora, to the bone church underground, where the bones of fifty thousand people had been strung into altars and chandeliers by a half-blind monk. The bones belonged to victims of the Black Death and the Hussite Wars. That some idiot had stolen Josephus Wynne's old silverware didn't seem very important, she told the detective.

She shut up—too much.

He asked her half a dozen more questions, but they weren't difficult ones. Grace told him that he'd made a mistake, that Riley could not have done that. He has such a good life, she said. We're happy. He doesn't need money. His parents help him. And besides, she said, *I* would have known. He couldn't have kept anything like that from me. He tells me everything. Everything.

Perhaps the detective was a man whose own wife believed that he told her everything.

What the detective did not tell Grace, what she learned days later in the news, was that Riley, Alls, and Greg had already confessed. The detective was crossing off his to-do list. He'd needed nothing from her.

This was how she imagined the robbery: Riley slipping a sweaty five-dollar bill into the recommended donation box and smiling at the tiny old docent on duty, following her through the downstairs rooms as she recited footnotes of Tennessee history. Riley had been through the house half a dozen times over the years; they all had. The Wynne House was the closest and cheapest school field trip. But on a summer Tuesday, the place was dead.

He stopped hearing the docent's voice clearly, as though he were underwater. He followed her upstairs. Her legs, ninety and blue and veiny in her whitish stockings, shook less than his did. At the top of the stairs she turned back and moved her mouth, looked at him expectantly. A question? She had asked him a question.

"Yeah," he said. "Yes, ma'am." He hoped it was the right answer.

He followed her from room to room, nodding and scrawling gibberish in his notebook. Outside the door to the tiny windowless study, he rolled his notebook and stuck it and his pen in his baggy front pocket. She opened the door outward and he followed her inside. He pointed with a trembling finger at the tiny print over the toilet table.

"Can you tell me who the artist is who made that?"

"That one? I don't remember. Let me get a better look."

She stepped forward and peered at the signature, which he already knew to be indecipherable. He held his breath and tried to back quietly out of the room. The edge of the rug caught under his heel and he stumbled.

She turned around. "Are you all right, hon?"

He jerked his foot free and made for the door, slamming it behind him. He grabbed the ladder-back chair that sat next to the door and wedged the top rung under the doorknob. He breathed.

Now that she was safely penned, he could hear her voice leaking under the door. Not screaming. Asking. She was asking again, something; he didn't know what—just the sensation of her tinny voice from far away, like a house cat trapped in a basement.

He went downstairs and opened the front door. Alls and Greg came in quietly with scrunched-up nylon grocery bags and three pairs of gloves. They dispersed into the rooms, filling their bags with needlework samplers, old desk clocks, a silver-hilted hunting knife. They had a carefully made list of treasures: nothing large or cumbersome, nothing one of a kind. They did not expect the front door to open. A man they had never seen before stepped in with a garbage bag to empty the small wastebasket by the door. He was the groundskeeper, and he always came on Mondays, never Tuesdays. But here he was, seeing them.

The groundskeeper, who was past seventy, fell to the floor.

The boys grabbed the bags they had filled and fled.

Because the groundskeeper was too long returning to the mobile home that served as the Wynne House's office, where he was supposed to leave his keys, the administrator who worked there came out looking for him. She found him sprawled on the foyer floor, and then she heard the warbling cries of the docent, still locked in the windowless upstairs study.

The prosecutor later said that the boys had intended to fence the goods in New York, but they had not even left the state. Grace watched the headlines change from her concrete dorm room in Prague: NO SUSPECTS IN WYNNE HEIST; WITNESS SUFFERED STROKE AT SCENE; GROUNDSKEEPER'S CONDITION STILL CRITICAL. There was a police sketch from the docent's nearsighted description, but Grace was relieved to see that the drawing looked nothing like Riley. It could have been anyone, really.

Grace knew that Riley would worry about the groundskeeper. She could imagine him pacing, holding his fist against his mouth. That the man could die would have shaken Riley from his fantasy: the rakish glamour of a small-town antiques heist by a gang of wild boys, an intricate prank. But they had scared an old man to near-death. If he lived, he would surely identify them. But if he died, was that manslaughter? Could they call it murder, even? Grace imagined Riley's spinning thoughts as though they were her own.

She was right to be worried. When the police found a suspect in Gregory Kimbrough, twenty, of Garland, Greg's parents said that was impossible because he had been at the family cabin on Norris Lake for the past several days. There was one cell phone with network activity on the Wynne property at the time, the police told them, and it's yours.

Grace hadn't even known they could do that.

He'd probably been checking a sports score or something.

The police took the Kimbroughs into custody too, as the phone was technically theirs, and drove to the cabin with Greg's parents in the backseat. Mr. Kimbrough was a criminal defense attorney. Greg wouldn't have an opportunity to say anything without a lawyer present. At his parents' urging, Greg rolled like a puppy. Alls and Riley were arrested hours later.

Grace watched the Wynne case through the foggy pinhole of the *Albemarle Record* and its local correspondent's maddeningly elliptical reporting. Cy Helmers had been three years ahead of the boys in school and four ahead of her. He'd gone to Garland College and become the county paper's cub reporter when he graduated. He reported the Wynne heist as if he were above gossip, as if he couldn't stand to make his old schoolmates look worse than they already did.

The Czech front desk matron sent her son to fetch Grace twice more. No other student had received a phone call, and Grace felt conspicuous and exposed as she conducted these conversations, despite the fact that the woman spoke no English. There was a plastic window over the counter, through which students passing through the lobby could see her. Grace faced the wall.

The second phone call was from Grace's mother, whose very voice seemed to go pale when Grace said that no, she would not come back in time for the sentencing; no, she did not know when she would come back at all. Her mother, whose maternal passions were seldom if ever directed at Grace, now implored her: How could she just abandon Riley like this?

"Abandon *him?*" Grace was incredulous on the line. "The person I built my life on, the last decade and my entire future, the one and only person I can call mine"—this was a dig—"just committed a whole parade of felonies with his idiot friends. And you think I should come home to *support* him?" She was shaking when she finished. Her mother had little to say after that.

The third and last call was from Riley's father.

The boys had been released into their families' custody, awaiting sentencing. It was evening in Prague, morning in Tennessee, and Dr. Graham was calling from his office at the college.

"I think I understand," he began, "why you would not want to come back for this."

Grace had nothing to say. It had not occurred to her that he would call. "I can't believe this is happening," she said. A truth.

"Us too. And him. He may be having the hardest time believing it."

"I don't think he knew what he was really doing," she said. "He couldn't have. People make mistakes without realizing—one bad decision can just carry you away. And the three of them together. You know."

"We should have checked him more," Dr. Graham said quietly. "I guess you seemed to keep him in line enough." He laughed, a little drily. "Grace, you know we love you as our daughter."

They had said this for years: not *like a* daughter but *as our* daughter, and Grace had bloomed under those words and their power to make her one of them. But it was Dr. Graham calling her, not Mrs. Graham, and he was calling her from his office, not from their home.

Grace remembered shooting skeet with the Grahams when she was fifteen, her first time. She had done well, as well as Riley and his brothers, and Dr. Graham had laughed with surprise and delight. "Goddammit, son," he had said to Riley. "You'll never do better."

"If there's anything you know that could help him," he said now, "anything at all—"

"I'm sorry you're going through this," Grace said.

Grace did not call. She did not write. Just before they went to Lacombe, she received a single letter from Garland.

Dear Grace,

Love,
  Riley

She never knew whether to read it as an indictment of her silence or a promise of his.

What he must think of her, what his family must think of her—what they must say. She hated to think about it. She worried less about what Alls thought of her now. He had known long before Riley how bad Grace could really be.

2

G race knew that a parolee had a keeper and a leash. They didn't know where she was; they couldn't. She *knew* these things, but that night, as she twisted under her sheet, her brain refused them. She took a sleeping pill at two but failed to submit. The night brain knew every trick.

What did she think, that Riley would murder her? That he was tracking her so he could throw lye in her face? Hanna had told her that story, from New York half a century ago. A man, Burt Pugach, had hired hit men to throw lye into the face of Linda Riss, his girlfriend, after she told him she wouldn't see him anymore. He told her, "If I can't have you, no one else will have you, and when I get through with you, no one else will want you." He went to prison for fourteen years, and he wrote her thousands of letters. He had blinded her in one eye. When he was released from prison, she married him.

It was the happy ending that most troubled Grace.

Tomorrow they'll be out, the night brain taunted her. She took another pill at four and begged for defeat. She went down at six and slept through her alarm.

When Grace got to work the next morning, Jacqueline was on the phone in her office, picking at her cuticles and blowing smoke from the side of her mouth, her door wide open. Amaury was already stooped in his dark corner, cooing at the pocket watch under his yellow lamplight. His table was as far as possible from the basement studio's high windows and the meager sunlight they let in from the narrow street. As far as Grace could tell, he lived his life underground: in this basement, on the metro, and in his basement apartment in Montreuil. Grace had seen him getting off the metro in the morning, blinking unhappily in the sun.

Hanna had tied a white smock over her clothes. She'd lined up Grace's worktable end-to-end with the two extra tables that were left over from better times, when there had been more work and more staff. Grace counted ten bowls and containers arranged along the tables, largest to smallest.

"Tu es en retard," Hanna scolded her. Hanna was never late, and her hands were never still. Whenever she and Grace had lunch together, Hanna bobbed her knee as she ate, always impatient to get back to work. "Are you ready?"

"As ever," Grace said, tying a smock over her own clothes.

"I didn't want to start and then have to stop again to explain it to you."

"Sorry to keep you waiting," Grace said. "The train was late."

"We're cleaning the beads. As you know, they've discolored from someone's shortsighted application of oil to their surface. But, as with hair spray or nail polish, this has only damaged them." She looked at Grace from the side, through the gap between her face and her eyeglasses, and Grace ran her thumb over her own clear-polished fingernails.

She and Hanna seldom worked on a project together. Until recently, there had been enough to do so that they each stayed late, piecing parts back together and buffing out scratches in satisfying silence. But Grace hadn't gotten anything after the birdcage, and she knew to worry. Jobs like this one were few and far between, and without a visa? She'd gotten lucky. If she were let go, she'd be a hotel maid again.

Hanna raised her chin toward the repurposed chafing dish at the end of the table. "Container one," she said. Hundreds of tiny dark beads were sunk in turpentine like coffee grounds, the dirty oil clouding around them. "Those have been soaking overnight."

"How late were you here?" Grace asked. Hanna's eyes were as red rimmed as her own.

"One, maybe half past," Hanna said. "Use the ceramic spoon to stir them around a bit, very gently, not breaking a single one. Then you will gently sieve them out, about fifty at a time, into container two." She pointed to the large metal mixing bowl next to the chafing dish. "Move the beads into the clean turpentine, clean the sieve, and begin again, moving the beads to container three. Four through six contain a castile soap solution, and seven through ten are water. There will be at least a dozen batches of beads like this to move through the system."

Hanna looked at Grace as though she were leaving her child in Grace's care. "I know I don't have to tell you how vital it is that you clean the sieve between each container, and especially between each solution." Her pale eyes glowed brighter against the bloodshot. "Yes?"

Jacqueline trusted Grace to regild and re-leaf holy relics. Once, she had called Grace her "little spider," and Grace, disturbed by the comparison, turned to Hanna to laugh about it and found her pink with jealousy. It didn't matter that neither Grace nor Hanna had any great respect for Jacqueline—Hanna still needed to be the best.

"Yes," Grace said now, smoothing her flyaways.

"I'll perform the hand cleaning," Hanna said. Her own table was set with a paper-lined tray of paintbrushes and magnifiers arranged like dental tools. "I'll begin when you make it to container seven. Until then, I will be constructing a sheep out of wool to replace this one with the cracked neck." She gave a dainty smile, showing her small, square teeth, and opened her palm to reveal what looked like a balled-up tissue held in a sweaty hand for two hundred years. The sheep's barely discernible ears were suggestions cut from felt, smashed flat. Only two legs remained, scabby sticks protruding from dirty gray stuffing.

"Sad little fellow," Hanna said, not concealing her glee. "No use rehabbing him. I'll have to start from scratch!"

Grace bent over the chafing dish of turpentine. The smell reminded her of Riley, but she hardly needed reminding. The *Record* had reported that he had been drawing some in prison, what Cy Helmers had called "charcoal lines and squiggles." Grace had winced at "squiggles," but Cy Helmers hadn't meant to become an art critic. Grace wished that she could see the drawings herself; they would help her understand Riley's state of mind. What kinds of squiggles? Anxious like Twombly's, dancing and light like Hockney's swimming pools, or lightless and grim like Fautrier's? Grace didn't know whether to blame herself or Riley for the fact that she could think of his artwork only in terms of copies, of either real artists or real objects or real life—what was the difference? But she blamed Cy Helmers for his poor descriptive abilities. "Squiggles" could mean anything.

That the drawings were at all abstract was at first a wonder to Grace. Riley had always been an insistent realist, painting the historic buildings around town. His father used to refer to their house as the Garland

Visitor's Bureau. Grace had tried to push him toward abstraction, or at least pull him away from Garland, to no avail. Maybe he'd changed his style because in prison there were no historic homes to observe. More likely, he didn't want to show off anymore.

He'd never painted his family's own house. He said it was too familiar. His family's house was far more special to her than it was to him, she knew.

Grace was not a Garland native. She'd been born in Louisville, Kentucky. Her mother was eighteen, her father nineteen. They'd met at a party after a Van Halen concert, Grace's father once told her, but such details were rare. Her parents were unwilling to discuss anything before their marriage, before Garland, as though Grace had been a witness they'd expected to remain silent.

Her father's parents had taken care of her until she was three, while her father was in college and her mother was somewhere else. She'd never been told where.

After that, Grace lived for varying stretches, some repeating, in North Carolina with her aunt Regina and her kids; in Smyrna with her father, after he dropped out of Tennessee State and took a job at the Nissan plant; in Paducah, Kentucky, with her mother and two other young women who, it turned out, were not willing to babysit their roommate's kid when she was kept late at work; in Memphis, briefly, when her father was married to a woman named Irene who had bald eyebrows and made Grace spaghetti sandwiches before her bartending shifts; outside Chattanooga with her mother and an older man named Alan, who wore collared shirts tucked into chinos every day and had two grown children who did not seem to like Grace or her mother very much; and in Ocean City, Maryland, where Grace's mother was waitressing when Grace's father came up for the season to try to talk to her and make things right.

Her father came in June, and by August, Grace's mother was pregnant. Her parents married and, together for the first time, they all marched back south to Garland. Grace was nine. She started fourth grade two weeks late and newly legitimate. When the teacher introduced her, Grace looked out from under her dark bangs and felt a thrill that not one of them knew who she had ever been before.

Grace's family moved into a small white-sided ranch house behind the grocery store. Her mother planted white begonias in circles around the two small trees in the yard, and her father surrounded them with dyed-red mulch, which Grace noticed as soon as she noticed that the people in Garland's nicer neighborhoods used mulch that was brown or black.

The house was nearly silent at first. The three of them had no idea how to interact. Any two people could be talking in a room, but when the third entered, the conversation would fall apart, all parties self-conscious and suddenly overwhelmed. Grace had always read a lot, and she'd seen so many adult faces slacken with relief when they found her engrossed in a book or a magazine, as though she had *un*intentionally absented herself from whatever forgotten carpool pickup line or tense phone call was in the background. Now she disappeared into her books again, hoping to ease the pressure on her parents, who even she could see were struggling to play the roles they had finally submitted to. She'd spent long stretches of her childhood in fictional worlds, and trapped in this new and uneasy diorama, what was real and what wasn't began to seem uncertain. When Grace found a box of her father's secret detritus in the basement that included several photos of Irene, she was relieved to see that she had not imagined that whole episode, among others.

Then the twins were born, identical colicky boys who absorbed her parents in family life completely. Her mother and father adored Aiden and Dryden—their names, aspirational and slant rhymed, embarrassed her before she knew why—with such obvious passion, imagining their thoughts and desires and fears before the boys could speak them. Her parents loved their baby boys in a way that even they had not expected. Grace had been practice for them, she concluded. She hadn't realized she was lonely until she began to understand that other people were not. Then she met Riley, and he brought her home to the Grahams.

The Grahams lived in a pale-blue-painted brick house on Heathcliff with a giant hemlock tree in the front yard. The tree was at least three stories tall, though it looked like ten when Grace and Riley were children. They climbed up the sap-sticky branches as if these were spiral stairs in an empty tower, until they got so high up the slender trunk that they could see the single green flipper at the bottom of the Monahans' leaf-addled swimming pool, they could peer into the skylight in the Wagners' bathroom, and they could feel the trunk swaying beneath them. Grace would wrap her body tightly around it, a death grip of spindly arms, looking out and looking over, never down. And then Riley would climb a little higher.

They kissed in the tree and on the rooftops, shortcut around the neighborhood by hopping from eave to eave. They lay out on the asphalt shingles in the summer, their fingers crooked in each other's waistbands, making out and burning in the sun. They skinny-dipped in the Monahans' swimming pool when the Monahans went on vacation and paid Riley five dollars a day to take care of their cats. Grace slept at home but otherwise lived at the Grahams' as best she could. Often their neighbors would forget that she didn't live there. She babysat their children and patronized their lemonade stands, and everywhere Riley was, she was too.

Even now, Grace could go back into these memories so completely that she was shocked when a noise, a voice, a heel on the pavement shook her out of the dream.

Garland had one high school and one art teacher. Mr. Milburn thought himself a backwoods talent scout, shaping young genius for what he called "the big leagues." "Don't forget us when you're famous!" he crowed to Riley, clutching his forearm. Riley was a splendid draftsman who could draw from life in the way that seems like magic to those who can't: still lifes of softening bananas with frayed stems and collapsing brown bruises, used tissues, messy garages, sleeping grandparents. She tried not to envy him. Grace had no talents of her own, but her attachment to Riley was its own kind of talent, wasn't it? She had a gift for pleasing him, and so his talent seemed to extend to her, like warmth.

Since the arrest, Grace had remade her life alone, administering now to objects: teapots too delicate for the stove, chairs too fragile to sit in. At night she went home to the far reaches of Bagnolet. She got off the metro at Gallieni, the end of the line, and picked up a bus to the end of its line. From there it was a kilometer up and around the hill to her flat. She rented a row house's upstairs floor, a small bedroom and bath, from an Austrian nurse in her sixties. Mme Freindametz claimed to feel more at home in the hospital where she worked. She had a little bunk, she'd explained to Grace, in the wing for night nurses.

Mme Freindametz kept no family photos in the house and almost no personal effects, except for an embroidered pillow that looked too loved to be anything but a family heirloom, and one wooden spoon so warped and burnt that it surely would have been tossed out long ago if it didn't have sentimental value. Grace was careful not to touch these things in front of Mme Freindametz. But Grace had few effects from her old life anymore, and so sometimes she would run her fingers down the length of the spoon's handle, ease her thumbnail into the split in the wood, and almost feel like it meant something to her.

At four o'clock, the turpentine in the chafing dish had turned the color of olive brine. The liquid lightened from bowl to bowl as the solution became less polluted, and the two rightmost bowls were clear of even the slightest film. She laid the first four batches of beads out on linen towels to dry. It was ten o'clock in the morning in Garland. Their day had only begun.

Grace had not spoken to anyone in her family since her mother's single phone call to Prague more than three years ago. She sent them e-mails every couple of months so her parents would have enough to say should anyone ask after Grace in the grocery store. Grace could never tell her mother where she really was. The chain back to Riley was always too short. In Grace's e-mails, she lived in Melbourne, Australia, and worked as a marketing assistant for a nylon luggage company. Travel to Garland was much too expensive, a handy excuse for them and for anyone who asked when they would next see their daughter, but Australia was also white and so, to them, *safe*, preventing inquiries about sex slavery, civil war, or drinking water.

Believing her was their choice. She had given them a gift in tidily constructing a busy, happy life on the other side of the world. Her parents could have pressed her about phone cards and webcams, but they didn't.

For a while after the boys' arrests, Grace's mother had sent regular updates on Riley's case. Grace was confused by this interest, which seemed out of nowhere. Her parents had never paid any special attention to Riley before, or even to her. But when Riley was sentenced and still Grace did not come home, did not write or call the Grahams, and ignored any mention of Riley in her responses to her mother's e-mails, their exchanges made the necessary transition into small talk. Grace knew they thought she was heartless.

Privately, she had scoured the web for information about the case. She checked in every day without fail, like taking a pill. Just once, and quickly, to get it over with. The compulsion didn't make any sense, she knew; there was nothing in her life to threaten anymore. She had no relationships to protect, no real career or reputation. And if some malevolent ghost from her past did discover her here in Paris, it wouldn't be Riley or Alls—it would be police about the painting; or Wyss, the collector or whatever he was, also about the painting; or the thug Wyss had sent to beat her up the first time. But Grace was never as afraid of the police or Wyss as she was of Riley and Alls, which was to say she was never as afraid of getting hurt as she was of having to look into the eyes of those she'd already hurt so much.

For obsession to be managed, Grace had learned, the object must be shrunk to a manageable size and enclosed within a manageable shape. Vast, hovering clouds must be packed into a small, hard mass or they would smother you. Now she didn't think about Mrs. Graham anymore, her bridal portrait with magnolias at the waist. She didn't think about Wyss's man and his bolt cutters, and she didn't think about where the painting was, and she didn't think about what her life should have been— pregnant in America with a Volvo and health insurance—instead of this one, and she didn't think of Alls at all. She had packed it all into one tiny box, and that box was checking the *Albemarle Record* every day, once a day, just quickly, to make sure there was no news from her old life that might show up in her new one.

The boys hadn't ever spoken to the press, not even to the *Record*. They could, though, and at any time. She could never stop checking up on them. She'd had to accept that the *Record* would report, dutifully but mildly, on the Wynne robbery for the rest of their lives. Obituaries now included achievements like "longtime donor to the Josephus Wynne Historic Es- tate, which was robbed in 2009." These mentions, though frequent, were benign. When there was no mention at all, she was rewarded with an ir- rational, temporary feeling of safety.

And then, one day in June, there it was: Riley Graham and Allston Hughes, the convicted robbers of the Josephus Wynne Historic Estate, would be released on parole, barring incident or compelling objection, on August 10. She thought she had touched bottom in her fear, and now it opened up beneath her.

A few days after the boys' parole was announced, Grace received an e-mail from her mother that broke their unspoken agreement.

Riley is going to get paroled soon. I didn't know when/if to tell
you but his mom told me at mass last week. She said he wants
to go back to school but not at GC. He has been drawing but is
being very private about it. They are probably relieved about
that. That poor family doesn't need any more attention.

Poor family left a messy sting. She still felt she was one of the Grahams,
though of course she had forsaken that privilege, and she resented her
mother's simple pity for them. But perhaps this was her mother's nasty
secret smirk: The Grahams were the poor family now.

The only objection to the parole came from the groundskeeper's family. Wallace Cummins had died in 2010 after a second stroke, at the age of
seventy-three. His obituary lauded him for his decades of service to the
Josephus Wynne Historic Estate, but made no mention, for once, of the attempted robbery of the estate the year before. But shortly before the parole
hearing, Wallace's daughter told WTQT that her father was murdered.
"That first stroke led directly to the second," she said. "My dad was killed
by criminals as surely as if they'd pulled a trigger." She did not want the
boys released on parole. She did not want them "loose."

They were out by now; Grace knew it.

At five o'clock, she left the beads and walked the nine circuitous blocks
to the nearest Internet café, one of the last remaining now that everyone
else had smartphones, and bought ten minutes.

She'd braced herself for a mention on parole day. She held her breath
as she waited for the page to load, but the *Record*'s top story was only the
ongoing debate over the condemnation of the public pool. She began to
type their names into the search field, and as she was typing, the page
reloaded itself. The front page changed.

A photograph.

The boys were coming out of Lacombe together. She could see Riley's
mother close behind and, she thought, Alls's father, but the face was
blurry. Alls hated his father.

What if she didn't recognize them, if they had changed that much? She
would see a man in a shop or in the park and wonder. The last picture
she had seen was from the first day of their prison terms. A local photographer had been waiting at the gates to watch them go in.

Now she was shocked at the sight of them. Riley was a man now. His hair was long again, faded to rust, and most of the curl had fallen out so that it fell in lank waves over his ears. It was dirty, maybe. His cheekbones were higher, his jaw sharper, his snub nose not so snubbed. He had two creases between his eyes, just like the lines his mother had called her "elevens." His eyes were down; she couldn't see them at all. She looked for his birthmark, a thumbprint under his jaw, but she couldn't find it in the shadows. He looked so much older, more than three years older.

Alls was behind, biting his lip as if to hold his tongue. She remembered his teeth knocking against hers and swallowed.

Alls was still Alls. Riley was Riley, but not.

In the reflection of the computer screen, Grace saw a boy coming over to her, throwing his dish towel over his shoulder the way she'd seen Alls do a hundred times in the kitchen on Orange Street, and she felt the wheels on her rolling stool skate out from under her. She grabbed the edge of the desk to keep from going down.

"Ça va?" the boy asked her.

She turned around. His eyes were blank, his mouth empty and concerned, and he didn't look like Alls at all.

"Ça va," she said.

She stared at the photograph, hovering over every detail. Riley had filled out in his arms and chest, but his face was thinner. His freckles hadn't faded—if anything, they seemed darker on his pale skin. She didn't know the shirt he was wearing. It was too tight, stretching across his chest and pulling at the buttons. His hands looked so familiar to her that her own hands shook. She couldn't help feeling that the gaze he was avoiding was hers.

Alls looked calm, smooth across his dark brow. He looked up at the camera, right at her from amber eyes. Maybe his release had brought him relief. It should, shouldn't it? But Grace better understood the lines between Riley's eyes, the incredible fatigue of the unknown.

Paris had been a mistake, she knew now. She should have gone to Tokyo or Mumbai. Someday, *someone* would see her. She'd had a scare once, at a wine bar almost two years before. She was on a date. Now the idea of a date was ridiculous to her—watching some poor boy imagine that *she* could make him happy!—but at the time she had been in Paris only a few months, and she believed she could fully become her new self.

Grace had been in Europe for almost a year then. She had stayed in Prague after the summer program. She was terrified to travel, as though she were invisible only as long as she was still. After they were sentenced in August she left for Berlin.

She worked any job she could scare up, from washing dishes and cleaning hotel rooms to modeling for expat artists. She was surprised at how resourceful she was, how quickly desperation eradicated her timidity, her fear. An antiques dealer whose small shop Grace cleaned at night had begun to train her in making minor repairs when her assistant disappeared. But Berlin, though big and anonymous, was lousy with New Yorkers, especially the kind of artsy twentysomethings who'd been her classmates during her brief time in New York. She already feared running into someone she'd known. She didn't want to be Grace anymore, even for five minutes.

She changed her name and bleached her hair, hoping this would also change her on the inside. She left for Paris. *Then practice losing farther, losing faster.* She kept a copy of the Bishop poem tucked into her passport, mocking the drama of her own loss. If she couldn't find Grace, no one else could either.

But she wanted a life, however small it would have to be. A bartender from Melun asked her to dinner one afternoon while she was reading in the Jardin du Luxembourg. He was deferential and friendly, and though Grace's French was still a bit tangled, he seemed uninterested in her American past. They had dinner and a glass of wine, and when they parted ways at the metro, Grace was euphoric to have done it—a date! Even lying to a perfect stranger could provide a sense of intimacy, if it presented the very limit of contact. She met him again four days later for dinner at Racines, and it was there that she saw Len Schrader, the father of her college roommate in New York, Kendall Schrader. She'd met the Schrader parents just twice, but she was almost certain.

She felt as if she'd seen a character from her nightmares. But why? Len Schrader was so far removed from Garland, and Grace looked so different—paler, thinner, another blonde dressed all in black. He would not recognize the college freshman from Tennessee. But if he did, he might come over to her table. He might say, "Kendi's friend? I thought that was you!" He might ask her questions about what she was doing there, and even if she answered them in the same vague way that she had for her date, Len Schrader would tell her what his daughters were up to these days, even if she didn't ask. He might remember that Grace had left NYU, and his daughter's life, quite abruptly.

Her date would ask why he had called her Grace. And hadn't she said she was from California? And Len Schrader might tell his daughter he'd seen Grace in France, and Kendall might wonder, again, what had become of Grace, and that boyfriend of hers. . . .

And on, and on.

So Grace had smiled at her date and suggested that maybe they weren't that hungry after all, maybe they should go, and then she sneaked out the side door like a psychopath or a sure thing, depending on his expectations. He followed her out and she went home with him. How strange it was to feel safe only with strangers! She had sex with the bartender, trying to fully participate in this made-up life she was so determined to have, and shared a cigarette in his kitchen under a yellow light. Grace didn't smoke, but Julie did.

Two weeks later, the bartender showed up near the Clignancourt metro. Grace was on her way home, and she saw him there on the sidewalk, smoking a cigarette and talking on his cell phone. She hadn't given her number. She had slipped out of his apartment while he slept.

"What are you doing here?" she demanded.

He'd laughed, a little meanly. "My sister lives here," he said, nodding toward the building next door. "I'm waiting for her to come down."

At first, she hadn't believed him. She understood that she was paranoid, but that didn't mean she held the cure. Her new life would have to be very small indeed.

11
Garland

3

A *bad apple.* Grace had first noticed her mother say it about the tabby kitten Grace's father had brought home when they'd first moved to Garland. He'd found it mewing behind the Dumpsters at his work. "There's coolant around there," he told Grace's mother when he brought the kitten home.

"He probably already drank some of it," Grace's mother said.

"Well," her father said, which was how they agreed to disagree.

Grace named the kitten Skyler—"How about Tigger?" her mother had asked—and watched it grow, under their haphazard care, into a mean adolescent who would beg to be petted, bumping his head against their legs, and then promptly sink his fangs into the wrist or fleshy palm of whoever fell for it and tried to show him affection.

"That cat is a bad apple," Grace's mother said. "He can't help it; he's just rotten."

That Skyler could not help his nature kept Grace tender toward him for longer than her parents were. Then her cousin, a boy of eighteen, went to jail for stealing credit cards out of the neighbors' mail.

"He's just a bad apple," Grace's pregnant mother said, leaning over the sink to wash her hands. She was a home health aide and always washing her hands of something. "He stole from his own mother. You know, I caught him once, going through her drawers."

"You got to drop that," her father said. "He wasn't any older than Grace is when all that happened."

Her mother raised her eyebrows. *Well.* "It isn't Regina's fault. They did their best."

Her father took the cat—he wasn't referred to by name once he was gone—to the shelter after he bit Grace's ankle, unprovoked. Grace's mother was nearly due; they couldn't have him attacking the babies.

In the grotesque chaos that followed the twins' birth, Grace had assumed there was simply not enough love to go around, and the babies needed all of it. Fair enough. But the more attention her parents gave them, the more attention the suckling tantrum machines demanded. Witnessing her parents' transformation into frazzled, intent, TV-censoring caretakers, Grace found herself evilly hoping that one of the twins would turn out to be a bad apple. She thought they were both rotten—their sopping faces, their gaping, toothless screams, their hanging drool, their fountains of diarrhea, their rashes and allergies and insomnia and sudden, terrifying squalls.

"We didn't think we'd have more children," Grace's mother said to a neighbor, who beamed back, nodding.

One afternoon, Grace was hiding out in the basement, where it was quiet, reading a pile of old *Life* magazines that a neighbor had thrown out the week before, when the idea, terrible and unthinkable, crept up her shoulder like a spider: She was the bad apple. That was why her mother didn't act right toward her, not the way she acted with the twins. It wasn't Grace's fault that she was a bad apple. It wasn't anyone's fault, but it did explain a lot of her feelings, her secret thoughts. Being rotten was like being poor, but in your heart. Nothing to be done. You get what you get and you don't get upset.

And she had done wretched things. That year, Grace had stolen a hundred dollars from a classmate, Deanna Passerini. Grace loathed Deanna, who would grab whatever she wanted from her classmates' hands and lunchboxes: markers, pretzels, colored-tissue stained-glass art projects. "You're going to break it!" someone screamed at Deanna almost every day. On her birthday, Deanna came to school brandishing a card from her aunt in Massachusetts. The card held a hundred-dollar bill, which she whipped around for all to see. How much money a hundred dollars was to a ten-year-old—a thousand! A million! That anyone would give horrible, grubby, grabby Deanna a hundred dollars seemed unholy, as if the universe had rewarded her for being so repulsive. Deanna said she was going to use the money to buy a crystal sculpture of a horse she'd seen at the mall. Grace knew she would have broken the horse right there in the store.

And then she thought: I'll show you how to take something, Deanna P. You don't *grab* it.

After lunch, when they all had bathroom break, Grace went into the stall next to Deanna's. The four stalls were full, and a few other girls were crowded around the two sinks, washing and chattering and cranking the paper-towel dispenser. Deanna had put her new troll doll, a half-eaten bag of chips, her list of spelling words, and her birthday card right on the bathroom floor. Grace sat on the toilet with her pants up, waiting, and when she saw Deanna stand and turn to flush, she took the card. She stuck it in the waistband of her jeans, in the back, and pulled her shirt over it.

She was at the sink when Deanna began to scream. Grace held up her empty hands, and Deanna immediately blamed Amber White, because Amber White was poor and dirty and often in trouble for misbehaving in some humiliating way—cussing obliviously or picking at her nipples through her shirt during reading circle. Grace thought then that another line on Amber's rap sheet wouldn't matter. Amber pushed Deanna, who roared in rage that Amber had *touched* her. Grace went to get the teacher and reported the theft.

Deanna got in trouble with her parents for taking the money to school. Amber couldn't produce the money and their teacher let the matter drop, but the other children tormented her with new vigor. Deanna, on the other hand, ascended in her victimhood. And while Grace had never seriously considered coming forward, once she saw how much further someone like Amber could fall, she knew she would never confess.

But she didn't know what to do with the money. She worried that it would incriminate her. She rolled the hundred in a couple of one-dollar bills and dropped it in the Salvation Army donation box just before Christmas, skinny Santa clanging the bell next to it. He smiled at her.

She remembered Skyler, probably gassed at the shelter, with a pang of commiseration. They may not have been able to change their natures, but she could hide hers. She would have to.

In middle school, Deanna began to straighten her hair and go to the tanning bed. Amber White's chest grew too big, too fast. Grace met Riley.

You could be bad and still be a good girl, if you tried hard enough. She hadn't tried hard enough before.

"Kids are shits," Riley said when she told him about stealing Deanna's birthday money. "You can't beat yourself up for that stuff." They were lying face-to-face on his family's trampoline, deep in the backyard under the shade trees, where it was cooler. Still, their hair stuck to their damp foreheads and they wiped trails of sweat from around each other's nostrils.

Grace cried. Stealing Deanna's hundred-dollar bill was the worst thing she'd ever done, and the worst thing she'd ever do, *ever*. Whenever she saw Amber at school, even now, two years later, she felt horrible all over again. Grace didn't even know the girl who'd stolen that money. She couldn't even fathom her.

"I killed a finch with a slingshot once," Riley said. "Me and Alls shot the nest out of a tree because we wanted to see the eggs, and then we shot the bird."

"The mother bird?" Grace gasped.

He winced. "We were just kids."

Riley made it easy for Grace to be good. Her mother didn't seem to like him much, but Grace suspected that had more to do with Grace than with Riley. But if everyone liked the Grahams, and the Grahams liked Grace, then maybe Grace's mother had been wrong about her.

The Grahams had given her a chance, and she was eager to show them that she could be worthy of their love. They treated Grace as if she belonged to them, and so did Riley, and she devoted herself to earning her keep. She left her frantic, lonely childhood behind to become the Grahams' daughter and Riley's dream girl, silky haired and shyly smiling. She knew to go wherever she was wanted.

One afternoon the summer after Grace's sixth-grade year, she wandered outside when Riley was playing video games and Mrs. Graham had gone out. Dr. Graham was repairing the lawn mower in the driveway, and he was startled at her appearance. "I never hear you coming, sweetie," he said. "I'm used to thundering boy hooves." Then she was handing him tools as he described them—"the long thingie with the spinny thingie," he said—and listening as he explained how the motor worked. When he finished, he ruffled her dark hair and said, "Thanks, daylily!"

"You're so welcome!" She beamed at him, ecstatic over her first nickname.

"My parents *love* you," Riley said when she told him. "My mom really wanted to have another baby after me. She always wanted a girl, but my dad said five kids was too many kids."

A few weeks later, Grace was curled up on the couch in the den with Mrs. Graham watching *To Catch a Thief*, one of Mrs. Graham's "glamour films," when Dr. Graham came in late from work and poked his head around the corner.

"I see you got your girl," he said, and Grace, as shy as she was eager, sneaked a look at Mrs. Graham, who was nodding to her husband as she reached to smooth the blanket over Grace's knees.

Grace couldn't see then what Riley saw in her, but he was like sunlight, shining easy faith on her and eliminating the shadows. His town, from the crossing guard to the college girls scooping ice cream behind the counter at Ginny's to the principals of their schools, adored him. He was the youngest of the four Graham boys, spirited and handsome, a prankster who liked to tell stories about the times he'd been caught and the times he should have been. He had wild red hair and uneven dimples—a face for boyish mischief—and freckles everywhere: a spray across his face, a blanket over his shoulders and down his arms. To Grace he looked vibrant, brighter than everyone else, as though sparks burst through those freckles and that hair. His manners could be almost comically courtly: He blessed strangers when they sneezed, and tipped the brim of his ball cap and said "take care" after the Ginny's Ice Cream girls handed him his change.

Dr. Graham was the physician for the college basketball team, a humble hero, and Mrs. Graham worked in the student counseling clinic. There was more money from the family lumber company started by Riley's great-grandfather. But it was never about money, Grace consoled herself in later years—except by then, she understood how desperation of any kind could turn you meager, mean. The Grahams were not meager in anything. In their stacks of books and rows of inherited photo albums, their jars of mysterious condiments and overfull crisper drawers, their inside jokes and bottomless well of traditions, their boxes full of extra coats and gloves and cleats and Boogie Boards, the Grahams had only abundance.

When she surveyed her pimply classmates—the girls who'd quickly shut her out, the boys who vacillated between buffoonery and cruelty—she felt a surge of pride, even victory, that she had Riley. Would she have wanted Greg, the overgrown baby whose father had promised him a Land Rover for his fifteenth birthday if he kept up honor roll? Would she have wanted Alls, who never went home of his own volition? No, of course not. She couldn't believe her luck that Riley wanted her, but she was grateful, and she loved him for it.

The June that Grace turned thirteen, she and Riley lost their virginity in an abandoned house at the edge of his neighborhood. They had been climbing through the windows of the house for months to poke around and write their initials in the dust, and they had begun to think of it as *their* house. They did it on the carpeted floor of one of the bedrooms— *their* bedroom. Neither of them was prepared for how much it would hurt Grace, and Riley kissed her all over her forehead afterward. Neither of them was prepared for the blood either, and Grace thought sex had brought her period, as if her body had rushed to catch up with her. When she got her real first period a few months later, the blood seemed both more disgusting and less substantial. It was only once Grace got older, when she was sixteen and found herself lying to a nurse about when, exactly, she had become *active*, that she realized she had been too young. If she and Riley hadn't stayed together it might have become a source of shame. Instead, every secret they shared was a double knot that bound them tighter.

Mrs. Graham clutched at Grace like a long-awaited gift. She bought Grace dresses, sweaters, books (none of her sons really liked to read, not the way she did, not the way Grace did). When Mrs. Graham laughed, she tilted her face up and her mouth opened in surprise, almost as if she were in pain. When she really laughed, at her husband or at her boys, she bit her lips together, laughing through her nose. Once, Grace, using the master bathroom, had tried on her lipstick, a shimmery plum called Crushed Rose that came in a gold tube, and tried her Mrs. Graham laugh silently in the mirror.

Mrs. Graham even took Grace to purchase her first bra. Grace had twice started to ask her own mother, but stopped—Aiden was screaming, then her father came in—and Mrs. Graham had not needed to be asked. She took Grace aside and said, quickly and softly, smelling like grapefruit, that she needed to exchange a jacket at the mall and Grace should "come with" to "pick up a few bras." She didn't even make Grace answer; they just went. Later, curled up in Riley's bed, Grace would sometimes notice one of those bras strewn on his floor amid the homework and sweaty socks, and she would feel overwhelmed with love for the Grahams, her real family. She sometimes fantasized a whole childhood as one of them—Grace Graham, the daughter Mrs. Graham had wanted—though she couldn't tell Riley this without making it sound as though she wished she were his sister.

4

Riley left Garland Middle for Garland High; Grace, left behind, worried that she would begin to seem too young to him, a babyish phase he should now grow out of. After school she rushed to wherever he was, always with Alls and Greg. Greg often accused her, even in front of Riley, of trying to take Riley away from them. She laughed and Riley rolled his eyes, but Greg was right. She was jealous. No matter how long she and Riley were together, the boys had been together longer. Sometimes, it didn't seem fair that Grace gave all her love and attention to Riley when his was spread so thin. But he wouldn't let her in with the boys, not really, even though all of them spent so much time together. When she did the things that she thought would earn her admittance—threw an empty glass bottle at the brick back wall of their middle school, called Greg out for farting—Riley scolded her. There was one time she remembered particularly. It was after Halloween, and they were all sitting on Riley's front porch eating leftover candy.

"What's a hillbilly's favorite thing to do on Halloween?" Alls started.

"What?" Grace asked first.

He looked at the floor, trying to keep a straight face. "Pump kin."

Riley's laugh was loudest of all. Then Grace, recovering first, said, "What did the leper say to the hooker?"

"What?" Greg asked.

It was too late; she was already grinning. "Keep the tip."

Alls cupped his hands over his ears in mock alarm, but he was laughing, and so was Greg. Riley was not. "Let's go somewhere," he said. "I'm bored out of my skull."

Later, when his friends had gone home, he told her that she'd embarrassed him. He framed his argument generously: "Quit trying to be a guy," he said. "You don't have to fake it. Just be yourself."

She wasn't faking it, she started to explain. She was just—

"But I don't like you like that," he said.

Just-be-yourself had its limits. She adapted to his vision. She liked that girl more than she had ever liked herself before anyway, so that was the self she became.

Starting that year, the boys often went to Greg's basement after school. Greg was already drinking hard then, stealing booze from his father, who had a wet bar downstairs and drank too much to keep track of his inventory. The first time Greg offered her a screwdriver, she told him to shut up, thinking he was making fun of her. "No, I'm having one," he said. "You'll like it, it's good." Greg kept his pot down there too, right in the drawer with the party toothpicks and restaurant matchbooks, as though he wanted his father to find it.

One night in early April, the boys were lit to the rafters and Grace was nursing her screwdriver when the boys decided to take Mrs. Kimbrough's car out for a drive. Greg took the keys from her purse, which was next to the bed where she and Mr. Kimbrough slept. Riley had never driven so much as a lawn mower, and Greg was too bombed to get the key into the lock. Alls had learned to drive a golf cart caddying that summer. Grace protested wildly, in a whisper. She wasn't even supposed to be there. She had snuck out of her house. Riley told her not to worry; they would drop her off at home. Alls backed Mrs. Kimbrough's silver sports car out of the driveway, narrowly missing the brick mailbox. Greg pumped up the bass and then locked the windows to hotbox the car. Alls jabbed at the window buttons, trying to roll them down. His dad drove an old car without power windows and he couldn't figure it out. Grace made them drop her off at the end of her block so her parents wouldn't wake.

The next morning was Sunday, and Grace biked over at eight thirty, per custom, to go to church with the Grahams. She found Alls, Riley, and his parents in the kitchen, all with their hands over their eyes. The telephone was in the middle of the table, no one touching it. Mr. Kimbrough screamed from the receiver that he would wring Riley's balls off. Riley's mother always put angry parents on speakerphone. She wanted neither to spare her sons their fury nor to have to regurgitate it herself.

"Tell him to get over here," he shouted. "I want your little shithead crying on the floor just like mine is."

Marmie, the Grahams' beagle, began to howl at the phone, and Mrs. Graham gestured at Grace to shush her.

"It's no use letting him lie to you." It was Tracy Kimbrough now. "Greg told us everything."

Greg had told his parents that he let Alls and Riley borrow his mother's car and that they had crashed it. He claimed to have stayed home. Now the car's front end was bashed in and there was vomit all over the backseat and floor.

"You could've killed someone!" Dr. Graham bellowed.

"It's a miracle you weren't arrested," Mrs. Graham said. "Really, I wish you had been."

"Alls, you need to go home now," Dr. Graham said.

Riley was sorrowful and self-flagellating as he promised to pay for his half of the damages. He didn't contradict Greg's ridiculous story to his parents. But he told Grace later that they had all driven downtown, what there was of it, where they were flagged down by two seniors from school. One of them was a locker-room pills dealer, freshly expelled. His name was a four-letter word on all parents' lips. They let him drive, playing autobahn on Old 63 until Riley puked on the floor. The older boy plowed the car into the pin oak on Dawahare Street, and they left the car there, bashed in and full of vomit. Alls went home with Riley, who discovered on his doorstep that he'd lost his keys over the course of the evening. Alls didn't even have a key to his own house—his father was always losing his keys and borrowing his son's—so he'd learned to pick the locks with paper clips when he needed to. He got them into the Grahams', and they collapsed on the couches in the family room.

Grace couldn't understand why they had let Greg off the hook, but Riley shrugged off her questions. She figured it out on her own: Greg had been buying the pot and supplying all the alcohol. He stole money from his parents all the time: He sold his belongings and claimed to have lost them, collected money for fake tutors and fake field trips. He paid for most of the damage to the car in exchange for Riley and Alls taking the blame.

But the blame assigned to Alls and Riley was not equally distributed. Mrs. Kimbrough focused her rage on Alls alone, and when his father tried to pay for the damages, the Kimbroughs refused his money.

Charlie Hughes was "having a hard time," everyone knew, meaning he was an alcoholic whose private struggles had become public. His wife, Alls's mother, had walked out on them just two months before, after Charlie's third DUI. Paula Hughes had worked at the United Methodist day care in the mornings and babysat the younger Turpin children in the afternoons, and when she left, Jeffrey Turpin started a rumor that Alls's mother had been deported. Alls was reconsidered by his peers: His complexion, though pale, had a strong olive cast that they now remarked on for the first time. Other than his coloring, he looked like a younger Charlie, long-nosed and lanky and ready to get into trouble. But Alls didn't correct the rumor. He must have preferred it, in its loud stupidity, to the truth that few knew: His mother had promised to return when her husband got sober. She had given up.

The Friday before the boys wrecked Mrs. Kimbrough's car, Charlie Hughes had made a scene at the boys' baseball game.

Riley didn't play, but since Alls and Greg did, Grace and Riley were there, hanging out with some other kids under the bleachers. In the third inning, they had heard Charlie hollering, "How's my boy doing?" as he ambled from the parking lot. He struggled up into the bleachers and began to loudly speculate about why Bradley Cobb, the third baseman, was still so small at fourteen. Grace and Riley scooted out from under the bleachers to watch Charlie. He made Grace nervous. Riley loathed him, bitter on his friend's behalf.

"Got a weak chin too. Must have been a preemie," Charlie Hughes said to no one in particular. The Cobbs were sitting two rows down.

"Come on, Charlie," Mr. Kimbrough said. "Let's just watch the game, okay?"

"Maybe his daddy didn't get a good toehold." Cackling, Charlie lurched forward, clapping the woman in front of him on the shoulder. "What do you say, Cobb?"

Grace couldn't see the Cobbs, but no one laughed. Charlie rummaged in his pants pocket and a bottle slipped out, clanging against the bleachers and then falling through the gap until it broke on the asphalt below.

"Whoops," Charlie said, looking down through his legs. "Careful, kids."

Grace looked out to Alls at first base. He was focused on the batter, his jaw tensed, and she couldn't tell if he'd seen. The broken vodka bottle hadn't been much bigger than a flask. That Alls's father was a *vodka* drunk was worse in Garland, where men drank beer or whiskey, and they drank it at home, jiggling squat glasses of ice on their porches, not at their kids' baseball games. Alls's father was usually working on Friday evenings. He shouldn't have been there anyway.

Charlie left silently after the next inning, and Grace and Riley cleaned up the broken glass before Alls came out of the dugout. Grace felt newly grateful for her own parents' disinterest.

When Riley, Greg, and Alls wrecked Tracy Kimbrough's car a week later, Grace was sure the episode at the baseball game was connected to the Kimbroughs' treatment of Alls. Mrs. Kimbrough, whose every surface was always affluently packaged, was in no hurry to have her car fixed. She ran the crumpled car all over town for weeks, telling anyone who asked that Alls Hughes had stolen her car and driven it around at night smoking marijuana. She omitted Riley's involvement as readily as she did her own son's, and this seemed to be her preferred form of compensation. Shortly thereafter, Alls was kicked off the baseball team for failing a surprise drug test administered to no one else.

"You have to tell them," Grace begged Riley. "This is all happening because of Greg's crazy mom. She can't tell when he lies to her because he *always* lies to her. She's ruining Alls's *life*."

"His *life*? This isn't that big a deal. Everybody'll forget about it in a couple weeks, and next time it'll be Greg's turn. You take turns getting the shit—you have to."

It's not like that for us, she wanted to tell Riley. People would forget about Riley's mistakes and Greg's mistakes because of their nice families in the background, but Grace and Alls didn't have backup. She didn't know how to explain this to Riley.

He put his arm over her shoulder. "Don't worry so much."

The cost of this mistake had ballooned, and Grace knew Alls couldn't afford it. She understood then how tenuous her own position was. If some grown-up decided that Grace didn't belong with Riley, her life could be gossiped right down the toilet.

Years later, when Greg ratted out his friends for a plea bargain, Grace was probably least surprised of anyone. She knew the rules.

While Riley practiced his chiaroscuro, his depth of field, his achievement of photorealism, Grace practiced the craft of love: cupcakes, mix CDs, impassioned encouragement, her fingers against the inside of his biceps, doubled joy at his victories and indignation at any slight. She loved the roaring crackle of his laugh and how it seemed to raise the temperature in the room. She loved that he was kind to his mother and kissed her on the cheek when he came and left, that he and his father talked at length, like old friends. She loved that his father gave him money to take Grace out to dinner. She loved the red-gold hairs on his arms and that he drove a stick shift. The way his body jerked right as he fell asleep and how he always woke up looking cross and petulant. She loved how people waved to him from down the block and called his name. And the sound of his name in her mouth, and his signature, how the R seemed to be kicking the rest of it off the page. She loved when he drew her. She loved when he left his friends to be with her. Even at fourteen she knew that she had him locked down and she loved that too. She had won—everything.

Only once had Grace worried about losing Riley. When she was sixteen, a bored blond nightmare named Madison Grimes showed up at Garland High as a senior, kicked out of her Virginia boarding school, and scared the devil out of Grace when she made it clear that she wanted Riley. Deanna Passerini and Colby Strote told her in biology, and not out of kindness. Then Grace heard it herself, approaching Riley's locker: Madison's low, husky laugh at something Riley had said.

"Can't take her home to Mother," Greg muttered within her earshot. Grace knew he didn't mean to threaten her—he was never that specific— but goose bumps prickled down her limbs.

By then Grace was often sleeping over at the Grahams' whenever Mrs. Graham decided it had gotten too late for Grace to go home. Mrs. Graham had fixed up the small guest bedroom in the attic for Grace with flowered quilts from her own childhood and a toile-shaded lamp. Riley snuck up the stairs at night, delighted at the creepiness of sex in that little rosebudded room. He sometimes grew frustrated at Grace's relationship with his mother and needed reminding that their closeness was exactly the thing that enabled his comfortable and unobstructed sex life.

Grace was lying awake in this bed one morning at dawn, Riley asleep next to her, when she felt a space open up in her imagination: What if Riley stopped loving her? What if she lost her room in this house? When she was at home, she was always waiting to come back here; her parents and brothers were strangers milling around while she sat watching the clock, looking for a reason to go. And if there were no reason for her? She felt suddenly haunted, the ghost the threat of becoming a ghost herself.

She watched Madison at school. It was the matter-of-factness in her demeanor—she never crossed her legs; she smoked at lunch—that Grace, in her yellow sundress, found particularly menacing. Grace had been challenged not by someone she could best, but by her opposite.

Grace contemplated anal sex, which she hadn't done and didn't want to do. Had she unconsciously saved it for a time like this? But then, late on a Friday night when Grace, Riley, Greg, and Alls were drinking amiably in the woods behind the Kimbroughs' house, Riley erupted with laughter. He handed his phone to Grace. There was Madison, tits out, begging for his attention from the screen.

"Christ," Riley said. "Some people have no manners."

Grace peered closely at the picture, comparing Madison's breasts to her own until she felt Greg's breath on her neck.

"The Kimbroner likes her," he said.

Grace smacked him away. *You stupid whore*, she thought, relieved and delighted as she watched Riley laugh. *You don't know him at all.*

Greg hooked up with Madison the next week—the perfect end, really—and intermittently until her graduation, when she vanished to the coastal South. Sometimes, Greg would pine for her a little. "It was more than it was," he would say thoughtfully. It wasn't, but his friends allowed him his delusion. Grace was especially generous, now that she felt certain there was no contest for Riley's love that she could not win if she stayed true to herself, the good girl, naked in the attic, sundress heaped on the floor.

5

The boys went to college together, though they didn't really *go* any-where. Of the hundred students in their graduating class, twenty-two had enrolled at Garland College. Children of GC faculty or staff received tuition waivers or reductions. Riley and his brothers went nearly free.

Alls had banked on basketball paying his way. He had every reason to think he'd get a scholarship to GC: The college had given a full ride to the two best players on Garland High's basketball team for the past twenty years, and Alls was the Ravens' star point guard. But in December, the Court Vision Committee offered its two scholarships to Clay Atkinson and Jeremy Bullock. Even the coach could not conceal his shock. Jeremy abso-lutely deserved the scholarship, but Clay was mediocre. He cracked under pressure and was easily pushed around by bigger players.

Grace was less surprised. Clay's father was Ike Atkinson, attorney at law, and his mother was Caroline, Realtor and breeder of labradoodles, and they lived in a big white house with green shutters. Jeremy Bullock, one of eleven black students at Garland High, had been raised by a single mother, and Grace had seen Jeremy's smile tighten when the committee chair, announc-ing his scholarship, mentioned this among the "difficult circumstances" Jer-emy had "overcome." But Alls must not have fit the vision. His mother had never returned. She called him yearly and asked him to visit her in Michigan, but he had gone only once. Good Time Charlie worked at a big-box sporting goods store in Whitwell between benders. Their story had no lift.

"You're calling them *racist?*" Riley asked. "But they picked Jeremy."

"And *Clay.* Look, what was that 'single mother' bullshit? They like that—on a black kid. It's very true to their vision. But on Alls, not so much. And Alls's mother is Colombian."

"Doesn't that make *you* the one who's fixated on—"

"It should have been Jeremy and Alls." She struggled to explain herself. "You know they are so happy with themselves right now, patting their backs for helping Jeremy. But then they look at Alls and see the town's most obnoxious drunk, the Latina babysitter he conned into marrying him, and a kid who's a *mix* of them. The one who refused to sell candy bars because he made more at his real job."

Riley groaned.

"Why else would they pick Clay? Clay sucks."

"Because he's a little shit," he said. "Because he never pisses anyone off, and Alls does."

"And why is that?"

She wished she hadn't said anything at all. If Riley was blind to Garland's social stratification, it was not in her interest to enlighten him.

What she didn't mention to Riley was that she had seen Alls get the call from Coach Backus. They had all been at the Grahams' house, pawing through the basement for discarded housewares they could take to the house the boys were going to rent for college. Greg had found a cache of old babes-with-cars posters belonging to one of Riley's brothers—Jim, they guessed, based on the vintage of both subjects—and they'd crowded around them, cackling, when Alls pulled his buzzing phone out of his jeans pocket. He looked at the number and ran up the stairs; there wasn't enough reception in the basement.

Grace went upstairs a minute later to get a drink. She filled her glass at the kitchen sink, and from the window, she saw Alls in the backyard, phone to his ear, pacing. She knew she was seeing something private but she didn't know what. He stopped and crossed one arm over the other under the walnut tree, his back to the house. Grace realized she was holding her breath. Even twenty feet away and from behind, she knew she'd never seen him so upset. When his arm dropped, it just hung there, limp, until he stuck his phone back in his pocket and stooped to pick up some rotting fallen walnuts from the ground. He began to whip them at the paint splotch on the fence, an old pitching target.

She wanted to go outside, to ask him what had happened or if he wanted to talk. But she couldn't talk like that to Alls. They didn't have that kind of friendship. He sometimes made her self-conscious and uncomfortable: When she was combing her hair with her fingers or laughing a not-awful laugh, he would give her this knowing look, a squint and a suppressed smile, as if he'd caught her at something. *You don't know shit,* she'd want to say.

Grace watched him until she heard the thunder of footsteps coming up the basement stairs. Greg and Riley blew past her into the backyard, where they, too, began to pick up fallen walnuts and pelt them at the fence, as if they were all obeying some boy command from above.

"What about other schools?" she asked Alls several days later. They were sitting on the back porch steps at Riley's family's house a few days after Christmas. Grace sat a step below Riley, leaning between his legs. When she said this, he squeezed his knees a little, telling her to hush.

"There are no other schools," Alls said.

"I mean UT, or State, Belmont—"

"I'm not good enough for UT," he said. "But I'm good enough for Garland."

"What about other sports? I mean, you've played pretty much everything."

Riley put his face in his hands. Grace knew that getting another scholarship was not as simple as she was suggesting, but Alls was the most graceful person she knew, long and leanly muscled. He moved with the careless elegance of someone always at ease in his body. She had never seen Alls Hughes trip. His body could learn, she thought, anything he asked it to.

"I'm going in," Riley said.

"You don't have to go to college," Grace said when the door had shut.

"I'm fucking going to college," he said.

She'd touched a nerve. "What do you want to be?" she asked.

He snorted. "What? Like, when I grow up?"

"Yeah," she said, glad he had laughed. "When you grow up."

"Uh, *away.*" He rubbed the crooked bridge of his nose. "Out of here."

"*Here?*" Grace said, disbelieving.

"Garland," he sighed.

"So go work on an oil rig. Or go to college in Kansas." Marmie hobbled up the stairs and parked her graying head on Grace's lap.

"Is that what you're planning? What do *you* want to be?"

Grace Graham. Smart, rich, mother of future Grahams. "I don't know," she said, stroking the dog's ears. "But my family is here."

He raised his eyebrows. "I've never even met your family. You know how weird that is in this town? There's nobody who sees me coming and doesn't think of my dad."

"I meant *here*," she said, tapping her finger on the porch step. There wasn't any reason she shouldn't say that, and yet she felt it had been a mistake.

A Riley whoop rang out from inside. They turned to the bay window and saw him dancing his mother across the living room floor, showing off for them, for her. They could hear Dr. Graham's Steely Dan through the glass. Riley gave them a goofy thumbs-up. Grace waved.

"Well, same," Alls said to her then. She was relieved. She could tell that he'd thought she just meant Riley.

Grace smiled. "You just need to figure out what you want."

"Like you did," he said, the corner of his lip twitching.

"I don't know what you mean."

"It's okay," he said. "You did good, and you know it. I fuck up, but you never do."

Grace laughed, out of both habit and self-defense, and Alls nodded, looking at her in a way she did not want to be seen.

"Stop it," she said, standing to reach for the icy doorknob. She could hear the opening chords of "Deacon Blues," and she wanted to join the dancing.

The next week, Alls quit the basketball team, right in the middle of the season. He couldn't see faking it through February, he said, with all those people pitying him. "I don't owe anybody anything," he told his coach.

Shortly after that, he started going to the college after school for fencing practice.

"Of all the sports that could get you a scholarship, you're going for one you've never done before," Riley said. "Makes sense."

"Like, with the mask and shit?" Greg asked.

"Yeah," Alls said. "And shit."

"What about track?" Riley asked. "You can run."

"No, you don't get it," Alls said. "See, they *have* a full track team. They have a full basketball team. GC has *one* available scholarship, and it's for fencing, so I'm going after it. They had a junior transfer up north mid-year. Your dad's the one who told me."

"I didn't even know they had a fencing team," Greg said.

Alls nodded once. "Now you get it."

Alls won the scholarship, possibly with a quiet assist from Dr. Graham, and would begin college only a semester behind Riley and Greg. In August, the boys rented the falling-down house on Orange Street. Riley gave her a key, and Grace made herself at home in his room upstairs, Alls in the room below and Greg down the hall.

At first, they all basked in the freedom the house afforded them. No one had to smoke out in the woods anymore; no one hurried to push the empties under the couch at the sound of footsteps on the stairs; no one needed to wear proper clothes, buttoned and zipped. Grace lived with her parents only technically now. She spent most nights at the house on Orange Street, and though her parents didn't like this arrangement, they were too late to intercede with any meaningful authority. When her mother protested that Grace spending the night with Riley all the time didn't "look right," Grace feigned confusion: to whom? The Grahams didn't mind that she stayed over, she said. She had her own room in their house. Mrs. Graham was only grumpy that she saw less of them now. Grace dragged Riley home for dinner once a week, and she sometimes visited on her own, too.

"Whose opinion are you worried about, Mother?" Grace asked with airy chill.

In the house on Orange Street, Greg ambled around stoned in his shorts, not even bothering to hide his morning Kimbroner. Alls left his pipe on the kitchen table and made out with Jenna from Ginny's Ice Cream on the sofa, not caring who saw them. Riley and Grace were as loud as they pleased. For the past four years they had been sneaking around together, and now there was no sneaking to do.

Grace planned to start at Garland College the next year. She was graduating second in her class and she'd scored very well on the SAT, and she was confident that she would get a scholarship. She would major in art history, a complement to Riley's talent. After college, they would get married. That was the plan.

At night she looked through Riley's coursework, greedy to learn something, anything. With the boys graduated, there was nothing left for Grace in high school. She'd already read *Beowulf* and *1984*; she'd read them last year, when Riley had, and now she had to listen to her peers' slow-motion jawing—"it's like our world, but *not*"—as if they were underwater. She should have petitioned to graduate early, she knew, but she hadn't, and now there was nothing to do but stare at the horizon and wait, both for graduation and for the three o'clock bell.

In December, Grace came back to the house one day after school, wheeled her bicycle into the shed, and went inside thinking that no one was home. She took a can of High Life from the refrigerator and flopped down on the green plaid couch in front of the picture window with *Macbeth* and a highlighter. She unzipped her jeans to get comfortable and flexed and pointed her bare feet in the sun. It was warm for December, warmer on the sun-soaked couch, and she drifted off with her highlighter in her hand. She woke suddenly, and she didn't know why until she saw, through the doorway, Alls in the kitchen on the floor, cleaning up the aftermath of a dropped take-out container. Sticky brown food was strewn across the vinyl.

"I was trying to be quiet," he said. "I spilled some on your book."

Macbeth was still resting on her stomach. Now she moved it to cover her undone fly. "What book?"

"Uh, *What Work Is?*" he asked, if it were a question. He nodded toward the paperback. "I don't know; it was on the microwave."

"It was?" She thought it had been on the floor at the top of the stairs. "Do you like it?"

"It's all right," he said. He came in and dropped the book on the couch next to her. "I didn't realize it was going to be poetry." But they were both looking at the cover as he said this. *What Work Is*, it read. *Philip Levine. Poems.*

"It's fine to read poetry on purpose," she teased him. "I won't tell on you."

He rolled his eyes. "I just read whatever's laying around."

"So, lots of poetry," she said. "Because all the books are mine."

She thought he would laugh then, but he didn't, and she felt that she had made a misstep. "I shouldn't be sleeping right now," Grace yawned, trying to help him. "How was work?"

"Fine. Smelly. Found a bat in a bakery oven," he said on his way back to the mess on the kitchen floor.

Alls helped two men out of Pitchfield repair commercial bakery equipment. He'd had the job since he'd gotten his driver's license.

"Gross! How long had it been there?"

"No eyeballs."

"Yikes," she said, but then she must have drifted off again, because when she awoke to a wet thumb wiping at her cheek, she thought at first that it belonged to Alls.

"You have a pink stripe here," Riley said. "Like a neon scar." She stretched out her arms and he groaned, happy to collapse in the sun with her. "You smell like sleep," he said, and she closed her eyes again.

That night, restless from napping, Grace woke up and watched the headlights from the street sweeping across the wall, only half-conscious of the noise from downstairs. Riley was stretched out next to her, flat on his back like a dead man, with his feet splayed out under the blanket. The highlighter hadn't come off when she'd washed her face. She reached for the stripe with her tongue, as far up her cheek as it would reach, and she thought she could still taste the ink. The noise was right under them, in Alls's room, a slow, insistent thud, and at first she wondered, blearily, if he was practicing, doing drills or something. Not until she heard a quick, shrill coo did she realize what she was hearing.

Alls had certainly heard *them* before; he must have.

Suddenly conscious of her own breath, embarrassed at the sound of Riley's gentle snoring, as though Alls might hear *that*, Grace swallowed and closed her eyes, trying to force herself back to sleep. But now she was holding her breath to listen. She heard his cursing laugh as his bare mattress slid across the floor, and she slid her hand beneath her underwear's elastic. In a minute she was silently flipping onto her stomach, already groping for an explanation should Riley wake as she shifted, but he didn't, and when they finished in the room beneath her, she was soon after, face hidden in her pillow, not quite deaf.

She left for school the next morning before anyone else was awake, stealing out of the house ashamed for the first time. That evening she and Riley went to dinner at his family's, and then she told Riley she would go home, sleep at her parents'.

"Why?" he asked.

"I need some more clothes. Look, I had to wear your shirt today. *And* it's dirty."

She managed to avoid Alls until the next night, and then she crossed him in the hallway. He was coming out of the bathroom, his shaggy hair dripping. He was in a towel, for crying out loud. She stared at the wet hairs down his belly. She wanted to slap herself at the stupid cliché of her desire.

Instead she went into the steam-fogged bathroom and sat on the edge of the tub.

What was this feeling? She knew lust. She knew lust well. Lust had been a friend to her, a good listener and a great talker, a fine mood on a sunny day. Lust belonged to her. She did what she wanted with her lust. But this feeling was not that feeling, so what the fuck was it? Like the sharp pain in her sinuses before rain began to fall, this feeling blinded and dizzied her, obscured her brain in clouds. She was invaded by lust.

This lust was like falling down icy stairs, like discovering blood pouring from her shin as she shaved in the shower. She'd known Alls for years! This lust couldn't be real—it was hormones, or her birth control, or something contagious from Shakespeare, or autumn. This feeling was too stupid to feel.

Suddenly worried that Alls might be listening to her, she flushed the toilet and then felt only more embarrassed. How long had she been sitting here on the edge of the tub? The smell of the steam had overwhelmed her. She had walked right into her own trap. What was boy smell but a choice of deodorant plus the sweat of whatever he ate and drank? Alls and Riley ate and drank all the same things. Their sweat was probably the same. She had just become confused in this half-Riley steam, that was all. She pulled back the shower curtain and grimaced at the grime along the bottom of the tub. She knew which shampoo was Riley's and she could guess which one was Greg's. The Head & Shoulders had to be Alls's. She uncapped the bottle and inhaled.

At the knock on the bathroom door, she jerked the bottle into her nose.

"Hey, you want ice cream? Want to walk up to Ginny's?" Riley asked her.

"Yeah," she said, her voice like a car horn. "Yeah, I'll be right out."

She washed her hands with her own lavender-and-vanilla-scented soap and waved her hands around together as she lathered them, trying to fill the room with her own smell and clear out the smell of Alls, which seemed incriminating. She kept a single perfume sample in her toiletry bag, rationing dabs of it for special occasions. She rubbed it into her wrists and the hollow of her throat, filling her nose with peachy floral relief.

Riley was waiting by the door. He flared his nostrils, sniffing. "What's going on?"

"Nothing," she said. "I'm just happy to see you." And she was—she was profoundly assured by the sight of him, the smell of him.

"You smell good," he said. "I love that."

At Ginny's, though, Grace watched Jenna's fingers around the scoop, her forearm raking through the mint chip, and felt a hot, nauseous revulsion. "Six dollars," Jenna chirped to Riley. She had the voice of a camp counselor and a chin like a dinner roll. Grace tried to smile.

Riley tipped the brim of his cap to Jenna and waved.

"See you later!" she sang.

That night Grace found herself blinking at the dark wall again. Some malicious part of her had shaken her awake. The room downstairs was silent. Not since silly, obvious Madison Grimes had Grace felt the tightening in her chest, the quickening in the air, that made her look for a predator circling above. But this time the threat was right inside her.

She shook her head against her pillow. The line from Grace to her future was as straight as she could draw it. She reached for Riley's hand, clammy in sleep, and held it tight in hers.

The next day she decided to buy the perfume Riley liked, as if it were a kind of armor. Grace had been blindsided by her feelings, but she would not be defeated by them. She borrowed Riley's car and drove to the mall. At the perfume counter, she found the twisted glass and silver bottle on a tester tray and sprayed her wrist. The wet puddle dripped in all directions. Too much.

"How much is this?" she asked when the saleswoman approached her.

"That one is sixty-five for the eau de parfum." She bent to retrieve the blue box from beneath the counter.

"Oh," Grace said. "Does it come in a smaller—"

"There's a lotion," the woman said. "But nothing smaller."

Grace hadn't thought it would be so much. "I guess I need to think about it."

"The bottle will last you a long time," the woman said, "if you just spritz a *little* of it."

"Right," Grace said. "Well, thank you anyway."

The woman bent to put the box back. Grace fingered the tops of the other perfume bottles. She was startled to find that her heart was pounding.

The woman was on the other side of the counter now, helping someone else. Grace picked up the tester bottle again and dropped it into her tote bag before she could give herself another second to think. She heard the bottle clink against her key ring and felt her head seem to lift off her body. She turned away from the counter and slipped into the racks of handbags, disappearing behind a Christmas-garlanded pillar. Her hands were on fire, trembling on the strap of the purse she pretended to examine.

In the parking lot, she hurried among the rows of cars, forgetting where she'd parked. When she finally sank into the driver's seat, she locked the door and then let her head fall back, her mouth open. The blood in her veins slowed. She closed her eyes and licked her lips, victorious and exhausted, her rite completed.

When she got home Alls was in the kitchen making a peanut butter sandwich. "I didn't know you wore perfume," he said.

"It's new," she said stiffly. "How's Jenna?" She winced at the sharpness in her voice.

"Fine, I guess." He shrugged. "Jenna. Jenna is always fine. Jolly Jenna."

"Yikes," Grace said. "She certainly likes *you*."

"What, you jealous?" When their eyes met Grace nearly lost all her courage. He had said that before, other times over the years, but it had been different then, a joke that came through the wire intact. She feared she was blushing, but she fastened her eyes to his and forced herself not to let go. She had to conquer this.

"I heard her the other night," Grace said. "*Liking* you."

He was screwing the cap onto the peanut butter jar. His eyebrows crawled together.

"She's pretty shrill," Grace said.

"So we're going there now," he said. "You know I've been deaf and mute in the next room for years, and now you're going there."

"That little cheeping noise was cute," she said. "Like a duckling."

His smirk of disbelief threatened to break. She'd made him angry. Good.

Instead he laughed. "You were listening pretty hard. You've given it some real thought." He covered his eyes, low laughter rumbling from his belly. "Jesus. You are such a psycho, he has no idea."

"Oh, he knows," she said quickly, as if that were a clever retort. She opened the refrigerator door, but there wasn't much inside. Her fingers were trembling. She took the nearly empty carton of orange juice just to have something to do. She raised the carton of juice and finished it there.

"Do you want to know how *you* sound?" he asked.

The lust spread like poison ivy, and as the itching got worse and worse, Grace worried that she wouldn't be able to leave it alone. Scratching was obviously out of the question; to do so would be to undo her life, to erase herself, to become Amber White. That was not a choice she would ever make. But the new lust crawled around her, forbidden but making a home. Neither she nor Alls ever brought up their conversation in the kitchen again, but when they caught each other's eyes, Grace was terrified that Riley would see a flash there, would sense that *something* had happened.

At Christmas, while foraging for extra wrapping paper in the basement, Mrs. Graham showed Grace her wedding dress, hanging in plastic on a rack. "Do you want to see?" she asked Grace, who said yes, of course she did. Mrs. Graham lovingly unzipped the plastic and fingered the lace. "I was just your size," she said. "Can you believe it?"

Ten minutes later, Grace was wearing the dress, blushing wildly, and Mrs. Graham was crying next to a pile of outgrown sports equipment.

"When you get married, we'll put flowers in your hair," Mrs. Graham said.

Grace embraced her, burying her nose in Mrs. Graham's shoulder and watching the basement stairs for Riley's feet. She didn't want him to see her in his mother's wedding dress. Mrs. Graham's bridal portrait hung in the dining room. Grace knew it by heart—her downcast eyes, the bouquet of magnolias at her waist. The image of Grace costumed as his mother might be a hard one for Riley to shake. But if Grace could have stayed in the basement wearing Mrs. Graham's wedding dress forever, she might have.

She had to get away from Alls.

Mrs. Graham unzipped the dress and Grace stepped out of it. She pulled her striped T-shirt back over her head and went upstairs to find Riley, bereft that leaving the house she loved was the only way to keep her place in it.

The next week, when Riley implored her to tell him what was wrong, why she'd been so cranky and irritable lately, she looked into his worried green eyes and told him she was bored and restless in school. That was true. And she'd begun to dread the four years at Garland College that would follow—Riley's schoolwork outside the art studio was her own thirteenth grade. She'd gone in to the guidance counselor to see where she still had time to apply. Riley could come visit her on the weekends, and she wouldn't have to live in that bedroom right over Alls and see him every day. Mrs. Busche was surprised by Grace's request: Was Grace all right? Had anything . . . *happened*? No? And Grace wanted to study art history still? Garland College, Mrs. Busche said with some pride, had an excellent art history faculty, several of whom were good friends of hers, so unless Grace wanted to go into lab sciences or medicine or something—

"I'm worried I won't get a scholarship," Grace said. "And if I don't, it'll be way too expensive."

"But honey, you *will* get a scholarship. I'd bet my own hat on it."

"That's what Alls Hughes thought too."

"You are *not* Alls Hughes." Mrs. Busche closed her lips. There was no gracious way for her to explain why she had said that.

Grace swallowed. "Mrs. Busche, I mean no disrespect at all. It's just that . . . I've looked at Riley's assignments, and I'm worried it won't be— that I won't—"

Only because Grace couldn't say it aloud did Mrs. Busche understand. "Ah. That you won't be challenged academically. Well, that is something to consider." She blinked several times, frowning, as if she were seeing Grace for the first time. "I just thought—well, you're too late for UT and Vandy, but have you thought about going out of state?"

"No," Grace lied.

"Well, if you want a truly rigorous academic environment, there is no reason you shouldn't apply to"—she moved the pile of glossy brochures at her feet into her lap—"Vassar," she said, pulling the top one open to display the inside as if it were a children's picture book. "Jane Fonda went to Vassar."

Grace shook her head. "I don't know," she said. She felt Riley slipping away with every word of this conversation. "There's probably no time, anyway."

Mrs. Busche held up another catalog. "New York University," she said. On the cover, a frowning boy with dark poufy hair touched a yellow-tipped paintbrush to a canvas taller than he was. "They have an excellent art department as well," she said. "And all those museums."

Grace could not imagine Riley coming to visit her in the nowhere wilds of the Northeast, but she could imagine him coming to New York City. Yes, Riley would come to her, and they would go to museums and art galleries together, and she would be able to teach *him* things, and she would hardly have to come home at all. And the feeling, which she had begun to think of as a secret disease, something progressive and debilitating, would wither, all those miles away. Maybe Riley would want to come too; maybe he would transfer or something. She would become one of those art people, whoever they were, and he an artist. The math was so obvious she wondered why she hadn't thought of it before. Of course.

"Woo!" Mrs. Busche said. "Look at you! Won't that be something?"

Riley made her case for her. "She's too smart for Garland," he said to Grace's parents, sitting on their couch and shaking his head. He looked at them one at a time. "*I* want better for her."

What could they say? This little chat had been a show. She didn't expect their support, any kind of it.

Grace's numbers were very good, but she had to invent her extracurriculars. She wrote an essay about overcoming her hillbilly upbringing, bogus Appalachian minstrelsy cloaked in upmarket vocabulary. NYU offered her a partial scholarship and suggested she borrow the rest, which turned out to be simpler than getting a library card. She and Riley gloated over her acceptance, but their peers were skeptical, particularly the girls. At the graduation parties, they held their red plastic cups in one hand and worried their promise rings with the other. She was leaving Riley here? *Without* her? Grace told herself they were just insecure and immature, tying themselves to Garland with their flimsy romances, to their boyfriends with diamond-dust rings from Palmer Family Jewelry & Plaques.

"Let's get married," Riley said the morning of her graduation.

"Yes," she said.

"Now," he said.

She would turn eighteen in two weeks. "It's legal on my birthday," she said.

"I should give you a ring," he said. "Come on, let's go buy a ring. I have eighty bucks." He laughed. "It might have to be a mood ring."

"Wait," she said. "Your mom would be crushed. We can't do it without them. It would be a slap in the face. They'll think I'm pregnant."

"You and my mom," he groaned.

"Then we'd have to keep it a secret," she said. "From everyone."

"We know how to do that," he said, kissing her collarbone.

"And we'll have the big thing later, like she wants."

"I love you so much," he said.

"They'll put it in the paper though. They run the marriages with the legal notices."

"So we go somewhere else, some other nowhere a few hours from this one."

On Grace's eighteenth birthday, Riley drove them to the Klumpton County courthouse, three hours away. They didn't know anyone in Klumpton County. They found witnesses among the people waiting for the DMV. Riley started to cry when Grace said "I do," and then she began to cry at the sight of his crying. Afterward, they split a fifth of Old No. 8 in the car and reclined their seats back, hands clasped and staring at each other, overcome with the weight of their love.

III
Paris

6

On Sunday morning, Grace lay in bed and listened to Mme Freindametz and her daughter, who came every Sunday to do her laundry, bickering in the kitchen about how long you could leave eggs out on the counter.

Grace's mother and the twins would go to mass this morning. Her mother wasn't even Catholic, but since Riley's arrest, she had taken to going to the Grahams' church from time to time, and she liked to mention this in her occasional e-mails to Grace. She couldn't have known how these mentions of Mrs. Graham and occasionally Dr. Graham—how they'd looked, what brief politenesses they'd exchanged, if Mrs. Graham seemed to have a new purse—pained Grace. They cut her right across the heel. Grace knew her mother wouldn't bring them up *just* to hurt her (although those sightings of the Grahams gave her mother a nasty kind of satisfaction, Grace was sure), but only because she was sure her mother couldn't possibly understand how much Grace loved the Grahams.

If Grace's mother took the twins to mass this morning, they might see Riley there. Grace wondered if the twins would recognize him on their own, or if their mother would point him out. Riley had almost never come over to their house. He'd wanted to be there about as much as Grace had. The twins were thirteen now, about to start eighth grade. Grace didn't even know what they looked like. She still pictured them ten years old. Her mother said they asked about Grace, but she didn't believe it. What would they ask? They had hardly known her.

Grace hadn't left the house since she'd gotten home on Friday night, but the boys had been out of prison for almost two days, and she had heard nothing.

I'm coming, Riley had said back then. *I promise.*

Unlike Grace, Riley had always kept his promises.

This was not just Sunday in Garland, though. It was Sunday in Paris too, and on Sundays Grace went to the flea market. This was the life she had left for, the life she was so desperate to keep, and here she was lying in bed like an invalid, as if this crudely stitched patchwork of hers were a quilt she could clutch and hide under. No. She pulled back her blanket and got her feet on the floor.

The Marché aux Puces was perhaps the only flea market in the world where a six-thousand-euro Louis XIV love seat sat outside on the sidewalk. Today the sky was overcast and the whole neighborhood was ghostly, almost no one there but the proprietors of the glass-walled rooms and their dogs. In August, Paris left.

The treasures in the glass rooms always seemed recklessly lavish: Chandeliers carelessly dripped crystals; gilded chairs reclined with legs splayed open, their deep seats exposed. Dogs ran up and down the aisles yapping to each other or snored lazily on their exceptional beds. In one three-sided room, a dachshund curled into a doughnut on a red plush pillow shaped like a pair of sunglasses, RAY-BAN embroidered across the surface. Across the way, a bichon frise dozed on a miniature chaise longue with claw feet.

Grace wandered to the end of the row and turned in to the street market. She combed the tables of the open-air stalls, turning away when the dust flew up, waiting for the glimmer of recognition that meant she'd spotted something of value. The moment of detection produced a high, a fizz of pleasure in her veins and in her ears because she had seen what no one else had seen, had known what no one else had known. At Clignancourt, she knew she was flattering herself; the stalls were so overflowing with treasure that treasure was common. This flea market was a stocked pond. When Grace found something a little damaged, she would repair it, lovingly, to sell. The money helped, but the thrill was in the spotting. It was how she imagined other people must feel when, from afar, they recognized a long-lost friend.

Grace ran her hands down the arms of a wheel-back chair missing one leg, a forgotten amputee from a dispersed estate. Her fingers came away with a faint green mildew that smelled like a cave. Her eyes roved over old jars, suitcases, juice glasses, rhinestone jewelry, and cardboard boxes full of wooden coffee grinders. She watched as a very tall man in a camel hair coat strode up to the coffee grinders as though he'd been waiting all week to visit them. He dropped to a low squat, pulled a bag of coffee beans from his coat pocket, and dropped a few beans into each grinder, pushing and pulling the handles, holding the wooden boxes up to his ear to listen. He didn't buy any, and the stall's proprietress cursed at him. He shrugged. "No good," he told her.

Grace was looking through a mountain of old hairbrushes when she saw a curiously shimmering box hiding behind some wooden shoe trees. Its lacquer was roughed up, the corners chipped and showing the wood beneath, but she recognized the soft, warm silver color of the paint. She felt the thrill flick up her spine. This little piece of tack looked like a James Mont cigar box, American, from the 1920s.

"Julie! Find something good?"

Hanna. She strode over, reaching for the silver box only because she saw Grace's eyes on it. Grace hurried to snatch it up herself.

"Just a china pig," Grace said, their term for something unimportant but charming, if slightly offensive to taste.

Hanna squinted. There was a good chance that she wouldn't know what it was. James Mont was an American designer for retro American palates. Still, Grace tried to feign indifference. She didn't want to get into a bidding war.

"I hate coming on Sundays. Everything good is gone by Saturday noon."

Not quite. "Better bargains, though."

"You'd rather paw through the leftovers. I'm only here today because I worked all yesterday. I'm just *loving* this project. It feels so endless and intricate, almost like building something from scratch." She cocked her head up the street. "Would you like to get lunch? I'd like to have an omelet and rest my eyes before I do the rest of the market."

Grace asked the proprietor for a price on the box. He knew her and said thirty, knowing she wouldn't pay that much. She got the box for twenty-two, but still Hanna whistled. Grace was pleased. Hanna had no idea.

Hanna used her knife to cut her plain omelet into a dozen narrow rows. One by one, she rolled each section of egg around her fork. Between bites, she set down her fork at the ten o'clock position and took two sips of water. Grace had seen this all before.

"So what is it?" Hanna asked her.

"James Mont," Grace said, relishing her small victory. "Turkish American, 1920s to 1950s. *Orientaliste*, shiny case goods, lots of velvet."

"I've never heard of him." She cast a dubious eye at Grace's tote bag.

"He was the decorator for the American Mafia. And he assaulted some poor girl, another designer, and went to prison for years. When he came out, people loved him more than ever."

"If only that were how it worked for the rest of us," Hanna said. "The rich and famous can put prison on their résumés."

Grace flushed at *the rest of us*, but when she looked up, Hanna's mouth was pressed into an inward smile. Hanna had meant herself.

"You?" Grace asked her. "Do you mean that you—"

"Unlicensed reproduction," Hanna said. "Fraud. A long time ago, in Copenhagen."

"You forged antiques?"

"You don't think I could do it?"

"I have no doubt." She thought of Hanna's fastidious sourcing, her obsession with glues and lacquers that were not anachronistic. *You're not going to tear the space-time continuum*, Grace had teased her.

"I had a gift," Hanna said with a shrug. "But I misjudged a client. I have better eyes for art than for people."

Grace imagined Riley sitting on his bed, paging through a college course catalog, his knee bobbing. She imagined him looking through his drawers for photos of them, of her, that had long been removed. She kept her eyes down on her soup bowl. "When you got out of prison, how much did you start your life over? I mean, how much did you try to return to, and how much did you have to, or want to—"

"Start fresh?" Hanna said with distaste.

"I understand if you don't want to talk about it."

"Other people are the ones who don't want to talk about it," Hanna said, pursing her lips. "Well, I had to find something else I could do. And restoration, as you know, is not so far from forgery." She smiled. "Except the work is half done for you."

"Why did you come here?"

"To Paris? I'm not allowed in Denmark, and no one would hire me there even if I were. Not now. But France has been very forgiving. Of course, I should be somewhere much better than Zanuso, but—" She shrugged.

"You should," Grace agreed.

"And so should you."

Grace was pleased by the compliment even as she felt the prickle of implication. She might need to give Hanna more of a story, but only if she asked. To bring it up before then would only sharpen Hanna's suspicions, whatever they were.

"How long were you in prison?" Grace asked.

"Almost four years."

"Four? For antiques forgery?"

"No," Hanna said. "For that, only two months. The rest was for assault. The matters got tangled up, legally."

"What did you *do?*" Grace hadn't meant to say it like that, and she didn't really expect Hanna to answer her. But she could see that Hanna was thinking about the question and choosing her words, which Grace had never seen her do before. Hanna's words always sprang neatly from her mouth as complete and orderly thoughts. Whatever Hanna was about to tell her was important, Grace knew, and she tried to keep her face relaxed. *I certainly won't judge you*, she wanted to say, but that might have far overshot the mark.

"What was it?" Grace pushed.

Hanna tore off a crust of bread and chewed it at her. "You can look it up," she said. "There's no secret." She cracked her neck from side to side.

Grace waited. Hanna drank from her glass and spat the ice chips, one, two, three, back into the water.

"A client," she finally said. "I injured a client who threatened me."

"He threatened to expose you?"

"She," Hanna said. "I cut her right down her neck." She pointed with her fork to her jawline and gestured toward her clavicle. "Down to her collarbone with my small utility knife."

Grace swallowed. Hanna cleared her throat. "She wanted me to sell her husband's inherited antiques, you know, that she had brought in for 'cleaning' or whatever, and make copies for her to take home in their place. I wouldn't do it. I won't *steal*." She frowned.

"But you forged," Grace said doubtfully.

"It's one thing to make something from nothing. If your eye can't tell the difference, I don't see how that's my problem. You get the same enjoyment and status from the piece."

"How did she know you could pull it off?"

"She had one of my pieces. A side table. She had commissioned it! She knew exactly what that table was, but she threatened to turn me in for forgery if I didn't do as she asked. She wanted me to help her steal from her husband—her own husband! Would you do it?"

"Never," Grace said.

"Right. But I hadn't made her sign anything for the repro, so, stupid me. I had no proof that she knew she'd paid for a repro except how little she'd paid for it. And I was very frightened of her. She was a very intimidating woman."

Grace nodded, though it was difficult to imagine Hanna intimidated by anyone. That was the benefit, Grace thought, of showing no affect. You couldn't manipulate someone if you couldn't see their feelings.

"But then," Hanna went on, "that night, she did something *very* stupid. She grabbed one of my knives and tried to threaten me with it."

"What?"

"I should have let her, of course. It would have been better. But in the moment, you know, someone has a knife to your throat, it's hard to think."

"So you defended yourself," Grace said.

"She was a very prominent citizen, and I was a criminal. She made my one small crime validate all her claims. You can guess the rest. If I'd cut her arm or something, I don't think I would have even been arrested. She wouldn't have risked the potential embarrassment. But the neck, you know. Can't hide that."

"My God," Grace said.

"And that is why I don't work in Copenhagen anymore." Hanna folded her hands. "Now I'm fastidious in my restorations. No one could be more scrupulous. Every scrap of paper, every mote of dust is accounted for."

"Jacqueline knows? About the assault?"

"I've told her no lies. I would be at a much better establishment if I didn't have this mark." She dabbed at her mouth with the corner of a napkin. "But Jacqueline will hire anybody."

Grace had come to Jacqueline with no references and no credentials, just wildly feigned confidence and an offer to work for free for two months, learning all she could, while Jacqueline judged her potential. Grace had been broke when she made the offer, but desperate with hope and determination. When Jacqueline said yes, Grace sold the only thing of value she still owned, an agate horse-cameo bracelet and Graham-family heirloom that Riley had given her for her sixteenth birthday. She had hung on to it all through Prague and Berlin as some kind of proof of her good intentions. When she dropped it into the palm of Mme Maxine Lachaille, a dealer in Saint Germain des Prés who sometimes referred work to Jacqueline, Grace had felt as though she were discarding her own handcuffs.

"And what about you, Julie? Why aren't you working somewhere better?"

"You know," Grace said. "Stray cat."

"But you want to stay in Paris?"

Grace nodded. "I love it here."

"It's so bizarre to me, you know? A lot of American girls want to live in Paris, but what we do is *not* what they have in mind. Sitting in a basement all day, in private crisis over a badly dried varnish. You don't look like someone who should be in this line of work. More like one of those art gallery girls—someone smiling by the door."

"Oh, and would *you* want to do something like that?"

"Not for five minutes."

They laughed.

"But why Paris? You work late every night, and here you are today, alone, and you say you come every week. What about Paris do you love so much? If you have visa issues, why not go to New York and make sacks of money? Relatively speaking, of course."

Grace laughed again, but Hanna was waiting for an answer.

"I hate Americans," Grace said, thinking that answer would certainly suffice, but she was wrong, or she had taken a beat too long to answer. Now Hanna was not smiling. She was watching Grace carefully, like a piece of veneer she had glued down that was just waiting for her to look away before it sprang up again.

Grace knew she needed to give Hanna more to satisfy her curiosity, but she also knew Hanna would not be easily assuaged now that her radar had picked something up.

"My ex-boyfriend," she said carefully. "He was just released from prison, and I don't want him to find me. So I won't go back."

Already she regretted it.

Hanna raised her eyebrows. "Abusive?"

Grace nodded, relieved at Hanna's willing suggestion. "I'll stay here all my life if it means I never see him again."

She had said enough. Hanna averted her eyes, suddenly respectful of Grace's privacy, and called for the check.

When Grace got home that afternoon, she sat cross-legged on her bed and looked up Hanna Dunaj online. She found dozens of articles, all in Danish except for one in English from the *Copenhagen Post*. In 2003, Hanna Dunaj had been arrested for the assault of Antonia Houbraken, twenty-four, and subsequently charged with fraud. The photo with the article was not of Hanna but of Houbraken, leaving a building wearing a black leather jacket and a light blue scarf. She was tight-lipped, with long dark hair. She was the wife of a football player, FC Copenhagen forward Jakob Houbraken.

Hanna Dunaj had been a furniture restoration specialist in Copenhagen and Kolding, the article said, who also sold restored antiques. "Houbraken suspected that a piece purchased from Dunaj was not the antique Dunaj had represented, but a forgery. Houbraken reported that when she confronted Dunaj in her studio, Dunaj attacked her with a utility knife."

Hanna was extradited to her native Poland, but the article did not say why, only that she would serve her sentence there and be barred from Denmark for a period of ten years.

Grace read the article several times. She wouldn't have thought Hanna capable of sudden violence. Her blood seemed to run too cool. Riley had been that way too, except about Grace. "I love you so much it scares me," he'd told her more than once. When they were kids he'd said it with earnest bafflement, and she'd felt drunk on her own romantic power. But as they got a little older, he would sometimes mumble it into her ear as though she were hurting him.

Grace slid the silver box gently out of her canvas bag and onto her lap.

She lifted the lid and ran her fingertips gently along each of the inside corners, feeling for any hollowness, any give. A secret compartment would be close to proof that she had an authentic Mont, but she had not wanted to look in front of Hanna. Now she caught it with her fingernail: the thin rim of a hidden slip, a secret envelope. She slid her fingers inside, thrilling at the possibility of what might be waiting. But there was nothing. The compartment was empty.

She'd first read about James Mont in an old issue of *The Magazine Antiques*, which she now excavated from the ziggurat of various back issues stacked by date against the wall under her window.

James Mont was born Demetrios Pecintoglu, and he had come to America from Istanbul as a teenager in the 1920s. In his twenties, he got a rewiring job in a Brooklyn electrical supply shop, and began to sell lamps there that he had designed. One day, Frankie Yale, neighborhood crime boss, stopped in with a girlfriend. Mont charmed the pair up to their ears, and soon after, Yale asked Mont to decorate his house. Mont then decorated for Frank Costello and Lucky Luciano; he'd found the client base to delight in thick, glossy lacquers and metallic glitz. Grace, too, loved his ballsy juxtapositions of squat rectangles and sweeping curves. He made armrests out of carved and gilded Greek keys, repeated them along lamp bases and upholstery trim. Either he or his clients were obsessed with the motif. Grace remembered something she'd learned from Donald Mauce, her old boss in New York: The nouveau riche loved classical shit. To their eyes, nothing made new money look older than naked white statuary and a few plaster columns propping up the roof.

Mont and his clients were completely uninterested in the round-spectacled efficiency of midcentury modernism that was springing up around them. In a Mont house, you blew smoke, fucked against the mantel, and drank gimlets until you passed out in the flared arms of a velvet chair. Modernism wasn't Grace's catnip either. Modernism had spawned the American suburb, its blank cul-de-sacs and houses with garages like snouts, square green lawns, and little clumps of impatiens. Grace had come to loathe the American lawn and all its flat propriety. She preferred Mont's excess: a chair's legs flaring insolently beneath a deep, plush seat; strong arms surrounding a narrow back that arched up and away. Every corner, every joint, and every inch of material seemed to announce his intentions.

During Prohibition, Mont designed case goods with hidden compartments: bars that folded down into baby grand pianos, desks that held hidden gun drawers. He was a gambler who made big bets and had trouble covering his losses, and he had a fearsome temper that was only stoked by working for gangsters. In 1937, when Mont had graduated to Hollywood clientele, he married Helen Kim, an actress eight years his junior. Bob Hope attended the ceremony. Mont had achieved the kind of life he'd designed for others. Twenty-nine days later, Helen Kim was found dead in their apartment, an alleged suicide.

Two years after that, Mont asked a pretty young lampshade designer, Dorothy Burns, to his apartment to discuss a contract. When she resisted his advances, he beat her to within an inch of her life; she was hospitalized for two weeks. Burns was so humiliated by the attack, the trial, and the publicity that she hanged herself. Mont did five years in Sing Sing for the assault. He sat out the entire war there, and upon his release, he returned to eager clients, either forgiving or forgetful.

The boys had been sentenced to eight, and they hadn't attacked anyone.

Grace's Mont box must have come over to France long ago, perhaps with some starlet in the 1930s who used it for her jewels or pills. Some of the velvet along the bottom of the inside had come loose from its backing; the glue had deteriorated. One of the hinges had a dent Grace would have to bang out, and all of the hardware needed to be thoroughly cleaned, down to the screws. She would have to teach herself his gilding process in order to convincingly fill the chips and scratches. She relished every injury, running her fingers very lightly over them as if they were sensitive bruises. Each one was a chance. She would repair them all.

7

Grace was first to work on Monday morning. She spread the last batch of beads on linen towels to dry. What had been a pile of murky clods a few days ago was now a speckled rainbow made of thousands of bright, worthless jewels. She pulled a pair of cotton gloves from the clean laundry. Latex gloves protected their skin from turpentine, benzene, and toxins; at other times, the cotton gloves protected the work from their skin. Grace rolled two clothed fingers over the glass beads and then examined her fingertips up close, looking for any remaining residue. She felt sudden warmth at the nape of her neck.

"You won't find any dirt."

Grace wheeled around, colliding with Hanna. "You scared me." She touched the back of her neck, calming the nerves there.

"Now that we can see the beads clearly," Hanna said, "I can source replacements from Kuznetsov for the cracked and broken ones. We'll have to go over each color to distress it reasonably so it matches. But today I will continue with the figures."

She picked up the sheep she had begun on Friday.

"Six sheep, two maidens, three swans, and an ox! It will take me days simply to gather the right materials! I need white wax, shell silver, gelatin, silvering solution, wooden dowels, gum arabic—did I tell you it's private? A collector."

Dealers had profit margins to consider, and museums had budgets, not that Zanuso ever did museum work. A collector meant a maniac with money. Hanna wouldn't have to cut a single corner.

She was the same Hanna, Grace told herself. Nothing had changed except what Grace knew about her. But all day, the sound of Hanna's chair grinding on the floor, the clip of her pliers, her quick exhalations of accomplishment—every noise from across the table seemed threatening. Hanna, her friend, beige and orderly, had slit a woman's throat and gone to prison. Hanna had neither hidden her past nor flaunted it. Grace had simply misjudged her, just as she was meant to.

Grace imagined shrugging over a sandwich and telling Hanna everything she'd done to end up in Jacqueline Zanuso's basement. Impossible. Hanna had not needed to unravel any lies; she was only filling in blank spaces. Grace had crudely, hurriedly filled in her own blank spaces whenever they appeared, and never with the truth. She was like someone faking a crossword puzzle by socking in random letters so it would look finished from a distance.

Grace started at the buzz of machinery and looked up to see Hanna with the keyboard vacuum. She had taken a break from the sheep to clean the field of wheat in the centerpiece's summer quarter. She moved the nozzle in tiny circles among the stalks in a trance. Grace had been shaken by Hanna's confession, but Hanna wasn't unsettled at all.

When Hanna went out for afternoon coffee, Grace went to the computer and checked the *Albemarle Record*—just once, quickly, crossing it off for the day—and then her e-mail. She used one address for work and another for her parents. Today there was an unwelcome e-mail from her mother.

Grace,

I saw Riley yesterday. He was at the hardware store with his father buying potting soil. I could hardly believe it, I practically fell on him hugging him, but I don't think he wanted to see me. I can't begin to imagine what he's been through since I saw him.

Here is the Graham's address in case you want to send a letter.

429 Heathcliff Ave
Garland, TN 37729

As if Grace didn't know that address better than she knew her own name.

Why did her mother send her these e-mails about Riley? Just to punish

her? To gloat that Grace's other family lay in shambles? Because she suspected that Grace was somehow responsible? Because she'd hoped that
Grace and Riley would marry and make Grace's family Graham-adjacent?
Because she was pretending, now that Grace was half a world away, to be
a different kind of mother?

Riley was walking around Garland now. She could see him walking by
their old college house on Orange Street and knowing that other people
lived there now, boys the same age he'd been. She imagined the sun in his
eyes, a car's steering wheel in his hands, the way a grocery store would
look when he hadn't been inside one in so long, the newly sharp smell of
the home that hadn't been his home in years.

When Grace got home that evening, Mme Freindametz was at the kitchen
table, drinking a cup of tea and doing a word search in a Polish magazine.
Grace smiled quickly and put her pot of water on the stove to steam rice
and green beans.

"What are you going to put in your nice box?" Mme Freindametz
asked.

"My box?"

"Yes, your new box, the silver one." She smiled approvingly.

At first Grace did not understand. She pointed to the tin breadbox she
had bought a few months prior, which was yellow and had a picture of a
topiary on it. "That? That box?"

Freindametz shook her head. "No, the one in your bedroom, the
new one!"

"You were in my room?"

"Yes," she said. "The vent was clogged, the vent behind your desk."

"Why would you—" Grace began, but Freindametz jerked the handle
of her teacup so that the tea sloshed against the side. Grace realized that
she had raised her voice. "How did you know it was new?" She tried to
keep her voice even, to stay calm or to sound calm. "Have you been in
there before?"

Freindametz opened her mouth but did not speak.

"How often? Every week, every day?"

Freindametz looked as if Grace had slapped her. "This is my house,"
she finally said.

"It's just a pretty box," Grace said slowly. "You don't put anything in it."

She turned off the stove and emptied the simmering water from the pot into the sink. She set the pot back on the burner, where it hissed, and then she went up to her room and shut the door.

Hanna was working exclusively on the centerpiece, and Grace was to help her whenever Jacqueline didn't have anything else for her. On Tuesday morning, all there was for Grace to do was fix a botched seam on a clumsy ceramic patch. They were often called upon to redo the shoddy guesswork of new clients who tried to repair their lesser antiques themselves and only worsened the damage. They brought these mutilated things to Zanuso et Filles, as helpless and embarrassed as people who have just tried to cut their own hair for the first time. When the beloved artifact was returned to them, they would run their fingers over the invisible repair, disbelieving. That moment often awoke some dissatisfaction, and they began to notice, in the antiques their families had passed down, flaws they'd lived with for decades. Suddenly, these marks of time were unbearable to them.

But because restoration could hurt the value of some antiques, Hanna, Amaury, and Grace had to be good enough that their work was undetectable to the human eye. Their clients wanted it that way, of course. Grace wouldn't ruin an Austrian compact with an American hinge, or gum up a two-hundred-year-old music box with an adhesive that had not been invented until 1850. For private collectors, they restored antiques that needed to look perfect only within the safe space of the home; for dealers, they restored antiques that would be sold to the public with little fuss—an old bureau improved from very good to mint. Grace seldom knew exactly where the pieces went after she finished with them. As long as Jacqueline's clients kept their valuables close, away from carbon dating and fluorescent spectroscopes, no one would be disappointed.

Hanna was telling Grace something about the antique linen she'd found to re-create the shepherdesses' dresses so they could convincingly herd the woolen sheep in the spring quarter of the centerpiece. Grace hadn't been paying attention. Jacqueline was on the phone in her office, yelling already, at ten in the morning, and Grace strained to hear her over Hanna. Grace was worried: The little patch job, which had taken her an hour at the most and was now drying, was the only non-centerpiece work she'd had since she finished the birdcage. There had been slow periods before, but usually because pieces were held up in freight or customs— they knew the work was coming. Grace couldn't think of anything coming.

The trouble at work had started when their most frequent clients, a cluster of four dealers from Clignancourt, had closed their shops after an export tax scandal. Grace didn't know how Jacqueline would make up the business. Grace had been at Zanuso the shortest time. She would be the first to go.

"Julie, are you listening to me?" Hanna looked over her glasses. "I need you to start on the orchard, in the summer quarter. You have to make the peaches." She held up a magnifier to one of her photographs. "These peaches are a little whimsical," she said. "More pink than is natural, and with a deeper groove. There are only two that are salvageable."

Grace nodded. "You need how many more, nine?"

"Eleven, and in different stages of ripeness."

Hanna handed Grace the photograph, a close-up of the peaches. Each was no larger than a pea, made from wax and painted in variegated shades of orange, yellow, and a rush of pink. Their stems were green-painted wire.

"Two should be broken, like this." Hanna said, handing Grace another picture. In this one, the peach had a bite missing, exposing the pit.

Grace knew the broken peaches alone would take her all morning, quite possibly longer. Like needlework, the centerpiece was intended to display skill. She and Hanna had to do the work even better than the eighteenth-century artisans who'd created it, if their work was to pass. Grace had begun here with easy things, learning on jobs too simple for Jacqueline to waste Hanna's or Amaury's time with: vases with cracked feet, jeweled compacts with bent clasps. She had since worked up to broken filigree, chipped enamel, and even, once, a reliquary with several slack gemstone settings that allowed the stones inside to rattle around like loose teeth. This week she would make pea-sized peaches; next week she'd be painting Bible verses on grains of rice. If there was a next week.

She rolled a ball of wax in her fingers, measured it, and recorded the diameter so that all the future peaches would match. She pinched and rolled and pinched and rerolled ten copies. When she had eleven equal balls of wax, she dug out her veiner, a plastic stem with a tapered end that cake decorators used to carve marzipan, and began to push a cleft down the side of the first peach. When all the peaches had clefts and pin-sized pits for the stems, Grace cut bites from two of them with her knife's narrowest blade and held her breath as she sculpted the round pits. She wheedled a few winding veins into the pits with the eye end of an upholstery needle.

Grace carved and painted peaches all day, stalling toward the end. She scumbled their shoulders with dry paint while she waited for everyone to go home. Hanna was last to leave. When she had finally gone, Grace pulled her James Mont box from the brown paper grocery bag under the bookcase where she had hidden it that morning. First, she removed all the hardware, and then she began to sand. Mont's gilding process required sanding each layer of paint or leaf down to nearly nothing before adding another. Grace worked softly down through the layers, pausing to take photographs as each hidden layer of color was revealed.

The studio computer had broken speakers, so Grace brought Jacqueline's laptop out of her office to listen to NPR while she worked. During the day, they tended toward Chopin, Schubert, and the news on the radio, but alone at night, Grace often craved American voices. She didn't care what they were talking about. Lynne Rossetto Kasper's voice, in particular, had a fatty American timbre that eased her expat melancholy. Grace snapped her goggles on and started melting powdered enamel with a torch while Lynne discussed the attributes of farmer's cheese. Minutes ticked by behind the tiny flame until Grace heard a door slam.

"I decided not to leave it uncovered overnight," Hanna said. "Even to dry. The dust."

Grace watched Hanna taking in Grace's secret project, their boss's computer.

"Please don't tattle," Grace said.

Hanna rolled her eyes and came over to look. "It is pretty," she murmured, running her fingers over the chip where Mont's gilt receded in mica-like layers. "What are you going to do with it?"

"Sell it, of course," Grace said. "I need something going when this place collapses."

"How much do you think you'll get?"

"Three, maybe four hundred."

Hanna giggled. "Is it even worth it?"

"He's worth more in the U.S.," Grace said, defensive. "You must make a lot more than I do here, if that's so paltry to you."

"How much does she pay you?"

"How much does she pay *you*?"

"Just under three a month," Hanna said. "Half what I made in Copenhagen."

"Three thousand?" Grace knew that Hanna made more but she had not known how much more.

"How much does she pay you? I know you get cash."

"*One* thousand," Grace said.

"My God, how can you live on that?"

"I barely do." Grace covered her eyes. "I don't know what I'll do if I lose this job."

"I didn't know you were so worried about it," Hanna said.

"Look around," Grace said. "You and Amaury have got the only work."

"Valois will open up again under some other name. He always does, and Lemoine too. The work will come back."

Grace nodded, uncertain.

"I'll talk to Jacqueline," Hanna said. "I'll make sure she knows how valuable you are."

Grace hardly slept that night, and when she did, she dreamt that she and Mrs. Graham were pulling weeds in her herb garden, and then Grace dug up some teeth and tried to hide them from Mrs. Graham, but she grabbed them out of Grace's hand and ran inside. Grace couldn't go back to sleep after that.

In the morning, when Grace got to work, Hanna was already hunched in a corner like a dead spider, her fingers bunched around a thread of beads. Grace sat down across from her and picked up a peach stem.

They worked silently until Hanna stood up and went to the sink. It was half past eight. When she came back with her mug of tea, she gently took the tiny peach from Grace's hand and held it up. "These were all finished last night," she said. "Whatever you're doing now is going to ruin them."

Grace tried to think of something she could say that would make sense.

She was too tired to reason. "I couldn't sleep," she said, as though that answered a question.

"Me neither." Hanna had switched to English. They'd never spoken English together.

They were the only ones in the studio. Hanna put her hands on her hips and looked toward the transom windows. "You know, today I have been away from Copenhagen for nine years. My anniversary."

"You want to go back," Grace said, now speaking English too. It felt strange and private, as though she'd suddenly shed her clothes.

"Doesn't matter if I do or not," Hanna said.

For a minute they were quiet, which was unusual only because neither woman was working. They were accustomed to long stretches of silence, but not idle ones. Hanna looked at Grace. Grace rearranged some of the tools in her jars.

"What was he in prison for? I don't think you told me."

"Robbery. Antiques, actually." Grace felt the blood rush into her cheeks. "He and some friends looted an estate."

"An *estate*?"

She didn't know how to describe the Wynne House, the likes of which did not exist in Paris. The nearest example she could think of was Versailles. "A big old house where no one lives anymore, and now it's open to tourists, but they almost never come."

Hanna raised her eyebrows. "Daring," she said. Grace couldn't tell if she was sincere.

"They were caught in five days. They hadn't sold anything yet. The estate got it all back." Except for the painting.

Hanna began to flip through her notes, but Grace could tell she wasn't really looking at them. "When did this happen?"

"About three years ago," Grace said. "Just after I first came to Europe." She folded her hands in her lap. "Now they're out and it's just got me a little . . . unsettled." She shrugged hopelessly.

"This is the one you're afraid of," Hanna said.

"Yeah," Grace said, her throat growing hot. She shifted uneasily in her seat. "I never broke up with him. I was afraid to. I went to Prague for a summer college thing, and a week later, I read in the local news that he and his two best friends had been arrested."

"I didn't know you'd been in Prague. Why didn't you ever tell me that?
Grace shook her head. "I don't know. Never came up."

Hanna frowned. "What did you do when you found out?"

"Nothing," Grace said quickly. "I never talked to him again. I was so
shocked and horrified, I just—shut down."

Hanna held a line of tiny beads threaded along a needle. She tipped her
hand and Grace watched the beads slip off the needle and down the thread
like drops of water.

"I never went home. I was supposed to go home after, but I didn't. And
I never wrote, never called. Not even to his family."

"You found out about the arrest on the *news*? You didn't talk to him?"

"We e-mailed each other. But I had no idea he was planning it."

"Then it's good you got away when you did," Hanna said.

"Yeah," Grace said. "You never know someone as well as you think
you do."

Hanna seemed to think this over. Grace didn't know what she wanted
to happen. She regretted lying to Hanna—how many times, just in this
one conversation? She hadn't meant to. It never felt like lying while she
was doing it so much as trying to tell the truth and failing.

And of anyone she had ever known, Hanna was the one Grace could
tell. Hanna would forgive her; she would have to. She had slit a woman's
throat. She knew how quickly a bad decision was born.

"It was serious?" Hanna asked.

"We'd been together since I was twelve years old," Grace said. She
could say *that* truthfully because she'd had so much practice saying it
before. "We lived together."

"And you didn't know they were going to do this crazy thing? What,
were you locked in the basement?"

"He didn't tell me anything," Grace said, angry with Hanna for joking
about abuse that, as far as *she* knew, was very real.

"You were an appraiser's assistant all through college, weren't you?"

Grace nodded. She had exaggerated her biography a little for Jacqueline when she'd started. Hanna thought Grace—*Julie*—was twenty-six.

"I think he thought I would help him," Grace said. "When I came
home."

"But he didn't tell you?" Hanna blinked at her.

"He only told me exactly what he wanted me to know," Grace said. "And I'd never had any reason not to believe him, you know?"

Every time she the missed the turnoff, it got harder to see the way back.

Amaury came in mumbling and took his spot, immediately bending over the collection of tiny brass movements before him.

Hanna nodded toward the computer screen, where she'd pulled up a photograph of the three trees in the centerpiece's fall quarter. "Acorns," she said to Grace. "Twenty." She held out the envelope of surviving original acorns, and Grace had to get up and fetch it from her.

Grace hadn't noticed how clammy her hands were until her fingers touched Hanna's.

Back at her table, she grabbed a fresh thumb-sized lump of wax and started pinching off balls the size of peppercorns.

"Too big," Hanna said.

Grace pulled over the magnifier and tried to disappear behind the lens.

She carved each bead of wax into an acorn on a needle mount, a T-pin stapled by its arms to a square of plywood. She perched a ball of wax on the upended needle and carved the groove that separated the cap, and then she pulled the end upward, tapering the nut. The first one took twenty minutes, but the second took her only ten, and then she cranked out nine more at six minutes apiece. She was grateful for Amaury's silent presence. Hanna wouldn't ask her any more questions in front of him.

The studio was quiet for the next two hours except for the tap and scrape of their tools. Just after eleven, Jacqueline opened her office door and stuck her head out. "Julie, I have some good news for you," she sang. "You're getting a visit from an old friend today." She laughed, and all the coffee Grace had drunk rushed up the back of her throat.

Jacqueline clomped out of her office in her heeled sandals holding a burgundy cardboard box that was warped at the corners. Grace knew it well: the ugly teapot, again, far more welcome than any real old friend.

Jacqueline leaned over Grace's table. She had a sunglasses tan, pale goggles across her face. "What are these tiny things? Are we making microbes now?"

"Acorns," Grace said, and her boss rolled her eyes. Poor Jacqueline, so disinterested in decorative arts, stuck in the business most obsessed with their minutiae.

Jacqueline flapped a hand toward the red box. "Do it now," she said. "She's coming back for it late this afternoon—needs it for a luncheon tomorrow, or something."

Hanna grunted as though losing Grace would present a great hardship for her project. Her hand darted greedily for one of Grace's acorns, and she began to inspect it.

"She's very good at this tiny work," Hanna said to Jacqueline, peering into her palm. "You should look at this. It would have taken me longer."

Hanna was trying to help, Grace knew, and she was grateful. If only it mattered.

The teapot was a trompe l'oeil cauliflower. The top half formed a nubby white floret, the lower half and spout a cradle of green cabbage leaves. Strasbourg, 1750, but who cared? It looked like something from a sidewalk sale in Garland, something that would sit next to a rack of leopard-print reading glasses. Perhaps it had once been a good example of its kind, but it was a Frankenstein piece now. The owners, entertainment lawyers in their forties, broke the teapot again and again. The first time, the bowl was cracked in three pieces; the second time it was the handle; the third, the bowl again. Why did they keep fixing it? What did the cauliflower teapot mean to them? A burdensome inheritance? The cracked hopes of their marriage embodied by an ugly wedding present?

There had been a time when a teapot was just a teapot.

Now the pot's lid was fractured, the knob broken clean away, and several of the porcelain cabbage leaves at the bottom were busted up along their green veins. A mess. In the box, nestled in the raffia frizz, was a plastic bag holding all the missing pieces and shards of broken porcelain, in sizes ranging from Communion wafer to steel-cut oat. Grace emptied the bag onto her blotter and examined the smallest shards, wondering who had done what to whom that they needed to punish their teapot like this, and why in hell they cared about it so much. She called it her Cabbage Patch Kid, but nobody here got the joke.

But the same couple had also given Grace the most beautiful job she'd ever laid hands on, more than a year ago, another teapot. Maybe they collected them, or perhaps they had one of those accidental collections forced on people after someone noticed they had two of something.

That teapot was too breathtaking to have been acquired casually.

Stunningly fragile, 1820s, sunlight-colored glass with finely detailed brass trim that formed the handle, a pheasant's graceful neck, and the spout, a lamb's head. On the lid, a swan reared back as if to attack. The animals looked alive, trapped and furious. That teapot was in near-perfect condition too, but for the tiniest speck of discoloration on the base. The surgery would be dangerous, and Grace was loath to risk it. She remembered the Hawthorne story she'd read in high school about the man who became obsessed with removing his wife's birthmark. The surgery removed the spot and killed her.

The teapot survived Grace's ministrations. She would give its owners this: When they threw a teapot across the room, they threw the right one.

She had hoped that if she could just keep the truth inside her, a nicer story than the real one would grow like a seed, taking root and getting stronger, until it grew around the truth and consumed it. The good twin would destroy the evil twin, or something like that. In her fantasy, no one, not even Grace, would be able to tell the difference.

But she had never forgotten the truth. She'd told shoddy lies. The story was pale and underdeveloped and looked like the impostor it was.

She took up a shard of green porcelain with her tweezers and slid it into the space she believed was its home. The piece just fit.

When Jacqueline had stepped out for her afternoon coffee, a man rang the bell.

"Puis-je vous aider?" Grace asked him at the door, but she knew. The teapot's owner was just how she'd pictured him. He wore a navy blue suit with peaked lapels and high armholes, and he looked ashamed. Grace slipped on some clean gloves, but just for show; the teapot was a salvage title at this point. She tucked it into its raffia nest and draped some tissue over it, as though she were putting it to bed.

"Don't touch it for at least twenty-four hours," she told him. "It looks solid, but it's still very fragile." He grimaced and took the box from her. "You really can't use it anymore," she said. "Especially not for coffee, okay? It will stain the cracks, and then everyone will know."

Amaury clucked from his corner. The man opened his mouth as if he were about to explain. "I hate this fucking thing," he said.

When he left, Grace thought she saw a smirk on Hanna's face.

"What?" she asked.

"Don't stain the cracks," Hanna gently mocked her. "Then everyone will know."

After everyone else had gone home, Grace checked the *Albemarle Record*. Nothing. She took out her Mont box. She began to painstakingly sand down the layer of gold lacquer that she had applied the night before so that it was just a warm metallic film that revealed the layer of silver lacquer below. She moved her fingertips across the wood lightly. If she went too deep and broke through completely, she'd have to do the whole layer over.

Three and a half years ago, she had thought the solution to all her problems was to disappear with Riley, somewhere enviable and romantic and *far away*, somewhere like Paris, thinking that if they could just be alone together, without interference from anyone back home, they would be happy again. His love for her, abundant as it was, would make up for everything she had left behind, and her love for him—if not as potent as it once was, at least as rigorous—would always keep him close to her. *He'll never leave you*, Alls had said. And now here she was, alone in Paris in a room full of antiques (the likes of which she could not even have imagined then), fearing that he would find her, that she would finally be alone in Paris with her husband.

Three silent years stood between them. She imagined that with each passing month, he tapped new reserves of rage. But those were the admissible fears. Uglier by far was the fear that he had forgiven her. She could see him convincing himself that they'd merely hit a rough patch. He would appear one day out of nowhere, yet another of his grand gestures, ready to be loved again. Finally, there was the fear of his eyes on her, of seeing in them a reflection of a girl she'd left in America.

It could have been worse, she reminded herself. If they'd found the painting he would have gotten ten years, twenty. Or he would have turned her in. She reached back and touched her bald spot, smoothing the hair down over it.

Just after nine, Grace was sanding the corners of the box, the places most vulnerable to too much pressure, when the sun went down all at once in a way that always spooked her. The windows became black rectangles, blurry feet passing across them.

Then she saw his feet. Standing, heels to the window. He was leaning against the building. Those were *his* feet. His shoes, canvas slip-ons with the heels tamped down. His ankles, the left one knobby from spraining it playing pickup basketball. His calves, long and taut, the red-gold hair she would know anywhere.

She pushed against the floor and rolled her chair back into the shadows, away from the windows. The casters on the concrete floor were loud, a rattling cough.

He couldn't see her. She was in the shadows all the way back to Amaury's corner.

She pulled her feet into her chair and her knees up to her chest. He couldn't see her. He would have to lie down on the sidewalk to look in. A cigarette butt landed on the sidewalk and the left shoe ground it out. Riley had never smoked cigarettes, but she had to remember that she didn't know him anymore.

She closed her eyes. When she opened them, the feet were just some kid's, some kid in slip-ons with the heels flattened. The ankles and calves looked plain and strange. They were not his, and he was not hers.

IV
New York

8

In August, Grace's father demanded to drive her to New York. She wanted Riley to drive her, but his classes began the same week. The trip was the most time Grace and her father had ever spent alone together. "Listen," he said in West Virginia. "I know you're sure you want to do this. But if it ever gets to be too much—"

"It's just college," she said.

"If it ever gets to be too much, don't be afraid to come home."

She rolled her eyes toward the billboards. "Thanks, but I think I'll be okay."

He squinted. "Of course you'll be okay. I never said you wouldn't be okay."

Grace and her father huffed up to the fifth floor of the dorm and shuffled past the loud families. In Grace's assigned room, a girl sat on one bed. Her hair was electric blue at the scalp and shining black below her ears. She wore white fake eyelashes and a T-shirt that read FUCK A MUSICIAN.

"Are you Kendall? I'm Grace."

"Gra-a-ace," she said. "Grace from Tennessee." She extended a hand with a different snake ring on each finger. "What's your thing? What are you working on?"

"Probably something in art hist—"

"I'm doing 'Bewildering Desire: Hentai and Idée Fixe.'" She laughed. Grace's father was struck mute, reduced to a porter. "You'll become one of us sooner or later." She looked at the quilted floral duffel bag that Grace had dropped on the floor. "Maybe later," she said.

Grace's father glanced at her shirt and reddened. "So you're a musician?"

"No," she said.

"Kendall's from Staten Island," Grace said, trying to change the conversation.

"Um, *Long* Island," she said. "But we lived in Manhattan until last year. Our dad still does. And I'm Jezzie. Kendall's my little sister. Oh my God—me, Kendall! That is *too* funny. She's currently napping elsewhere. Big night. I'm just back here for nostalgia reasons." She paused. "I do some theater," she said.

"Is Kendall a—is she an actress too?" Grace's father asked.

"Ha ha! Oh my God, you are charming. No, she's business school. Big desk, dolla-dolla-bills, all that." She stood up and hoisted her bag to her shoulder. "But I must leave you now," she said, collapsing her knees together as if she had to pee and frowning like a party clown.

Kendall was tiny, shrewd, and oddly maternal toward both Jezzie, who often came to their room to flop on her sister's bed and whine, and Lana, Kendall's loose-cannon best friend. Lana Blix-Kane was rich and terrified of being ignored. Grace couldn't see that then, only luxurious confidence. No matter what Lana did—guzzled vodka until she passed out in a strange apartment, spent thousands in a single shopping day, bought a puppy on Saturday and returned it on Monday morning—she was unpunished and unchanged, as though her parents had also bought her an *undo* button.

Grace met Lana her second night in New York. Lana came in with Kendall, but she didn't introduce herself. She sat on Kendall's bed and slumped back with fatigue.

"Mmm, you," she said to Grace. "You're a *serious girlfriend*." She turned to Kendall. "Right?"

Kendall shrugged. "You're the expert."

"There's this, like, ether of contentment," Lana said. "Like a house cat."

Grace opened her mouth to protest, but she didn't know what to say.

"I mean, you are obviously a fish out of water here," Lana said. "But you probably don't even know that. So you must have a boyfriend. Know what I mean? Well, probably not, right? You wouldn't."

Lana wore her fine blond hair impossibly teased, and Grace would later learn that if Lana had not just rolled out of bed, she worked hard to look as though she had. Her nail polish was always chipped, her eye makeup smudged and flaking. "You want to look like you're just getting home from a really good time," she once explained as she came at Grace with a clotted mascara wand, trying to fix her. But for now, all Grace knew was that Lana looked like she really had just come home from a really good time.

Grace squinted, buying time. She didn't yet know whether she cared if this girl liked her or not. "What about me? Aside from the hand-me-down bag."

"Your hair!" they said at the same time. They looked at each other and laughed, adoringly, and Grace felt a pang of jealousy ring from deep within.

"You have girlfriend hair," Kendall said. Her voice, deep and dry, was disconcerting coming from such a small person. "It's so long, indicating resistance to change, and thus monogamy." She sipped coffee from an enormous camping thermos. Her own hair was dark and short, as if she wouldn't let it tether her to anything.

"Fair," Grace said.

"Two," Kendall said. "It's very brown."

"So brown," said Lana.

"Not hazelnut, not toasty clove or whatever. Just plain brown. It's not a color anyone would dye their hair," Kendall said. "It *screams* nature."

"But nature whispers," Lana said. "*Nature*," she hissed. "What I was saying: You have virgin hair."

"Oh, no," Grace said, blushing. "I'm not a virgin."

Kendall shushed her with a hand. "It's, um, school picture ready. And if you came all the way from backwater mystery or wherever and didn't change your hair—"

"You've probably had the same boyfriend for, like, three years," Lana finished.

"Unless he's some old creeper," Kendall said, raising a finger. "Who's into *virgin* hair and Peter Pan collars."

"He's not," Grace said quickly. She was ready to shock them. "He's my husband. And we've been together for six years."

Lana's eyes went wide. "You're *married*?"

"His name is Riley, and he's a sophomore in college."

"Where?" Kendall asked.

They would know too many people at Harvard, Princeton. "The Sorbonne," she said.

They demanded evidence. Grace brought over her new laptop and settled between them on the bed. She showed them photos of her and Riley together until they looked seasick.

"They don't make ones like that up here," Kendall said when they had finished.

"You sound so surprised," Grace said.

"I just thought you'd be with someone really, I don't know, serious-looking."

"Seminary student," Grace added, but their faces showed no recognition. She tried again: "Eagle Scout?"

"It's so fucked up that you're married, though. Are you, like, hard-core Christians?"

"No," Grace said. "We knew we'd spend the rest of our lives together, so why not? But it's a secret. No one knows."

Kendall nodded, uncomprehending.

"Who's that guy?" Lana pointed to the last photo, in which Riley, Greg, and Alls were fishing from the Kimbroughs' dock on Norris Lake.

"That's Greg, one of Riley's friends since they were little kids."

"He looks like a glazed doughnut. A fat baby-man," Lana said. "Look at those blond wisps."

"He pulls the crust off his sandwiches," Grace said.

Lana pointed again. "And that one?"

"Alls. His best friend."

"They have super-weird names down there," Kendall said to her. "Last names as first names—what's the one you told me yesterday?"

"Tipton Hartley," Grace said. "Goes by Tip. 'Just-the-tip' Hartley."

They laughed, all together this time, and it felt good to Grace.

"Wait, tell me another," Lana said.

"Um, Malone." Grace said. "Vines."

"*Vines?*" Kendall howled, and Grace felt a weight lift.

"Tell me about Allllls," Lana said. "I like him. He looks disturbed."

"He's not disturbed, he's just had a hard time." She swallowed. "It's short for Allston, Allston Javier Hughes." She didn't want to talk about him, so she told them about the Kimbroner instead.

Lana was an artist. Kendall mentioned it in passing, in the same tone she might say someone was a Pisces or ten pounds overweight. Not in the reverent way people talked about Riley.

The previous year, when Lana was only seventeen, she'd gotten one of her videos into a Chelsea gallery group show. Her piece was a three-minute loop of Lana, naked and sick with the flu, lit in gauzy, softly glowing peaches and pinks. She blinked wet lashes up close to the camera lens and licked her chapped lips until they glistened. Too congested to inhale through her runny nose, she breathed audibly through her mouth. At two minutes, Lana hacked up phlegm and spat, strings of saliva clinging to her chin. At two and a half she stood up, weak and unsteady as a fawn, her naked body rising through the frame in fluid latitudes. Knees shaking, she turned and walked away from the camera until the whole length of her body filled the frame, and she disappeared through a doorway. Seconds later, she could be heard retching into a toilet.

The video had been pulled from the show on its second day when a critic discovered the naked subject had been only sixteen at the time of its filming. The gallery could have been charged with distributing child pornography, which had seemed to be Lana's intention. Grace wanted so much to ask her about the video, which both fascinated and troubled her, but she was worried her questions were too basic. When she finally did, Lana nodded as though she'd been asked these same questions a thousand times. "I'm interested in 'prettiness,' debasement, and self-objectification," she said. "But subverted through entrapment and the transference of contagious shame."

To make her art, Lana lived it, playing the dumb damsel in front of her camera as well as the director behind it. Grace thought Lana was the most calculating person she had ever met. She could hardly look her in the eye for days after seeing the video, not because she'd seen Lana naked, but because she was ashamed to have so underestimated her.

On Grace's first day of Western Art I, the professor's voice heavy in her ears, she looked around the darkened theater and saw a hundred girls like her: nails clean, notebooks out, eyes screwed up at the screen. But their hair was slicked back in ballerina buns or wild and loose, and their ears held pearls or bold feathered hoops, wooden disks. She saw that they all wanted to be versions of the same thing, only they were so much further along.

Grace began to spend her Saturday afternoons wandering around Chelsea galleries, taking notes on free postcards and press releases. She ignored the heavy ache in her legs as she wound her way up metal staircases that looked as though they went nowhere promising. She learned to push through unmarked metal doors into spaces two stories high, white and hollow, that housed what she had begun to realize were ideas. Art was not there to look nice. Art was there to scratch at people's brains, to help ideas find traction in metaphor that they could not when made explicit. She was exhausted with thinking and with unlearning so much of what she had thought before.

She returned to her dorm at dusk, her brain abuzz. When she saw something and really got it, she knew it, she *felt* it, and it thrilled her to slip into the crawlspace of someone else's mind.

Though she couldn't quite position Riley's careful oils of historic buildings among the work she saw now, she assured herself that this was only because she didn't know why it so compelled him or what his intentions were. How could she? She hadn't known enough to ask. She was only just learning about art and intent. It didn't matter if Riley's paintings looked sedate, as long as the idea behind them was not. That mystery excited her too: that Riley had ideas that were still opaque to her, corners of his brain still unexplored.

She tried to explain Lana's video to him on the phone. She couldn't bring herself to show him Lana's naked body, a jealousy she knew would please Lana to no end. "But where is the skill?" Riley asked. "Anyone could make that." Anyone couldn't, Grace tried to explain. Only Lana could make her art because it was her idea. Then Grace changed the subject. Maybe it just didn't translate into words.

She began to look for a part-time job and to reform her appearance for New York. She middle-parted her hair and sprayed it with Kendall's various glosses: *Shine! Glass! Mirror!* She bought draped, slinky knits from the ten-dollar stores on Fourteenth Street and painted her nails the same metallic black that Kendall painted hers. Lest Kendall charge Grace with imitating her, she waited for Kendall to make the suggestion. She always did, and Grace was grateful for her diagnoses.

When Grace got an interview for a position as an art appraisal assistant, she bought an eight-dollar polyester blazer at Goodwill. She tried it on for Kendall that night, shrugging it on and sticking her arms out.

"Jesus," Kendall said. "That is repugnant. Do you want to borrow something?"

The seams dimpled, but Grace hadn't thought it was that bad. She happily let Kendall reconstruct her into what Kendall called "Grace 2.0." When Kendall got to Grace's shoes, she bit her lip and sighed. She wore two sizes smaller than Grace did, so she couldn't save her there.

The next day, Grace rode the 6 train uptown from their dorm to the East Sixties, a part of the city she had not yet had any reason to see. On the train she stared at her shoes, twelve-dollar ballet flats in imitation patent leather with ragged bows. They looked like children's shoes, first Communion shoes. It was raining, and the gum around the sole had begun to give up. The sole drooped open at the toe like a mouth.

Grace knew that no one would hire her in those shoes.

When she got off the train, she ran down the block through the rain hoping to find a shoe store. Every block in Manhattan seemed to have a shoe store, a nail salon, and a bank branch. She found one and headed straight for the back, where any sale racks would be, and there she saw a pair of boots standing tall among the other shoes. They were black calfskin, almost knee-high, with zippers running up the outside. They had heels high enough for a subway rat to run under. The boots were 60 percent off and still two hundred dollars. She had never had shoes half as expensive. They would wipe her little bank account clean. She remembered the photos of the office she had seen on the appraiser's website: the giant windows, the glass-fronted bookcases, the long brocade curtains that puddled on the floor. These boots could get her this job.

She dropped her plastic flats in the trash can on the way out. She wasn't used to wearing heels and felt herself walking differently, like a racehorse stalking to the gate. By the time she stepped out of the elevator on the ninth floor of the office building, Grace had become a different person. The door read MAUCE FINE ARTS APPRAISAL in gold stick-on lettering. She rang the bell, smoothed her hair, and rubbed her lips together.

He pulled the door open and looked her up and down. "Nice boots," he said. "Donald Mauce." He opened his mouth wide enough to fit a whole egg in it. He was tall and very thin, with pale, waxy skin and wet eyes. His sparse silver mustache flared out over fleshy lips. Grace was reminded of a white catfish she'd once caught at Norris Lake. "Bethany will be here in a sec. She's our vice president, just ran out for soup."

Donald sat down behind a green metal desk and gestured for Grace to sit in a rusted chrome chair in front of it. This was not the office in the pictures, but a single stale room. Donald's desk was piled with papers and receipts surrounding a plastic barrel of peanuts. She could smell the shells in the trash can. She felt him looking at her, grinning, and she dropped her eyes to her boots on the stained carpet. She'd worn a black dress and lipstick, downtown-college-girl red.

Donald asked her about her art history classes, how she liked school so far. He asked where she was from and she told him Tennessee.

"Oh, wow," he said, leaning forward on his desk. "What's *that* like?"

The door hinge whined, and a woman stepped in with a deli bag. "You must be the new girl," she said. "I'm Bethany." She smiled barely, as though it hurt. She wore tinted eyeglasses and white running shoes with her office pants. Her hair was a beige mushroom.

Donald nodded. "We're just getting to know each other."

He gave Grace the job. She left with a handful of peanuts and two Sotheby's auction catalogs on nineteenth- and twentieth-century decorative arts. He winked at her and said there would be a quiz.

9

Grace spent her first day working for Donald Mauce alphabetizing his bookshelves. Bethany was out and Donald didn't know how to teach her anything. He sat at his desk, reading and leaning back in his squeaking chair, as Grace heaved the books around on a stepladder in front of him. Yellow dust flew up from pages and she coughed. Donald packed up at four. He said he had a wine group at six and if he was late they would start without him. What was Grace's favorite wine, he asked. Whiskey, she said, and he horse-laughed and shook his head. Very clever, very clever, he said. She learned never to make even a small joke around him. He would embarrass it with appreciation.

On the second day, she arrived a bit early. She returned to the stepladder. Bethany came in, threw down her bag, and groaned as though she'd been saving it since she woke up.

"I forgot you would be here," Bethany said.

"I started yesterday."

"I know."

Grace was on the top step and Bethany hadn't raised her eyes above Grace's knees. "Donald asked me to alphabetize the books," she said. She heaved the acid-rotted volume in her arms into place. "I'm on Wegner, Hans."

Bethany nodded slowly. Evidently, she wasn't one to smile out of politeness, but coming from the South, Grace took this for seething hostility. She could tell Bethany didn't like her, but she wished the woman would just fake it, like a normal person.

Grace's left knee twitched and Bethany blinked. "Tell me when you're finished," she said. "I'll teach you how we work."

The work was called *comps*. Grace's job was to value the client's things (vases, paintings, rugs, silver) by finding comparable things that had been sold within the past few years, either retail or at auction. Bethany started her with easy ones, B-list twentieth-century American artists. First Grace would read the specs as noted by Bethany or Donald: *Jerome Myers, drawing, 1908, Ashcan School, 11 by 16 inches, no damage, tenement motif.* Grace crawled around the Internet looking for matching specs on gallery or members-only auction-house websites. Sometimes she ran into "price upon request" and had to call the galleries on the phone. She made these calls in a quiet, downturned voice, trying to smother her accent.

When she turned in her first report, Bethany skimmed the thirty pages of comps, changed a few of Grace's words for prissier ones, and circled some typos that made Grace cringe.

"This is fine," Bethany said. "On Monday I'll give you a new one."

Grace liked the work. It was easy to tell when she'd found the right answer, and she got to look at art all afternoon, even if at first it was all smudgy Ashcan snores. She felt a prickle of guilt at that particular judgment, trying as she was to reconcile all her new opinions with the reality of Riley's artwork. After her failure to explain Lana's video and her reaction to it, she had kept her burgeoning art criticism to herself.

Private *from* him felt wrong; private used to mean *with* him. They talked every night for an hour (or until Kendall came back), everyday talk but laced with the mournful mating calls of the newly separated. Afterward, she usually went to the bathroom and cried at how far away she felt.

Grace worked for Mauce three afternoons a week, at first. When she got her first paycheck, she bought a few of the textbooks she'd been reading only at the library, as well as some dark nail polish of her own.

By October, Bethany was giving her more interesting work. One week Grace was given an assortment of French botanical watercolors, which required anxious, stammering phone calls to Paris in her high school French. Another week she got a man's personal collection of watches. *Given* and *got* were Bethany's words, but Grace quickly adopted them. Given and got described her temporary relationship to these things she didn't own and never touched—for the short time she worked on the botanical prints or the watches, they were hers.

The watches belonged to a man named Andrew F. Pepall. He had purchased one each year since 1959, some new and some as antiques. He had kept meticulous records with receipts and notes for five- or six-year stretches, and then the notes would disappear, and Grace had only photographs to identify the watches. Pepall lived in Ann Arbor, Michigan, and he had mailed Mauce seven rolls of film documenting his collection chronologically by the year purchased.

Over time, Pepall had grown to favor brushed gold faces and reptile bands, but his taste sometimes changed abruptly before circling back to the stately. In 1966, he'd become interested in calendar watches. Grace was particularly taken with a romantic 1940s Jaeger-LeCoultre with illustrated moon phases on the dial. The year after, he bought a 1946 Pierpont that displayed even the days of the week. Grace adored the watches' delicacy and fine workings, their quietly haughty attitudes. She felt an odd sense of gratitude toward Pepall for exposing her to such things, as though he had taken her under his wing of good taste.

"Who is that sad old man?" Kendall asked from her bed in their dorm room. She opened a new bottle of water and sucked the whole thing down in one breath, the plastic constricting in her hand. Lately she had been taking Lana's Ritalin as a study aid and lying immobile with her textbooks for hours at a time. Now she stared at the online video streaming on Grace's laptop screen as if she'd be tested on that, too.

"Andrew F. Pepall," Grace said. "He's giving a speech at his retirement dinner."

"And he is?"

"An oncologist noted for his valuable contributions to the study of fatal bone marrow suppression from chemotherapy. I'm researching his watch collection at work."

"What the fuck."

"I just wanted to know what he was like, apart from his watches." Grace's explanation sounded even weirder out loud than it had sounded in her head.

"It's not the years in your life that count," Doctor Pepall read from his note card. "It's the life in your years. In cancer treatment, we must remind ourselves of that every day."

"No offense," Kendall said, "but it's kind of fucked up for you to stalk him like that." She screwed the plastic top onto the empty water bottle and tossed it toward the wastebasket, but the bottle bounced out. Grace noticed her watch slip on her wrist. Cartier Miss Pasha, stainless steel, worth about three grand in mint condition. Her heart quickened with the thrill of recognition.

In November, Donald began to talk of taking Grace along with him on outcalls. He brought friends and colleagues back to the office for no purpose she could discern, except to test her ability to socialize with noxious people. Why else did they come all the way up to the ninth floor if Donald was meeting them for lunch four blocks away?

Craig Furst was about thirty, just over five feet tall, open-pored and tan. He wanted to specialize in Indonesian and Malaysian antiques, he said, but the market wasn't there yet. He came by at least once a week, sometimes unannounced, to talk to Donald. Donald would hold up a finger to say he was on the phone, and Craig would set his briefcase down by Grace's desk and unwind his linen scarf, his leather-and-clove cologne wafting out over them.

"I'm just back from Thailand," Craig said one afternoon. "I got some *great* shots." He took out his laptop and opened it on Grace's desk, pushing her keyboard to the side. He began clicking through slide shows. "Isn't that fabulous?" he asked.

"Wow," she said, trying to sound appreciative but noncommittal. Bethany wanted her report on Nicolai Fechin within the hour.

"I'm giving a talk in Miami next month," Craig said. "West Javanese vessels and pots. It's going to be a real stunner."

"Cool," Grace said. "That'll be so great."

He put a hand over his mouth, his pose for thinking hard. "What does Donald have you doing then, I wonder? I could really use a helper. Do you enjoy Miami?"

Donald appeared then with his coat on, and Grace was spared having to answer.

When they left, she groaned. "Oh my God," she said. "Do I *enjoy Miami?*"

"Hmm?" Bethany's desk chair backed up to Grace's, but she didn't turn around.

"How many photos before you say you have to go to the bathroom?"

"Sorry," Bethany said wearily. "I wasn't listening."

Grace knew that Bethany, silent and reproachful behind her, thought she'd encouraged Craig. But how? Grace had tried to brush off Bethany's obvious dislike, and yet she found herself wanting to please her the same way she used to want to please her teachers, so often women of mothering age. Grace wasn't sure how many children Bethany had, but she was certain that at least one of them was a teenage daughter a few years younger than Grace. She'd heard them on the phone, but Grace could also sense the daughter in the way Bethany looked at her, searching for clues and warnings about the years ahead.

Craig made sense to Grace in a way Bethany did not. Over-fragrant and cloying, accessorized and faintly leering, he *looked* like someone who would sidle up to you with his card and offer his expertise on insuring your collection of daguerreotype erotica. But Bethany, whose only decorations were the small cross pendant that hung over her turtlenecks and a plain gold wedding band? This business depended on ornament and excess. It made no sense that someone so resolutely undecorated would devote herself to it.

But Bethany looked at her as though Grace were a whore who didn't know it. She possibly believed Grace's naïveté was cultivated. Bethany was from Queens.

Grace hadn't expected to be lonely. She'd thought loneliness was just a word for being alone and wishing you weren't; she'd forgotten the sucking thinness of it. She hadn't been lonely since she'd been a child—untethered, floating around other people like a ghostly houseguest.

In class, she watched her fellow students perform their garbled interpretations of Derrida and Foucault. It wasn't theater school, but they were all there, she saw, to learn how to act. Everyone, whether from Singapore or Oregon or New Jersey, had come to Manhattan to transform, and each day they tried on their costumes, testing their characters in the classroom before they tried to pass in the real world. They were prototypes of New Yorkers.

Donald Mauce was the worst imitator of all. The photo of the Mauce Fine Arts office that Grace had seen on the website—the brocade, the velvet, the Chippendale chairs—actually depicted the study of the British novelist Anthony Powell, circa *A Dance to the Music of Time*. Upon closer inspection, Grace saw the little dog napping on the corner of the rug.

"My niece did the whole website," Donald told Grace one Monday morning. Grace was now working some mornings too, when class was just lecture and she knew she wouldn't be missed. "I'm a huge fan of Anthony Powell, hence the homage."

"It's pronounced *Poe*-el," Bethany said.

"Have you tried these?" he said, holding up his half-eaten bear claw. "Truly the sine qua non of Danishes. How was your dinner party? Did you go with the rioja?"

The Friday before, he'd grilled her about her weekend plans, hoping to hear something wild and young. He was lonely, she knew. Donald was a widower, and he had no children, which Grace found to be a relief. She didn't have to comport herself as someone's child. He didn't see her that way. Grace told him a friend (one of Kendall's, of course) was making paella. Grace wasn't even sure she was invited, but she felt obligated to give him something. Just the word *paella* had been enough to cue a breathless wine advisory.

"No," she told him now. "A cabernet, I think. We just cooked with it. It was pretty gross."

"Cooked with it? In *paella*?"

Bethany put on her headphones.

"She couldn't get a big enough pot, so they made something else."

"But it wasn't good? Did you take it back to the store? All wine should be drinkable!"

Grace shrugged. "No, we just—"

"Was it spoiled?" He looked genuinely concerned, as though the wine had come from his own vineyard. He crossed his arms. "Or too much citrus? Too much wood? Oak?"

"I don't know," Grace said helplessly. "It was just really cheap and dusty."

"Dusty, like an earthy ground?"

"No, the bottle was dusty."

"Okay, but the bad taste—was it creosote? Maybe an undertone of petrol?"

"Donald," Grace finally said in a frustrated apology, "I'm eighteen. Wine doesn't taste like wood and lemons to me. It just tastes like wine."

His phone began to ring. "In Europe you'd be an oenophile by now," he argued. "Just be honest with yourself. No need for discomfiture. Ask your-self: What are these flavors to me? What in my life? It can be anything!"

Grace was sorry to disappoint him. She felt more comfortable around Donald than anyone else she'd met—he was even more clueless than she was. But how? He was in his sixties, she guessed. He'd had plenty of time to assimilate, and he certainly tried: He belonged to a dozen wine, cheese, symphony, and gardening groups, all promising to cultivate him.

"No," Donald brayed into his telephone. "Down the block, kittywam-pus from the Guggenheim!"

Bethany pulled off her headphones, the cartilage pinchers people wore for jogging, and rubbed her red ears.

"Where is Donald from?" Grace asked her quietly.

"Indiana," Bethany said. "Ohio? One of those. He moved here three years ago."

Grace remembered her interview, the way Donald leaned forward when she said she was from Tennessee. *What's that like?* It had been his best performance.

"He used to be an insurance appraiser," Bethany said, watching Grace from the corner of her eye. "A company guy, the one who came out after a flood."

"Not French watercolors and portraits of gentlemen."

"Not quite," Bethany said, smiling a little as she turned away.

Grace had taken Bethany for only one kind of snob, the woman who sneered at pretty young women for trying to be prettier, and assumed that she had fallen into this line of work—a former church secretary respond-ing to an ad or something—but now she wasn't sure.

"How did *you* end up here?" she asked, shuffling through her papers as though she weren't really listening.

"I was finishing my dissertation, and I lost my funding," Bethany said. She didn't turn around.

"You want to be a professor?"

Bethany picked up the phone. "I need to call my sitter," she said. "Let me know when you're finished with that pottery."

When Grace chatted with Kendall about work or talked to Riley about school, she let all the personas—hers, her classmates', Donald's—stand without scrutiny. If she believed in their acts, they might believe in hers, and so, in turn, would Riley. She refused to admit her loneliness to him.

"What are you wearing?" he would ask her at the end of a halfhearted extrapolation of Susan Sontag or Clement Greenberg. "I want to see you. Or at least picture you."

If Kendall was out, Grace could humor him. "I'm in bed," she would say, making up something about her unbuttoned jeans and yanked-up tank top, her underwear or lack thereof. It was always a lie. Every night she slept in an old T-shirt of Riley's, stretched and faded, with holes in the armpits. GARLAND MIDDLE SCHOOL TRACK AND FIELD, it read across the front. On the back: GO STARLINGS! She also wore his shorts. She'd snagged two pairs of his boxer briefs before she left Garland.

"Are those *his*?" Kendall had accused her upon barging into their bathroom, where Grace stood brushing her teeth in the sagging shorts. "That is gross and possibly creepy."

Grace bent to spit out her toothpaste. Kendall was a rich New Yorker and Grace was not. Kendall had friends, and Grace did not. But Grace had something Kendall did not.

"I'll tell you when you're older," Grace said.

10

At home in Garland, Riley seemed to be holding up his end of their bargain. Infinitely patient, he would spend weeks building a house on his canvas, brick by single brick, the Tupperware lid he used as a palette on one knee, a joint resting lightly on the rubber edge. From the calmness in his voice, she could tell right away when he was painting.

One of his mother's friends, Anne Findlay, ran a small local gallery, and she had offered to put up Riley's work in January, her slowest month. She'd never shown a student before. "It's kind of good that you're not here," he said to Grace. "I have literally nothing to do but go to class and paint for this show."

Grace's mind was wallpapered with the diverse and ambitious artwork she had seen in the past three months, but she funneled her still-unspoken doubts about Riley's subject matter into concern that he might run out of buildings. "You could paint something else," she said. "You know, branch out." She didn't know how to pose her questions so that they didn't sound critical.

"Nope," he said. "I only paint what I know." He inhaled sharply. "It's about the process. I'm going to paint this whole fucking town."

Process! Painting the entirety of their small southern town! This was something she could say to Lana when asked about Riley's artistic "interests." *Process*, Grace imagined saying. *Outsider art and changing small-town landscapes.*

"Have you found our New York gallery yet?" They played this game now, the same way they used to walk around Garland and pick out their dream house. "The one that peddles the toothless and shoeless southern Gothic movement?"

She pictured his careful canvases of Queen Anne mansions with brass plaques from the historic society. "Hardly," she said.

"Whoops, gotta go," he said, his rounded, graceful drawl contorting into something backwoods. "Alls is here and we're gonna go romance some livestock."

He'd never met a cow in his life, and his hillbilly shtick was a new thing. He'd never done it before she left for New York. "Wear a clean polo," Grace said. "You don't want to scare them off before you get to first base."

"I love you," they said together, a timing they'd perfected as children. They'd never grown out of it.

Grace skipped class to take the train to Chappaqua with Donald for her first outcall. He had been hired by a widow who lived with her adult daughter in a 1950s Tudor revival. Grace remembered some boys in pea-coats she had met at the party Kendall threw in their room, the way they said they were from Chappaqua with their chins out, as if it deserved a reaction. But Grace didn't think this house, clad in thin stucco and fake leaded glass, was anything so special.

Inside, the house was carpeted, with low ceilings. The walls were papered in a dank blue damask. The widow, Debbie something, immediately sat down on a couch as if just letting Grace and Donald in had exhausted her. Her daughter, Nicole, had picked them up at the station. Now she stood with her arms crossed, her eyes narrowed at Donald.

"Where should we set up?" he asked.

"It doesn't matter," Nicole said, unhappy to see them and unwilling to hide it.

Grace sat down in a lumpy slipper chair and opened the laptop, her knees tightly together beneath it. In Garland, no one would ever have someone into their home without offering something to drink or asking how their drive was. Was this a Chappaqua thing or a northern problem in general? And, she scolded herself, just what did she mean by comparing anything to Garland, as if it were someplace to brag about?

"I'll just walk around your house and inventory your collections," Donald said. "Grace, my assistant, will take notes on the computer." He picked up a small statue and turned it over to look at the bottom. "Jade," he began. "A jade sheep statue, Chinese, probably Qing, probably late nineteenth or early twentieth, sleeping sheep, wooden base, rosewood." Grace tried to keep up, typing as he talked. He took a tape measure from his pocket and stretched it first top to bottom and then around the statue. "Nine inches plus a two-inch base, sixteen-inch circumference. Picture?"

Grace handed him the camera, and he photographed the statue from each side.

Debbie took her hand from over her mouth. "My husband gave me that. For our tenth anniversary."

"It's a great piece," Donald said. "Good color, good feet. Did he buy it in the States? How much did you get it for?"

"No," she said. She didn't look at him. "We lived in Mukden— Shenyang—for two years, in the late seventies." Her voice cracked as though he had forced these details out of her.

Donald nodded. The daughter turned and walked out of the room without comment, and it dawned on Grace that it was upsetting to these women for Donald to be there, weighing anniversary presents in his hand. And they didn't even know that it was the teenager sitting on the couch who would suggest prices for all their family treasures.

Donald leaned over a vase next to the jade sheep. "Jar," he said. "Chinese, porcelain, rosewood cover. Double happiness motif, top-heavy hourglass shape, flared rim." He ran his pinkie along the edge of the lid. "There's some slight chipping along here." He turned to Grace, clasping his hands behind his back. "Condition: good." He looked at Debbie and smiled.

Grace followed him from room to room, filling up pages with hastily typed notes. She cataloged vases, boxes, ceramics, furniture, books, rugs, drapes, paintings, prints, and finally jewelry, which felt far too personal and intrusive. Everything had a story, whether Debbie told it or not. Donald and Grace finished the downstairs in two and a half hours.

"Should we call in some sandwiches?" Donald asked Nicole, closing a music box on the nightstand in the master bedroom. "It's getting close to lunch."

"There's a deli a few blocks in," she said, "if you need to take a break."

"Oh, we'd lose too much time. I was thinking you could just order some delivery."

She shook her head. "We're not really hungry."

Grace looked at the carpet, mortified. Her secret gratitude toward Donald for his poor manners, his obliviousness of his own social ineptitude, was wearing thin. She watched him leave his smudgy fingerprints all over Debbie's things, cringed at his carelessly probing questions, and she was embarrassed to be associated with him.

At the station, Donald told her that he wasn't coming. He had a dinner date with a woman who lived in Scarsdale. "We've been corresponding online," he said. "Her screen name is 'Floria T.' She said I was the first one to get it." He waited for Grace, but she shook her head. "Tosca? *No?*" He gaped. "Well then, I wish us *both* luck."

On her way back to Manhattan, Grace listened to her messages, both from Riley.

"Hey, it's me," he said. "My crit was crap, as usual. Josh showed off a heartwarming nude portrait of his younger siblings, and Jessica Sunshine painted a forest scene with glitter snow and, no joke, feathers glued to the trees. And then I got reamed for not doing anything playful with materials in my Fiske Tobacco Warehouse piece." He inhaled. "Not my favorite day, this day. On the other hand, if these people actually *liked* my work, that would be worse. And then I thought, you know what, man? Grace is up there, being all smarty-pants with fancy folk—"

The message cut off, but another one began. "What I was saying is after a day like today, and Greg put empty beer cans back in the fridge because the trash was full, and you're not even here? Alls keeps saying you'll cut your hair and leave me for a professor. And my mom wants your dorm address; she wants to send you something. I'll be around until seven or so and then we're going to Ryan's to watch the game. Love you a thousand."

The man next to Grace shifted uncomfortably in his seat, and she realized that she'd begun to cry. She called Riley, but it was already seven thirty, and there was no answer. She opened her Critics in Context course pack and tried to concentrate, and when a fat tear splashed across a photo of Slavoj Žižek's shaggy face, she was glad she had the sense to laugh at herself, just for a moment. The man in the seat beside her drew his arms across his chest.

Riley called her back as the train was leaving Bronxville. She could hear a chorus of groans in the background and guessed he was standing in

Ryan's kitchen, his back to the TV. She could see him hunching over and covering one ear to hear her.

"How was it?" he said. "Was it a castle?"

"No, just a house." She thought she heard Alls talking to someone. "It was very weird, going into some stranger's house and touching all their stuff while they just stand there, watching."

"Are you crying?" he asked her.

"Riley! Don't say that in front of people!" She pictured boys' heads turning around from the couch.

"Sorry," he said. "Hang on."

She heard the screen door slam and then he was in the backyard. She tried to explain how unsettling it had been, but Riley couldn't see what the fuss was about.

"Darlin'," he said, "you're making too much out of this. How was class? Don't you have class on Tuesday morning?"

"Fine," she lied. "Good. Taste is class. The Real is not reality. I am a social construction."

"All cats are black in the dark," he said. "Can I call you later?"

Around two in the morning, Kendall and Jezzie came in with Lana passed out between them. They'd lugged her out of the elevator and down the hall, and now they had her slumped on Kendall's bed. Grace was cross-legged in bed with her art history book.

Kendall stumbled out of her heels and sat down on the floor, leaning against Lana's dangling shin for support.

"Jesus," Grace said, getting up to peer at Lana. "Is she okay?"

"Poor baby," Jezzie said. "She looks like a melting sex doll."

"That's what she wants," Kendall slurred. "I worry, you know?"

"How much did she drink?" Grace asked.

"Three vodka sodas," Kendall said. "Same as me. Three is the magic number."

A strip of false eyelashes was crawling up Lana's left eyelid. "Are you sure?"

"Somebody put something in her drink," Jezzie said. "She'll drink anything if it's a gift."

"Jay," Kendall mumbled. "It was Jay. Or Marwan, that shit-show."

"She went out with Jay last week," Grace said. "She said she liked him."

"She does like him," Jezzie said.

Kendall nodded. "She just doesn't *know* him."

"I don't know how you guys do it," Grace said.

Jezzie, suddenly sober, gave her a disbelieving side-eye. "Do *what?*"

"Deal with these guys," she said, shrugging. "All these creeps you don't know. I'd just stay home."

"No, you wouldn't," Kendall said. "You'd talk to creeps too, to find the semi-creeps."

"You're still with your middle school boyfriend." Jezzie snorted. "Your whole worldview is crippled. It's like you never stopped playing with dolls or something. We'd die of boredom, being you."

"I'm after depth, not breadth," Grace said, blocking Alls from her mind. "I'm not collecting baseball cards." Riley had been sixteen when the first hair on his chest appeared, and Grace had been first to notice it. She watched his freckles fade and reappear every summer. She was finely attuned to his satisfaction, anger, embarrassment. She knew the exact moment before he came.

"Good luck on your dissertation," Jezzie said. "Sounds super fun."

Lana's ankle twitched. Grace sighed. "You're sure she's okay?"

"She is now," Jezzie said. "But only because we were there."

Grace reached over and pulled the band of eyelashes from Lana's shimmered-up eyelid, a caterpillar from a petal. Grace trusted nobody except for Riley, not even herself.

The next week, at work, Grace received an auction catalog and invitation from Phillips de Pury, the swanky auction house on Park Avenue. The auction was a Friday evening sale, half-commerce and half-party. The catalog promised Cecily Brown, Georg Herold, Ryan McGinley. The glossy, oversize pages showed furious paintings of tangled bodies at a lawn party-cum-orgy; sculptures of bent-over ballerinas made of wooden lathes, painted pink; photographs from a road trip taken by rich, skinny, naked twenty-somethings. And Grace had received an invitation. How had the people at Phillips de Pury mistaken her for one of them?

"Oh, that happens all the time," Bethany said. "When you register for any of the auction record websites, your name gets dropped into their piggy banks."

"It's not a real invitation?"

She looked up over her glasses. "Um, no, it's a real invitation. It's a public auction."

"You should go!" Donald hollered. "Get dressed up, take a girlfriend! You'll have a blast!"

Bethany rolled her eyes. "I mean, if you're interested in contemporary." She glanced at the catalog's cover, a pornographic neo-Expressionist painting by Marcus Harvey called *Julie from Hull*. Then she looked at Grace and her tweed miniskirt and vintage blouse with the ironic Peter Pan collar. Grace wasn't dressing like a girl from Garland anymore.

"God," Donald moaned, suddenly wistful. "What it must be like to be young and beautiful in New York City."

11

J ust before Thanksgiving, Kendall overheard Grace on the phone with Riley, cooing how she couldn't wait to see him.

"Isn't it, like, three a.m. in France? Are you going to Paris for break?" she asked Grace.

The Sorbonne, right. Grace turned away in case her face was reddening. "No, just home. Riley's coming home."

"Just for Thanksgiving? Is he not coming in December?"

"He's probably home for the rest of the year. His mom is really sick."

"Oh my God! What's wrong with her?"

"Breast cancer," Grace lied. "It looks really bad."

She flew home the Tuesday before Thanksgiving. They had told their parents that she was coming in Wednesday evening. Riley picked her up at the airport, standing at the curb next to his old green Volvo. She ran to him and he hoisted her up by her butt. She split her jeans wrapping her thighs around him, and the cold rushed at her skin as they laughed and clutched at each other. He set her down on the trunk of the car and pressed his forehead to hers. She wanted to get her whole body inside his, held tight beneath his skin. He drove, and Grace kept her hand on his thigh, her nails crooked into the inseam of his jeans.

When they pulled off exit 227 to Garland, he took a turn that she didn't recognize.

"Aren't we going to your house?"

"Going a different way," he said. "I don't want to risk anybody seeing us at a stoplight. Got to keep you a secret."

When he pulled up to the light at Dunbar Road, where they had no choice but to funnel into the only route home, he looked to his left and right and behind him, then reached over and gently pushed Grace's shoulder down.

She hunched but turned her face toward him. "Are you kidnapping me? Are you going to transport me across state lines for sex purposes?"

He nodded and pressed his lips together. "There's nothing I'm going to do to you that *isn't* for sex purposes," he said. "You'll have to escape out the window when you're sick of me."

"In a hundred years," she said.

"Won't be long enough."

She sat up and brushed the hair out of her eyes, but she slunk down low. She didn't want anyone to see her either. "We're disgusting," she said. "We must make people so completely ill."

"It's not our fault," he said. "We can't help what we have."

Sitting in his car with her knees against the glove box and her spine bent deep into the seat, she may have looked helpless, but she felt superior to the people she couldn't see riding in the cars around them.

Riley pulled up to the house on Orange Street, clapboard with chipping peach paint, a color out of place anywhere but in a nursery. The porch sagged in the middle and there were several crumpled beer cans in the front yard, one perched in the crotch of the struggling apple tree as though it were growing there. Wet and wrinkled junk mail was plastered to the front steps. In the front window, a faded devil mask grinned out at the street, a leftover from Halloween. The front screen door was busted through the bottom half, where someone had probably kicked it. Grace had never seen a place as dear.

Together, they hurried up the front walk and inside, through the dark living room with its curtains always drawn, past the horrible bathroom, and up the stairs. He slammed the door behind them. Grace kicked off her sneakers and Riley ran to the stereo to turn on some privacy music. The bass line shook the desk lamp and Grace started to laugh. She heard hooting from the kitchen: They knew what that music was for. Alls was down there. She swallowed.

"My wife," Riley murmured, "you better not make any plans this week."

"Quit bossing me around," she said. She pushed him down on the bed and he pulled on her belt loops. Every drop of confidence she had missed in New York was here, waiting for her. She had left it all in his bed.

She straddled him and rocked back, pulling off her sweater and T-shirt together, and she shuddered when he slipped his hands over her breasts, his palms almost floating over her nipples. She fell forward and pushed into his hands, and he wrapped his arms around her and kissed her, nosing down her neck. She slid her hand between their bodies, down his fly. He groaned and shook his head. Not yet. He rolled her onto her back and pushed her thighs apart. She laid her hands on his shoulders, waiting and aching, and then, when she expected to feel his tug on her waistband, she felt his warm breath through her underwear, his thumb pulling it aside, and then his slow licking and licking. She had forgotten about the rip in her jeans.

Grace woke up in the middle of the night with Riley's bent knees crooked inside hers. She pulled on a dirty T-shirt from the floor. It smelled like green-top Speed Stick, Volvo, sweat, and turpentine: her husband. She went down to the kitchen for a glass of water and when she came back upstairs, she saw the canvases, more than a dozen of them, leaning against the wall just outside his door frame, all facing the hallway wall. Her heart quickened a little with excitement. His show at Anne Findlay would begin just after Christmas, the gallery's slowest time of the year. His work would go on sale along with the holiday decor and discontinued electronics. Lana had told Grace that in New York the slow season was summer, when the city emptied of rich people.

Grace knew that she should wait for Riley to show her. She should let him pull out the canvases in the order he wanted and point out the details he wanted her to see, but she couldn't wait. She had learned, from all her silent Saturdays looking at artwork by herself, that she could see better alone.

She could always pretend, tomorrow, to be surprised.

She crept into the bedroom and took his cell phone from his desk. She could use it as a flashlight. She turned around the first canvas and shone the little blue swatch of light at it, moving the light up and down and around. The house was one she recognized, an old Victorian, redbrick, with a turret in the front and tulips up the walkway. The next painting was the downtown block where Norma's Sunday Grill was. Wrought-iron tables. Menus. The painted cursive on the windows. Grace grimaced and flipped back a third canvas. This one was the library, omitting the ugly 1980s addition.

She put his phone back. Carefully, she lowered herself into bed. His arms tightened around her and she blinked in the dark. Last week, Lana had shown her a work in progress, a video she had shot the night before. She'd had her nipples pierced on the Bowery in the middle of the night, wasted and alternately puking and laughing, propping her head up with her hand. The piercer was a fat old punk with graying temples and a pointy goatee. Jezzie had gone with her to film the piercing. The next day, Lana had watched the video hungrily, bent over Kendall's desk, soaking her breasts in Dixie cups of warm salt water. "I like to plan things," she had told Grace, "and then get too fucked up to know what I'm doing. Then I have to watch the film to find out what happened to me."

Maybe Riley was making an ironic critique on the predictability of small-town life, the sweetness of it. The staleness of it. There were no people—maybe he was speaking to some kind of emptiness. Or the opposite—that the buildings themselves were the characters. She clutched at meaning. Maybe he'd left off the library addition to comment on the rose-colored-glasses vision of Garland's citizens, and not because it would ugly up his nice painting.

Process, he had said. Grace had seen a show a few weeks ago of quick, unimpressive sketches of a haystack, like Monet's haystacks, all done with black marker on cheap computer paper. The artist was in the gallery's back room, robotically sketching these hundreds of haystack drawings littering the gallery, gleefully proving how an image's fame made it into an impotent cartoon.

In the morning, they ate old cold leftover pizza with hot sauce. Riley liked green Tabasco but had bought a bottle of Cholula for Grace and presented it with much fanfare. She asked him about the show. When would she get to see what he'd been working so hard on?

"A lot of it's already at the gallery." He peered at a plate to see if it was clean enough.

"Already?" She felt hopeful and relieved. What was upstairs had not made the cut.

"Yep." He came up behind her and squeezed her sides. "That's my big news. Surprise! She's putting me up in December."

"What? Why?"

"Why do you think, smarty-pants? She thinks she can sell it. She saw what I was working on and said she wanted to put me up in a big month, not a small one."

"Wow," Grace said. "That's wonderful."

"It is. It is fucking *wonderful*." He turned her around and pulled her close. "Grace, this could be—*will be*—the beginning of my real career. Not a favor, not a 'student' show. She thinks she can sell me as a real, working artist."

"That's fantastic," she said, turning her face up to kiss him. "I'm so happy for you."

Riley grinned wildly, a little boy on Christmas Eve. "I wanted to see your face when I told you." He was watching her closely, and she beamed back at him, putting her arms around his neck.

"So when can I see?" she asked him. "I want to see everything you're working on."

Grace wished that when they'd gone to Anne Findlay that afternoon, Riley had unveiled an investigation into perceptions of change in familiar public spaces. That he had taken hundreds of photos of familiar buildings, places he walked by every day, and mounted them on boards at angles just improbable enough to make the familiar unfamiliar. That he had braced up these assemblages with concrete blocks, two-by-fours, and wooden pallets, creating rooms and tunnels within the gallery walls that allowed people to walk through these semi-familiar spaces, noticing here what had changed too slowly and incrementally for them to notice in the real world.

But that was not her husband's artwork. That was Isidro Blasco, an artist whose work, about his block in Jackson Heights, Queens, Grace had seen the month before. She had read about the show in an *Art in America* that Lana had left in their room. "A strength of Blasco's approach," the critic wrote, "has been the emotional restraint behind its formal innovation, conveying not destruction but disorientation, the unsettlingly simultaneous expansion and compression of space that the urban dweller experiences."

Riley Graham's work at the Anne Findlay Gallery was very pretty. Findlay must have had a buyer in mind for each and every piece: the owner of the property painted in it.

The night before Thanksgiving, the Grahams always ordered Chinese. Dr. Graham or one of the boys drove to Whitwell to pick up their order. Riley didn't want to leave Grace, but Mrs. Graham shooed him off. "Go with your father and Jim," she said. "Leave Gracie here with me. I've missed her too, you know."

Mrs. Graham was mixing sausage stuffing with her hands and couldn't hug Grace properly. "Oh honey," she said. "You're all skinny! And I look like an old kitchen hag. Lipstick me, would you?" She nodded toward the microwave. She kept a gold tube of her lipstick in a big seashell on top of it, with recent receipts and pocket detritus. Grace uncapped the lipstick and, giggling, clumsily applied it to Mrs. Graham's puckered lips. The whole house smelled like sausage and celery. Really, the whole neighborhood did.

"What can I do?" Grace asked, tying on a striped apron. "Sweet potatoes?"

"Done. Can I put you on pie? The dough's chilling. We're doing pumpkin, pecan, and broccoli quiche."

"Quiche?"

"Colin's bringing a girl, some little thingie he met at physical therapy. And she's a vegetarian. I was worried she wouldn't have enough to eat, so I was going to do the stuffing vegetarian—"

"Oh no," Grace said.

"Oh no is right. You'd have thought I threatened Tofurky. So, broccoli quiche. Colin said it was silly, though. You can't win!"

"But it will mean a lot to her," Grace said. "That you went to the trouble."

"Well, I bought the things and I made extra dough, so we might as well."

Mrs. Graham never fully put away the Thanksgiving groceries. She bagged them by dish and set the bags on the dining room table or in the fridge, if they included any perishables, sometimes several days ahead. Grace found the pie bag and started to mix the pumpkin filling, following the recipe on the back of the can, while Mrs. Graham asked her questions about school and filled her in on the local gossip. She seized on the New York art galleries when Grace mentioned them; she wanted to know everything.

"Isn't that wonderful," she said when Grace described an installation made of old film. "And you can walk right inside it?"

When Riley and his father and brother got back with the food, they sat on the floor of the family room and passed around the cartons. Grace, full of fried food and sticky sauce, remembered when Lana had compared her to a house cat. "An ether of contentment," she had said. Grace felt it keenly now. She caught Riley's eye and smiled. She thought of the girl Colin was bringing tomorrow and hoped she was awful.

After dinner, Grace pulled the pies out of the oven, slid the quiche in, and set the timer for Mrs. Graham. Riley was restless, itching to get out of there and back to the house. He went out to the car to wait, and Grace wiggled into her shoes and struggled with her jacket's zipper, which kept catching her hair. She heard Dr. Graham on the stairs. He always clattered down in a two-step rhythm, like a horse. He had an envelope in hand.

"Give this to Riley, would you?" he said.

"Sure," she said, tucking it into her jacket pocket. "Thank you."

"He mentioned he was running low on supplies, and I know this show means a lot to him." He kissed her on the cheek. "Good to see you, sweetie."

"You too," Grace said. She pushed open the front door. "It's good to be home."

The day before Grace flew back to New York to finish the semester, she and Riley were lying on the couch watching *The Sopranos* and drinking heavy hot toddies of orange-spice tea and bourbon. The house was quiet except for the TV and the sounds of their sipping, and Grace was trying to find a way to ask Riley about his artwork that didn't make her sound as though she doubted him.

"So what do you think you'll take on after the show?" she finally asked.

"What do you mean?"

"I mean, once you've painted every building in Garland . . ."

He nodded. "Yeah, I know. Well, I've been thinking about going bigger or smaller."

"Like bigger canvases?" Her mind filled with a vision of life-size brunch awnings.

"No—well, maybe. That could be cool. But I was thinking about trying interiors."

"Interiors?"

"Yeah, rooms. The insides of rooms."

"Like this room?" She looked around at the pine paneling on one wall, the dusty electronics, the coffee table piled with junk mail and idle sketches. It could be interesting.

"Yeah, just regular rooms. Some fancy rooms, some crappy rooms." He laughed. "Like this room. And I hadn't thought about size yet, but life-size rooms would be pretty dope."

"Ones you could almost step into. Like a really old-fashioned virtual reality."

He squeezed her foot. "That's kind of a sweet idea."

Grace was getting excited. What he was describing sounded ambitious. "There's this book I had to read for school, Baudrillard? He said we make fake realities to avoid the real one, the *real* reality. Hyperreality. That society is a prison and we make these fake mini-prisons to hide that from ourselves, like Disney World—"

"Whoa," he said. "Hold up. Don't come at me with a bunch of jargon and French guys."

"What? We're just talking about ideas, what you want to say—"

"And anyway," he said, "whatever I do next depends on Anne. If she sells all my stuff and wants more, I'll make more."

"Well, you can't just paint houses forever," Grace said. "Not unless you're *saying* something about, you know, the endless—"

"I'm not saying anything, Grace." An edge had crept into his voice.

"Not that you have an agenda, but a purpose, a kind of reason for—" She stopped to choose her words. "I'm just saying that maybe after this, you might want to try something more—"

"More New York." He nodded. "That's what you mean."

"No, it's not. But don't act like you didn't want me to go there. You wanted me to go there, for us."

"Not if it's going to turn you into a snob."

"I'm not turning into—"

The front door slammed and Alls tromped in, still wearing his white pants from fencing practice. Grace had been relieved, this weekend, to find herself mostly untroubled by Alls. She'd wanted to come *home*, after all, and Riley and the Grahams were home. That the pull of home was more powerful than any other felt profoundly reassuring.

He was breathless. "Don't stop fighting on my account," he said. "Nothing I haven't seen before."

"We're not fighting," Grace said.

Riley raised his eyebrows, looking at the floor.

Alls looked from Riley to Grace, grinning. "I'm going to New York," he said.

"What? Why?" Riley asked.

"Nationals," he said. "They're at NYU this year. You may not know this, Gracie, but your school is a big deal in fencing."

"Haven't you only been fencing for, like, a month?" Riley asked.

"A year," Grace said. There was no reason for Riley to get bratty at Alls. "And he's already headed to nationals. Congratulations!"

"I got really lucky. I've been killing it the last month or so, and I thought I had a chance, and then today one of the juniors fucked up his knee."

"Lucky you," Riley said. Grace pinched his ankle.

"I mean, I'm sorry about his knee. But he can go next year."

"When is it?" Grace asked.

"December tenth to thirteenth," he said. "But they can't keep us locked up the whole trip. You'll show me a good time?"

"You bet I will," Grace said, regretting the phrase's blowsiness even as it left her lips.

"You bet she will," Riley said, his voice clipped and transparently pissed. He lifted her ankles from his lap, stood up, and stalked into the kitchen.

Months ago, before she'd left Garland, she'd worried that Riley would see the gathering, darkening cloud of lust that followed Grace around all the time, threatening to burst. But he couldn't see that, only that Grace was walking and talking beyond his gaze and its particular tastes.

Alls was embarrassed. Grace shook her head: *Don't worry.* But she was worried, about Riley. A relationship that had grown up in a single cozy zip

code was being asked to stretch hundreds of miles. If only Riley were coming to New York instead. She could take him to some galleries and show
him what she was talking about. He needed new, jittery, excited ideas, not
more house paintings. And she hoped, meanly, that Anne Findlay wouldn't
sell a damn thing. That would be better for him, in the long run.

12

When Grace returned to New York, Kendall happily agreed to attend the Phillips de Pury sale with her. She said drunk commerce was her favorite kind and let it slip that this would not be her first art auction. Grace couldn't have been wholly surprised—she had asked Kendall to come as a part of her ongoing cultural tutoring. But such indications of their very different frames of reference were constant, and they had begun to chafe at Grace in a way she had not expected. If Kendall had been Swedish or Pakistani or Zimbabwean, Grace was confident they would have delighted in discussing their cultural differences, in "unpacking" them, as her professors were always harping on her to do. But they did not. Was it because the differences in her upbringing and Kendall's were impolite subjects to discuss? Or because interclass curiosity went only one direction? Aside from some passing amusement over Southern naming conventions ("You tell me a name, I guess the gender, and the loser takes a drink"), Kendall's interest in where and how Grace had grown up was limited to general bafflement and occasional caricature.

Grace absorbed what she could and muted her ignorance about what she couldn't. When she reported excitedly that the dining hall now had spicy mayo on the sandwich bar five days a week, she learned that Kendall had not set foot in any of the dining halls. She did not even know where they were. All freshmen had mandatory meal plans, and yet Kendall's parents gave her a weekly allowance for food. Grace omitted, then, her discovery that they had reduced security at the exit of one dining hall, making it easier to sneak out an extra sandwich or bag of bagels. Instead, she performed her disbelief, placing her hands on her hips and saying, "Well, I never!" in an exaggerated accent.

In early December, Donald took Grace on an estate appraisal, her first. An old lady had died, leaving behind the penthouse where she had lived for the past fifty years and its contents. A distant cousin had flown in to *execute* the estate, a word Grace found increasingly apt.

The apartment building was a 1950s brick box, glazed white in part to reflect any snatches of sun onto the gray buildings around it.

"Oh my God," Donald said as he and Grace walked down the hall from the elevator. "Can you even imagine what this place is worth? And she bought it in the sixties." He cackled and knocked on the door.

The apartment was dark and crowded with broken furniture, books, and ornaments, and the air was stale and still. They were on the twenty-fourth floor, and it smelled like the windows had not been opened in decades. The distant cousin was a woman in her fifties wearing jeans and a red sweatshirt. Her husband answered the door and then darted back to his wife, who stood across the living room on the other side of the sofa.

"We got in yesterday," the man said. "We live in Houston. We only have two days."

"This is really a—we didn't know her well," the woman said. "I know it sounds awful, but I only met her a few times, when I was just a kid."

"We just want this done as simply as possible," the man said. "I have to be back at work on Wednesday."

Donald nodded. "Got it. Right off the bat, it doesn't look like there's anything difficult to deal with here. It looks like, you know." He shrugged. "Junk."

The couple's shoulders fell in relief. Grace didn't understand. How could *that* be what they wanted to hear?

"Where should I set up?" Grace asked, unfurling the laptop cord.

"I doubt we'll need that," Donald said. He turned back to the couple. "I know a great broom cleaner. If it is all junk, I'll give you her card and she'll be here by six with a crew of four. In twenty-four hours the place will be totally hollow." Donald smiled, and the couple smiled back.

Taxes, right. They'd make a fortune selling a penthouse in the East Eighties, but they didn't want to fool around with its contents.

"Well, we'll leave you to it," the man said, and he and his wife left the room. Usually, the clients watched, protective of their belongings.

Grace felt the heavy loneliness in the room. Someone had died in here only a few weeks ago. Her collection of paintings and drawings covered the walls and leaned up against them. But then Grace noticed that there were no photographs on display, and the paintings and drawings were mostly reproduced landscapes of old European streets and cathedrals.

"She doesn't have children, or anyone?" she whispered to Donald.

He shook his head. "I think there was a longtime maid, but she's moved out now."

Grace had not realized that there were still live-in maids in America. She wondered when the maid had left—before or after her employer died? How long had they been together? Decades? The apartment was not clean, though Grace felt guilty for noticing. Perhaps the maid had retired and stayed on as a companion. Perhaps she had no family of her own. Had she found the woman dead? Had they known she was dying? Where had the maid gone now? She began to seem more like a widow, the more Grace thought about it.

That night, Riley would half-console, half-correct her on the phone. "She was working for ten bucks an hour, babe. Just like you, just like me."

"I make thirteen," Grace reminded him.

"Those three extra dollars aren't for speculation."

"Insight."

"Fantasy."

But in the afternoon, Grace's particular discomfort was still developing. For nearly two hours, she followed Donald as he walked through the rooms of the apartment, opening and closing all the closets. "Nope, nope, nothing," he said, thumbing through the coats and sweaters, shaking his head at the peeling vinyl chair cushions. Grace knew it was true, but she hated hearing him say it, as though the dead woman could hear him too.

"We haven't packed anything up," the man called from the bedroom.

"It's all just like when we got here," the woman said, returning to the living room, where Grace and Donald stood by a radiator. "We haven't moved anything."

Donald picked up a small figurine, a shimmering porcelain horse. One of the hind legs was broken off at the knee. "Isn't this cute, like a little Lalique." The woman shifted her weight. "But it's broken."

Grace knelt in front of the bookcase. *A Picturesque Tour of the English*

Lakes. China: In a Series of Views, Displaying the Scenery, Architecture and Social Habits, of That Ancient Empire. Travels from Buenos Ayres, by Potosi, to Lima. The last was bound in marbled linen but coming apart.

"Donald," she said. "What about the books?"

"What?" he said. "Clearly heat damaged. The spines are falling off."

"But they could donate them," Grace said. "Maybe a library or even—"

"Is there coffee?" Donald asked the couple. The woman nodded. "Grace, can you get us coffee?"

She stood up and brushed off her skirt.

In the kitchen, she opened the cupboard and took out a mug with a basket of flowers cheaply screen printed on the side. She found a box of sweetener packets and then began opening drawers, looking for a spoon. Every drawer was a jumbled mess. Had the cousins looted the apartment before Donald and Grace got there, was that it? And they didn't want to pay estate taxes on all the undamaged Lalique figurines they'd wrapped in old socks and stuffed in their suitcases? Or was the resentment Grace felt of another kind, a strange identification with the dead woman or her maid? She knew she was being ridiculous: Their job was to locate items of value, and here there were none. And yet she felt sick, as though they had appraised the woman's life and and found it worthless.

Grace heard the woman's voice from the living room. "I really do appreciate you coming on such short notice. We're trying to get the place on the market as soon as possible, and it's so overwhelming with all this—all this—"

All this *what*? Grace jerked open another drawer and found it jumbled with flatware, cheap stuff with split plastic handles tangled up with some tarnished silver, as if everything had been dumped out of a box. There were some tiny spoons like the ones Mrs. Graham had inherited from her mother-in-law. She kept them in a glass on the windowsill in the kitchen. Once, dishing up ice cream for everyone, Mrs. Graham had given the regular deep and sturdy tablespoons to her boys and her husband, and then plucked out two of the tiny silver spoons for herself and Grace. She had known Grace would like them. Grace had often helped herself to a tiny spoon after that. She'd even brought one with her to New York. She ate her yogurt with it.

Now Grace picked up a spoon and turned it over. She had worked on silver the month before and learned about the hallmarks stamped into the undersides of the handles. This spoon's hallmark was a Dianakopf, a raised profile of the goddess Diana set inside a recessed clover shape. Easy even for a novice to spot. Austrian, probably late 1800s. Grace was so pleased with herself that she knew what it was.

The woman who had lived in this apartment liked old travel books and *South Pacific.* Grace had seen the videotape on a shelf, the label home-made. She ate Ritz crackers and drank orange spice tea. Boxes of both were still in her cabinets. The novels on her nightstand were by Rosa-munde Pilcher. There was a Christmas card on the fridge with a photo of a grinning, cake-smeared toddler. *Happy Holidays from the Reeses in 14E.* Did they even know she was gone?

Grace slipped the tiny spoon and the four others just like it into her pockets. They weren't worthless to her.

The sheer amount of stuff in New York had begun to overwhelm her. She had always liked things, the specialness of unusual things, like Mrs. Gra-ham's little spoons and the horse-cameo bracelet Riley had given her, which was as interesting as it was ugly. But here, there was so much finery to name and quantify. That's why people brought in Donald, the truffle hog, to sniff out hidden valuables so they could insure them. Grace hadn't realized what a narrow slice of the economy she had grown up in until she had been begged for a dime on the sidewalk and then, ten seconds later, stood in a penthouse taking notes on a piece of lumpy pottery that cost more than a year of her tuition.

Grace could think of better things to do with that kind of money than go to private college. There were the people on the sidewalk, for instance. But when Grace walked around her new city and saw the panhandlers— the runaway teenagers with cardboard signs and skinny dogs, the Vietnam vets with swollen eyelids and no teeth, the man who once stood outside her dining hall with two small children and asked her if she would smuggle out some bagels for him in her backpack—she did not really *consider* them. To do so would be to admit that they were people like her, and at eighteen, she was unable or unwilling to do that. Clearly, most other people didn't think of the poor as real; they walked around them. Grace had snuck out a dozen bagels in her bag for the man outside the dining hall and pointedly handed the sack of food to his young son. She resented the man's exposing his children to the severity of their need. He should, she felt, have protected them.

She didn't think of that man again until about a year later. She was nineteen then, penniless in Prague with only a stolen oil painting she couldn't sell, and her pickup English tutoring had all but evaporated. Her only remaining client asked her one day to meet him at his home. On the subway, she knew. She knew what would happen. And when he locked the door of his apartment behind her, poured her a glass of water, and then shoved her over the back of his couch and offered her ten times her hourly rate to hold still, she said yes. To say no would mean what, to be raped? But she might have said yes even if it had not. She needed money. For the four minutes he fucked her, she stared at the blank black screen of the TV and her disbelieving face in the reflection. She thought of the rich people and their rugs and vases, what they could buy for her now, and then she remembered her snooty charity, handing the sack of bagels to the little boy instead of his father. All she needed now was to pay rent and feed herself, only herself, and here she was, allowing the formerly unthinkable.

It was perhaps peculiar, then, that when Grace was working for Donald, she didn't resent the stuff itself. She loved the stuff; it gave her such a thrill to know the history, value, and intimate details of things when their owners did not.

The owners she either envied or despised. A man in Tribeca had Donald and Grace appraise his collection of "rare African masks." His interior designer had bought them as a collection so that the client could be a collector. Grace was offended by how little he knew about them. The masks weren't even African; they were Guatemalan animal masks from the 1970s. Writing the report was painful; she hated to educate him. She wanted the man to go on telling his guests about his African mask collection until he could be humiliated, to his face, by one of his own.

13

Grace didn't see Alls the first day he was in New York. The fencing tournament ran from eight in the morning until ten that night, and she was grateful he was tied up; she was trying frantically to catch up on her neglected course work, writing final papers and cranking out forgotten assignments for partial credit. She'd been too busy with Donald to notice how far behind she had fallen. She was always studying, just not the right material. Now she learned that cramming didn't work with Roland Barthes and Judith Butler. You couldn't just watch the movie.

"What do you mean, you're too busy?" Riley protested that night. "You wouldn't be too busy if *I* came up."

"That's not the same thing at all." She felt her face reddening and was glad he couldn't see her.

"Make time," he said. "If *your* best friend came to visit—"

"I wish you would," she said, and then she was embarrassed.

She and Riley almost never talked about school anymore. The long distance forced her to narrate her life to him, when before he had experienced it with her, and this in turn forced her to choose what was worth telling. And after Thanksgiving, she knew not to highlight the differences in her life in New York—her work and her education. She should focus on what they shared. But then what had been the point of her coming here, besides getting away from Alls?

Not that Riley noticed what she left out. He had his own distractions: Anne Findlay had sold nearly half his paintings by the second week of December. He was over the moon.

On Thursday after work, Grace made her way to the athletic complex to find Alls. He'd said he had a lot of downtime, hours spent waiting to compete, and she expected to find him among the dozens of fencers stretching against the walls or clustered in packs around outlets, tapping at their laptops. She wandered up and down the halls looking for the Garland fencers. When she found them and asked after Alls, a boy in headphones and wrist supports inclined his head toward the middle of the gym: Alls was competing now. The whole town had attended the Ravens' basketball games. Now Alls was fencing in nationals, and not even his own team was watching.

She spotted the Garland coaches first, one close to the mat and another farther back, taking notes. Only a handful of other people were watching. The two masked fencers dressed in white scuttled up and down a length of the mat, and not until he was right in front of her did Grace know which one was Alls.

She recognized his body, the way he moved. He bounced lightly on the balls of his feet, as if he were keeping a beat, while the other fencer's stance was low and deliberate, like that of a crab. They moved to the left a few feet, then right, the distance between them unchanging.

The coach with the clipboard saw Grace watching and beckoned for her to come closer. Alls's opponent lunged forward and Alls rushed him, flicking the tip of his foil at his opponent's hand. The score was 3-0. The coach clapped lightly and leaned over to Grace.

"You a fencer?"

"No," she said. "Just watching."

"You picked a lousy one to watch," he said quietly. "He's cleaning this guy's clock."

He meant Alls. "That easy?"

"This poor kid's made of wood, learned from a book." Then he nodded toward Alls. "See, he never shows you what he's about to do. I can't even tell half the time, and I taught him."

Grace watched Alls's shoulders flex under his jacket as he raised his foil and lowered it, dashed forward in a blur of limbs and clipped his opponent's hip, then his shoulder: 4-0. They each made a tight loop, and Alls cracked his neck from side to side. The boys faced each other again. Alls looked weightless, his muscles tense and alive.

"Because he doesn't stop moving?" Grace asked.

"See how quick he responds? You can't surprise him." He shook his head. "And you can't tell what he's going to do until he does it—no patterns, no hints."

The timer showed just under a minute left, but Alls didn't want to wait. He shot forward and closed three feet in a split second, then doubled back as his opponent lurched forward to meet him. He thrust his foil toward Alls's chest, but Alls arched backward, and the other boy, caught in his own momentum, was still pulling back his foil as Alls's darted to touch his belly.

Alls flipped off his mask and looked for his coaches, who were clapping. Grace waved.

He came over to hug her. "I didn't know you were coming tonight." He was barely out of breath, but she smelled the sweat on his neck and quickly pulled away.

"Just for a minute," she said. "I'm actually on my way to work." This wasn't true. She had planned on showing him around after he was finished, but standing with him there in the gym, too far away from the house on Orange Street, too far from Riley, she felt jumpy and unsettled. She heard a bell of warning sound within her.

"Now? Well, see you tomorrow then?"

"Definitely." Grace was already moving toward the door. "I'll call you in the morning," she called over her shoulder.

She went home. A couple of hours later, Riley called her, furious. She promised to make it up tomorrow.

The next morning, Grace called in sick. Alls met her in the lobby of her dorm. She took him upstairs and introduced him to Kendall, whom she had instructed not to talk about Grace and Riley's marriage. She wasn't used to asking people to keep her secrets, because she wasn't used to telling them.

"Your dorm room has its own bathroom," he said while Grace dug around her desk for a subway map.

"It used to be a hotel," Kendall said. "So how'd you do last night?"

"I made it to the semis and then got raked by a kid from the Air Force Academy."

"And you just started last year?" Kendall gaped. "That's kind of amazing."

"But I've hit the curve. The guy who won my event has been fencing since he was six."

"What were *you* doing when you were six? Catching crawdads or something?"

"Making moonshine in an old boot," Alls said, and Kendall laughed ferociously. In Garland, Grace might have rolled her eyes. Here, his presence was so surreal and discomfiting that she could only stare at his feet. Kendall seemed to have arranged herself yogically, her shoulders thrust back as if in mid-stretch, her thighs splayed apart.

"So," Alls said, "what are we doing? What are we doing *tonight?*"

"Well, I've got all day to hang out, but then tonight I have to go to this auction." She didn't look at him. "Sorry, it's sort of work related."

"What kind of auction?"

"Art. Paintings and photography."

"You should come," Kendall said. "I'm going too."

"Well, I don't know if—I mean, I just have one invitation." Alls was wearing a GC sweatshirt and a Carhartt coat. He'd make Grace look country by association.

"It's open to the public," Kendall said.

A certain public. "But he'd need clothes—"

"It's fine," Alls said, giving her a wary look. "I'll do something else."

"No, it's not that," Grace said. "My work is kind of weird—"

"Seems pretty important," Alls said. "Seems like you've got a real important job."

"You're coming," Kendall said. "I'll borrow a jacket for you." She licked her lips and started texting. "So not a big deal. Then we can all party after."

Alls didn't look at Grace. "Cool," he said to Kendall. "Thanks a lot."

"I just hope you don't get bored," Grace said.

That day, Grace and Alls zigzagged the city until she had shin splints. She threw everything at him: bubble tea, Gray's Papaya, Cory Arcangel's Super Mario video installations, the trapeze school by Chelsea Piers, white ghost bicycles with memorial plaques, Ernesto Burgos's cast-iron bathrobes, rugelach, beef-head tacos. They counted French bulldogs, double strollers, and people wearing underwear outside their clothes. She kept them busy, always moving, and she talked too fast, as if she really were a tour guide.

They took a picture of themselves to send to Riley. They talked about him all the time, as if he would join them later. Riley would like this; he would laugh at that. He was all they had in common. But picking through the construction debris along the High Line, ducking to spy into the apartment windows below, Alls was the one standing next to her, laughing, rubbing his hands together to keep them warm. They shared a cigarette and a flask of Old Overholt as they looked down at the cobblestones, watching people shop, and Grace ran out of things to say. She had been careful not to let that happen—space in the conversation felt dangerous, like the heavy stillness just before a thunderstorm. She realized she was gripping the rail.

"Do you . . . do you like it here?" he asked her, as if they had just met.

"Here, New York? Yeah. It feels so big, and—I don't know. Like everything here is more important. Like even buying toothpaste is somehow more special here than anywhere else." He winced, but she went on. "Like something's happening, and I'm just part of it."

"You feel both more and less important?"

"Yeah," she said. "Like I'm less in charge of my life, really, but the life is more interesting."

"Why do you want to be less in control of your life?"

Don't you? she thought. *You trust yourself to steer this rig?*

"I didn't. I mean, that's not why I came here," she said, though she could hardly tell him why she had. "But it does make you feel smaller, which is a relief in some ways. When you screw up, it seems less terrible. All these people, everybody screwing up."

What was she talking about? In Garland, she was practically camouflaged by Riley. She'd been greedy for the disguise. And yet, sometimes the weight of Riley and herself seemed to rest on her alone, as if *she* had become their scaffolding. She'd been the creeping ivy that needed a brick wall to grow along at first, but now the brick would crumble without it.

"He told me he got a tattoo," she said. "But he won't show it to me."

"It's Marmie," he said. "Running down his forearm."

"*What?* Like, her name?"

"No, a picture of her. He drew it after she died. She's running, kind of a trot. It's not bad, but it's *huge*," Alls said. "He regrets it already."

"It's sweet though," she said, and he nodded.

"You never screw up anymore," she said.

"No," he said. "Not anymore."

"Did you grow up, or what?"

"I don't know. Maybe." He shrugged. "When you're a kid you do what your friends do; you think you're all the same. But at some point you get that you're not. You see the lines. There's nobody standing behind you to smooth things over. You can't do what they do. So now I don't."

"You can get a dog tattoo," she said, wishing he wouldn't be so serious, not alone with her like this.

"It's really strange to see you without him," Alls said.

"Yeah," she agreed. "You, too."

She hurried to think of something else to say. "I worry about him," she said. Not true, not the way she'd said it.

"You should. He's so fucking *tense* without you."

She covered her mouth to hide her smile. "He is painting a *lot*." This was an inside joke. They all knew that Riley didn't jerk off. His friends had deduced it from his suspicious lack of masturbation jokes over the years, and they teased him about his snobbery. "Master Riley doesn't care for domestic automobiles, cheap sandwich bread, or self-pleasure," Greg would say in a mangled British accent. Riley didn't argue.

"The other day he blew up at me for throwing a ball against the ceiling," Alls said now. "He said I was *leaving marks*." Grace was laughing silently, so hard that she couldn't breathe, and Alls kept on. "But then he left this art book in the *bathroom*—"

"No, no, don't tell me—"

"Open to this page with a painting of a naked woman—who's the guy who does the slits for eyes?"

"Modigliani," Grace wheezed.

"Greg comes crashing down the stairs holding this book, screaming that it *broke* Riley—"

"Stop, you can't tell me this." She pulled herself together, suddenly alarmed—not about the possibility of Riley jerking off to a picture of an oil painting, but that she and Alls were laughing at him like this, without him, alone together. "Are you hungry? I'm hungry."

"No," he said. "About this auction."

"I'm sorry I was weird about it," she said. "I'm glad you're coming, really. It'll be nice to get some fresh eyes on all the madness up here."

"You think you're losing your Southern ways?" He had affected a bloated George Wallace accent. Displaced southerners were so quick to ape their own stereotypes. She did it too.

"You'll see," she said, unsure of what, exactly, she wanted him to see.

"I'll try not to embarrass you," he said, and she knew, unhappily, that he meant it.

Toward evening, Alls went back to his team's hotel to clean up, and Kendall and Grace got dressed for the auction. Jezzie lent Grace a black wool dress, sharply tailored, with a pencil skirt and a deep keyhole back. Grace had not known black wool could be sexy. When Kendall fastened the small hook at the back of her neck, Grace looked like everything she wanted to be.

"Where do you wear this?" she asked Jezzie, who was wearing a bustier and leather shorts.

"Temple," she said with a shrug.

Grace pulled on her boots, approved by both Schraders. Kendall drew black liquid eyeliner along Grace's eyelids with a steady hand, flicking her wrist at the edge to make a cat eye.

"No jewelry," Kendall said. "This look is all about the architecture."

Grace reached for her red lipstick and Kendall shook her head. "Bare. Like you're not trying so hard," she said, a bit impatiently. She tousled Grace's hair. "There. Like a sixties Bond girl, precoital. One of the smart ones from the beginning of the movies."

Phillips de Pury was on Park Avenue and East Fifty-seventh. A security guard opened the glass door for them and nodded toward the elevator. Already, everything was different from what Grace had pictured. In movies, art auctions were held in windowless, wood-paneled rooms where a few hundred people were arranged neatly in chairs before a man in a bowtie, who looked out over his nose at a sea of waving paddles. Phillips de Pury was a two-story chamber with marble floors, steel beams, and a loud echo. Voices rumbled in a low, knowing chorus of brazen opinions and echoing, throaty cackles. She thought of the doughnut fellowship hour held in the undercroft after mass at the Grahams' church and looked nervously at Alls, but Kendall had him by the elbow. He was laughing, too, at something she had said.

The pieces up for auction hung on the walls or sat on fat white columns. People weaved between them, hugging each other and gesturing with their wineglasses. A woman with a spiked crest of silver hair debated quietly with her husband over whether a McGinley would be an appropriate wedding gift for their niece.

The auctioneer wore a white shirt unbuttoned to his sunburnt chest. He took his place at the podium, and Grace expected people to quiet and settle into the Louis Ghost chairs scattered around the room, but the chatter only dimmed slightly. A man of a type she had begun to recognize, probably a decade older than she was but a decade younger in appearance, pushed around a chrome drink cart stacked high with oversize glossy auction catalogs, each as heavy as a high school yearbook.

"Lot one," the auctioneer said. "Untitled, David Salle. We'll start at ten thousand. Do I have ten thousand?"

The screen next to him displayed numbers spinning upward in rows of different currencies, fast as a slot machine, as he pointed around the room. Some people carried on conversations, standing in groups or turned around in their chairs, as if this were only a cocktail party. The painting went from $10,000 to $120,000 in about six seconds. Grace's heart sped up. Alls took the seat next to hers, his legs splayed wide as if he were on the couch at home.

"For one hundred and twenty thousand? Do I hear a penny more?" The auctioneer made a joke off-mic into his cupped hand, and the people in front laughed. "Sold for one hundred and twenty-two thousand dollars."

The crowd applauded. To Grace's left, two men in their midforties wearing matching navy sport coats, jeans, brown oxfords, black glasses, and salt-and-pepper hair kissed each other and then clapped with everyone else. She wanted to be them, superior in both their love and their taste, and able to act on it. She looked past Alls to Kendall, who was at the side of the room with an older couple, perhaps friends of her parents.

Grace realized that Alls was watching her. She expected him to open his mouth and say, "Scoot over," or "I'm hungry," something familiar from the house on Orange Street.

"You're sweating," he said.

After the auction, Kendall took them to a party at a friend's parents' apartment. A dozen people lounged on three couches, drinking and smoking. Grace read the spines of the books on the shelves and Alls followed behind her, too close. They drank vodka tonics out of coffee mugs. Whoever had grown up in that apartment was worried about breaking the good glasses. Kendall made sure everyone's mug stayed full, and when Alls sat down on the couch, she promptly snuggled in next to him and flopped her head onto his shoulder. Grace had never seen Kendall like this. Drunk, sure, but not desperate. "Some little thingie," Mrs. Graham would have said. "Some little trampette." Kendall whispered to Alls with her lips pushed out, a floppy pout that made her look doped up with novocaine.

If anything happened between Kendall and Alls tonight, Riley would be delighted with Grace. He would be as pleased as if Grace had set it up on purpose. And as for Grace herself, well. The picture of Kendall and Alls together, making out on the couch where they sat now or even later, in Kendall's bed—Grace would not be able to rid herself of such an image. Her stomach rolled just thinking about it.

Now Kendall had her hand on Alls's thigh. In the gap between two songs, she heard Kendall speaking. "So sad about Riley's mom," she said. Grace couldn't hear the rest, but she saw Kendall's lips, *something-something-Paris*.

No, she begged. *Not that*.

Alls's head twitched, and then he caught Grace watching.

"You ready?" she mouthed.

He cocked his head toward the door, and she nodded. He asked Kendall if she wanted a refill, and she smiled and stretched like a cat, nodding yes.

"What's wrong with Riley's mom?" he asked in the elevator.

"I can't talk about it," she said, looking up toward the mirrored ceiling. He raised his eyes to hers in the reflection.

"You told your roommate."

"That's different, she doesn't know him." In the mirrored elevator, there was nowhere to look away.

"Does he also not want you to tell anybody he lives in Paris?"

"What?" Grace shook her head. "She's thinking of someone else."

"You don't know *anyone* who lives in Paris."

"You don't know everyone I know," she huffed.

He groaned. "Stop," he said. "Just stop. You told her Riley went to college in Paris. She said so. You must not have caught that part."

Grace felt her throat closing up, like her own body was strangling her. "It wasn't—I didn't—" So many feeble starts, but nowhere to go.

"Don't worry," Alls said. "I wouldn't tell him that."

Alls knowing she had lied about Riley was almost as awful as Riley knowing. In one way, worse: She still wanted Alls so horribly. *Concentrate*, she thought. They needed to get to a diner. They needed to sit on opposite sides of a big white table under fluorescent lights and drink Coke. Grace would flap at her pit stains and Alls would say stupid things about the artwork at the auction, and everything would snap back into place. The auction. Someday it would be her and Riley there, buying, selling, whatever. They would win and they would squeeze hands, kiss.

Outside, she and Alls walked a yard apart, Alls following Grace to the subway, though she wasn't certain exactly where the nearest station was. Almost no one else was out on the Upper East Side. A man in a trench coat, his face tight and shiny, wove unsteadily down the sidewalk behind them like a toddler learning to walk.

"Hey, Nebraska," he called. "Nebraska, you slut."

Alls grimaced and took her arm, and they walked faster.

"I know what those slutty boots mean, Nebraska. Is that where you're from? Or fucking Ohio?"

Grace stopped and turned around. "Get the fuck away from me."

The man laughed to himself and then pulled out his cell phone, as though he'd forgotten that Alls and Grace were standing there and that he had been harassing her. He mashed some buttons and groaned.

"You done, man?" Alls said. "You need to turn around, go the other way now."

The man stepped forward, casually, easily. "Who's this, your brother? Your brother come up from the farm?"

"I told you to get back from me," Grace warned.

"I'll tongue-fuck you till you can't breathe," he slurred quietly. "In your little boots." He stepped into the light from a street lamp and seemed to wilt there, his body slumping forward. Grace grabbed Alls's elbow and they stomped down the sidewalk, Grace's heels hitting the concrete hard enough to send shocks up through her shins, her thighs, into her hips.

"Has that ever happened before?"

"I'm not usually out so late." Usually she was on the phone with Riley by now. Boys never seemed stupider than when they were surprised by the bad behavior of other men. "But it's not exceptional," she said. Part of her felt grateful. The man had shaken her up. She felt less vulnerable now, less caught.

On the subway, they kept a seat between them until they hit Grand Central and the train grew crowded. When he slid over toward her, she felt the tiny hairs along her forearms stand up, as if they were somehow reaching for him.

They should call Riley. They should have called him already, could still call. She felt an ache deep in her insides that was not allowed. *You're drunk*, she thought to herself. But she wasn't, not really.

She did not say anything when they passed Twenty-third Street, the stop for his hotel, and he didn't seem surprised when Grace stood up at Astor Place. He followed her up the station stairs and they crossed Fourth Avenue. Neither said a word.

When they stepped into the fluorescent light of the dorm, Grace signed him in. They waited for the elevator, and once inside, they leaned against the back wall, away from each other. She wondered what he was thinking right then. *Stop it*, she told herself. They were just going to talk. They'd had a thousand late-night boozy talks, usually with Riley there too. A girl in pajama pants got in on the second floor holding an *Amélie* DVD and then got off at the fourth. The doors opened on the fifth floor and they walked down the hall to Grace's room.

"I should leave this jacket for your roommate," he said when Grace opened the door.

"For Kendall, right."

He draped the jacket on the back of Kendall's desk chair and then sat on the bed. Grace's bed. She didn't turn the lights on. Instead she sat down on the bed next to him.

"Riley," she said.

He nodded.

"We should call him and tell how our day was, what we did."

"We should," he said.

"We could call him right now. But maybe—"

"It might be weird," he said. "That we're, you know, just here. By ourselves."

"Drunk," she said. "Drunk after the rich-people art party."

"Are you drunk?"

"No," she admitted.

"Me neither," he said.

"Do you want a glass of water?"

"Yeah," he said. "That would help."

She filled up the jar from her desk with water from the bathroom and they passed it back and forth.

Grace was still wearing her coat, zipped up. As long as she was still wearing her coat, nothing could happen. She could smell him.

"What do you want?"

She shook her head in the dark.

He turned toward her and got close. "How long?" he asked. "How long have you felt this way?"

"We can't," she said, pulling away. "We can't. We can't."

"Why do you think we're here, then?"

"I feel sick," she said.

"It's a sickness," he said.

"This is new," Grace said. "This is new to me."

"No it isn't."

She swallowed.

"You get to be who you want," he said. "I don't get why you let him decide for you."

"Fuck you," she said. "Don't tell me about me, okay?"

"Sorry," he said.

"Besides, you think *this* is who I want to be? *This* girl?"

"Does it matter anymore?"

"You've thought about this a long time," she said.

"Not because I wanted to."

She was aching and wet and didn't miss Riley at all. Riley was a world away, a souring memory that she couldn't catch the details of and didn't want to.

"We can never tell," she said, and his shoulders collapsed. He'd expected her to shut it down. He might have been testing her, she realized, her loyalty to Riley.

He wasn't.

"We can never tell," he repeated.

He unzipped her coat and slipped his hands inside, around her waist, clutching her as if she might disappear. She pulled him down on top of her, and his face hovered just above hers, his eyes shining in the dark. They knew, in that moment, that they had not done anything irrevocable. They could still go back. But she could feel his breath on her lips; she could taste it. Then she raised her mouth to his and breathed him in.

And when she ran her hands up to his chest, under his shirt, she told herself that this wasn't real. When he rolled her over him and she reached back to unclasp the neck of her dress, she knew that this could not be happening. It was not allowed and so it was not real. She slid his jeans down his thighs as if she were in a dream. She sucked on his earlobe and ran her wet fingers around the head of his penis as if she were just wondering what it would be like, to do that to him, and he pulled her dress up over her head in a blind tunnel where she floated, hoping she wouldn't wake up. She got up and locked the door. He sat up on her bed, leaning against the wall. She climbed onto him and he cupped her ass in his hands and groaned into her neck and none of this was real, not the unfamiliar fingers sliding between her lips, not her sense that she'd known him always and somehow not at all, and then she sank down onto him and lost her breath completely.

They lay there next to each other afterward, not touching, as though by keeping still they might stop time. She saw his arm next to hers, his chest rising and falling, but she couldn't turn to look at him directly. To do so would be to acknowledge both the sharpness and the depth of their betrayal: sharp like a cut where before there had been only an ache; deep as a sudden drop-off from shallow water.

He didn't smell like Riley at all. He smelled like black pepper and burning leaves.

This will destroy you, she thought.

She didn't know what he was thinking, but as they lay there she felt the weight growing heavier with every second.

When Grace finally spoke, her voice was as rough as if she had just woken up. "You need to go now," she said.

He didn't answer her. Grace closed her eyes. Finally, she felt the bed move. She listened to the sounds of his dressing: legs shuffling into pants; the mocking zip of his fly; his feet shoving into shoes; the relief, finally, of his arms shrugging into his coat. When she heard the door click shut, she turned toward the wall and began to sob.

She had her pillow over her head when Kendall came in the next morning, but she wasn't asleep. Grace pushed off the covers and got to her feet, wanting to pee before Kendall got in the shower.

"God," Kendall said as Grace passed. "What happened to you?"

When Grace came out, Kendall was wrapped in her bathrobe, her dress slung over the back of her desk chair. Grace saw her glance at a pile on the floor and realized that it was her dress—Jezzie's dress—lying there in a sloppy heap.

"Oh no, sorry about that," she said, shaking it out to hang it up.

Kendall raised her eyebrows. "It'll need to be cleaned anyway." Grace must have flinched, because Kendall quickly added, "Mine too. Smoky and sweaty and disgusting."

Grace sat on her bed and stared at her thighs, which looked as frail and dry as if she'd had the flu.

"What is it?" Kendall said.

"What?"

"Wait, did you—"

Grace shook her head furiously.

"No, no," Kendall said, a glint in her eye. "Something happened."

Someone began to pound on their door. "Don't move," Kendall said, slipping into the hallway as if Grace might try to escape. She came back with Lana, whose face gleamed with excitement, though Grace hadn't even heard them whispering.

Kendall stood at the foot of Grace's bed, her hands on her hips. She had the faintest smile on her lips. "Did you *fuck* him?"

"No!" Grace said, her voice all air.

"You did! Oh my God, you so *did*!" Kendall cried.

"Shit," Lana said. "This was the friend?"

"*Best* friend," Kendall said. "Of her *husband*!"

When they saw that Grace was crying, they sat down on either side of her, and Lana rubbed her back. She put her head on Grace's shoulder and shushed her maternally.

"Wow," Kendall said. "Who would've thought? Little Miss Small-Town America. *Mrs.*, I mean. Come on, stop crying. Nobody died."

"I'll get you some tissue," Lana said. Grace nodded, snot running down her lip.

"Well, something like this would have happened sooner or later," Kendall said. "Long-distance relationships are doomed."

"Please stop," Grace blubbered. "I can't—"

"I mean, I didn't realize you were even *into* him—"

"Kendall," Lana scolded from the doorway, but when Kendall stopped, Grace began to sob again, bigger and bigger, as if a magician were pulling a mile-long scarf from her throat. She gasped for breath, and when she looked up, she saw that Lana was standing in the doorway with her video camera.

"It's okay," Lana said, encouraging her. "Do what you feel."

V
Paris

14

He might have forgiven you," Hanna said.

Grace laughed sadly. She hadn't wanted to be forgiven. She hadn't wanted him to find out. They were irreconcilable desires. You had either one impulse or the other, and Grace had always had the other.

She and Hanna were sharing a bottle of Hanna's wine on the balcony of her minuscule Belleville studio. Grace was accustomed to spending her evenings by herself, and she was surprised when she accepted Hanna's invitation. But Mme Freindametz was off this week, and she had not forgiven Grace for snapping at her. Now that Grace had put a lock on her bedroom door, her landlady was visibly hostile.

Tonight, when Hanna had asked Grace if there was any news from home, Grace had taken a glug of her wine and told Hanna that she had slept with a friend of her husband. The cliché was painful to spit out.

"No good would've come of telling him," Grace said now.

"You would have broken up, like people do. You think he knows?" Grace nodded. "He must."

"And that's why you're so terrified of him," Hanna said to herself.

Grace knew this fork in the road: to tell Hanna that Riley was no one to be afraid of, or to nod easily and say *Yes, exactly.* Don't think, she told herself. Just do it.

"He wasn't abusive," Grace said. "I'm sorry I told you that."

"Oh." Hanna blinked in surprise. "I see."

"He would have been devastated. I thought lying to him was kinder—protecting him." Ah, that wasn't quite right, but she had said the main thing. She had made the correction. She was trying.

"Well, to protect his love for *you*." Hanna sounded older suddenly, and newly prissy.

"I'd worked so hard to earn it," Grace said. "And then to lose it over *one* thing—"

"Earn it!" Hanna cried. "What an American way of looking at it. You people think you deserve every happiness."

Grace tipped up her glass of wine and finished it. "Our founding fathers said we do."

Hanna peered at her, unsure if she was serious. Grace rolled her eyes, and Hanna sat back again.

"I've never told you about Nina," Hanna said.

Nina—it sounded familiar somehow. Then Grace remembered: Antonia. She waited, anxious for Hanna's confidence. Grace had confided in *her*, after all.

"I was helpless to her," Hanna said. "Every hour I spent near her seemed to vanish in a second. I could never get enough."

Hanna tilted her head back to rest it on the couch behind her and blinked up at the ceiling. "As soon as she left the room, it was as though the heat were switched off. I wanted to know everything about her, every detail of her life, her biography, her interests, her movements. Each thing I learned was a little piece of candy. And I always wanted more."

A week ago, Grace couldn't have imagined Hanna in love. To be in love was to lose control, and Hanna, on the surface, at least, always exhibited perfect control.

"The way you are in love is the way you are in all things," Hanna said. "And the way you are in all things is the way you are in love. Sloppy, messy in life? Sloppy in love. Need to pin down every detail?" She pointed at herself. "That's me in love—no laziness."

Grace didn't want to think about how she was in love.

"The woman I loved was a liar. So in life, in love. I see it in you too." Hanna pointed at Grace. "Untrustworthy."

Grace's mouth fell open. Hanna had accused her as if it were a joke, but she hadn't meant it like one.

"Lies beget lies," Hanna went on. "Like little bunny rabbits. They make more lies, wherever they go. They can't help it—pop, pop, pop, all over the place, little baby lies that grow up into big lies and make their *own* lies—"

"Look," Grace said. "I was young, and I fucked up, and I left, and I'm sorry. People make mistakes. They do crazy things when they're *in love.*"

"You've told lies, I bet, you don't even realize you've told. Like an addict! They just fall out of your mouth, like you're breathing them."

Grace recoiled. "What is this obsession with *lying* all of a sudden? Everyone lies. You try not to but you do. I'm no worse than anyone else. You're a forger, for God's sake."

"Used to be. Now I'm very frank, all the time. Now I don't bet what I can't afford to lose."

One week had passed since the boys were paroled. Nothing.

Grace saw the possibility that there would always be nothing, but she couldn't really grasp it. She tried to settle into the ambiguity, which she knew could last forever. If she didn't, the terrible uncertainty of where they were and what they were doing, feeling, thinking, saying would surpass anything they could ever do or think or say.

So much of her life since she had left Garland, even the first time, had been a series of tragic errors. She couldn't imagine that she'd gotten away with it. She didn't feel as though she had gotten away with anything— more like she'd gotten away *without.*

Grace was painting the hooves of one of Hanna's sheep when Jacqueline called her in. Usually her boss came out of her office when she wanted something, looking over everyone's work as she talked. Grace stood up, but her left leg had fallen asleep and she started to tumble. Hanna shrieked, high-pitched as a scared rabbit, and Grace grabbed the corner of the table to right herself. Amaury had leaned over to cover his workings with his arms, like a hen protecting a brood of chicks. His table was eight feet away.

"Pardon," Grace said.

She hobbled into Jacqueline's office, and Jacqueline shut the door.

"Asseyez-vous," she said. "I have something new for you."

"What about the centerpiece?"

"Hanna will be working on it for weeks," Jacqueline said. "In the meantime, we have to get paid." She unlocked her desk drawer and pulled out a velvet jewelry box. "Hold this," she said, handing Grace a giant cocktail ring set with brightly colored jewels. Jacqueline pushed her finger into the jewelry box's crease, peering into it. She turned the box over and shook it into her lap. Two pearls bounced across her skirt.

"The pearls fell out," she said, placing them in Grace's palm.

"I don't know what to do with jewelry," Grace said. "I don't know anything about jewelry."

"Just pretend it's a jewelry box instead of the jewelry, okay? You've done pearl setting before. The minaudière, remember?"

"But that was costume," Grace said.

"This is costume."

"I don't think it is," Grace said, rubbing the thick gold band with her thumb.

"It might as well be. Pearls, peridot. Nothing so *very* precious. The centerpiece is worth five times what this ring is worth."

"The centerpiece? How much? Nine, ten thousand euros?"

"More like fifteen, even as partial reproduction. Nothing like it, and the collector's a little crazy. So who can say?"

The green center stone was a huge oval cabochon, rounded as an eyeball. Jacqueline had said semiprecious, but Grace was sure she was looking at an emerald, flanked by stacks of amethyst baguettes. The ring looked like formalwear for a Mardi Gras parade, like the fantasy jewelry of a six-year-old who wanted to be a princess. At the top and bottom of the emerald were empty sockets where the pearls were to go.

"Amaury, do you have any pearl cement remover?" Grace waggled her finger, weighed down by the heavy ring. "I need to clean this up a bit."

Amaury cocked his head toward the shelf behind him, which held all manner of solvents and cements that Hanna and Grace seldom required. Amaury more often dealt with jewels, working on watches, and Grace wondered why Jacqueline hadn't asked him to do the ring.

Grace had the ring fixed in fifteen minutes. Dissolving the old glue was as simple as removing polish from a fingernail, and then she dabbed a little cement into each setting with a toothpick and pushed the pearls in. Three thousand euros, held together with glue.

When she gave the ring back to Jacqueline, her boss ran her fingers over the pearls and around them, feeling for any roughness. She squinted at the ring under her desk lamp. "Good," she said.

Then she took a brown paper sack from her purse and upended it into her palm. Out tumbled a jeweled bangle, a fat gold tube striped with red and white stones. "Same with this bracelet," Jacqueline said. "Some of the stones have come loose from their settings. It's an older piece." The gold was discolored and the remaining stones were dirty. Jacqueline held the bracelet out to Grace, who hesitated.

"Did you want me to ask Amaury? He's busier than you are right now—"

"No," Grace said quickly. "I'll do it."

Jacqueline handed Grace a small envelope. She could feel the stones through the paper. She knew that when she opened the bag, the stones inside it would be bright and clean.

At her desk, Grace looked closely at the gem settings. The lights buzzed overhead, and she turned on her brightest lamp. She picked at the crooked metal prongs that had given up their diamonds and rubies. Grace had been so eager to prove herself to Jacqueline, and *this* was what she'd done it for? She hadn't stolen anything in years, not even a pack of gum. She looked at Hanna's little sheep and their half-painted hooves with longing.

Grace and Hanna communicated in single words—Salad? Omelet?— until they were sitting next to each other on a park bench, staring together at a bird foraging from the rim of a garbage can.

"Oh, I don't think it's *that*," Hanna said when Grace told her about the jewelry. "She used to take in jewelry work from time to time. There hasn't been any jewelry since you've been here?"

"No, just watches," Grace said. "Amaury's things."

"She used to have a jewelry person here. Angeline. She left when her eyesight got too bad, and I guess that was the end of the jewelry. But I'm sure you'll be very good—you do all the microscopic work very well. You should get reading glasses, though. You'll ruin your eyes."

"It's just bizarre for something so expensive to be in a paper bag like that."

"You know as well as I do that people don't always take very good care of their things."

Grace nodded.

"I mean, it *could* be," Hanna said. "Stolen, I mean. We wouldn't know. Would you really mind if it was?"

"Of course I would."

"Funny that this would suddenly bother you," Hanna said. "You know she's not running a spotless operation."

"No one in antiques is," Grace said. "But there's a line. I'll do whatever I'm told as long as I can reasonably believe that it's okay."

"*Reasonably* believe? That's not belief; it's the opposite."

"Hanna, we don't *know* what happens outside the studio," Grace said.

"That's what I've been saying."

Grace sat in doubtful silence, picking at her salad. She thought now about Antonia and Nina and wondered if they were the same person or if these names, unusual sounding to her, were as common in Denmark as Madison and Emma were in Tennessee. So often she'd felt on the edge of knowing something, and as many times as she had leaped over that edge she had scrambled backward, covering her eyes. She didn't want to know about the jewelry but it was too late. She wanted to ask about Nina and Antonia, but Hanna's temperament seemed to forbid it.

Then Hanna asked her why she had cheated on her husband in the first place. Whatever limits *she* felt, she clearly ignored.

"The same reason anybody does," she said. "I was lonely and disappointed."

"Or bored and entitled."

"Maybe bored," Grace agreed.

"People always say the other person didn't *mean* anything."

"No, he meant a great deal to me," Grace said. "I loved him horribly, if you can say that. Like I was sick with him. I knew I'd made the right choice, marrying my husband, and some evil part of me was trying to ruin everything, and she needed to be silenced." She grimaced. "I sound like I'm describing a psychopath."

"Two selves."

"Everyone has them, I think."

"Public and private."

"Right and wrong."

"I find it so strange that you were married. You're such a remote person. I can't imagine you as a passionate teenager."

Grace could hardly imagine herself as a passionate teenager. Until that night with Alls, she had never been at a loss to explain, to herself, her own decisions. She had never confused self-interest with self-indulgence. She knew the difference.

When they came back from lunch, Amaury was in Jacqueline's office. They could hear him. Hanna put her finger to her lips, and Grace tiptoed back to her table.

"Whose is it?" Amaury demanded.

"Go back to your desk," Jacqueline said. "Stop asking me questions if you don't like the answers."

"You made a promise, and I won't work here anymore if—"

"Nobody's making you work for me."

When Amaury came out, Grace and Hanna dropped their eyes, their tools suddenly clacking. He took his jacket from his station and left.

Grace clanked the handle of her pliers loudly on the edge of the table. She wished she hadn't overheard.

15

On Monday, Grace was winding the centerpiece's tree trunks with bronze-beaded wires, spiraling from the base to the fine branches. Applying these beaded wires was the easiest thing they'd done to the centerpiece since cleaning, and Grace didn't want to rush. Jacqueline had left her alone after she'd finished the bracelet, and Grace wished she could work quietly on the centerpiece with Hanna. She was proud of her work: Her peaches, now bound to the branches, looked soft and fragrant, though they were neither, and her acorns were so small and precise that no one would even see them until they looked very, very closely.

She'd also done quite good work on the ruby and diamond bracelet, but she didn't want to think about that.

Hanna was clipping serrations along the edges of her silk leaves with minute scissors, the sharp blades short as a pencil tip, when Grace asked her what Nina had lied about.

Her brow furrowed, but she did not ask Grace to clarify.

"Real liars don't lie *about* anything," Hanna said. "They just lie. 'About' is a word liars use to justify their lying, to make it seem like a localized problem."

"You've made quite a study," Grace said, trying to sound light and wry.

"But I still don't know," Hanna said. "And that upsets me. With a liar, you can never know the whole truth, ever. You can't ever be sure that *this* version is the real version. There is no end, no bottom. Sometimes I wonder if the whole thing was a hoax."

"The whole thing?"

"Our whole affair. I'm not sure she was even conscious of lying, or if lying had become so much of her nature that she lied without thinking. So, yes. If I was just another object for her lying."

"And if you were in on it," Grace said, standing to get closer to the tips of the trees. "Lying to yourself, or wanting to believe too much."

She had meant to commiserate, to empathize, but Hanna was too quiet. Grace looked up to see Hanna's eyes tightly screwed onto her leaves. Bits of fabric small as dust floated down into her lap.

"I don't know what you mean," she said. "Nobody wants to be lied to."

"Of course not," Grace said apologetically. "Not consciously. It's just that you know the person wants something that isn't—"

"Yes," Hanna said. "You lie because you know, when asked the question, that there's a good answer and a bad one."

"You want to give the good one," Grace said. "To be good. And they want you to, too."

Grace had never talked like this with anyone. She looked down at the wastebasket and saw in its lid Hanna's reflection. She had leaned back from the table and turned her head toward the stairs and Jacqueline's door. Grace heard it open.

Jacqueline strode over with two jewelry boxes. "Hello, ladies," she said. "How's the gossip?"

Grace smiled weakly. "Fine."

Jacqueline sucked her teeth. "Amaury's going to come back to locked doors. That man." She laid a cool hand on Grace's bare shoulder, her jasmine perfume drifting forward. "Not that we need him anymore, right, Julie?"

She opened the first jewelry box. Inside was a watch, a jeweled pink monstrosity.

"Just the clasp needs fixing. I have an appointment, but I'll be back to close."

"There *is* no clasp," Grace protested.

"Relax," Jacqueline said. "It's right there." She split apart the jewelry cushion and dug out a jeweled crescent, a clasp in the shape of a single paisley. "The missing stones are in there too, but you can pull them out with tweezers. I can't get in there with my fat fingers."

It didn't even make sense for a watch to be in a cushioned box like that. "I'm not sure I can fix this," Grace said.

"I am," Jacqueline said.

The watch was the sort of bauble that a Disney princess would wear if brought to life. Platinum; candy-pink crocodile strap; diamonds surrounding a pink teardrop face. Grace found a comparable watch for sale at a shop in Connecticut for ninety-five thousand dollars.

The clasp had been torn from the band, as though the watch had been ripped from its owner's wrist, but the stones missing from the clasp would have come loose gradually. There were nine diamonds, each no larger than a mustard seed, and only eight sockets.

Grace was furious at this, that Jacqueline had been too sloppy to even count, to make it *look* right for her. There was no question that Jacqueline was stealing stones. Was there a partner somewhere, a jeweler who took in pieces for cleaning and returned them to owners sparkling with fakes? Or were these lifted right out of dressers and drawers?

"How come she doesn't ask you?" Grace lamented.

"She did once, but I refused. It's such a slippery slope for me, back to my old habits. I can't mess around even a little. I don't work on anything that doesn't have good papers."

"What? I've never seen any papers. What do you do when there are no papers?"

"I either get them myself, or get something via e-mail. If I can't, I tell Jacqueline I won't work on it without papers, and then she finds someone else."

"Me."

"Sometimes."

"How could you? And not *tell me*?"

"Julie, I thought you didn't mind. You've never asked about papers."

"I didn't know I could." Grace's mouth had gone dry.

"I thought that was why you were here, why she picked you. To do the jobs that are a little . . ." Hanna wiggled her fingers.

"And you never said anything. All this time."

"I didn't think you'd want to talk about it," Hanna said. "It's not the kind of thing people *say*. I'm sorry, I had no idea you were so—"

"Was there even an Angeline?" Grace asked, disgusted.

"Yes," Hanna said. "She left."

"Does Amaury do it?"

"He used to," Hanna said. "Not that they ever spoke of it in front of me, but it's obvious enough. But he got spooked or something. He only does clocks and watches now."

"What happened? What scared him?"

"Nothing much. We're all here, aren't we? Maybe he didn't have the stomach for it. He has a kid. He has to be cautious."

"I thought he lived alone."

"His son lives with his mother, I think in Montreuil. In his teens by now."

Amaury had been here since before Jacqueline took over for her father. Grace had only been here two years. Trusting her must have been a last resort.

"These aren't just little snatches from regular commissions," Grace said. "This is a hundred-thousand-dollar watch."

"So tell her no."

"If there's no one here under me, she'll probably fire me if I don't."

"There's no one here under you."

Grace knew she was at the very bottom of any ladder. Jacqueline probably wouldn't dare switch out the stones herself, even if she could. She wouldn't want to dirty her hands. So she gave Grace the materials, the instructions, and a smile.

Her? Jacqueline could say to the hypothetical interrogators who bothered Grace's imagination. *This girl? American. Hired her off the street. She betrayed me—a thief!*

Rage spread from Grace's fingertips up to her ears. She was disgusted that she could still be so naive.

Jacqueline's office was neater than usual. Grace started with her desk drawers. Cigarettes, pens, hair ties, a melted lipstick, busted sunglasses, mints, dozens of crumpled receipts, dirty centimes. In the filing cabinets, Grace peered over the papers for bulges. She rummaged in the pockets of the silk jacket draped over the chair. She checked behind the books, lifting them by the spines to check for false compartments. She ran her hand under the desk in case anything was taped there. When she was done, there was only the safe, but that was hopeless.

Grace sat in her boss's chair. Hanna would be back from lunch soon; she didn't have much longer. The clock ticked. The chair creaked. The inkjet printer was unplugged. Grace leaned forward and lifted the lid, and there, as goofy and bright as a little girl's bead set, was a plastic bag half-full of cheap stones. There were hundreds, all zirconia or something like it, all on the small side, pencil-eraser size or less. No, Jacqueline wouldn't risk the big central stones of a piece; she'd just swap the smaller ones. Grace raked through the bag. There were cuts in every style—round, square, emerald, baguette. An impostor ready for every role.

She went back to her desk to retrieve one of the replacement diamonds Jacqueline had given her. From the plastic bag, she took three more just like it.

And now to work: She blew out the eight empty sockets and emptied three more, leaving the little rocks loose on the table. When she heard Hanna at the door, Grace brushed the three diamonds into her lap with her forearm. She spent the next hour popping the zirconia into the eleven sockets and clamping them shut.

She picked up the clasp, now filled and glittering, and banged it against the table. Hanna yelped and jumped.

"Do you *mind?*"

"I'm testing the settings," Grace said. Nothing trembled, nothing budged. She inspected the clasp under the lamp, looking for differences in luster or color or sparkle.

"Looks good," she murmured to herself.

"Watch yourself," Hanna said. "It's a slippery slope, *petite voleuse.*"

When Hanna left at seven, Grace worked on the Mont box for an hour, listening for the door in case Hanna came back and surprised her. When the box was dry enough to put back in the paper bag, she pulled the three diamonds from her skirt pocket and arranged them under her magnifier. Incredible, that some speck of mineral could command so many hearts and wallets, just because it threw the light around and made a rainbow on the wall. So did the face of her Timex.

She hadn't stolen anything since the painting and now she'd stolen diamonds.

They were just chips, really. Very small and not worth much. And Jacqueline deserved it. Stealing from her was hardly stealing.

Grace pulled her hair back and started up the computer to run her daily check on the *Albemarle Record*. The computer took ages to boot up, and Grace was impatient, freezing the screen by clicking too fast. She waited restlessly for the *Record*'s page to load.

And there, the day's update: Riley and Alls had vanished from Garland. Riley had last been seen by his family on Saturday; Alls, by his parole officer. Greg refused to comment. Where they had gone, the *Record* did not speculate.

Grace had a bad night. She blinked right through the pills' attempted shutdown like a trick birthday candle. She counted backward from a thousand, twice. She got out of bed and did a hundred sit-ups, trying to tire herself. She drank another glass of wine and read about marquetry from a ten-pound text that was usually as soothing as a lullaby. She thought about calling Hanna, but she didn't.

This wasn't exactly what she had feared, but twice what she had feared.

At four in the morning, she gave up. She startled Mme Freindametz in the kitchen when she went down to make tea; she had been working nights before her break and now she couldn't sleep either. They exchanged a look of grudging sympathy.

She was gilding another layer on her James Mont box when Hanna came in at eight. Grace was in no hurry to revisit the watch, though Jacqueline would be waiting for her to do the strap. She had locked up the watch itself before she left. Grace knew that she would not scrutinize it in front of her.

She and Hanna worked on the centerpiece in silence, threading the leaves onto the branches. Grace was lost in the brambles of her thoughts, and perhaps Hanna was too, but she didn't show it. "Tighter," she said to Grace. "Softer angles."

"I've read about this woman," Grace said. "Heather Tallchief."

"I don't know her," Hanna said.

"She and her boyfriend stole an armored truck together. Three million dollars inside. The truck company hired her as a driver."

"Go on."

"She was only twenty years old. She'd run away from home a few years before, and she was working at an AIDS hospice and then going to dance clubs at night. She met this guy, Solis. He was forty-six. He was a poet."

"First love," Hanna said drily.

"He'd gone to prison decades before, for killing an armored truck driver. But she didn't know that yet, not until she'd moved in with him, and by then, she believed anything he told her. That it was all a misunderstanding. You know."

Hanna nodded.

Grace told her the rest of the story: Solis planned the Loomis heist stitch by stitch, Tallchief later said, so slowly that she didn't know what she was doing until she was doing it. She said that Solis *hypnotized* her every day, and not until she drove the truck off route, to the abandoned warehouse where he was waiting for her, did she realize what she had just done. When she climbed out of the truck, she was terrified. No one had any idea where she was. When he threatened to kill her unless she stayed with him, she did as she was told.

They fled Las Vegas on a plane Solis had chartered. He pushed Tallchief onboard in a wheelchair, disguised as an old woman in a wig and dark glasses. She had a crocheted blanket draped over her lap. But when the plane landed, she stood up and walked off, tall, strong, and young. The pilots remembered that, when police questioned them later. But she and Solis were long gone.

He shipped the money overseas in unmarked freight containers. In a few months she was pregnant, and as soon as she had the baby, she bundled him up and ran away.

Grace had watched the interview over and over. "Were you afraid he'd try to find you?" the reporter asked.

"Yeah," Tallchief said.

"And did he?"

"No."

Tallchief faked an English accent and made up a new name, and she found work first as a prostitute and then as a hotel maid in Amsterdam. She brought up her son there. She went to work every day, volunteered at her son's school, and became someone else.

When her son was ten years old, she came back to the United States. She stated her true name and turned herself in so that her son would have citizenship somewhere, some legal identity. She'd been hiding for twelve years.

In the courtroom, the judge likened Tallchief to the hundreds of girls who'd stood before him. Grace imagined all the women who carried drugs in diaper bags, screened phone calls, drew the blinds, smashed the cameras, lied, lied, and lied some more but who forgot to look both ways when they walked their own bodies across the street. They took the fall for their boyfriends and husbands and men they wished were their boyfriends or husbands. The judge invoked that tired sex-work cliché: A bad childhood, a bad father, and bad boyfriends created a woman who was doomed to be a shadow of all her experiences. Women, the argument implied, were weak: They would do anything for what they believed was love.

Tallchief wept in the courtroom, but she did not beg. "I want you to understand that it's not in my nature to steal or to plot intricate thefts," she said. "I am not a thief. I am not a lifelong criminal."

Her lawyer showed video of her loved ones in Amsterdam, offering testimonials. They wept as they remembered Tallchief coming to them with the truth, one by one, and begging their forgiveness. *Forgive her,* they pleaded. *She is not who she was then.* Her ten-year-old son wore a sweater and necktie, the knot too large above his narrow chest. He said he hoped that he would see his mother again soon, that he missed her so much.

The prosecutor asked the judge to think of the armored car company whose business was destroyed by the burglary, and of the casino whose money they had stolen. The judge sentenced Tallchief to five years in prison and ordered her to repay the three million dollars—the entire amount, since Solis was still at large. She was led from the courtroom in leg irons.

"I'd like to believe he actually loved me," Tallchief said after the trial. "I loved him. I feel foolish and hurt now, but that's the past."

"What an idiot," Hanna said when Grace had finished.

"Hardly," Grace said. "I don't think she was an idiot. What good would it do her now, to believe he never loved her?"

"What *good* would it do her? It's not a choice; it's a belief. She got conned and she should have stayed gone."

Grace agreed with that part. Some people watched the parade of faces on *America's Most Wanted* and fantasized about catching one of them at the local gas station, buying cigarettes and SunChips. They wanted the watchdog's glory, holding tight to the burglar's pant leg with their teeth. But there were other people who didn't want them punished. There were other people who looked into the blurry eyes of the same faces and breathed *Go, go, go.*

"They're gone," Grace told Hanna, her voice catching in her throat. "The boys."

"They can do that? No."

Grace shook her head. "They absconded. Together."

"Where do you think they've gone? Mexico?"

Grace was exhausted enough to be confused; it took her a split second to remember that Hanna thought she was from California.

"I hope so," she said.

"Why, where do you think they went?"

Grace could only shake her head.

"What, you think they'll come *here*?" Hanna stabbed her index finger at the table. "Do they even know you live here?"

"They shouldn't," Grace said.

"Why would they—what do you think is going to happen?"

A hair had fallen into the silver paint on her Mont box. Grace no longer bothered to hide it from Jacqueline. She reached for the tweezers, but she knew she'd have to sand off the whole layer. The paint was too dry already.

Grace scraped at the wood, gathering the metal paste under her finger-nail. She pulled the hair out. It was hers, fallen from her clip.

Hanna was staring at her. "Julie, what did you do?"

Grace opened her mouth and closed it again. They were coming for her; she knew it.

"Well," she began. "I stole from the Wynne House first."

VI
Garland

16

"What do you mean, not going back?" Riley had asked her.

They were lying on his single bed at his parents' house. Downstairs, the Grahams' annual holiday open house was in full swing. All three leaves were needed in the dining room table to make room for the food: sausage balls, country ham biscuits, pepper jelly, hot crab dip. Grace had rolled the cheese straws with Mrs. Graham in the kitchen that afternoon. "Oh, my Gracie, how we all missed you," she had said. "I'm so glad to have my girl back for a few days."

Grace had wept, inexplicably, into her shoulder. "I missed you too," she said. She'd only been gone two weeks. Grace had flown home, frantic and despairing, the day after Alls left. She needed to be with Riley, safe, and that was as far as she could think. She hadn't turned in any final papers and she would miss the exams. Grace hadn't had a B since sixth grade and now she would flunk her first semester of college, but that didn't matter a tenth as much as her other failure did.

At the party, Dr. Graham ladled whiskey sours from the punch bowl, none for himself. An ice ring full of holly leaves bobbed in the middle. Riley's great-uncle Gil had eaten most of the rum-soaked maraschino cherries already; Grace had seen him furtively replenish the bowl. Grace and Riley had made their rounds as a couple, hands clasped, to let the guests look Grace over and remark on how she had changed after just a few months in New York City. Sometimes they said, very satisfied, that she had not changed at all. His aunt Holly, she of the agate cameo bracelet, treated Grace like a riddle to be solved. Was she thinner? Had she changed her hair? Were her clothes different, because *something* was. Grace shifted uncomfortably, remembering an inanity she'd heard as a girl about virgins walking one way and not-a-virgins another. Grace hadn't been a virgin for many years, but she felt sure she knew what the *something* was. Maybe, Aunt Holly concluded with a wistful smile, the change was in Grace's attitude: She was coming into her own as a young woman. Grace felt as though she were auditioning all over again, this time to stay.

She and Riley had snuck upstairs when the guests coaxed Mrs. Graham to the piano, where she was now banging out carols, speeding them up with each verse until the singers were breathless trying to keep up. Always, these carols collapsed into tipsy giggling. The last singer standing received a peppermint pig, tied with ribbon to a tiny hammer. Riley and his brothers were never allowed to win, but the Graham boys always sang in the contest anyway, pushing the tempo, like false bidders driving up an auction price. Grace could hear Jim and Colin now rushing through a tongue-twisting "O Come, O Come Emmanuel."

She and Riley stared at the glow-in-the-dark stars on his ceiling.

"I'm not going back," she said. "I want to stay here, with you."

"And drop out of school?

"I can start at Garland in the fall. I hate it there. It's snotty, and the people aren't even that smart. Everyone's faking something; you just have to figure out what their thing is. I'm not learning anything there that I couldn't learn here."

"Well, *that's* not true. I go here, and I can tell you—"

"Fine. Nothing that I couldn't teach myself."

"You're not making friends," he said. "Everybody who goes away to school without knowing people has a hard time the first semester. You just need to put yourself out there more, join clubs or something."

"Clubs? You want me to join *clubs?*" She pulled her hand from his hip. "Do you not want me here, or what?"

"You know I want you. But you worked hard for this, and I don't want you to give up—"

"Giving up would be staying there, for fifty grand a year, miserable, just because people expect me to."

He groaned. "This is my fault. You're on the phone with me every night instead of meeting people."

"I don't *want* to meet people," she said. "What, like you're meeting new people? Are *you* meeting new people?"

"This is Garland. There are no new people." He grimaced a little. "Did something happen?"

She hadn't seen Alls since she'd gotten home.

"No, nothing happened. But everything I want to happen to me is here, not there."

"I knew you were having a harder time than you were saying," he said. "But I didn't know you were, like, depressed."

"I'm not depressed! I just want to be with you, not with a bunch of snotty posers talking about the aristocratic diaspora."

"This is not good," he said, rubbing his eyes. "I was supposed to come to you. I'm only at Garland because it's free, and I have to paddle around in the baby pool until I graduate, but then I can come over to the deep end, with you." He rolled toward her and propped his head up on his arm. "You're not supposed to come back to the baby pool."

"You sound like one of *them*," she said. "New York is not the deep end of America. It just thinks it is."

He sighed.

"I'm staying." She touched her nose to his. "*You* are my home. We're married. We're not supposed to live apart."

He was quiet for a long time, and she knew, with every silent second, that she was winning. His brow slackened, and they kissed on his twin bed like the teenagers they were, and when his mother called his name from downstairs, they stood up, straightened their clothes, and went downstairs to smile at all the neighbors.

For Christmas, Grace had bought Riley a gray sweater and a book about historical houses. She'd picked them weeks before, and they now seemed cruel, as if she were mocking his Garland tastes, his Garland comfort. Alls walked through the kitchen as she was wrapping them, and her face burned. He kept going, right out the back door. They hadn't spoken at all. As she gathered the paper scraps to throw away, it occurred to her that both she and Alls had always wanted Riley's life, and whatever desire Alls had felt for her had only been an extension of his envy.

I am Riley's cunt, she thought.

He hadn't wanted Grace, but Riley's Grace, and not even Riley's Grace but Riley's cunt. He'd only wanted Riley's cunt.

Riley had gone to fetch her presents, hidden at his parents' house, and he would be home soon. She tied the bows, curled the ribbon. How stupid she had been. She was ashamed at this turn in her misery.

You didn't get two. She was lucky to have one, lucky he was the right one.

That night, Riley gave Grace a monograph on Van Gogh that she'd coveted the summer before. Now she was embarrassed by it. Van Gogh was just one cultural rung above the lamplit fairylands of Thomas Kinkade. But then Riley presented her with a painting of his own, a watercolor portrait of her. Her face nearly filled the paper as she leaned out toward the viewer. She was naked, but not much of her breasts could be seen at that angle. The paint itself was pale and delicate, dozens of layers of thin, filmy washes.

"What is this?" she whispered, running her fingers along the paper's deckled edge.

"It's you," he said. "From the webcam. A screenshot. I hope you're not mad—you were talking, and the crappy computer light had you totally washed out; you were almost glowing white, but you looked—"

Grace looked closely at her face. She must have been completely lost in what she was saying; she looked so unself-conscious.

"Beautiful," he said. "You're always beautiful."

She was sure that this idea, a sincere watercolor portrait of his girlfriend based on a screenshot of a naked webcam chat, was the best thing Riley had ever painted, and far beyond what she'd thought him capable of. But the painting was also incontrovertible evidence that she was loved. He could never, ever know what she had done.

Why was it different, what she felt for Alls? Grace had loved Riley so much. She was an expert, an artisan, in the twin crafts of loving him and of being lovable. How was this any less honest than the other feeling, which felt more like the line in her fishing reel was spinning out away from her and she couldn't stop it? That didn't feel like any kind of love she knew. The line had all run out and the jolt had pulled her overboard.

Grace had learned to say *I love you* when she was just a child: first to her mother and father, then to Riley. Children learned to say *I love you* before they knew what it meant. They said *I love you* because their parents said it to them, and they returned it, a small gift passed back and forth.

She had thought love was not so different from those other truths that became so once spoken: "I swear," "I quit," "I now pronounce you husband and wife."

"I love you," she told Riley then, and she meant it. She always had.

Grace only slept at her parents' house for Christmas Eve and Christmas Day, when Riley slept at his family's house. The twins ran in and out of the house in muddy snow boots with school-holiday urgency. Grace did her best to offer her parents cheerful thoughts about her semester and New York, a little about her job. She presented a few tidy anecdotes. Her father asked about that girl with the crazy hair.

At first, she didn't tell them she wasn't going back. She didn't know how to say it, and they would see, soon enough. But on Christmas Day, she was alone in the kitchen with her father, his back to her, and he asked what classes she was taking next term.

"I'm not going back," she said. "I'm enrolling here."

He turned around, his hands dripping dish suds. "What? Why?"

"It's too snobby," she said. She could have sworn he looked proud.

The day after New Year's she went to her parents' again to paw through her childhood dresser for talismans: old pictures, trinkets, silly gifts that represented who she had been and who she should've stayed. She could hardly remember her life before him, just the lonely murk of childhood, and so she couldn't imagine being without him now. It was like being told that you wouldn't mind dying because then you'd be dead. If she and Riley were not together, she would cease to exist.

She found photos of her and Riley when he still had braces, small drawings he had given to her on the backs of receipts, ribbed cotton sweaters so boring that she'd known to leave them behind. She took anything Kendall would laugh at, anything Lana would pity. Maybe they were worldlier, in a cultural sense, but really, they were babied by their parents and their trust funds and would be forever. Grace was an adult doing the adult thing: admitting defeat, moving forward.

She heard her mother's voice behind her.

"Clearing out, I see."

Grace started. "Oh, hi. I'm just picking up a few old things."

Her mother uncrossed her arms to pick a piece of lint from her sweater. Grace had not really looked at her mother in such a long time, and now she was surprised at how girlish—soft, even—her mother looked. She had bobbed her hair, and in her ears were pink pearl studs. It was difficult for Grace to reconcile the woman in front of her with the image she held in her mind, the Ocean City party girl with bleached hair and sunburnt cleavage.

"I did what you're doing," her mother finally said. "When I was pregnant with you. I imagined showing you things from my childhood, you know."

Then why hadn't she? *When did I first disappoint you?* Grace wanted to ask. *When you peed on the stick?* Grace was now the same age her mother had been when Grace was born, and her mother, life derailed and forever resentful, had never so much as uttered the phrase *birth control* to her daughter. Now Grace wondered if her mother, in some dark corner of her mind, had wished that Grace *would* get pregnant. Then she would see.

"I knew you'd grow up," her mother said. "It's not that I didn't think you'd grow up. You've always been very confident."

"I don't think that's true," Grace said. By *confident*, her mother meant *uppity*.

"You didn't need me," her mother said.

How dare she, *now*? Grace had asked her parents for so little. She had mostly raised herself. And now that she was grown, her mother was going to blame her for it.

"You were very busy," Grace said, her teeth clenched. "With the twins, with work."

Her mother shook her head. Her arms were crossed, her eyes far away. "You didn't need me," she said. "Even when you were a little baby, you were very calm, very sensible. You didn't mind who held you, if it was me or not. You'd go to anyone." She laughed a little. "Babies are not sensible."

You stupid, loveless woman, Grace thought.

"I'm sorry," Grace said. None of this bore discussion.

Grace couldn't get a job in Garland as easily as she had planned. Every post at the college was filled by work-study students, and in January, none of the local boutiques were hiring. Grace wouldn't have been hired anyway. Local businesses only hired relatives. She applied at the three nearby art galleries, listing her lone art history course, Western Art I, which she had not even completed, as a qualification, along with four months of experience at a fake appraisal office whose e-mail address she made up and would have to monitor herself. She didn't want them calling Donald. She did not ask for help from Riley or the Grahams, who she knew were confused at her return anyway. She would find her own job, without writing *Riley Graham's secret wife* on the résumé she left with Anne Findlay's assistant, a girl who looked a little like Grace, but happier.

The second week of January, she was hired part-time at the T.J.Maxx in Pitchfield. She had to drive Riley's car to get there. He didn't like that she worked at T.J.Maxx. Grace as a discount cashier didn't fit into his vision.

"It's a job," she said. "My mom used to work at a T.J.Maxx." She didn't know where that had come from. It was true, but the comparison was unlike her.

"You're not your mom," he said, and there was nowhere to go after that.

Riley had made almost nine thousand dollars in his December show at Anne Findlay's gallery. Grace didn't believe him until he showed her his bank statement. He was dying to spend the money. When she came home at night, she found him obsessively looking at cars online. He bought a pair of white nubuck wing tips. He wouldn't save the money. He talked as if he would, as in *of course* he would save the money, *most* of it, but his math was magical.

"Do you want to go on a trip?" he asked her. "Like a real vacation. Like adults."

"Where?"

"Anywhere. Anywhere you want. Paris. L.A. Shanghai!"

"Do you?" she asked wearily.

"All by ourselves," he said. "We could check into hotels." This was the idea that really thrilled him—making reservations, signing his name.

She knew he was disappointed in her. Who was this tired, defeated knitwear cashier who dreamed of nothing? She couldn't explain. She was stunned by how much of herself had become secret from him. It didn't help that when she and Alls slipped past each other in the hallway, her neck tensed up for an hour. Once, she had gone to shower right after him and found herself holding his damp towel, breathing in the steam. Greg had knocked on the door to ask her how much longer she would be. She was naked and the shower was running, but she hadn't yet stepped into the tub. She didn't even know how long she'd been standing there.

More than a year had passed since she'd first stood in this bathroom, drugged by the steam, and how guilty she'd felt *then*.

When Riley told her one night that he had a surprise, Grace thought for a moment that he was about to pull out an engagement ring. Instead, she unwrapped lingerie, a red satin bustier with black lace trim.

She lifted the bustier from the tissue by its delicate straps. She didn't know anything about lingerie, but she could tell by the soft sheen of the fabric and the intricacy of the lace that this had been very expensive. She hated the red, but she knew that gift lingerie seldom expressed the aesthetic of the recipient. As she stared, Riley watching her from the other side of the corset, she felt criticized by him, soberingly so, but she didn't know why at first. The matching thong sat coiled in the box, a limp rubber band.

"It's beautiful," she said, because what else could she say? Lingerie! Grace was eighteen and her husband was barely twenty. She thought of lingerie as something for old people, bored with each other's bodies and habits, trying to fake themselves into seeing something new.

He needed her to be new. She'd been so afraid of losing him because of what she had done that she had neglected the rest. She had disappointed him, coming home to wrangle the carts at a Pitchfield strip mall. In trying to seem pure in order to *be* pure, she'd bored him.

She smiled—shyly, he probably thought—and took the box into the bathroom. The lid had long since broken off the toilet, and she balanced the box across the seat. This was who he wanted her to be. She pulled the corset over her head, struggling to get the waist over her shoulder blades. She lifted and dropped her breasts into the seamed cups. She looked over her shoulder at the mirror and adjusted the thong so that it arced perfectly over her ass, now a dark clefted peach. Her face looked too pale and too tired. She rubbed her lips together and raked her fingers up her scalp to fluff her hair, and then she went back into the bedroom.

17

B etween shifts at T.J.Maxx, Grace read as if she were still in school, though it was too late to impress anyone. She'd failed three of her classes through sheer neglect. She hadn't responded to either of the e-mails from her adviser, a harried adjunct she'd only met once anyway. She hadn't even responded to the texts from Kendall. She imagined Lana, wide-eyed, describing Grace's "nervous breakdown"—or was that a Southern phrase?

She tried to read her giant art history textbook, which had cost ninety dollars, but the words just settled around her, dead as dust. Instead she buried her mind in Shakespeare, feeling that she finally understood the histrionics of betrayal, and fat old novels that all seemed to be about doomed women, both the wicked and the duped. She missed working for Donald, magnifying the photos to find chips and scratches and signatures, pinpointing a silver hairbrush in time and by place. Donald and Bethany had both e-mailed her, and Donald had called a few times, but Grace hadn't answered. What could she say? That it had all been too much for her? She had no way to explain her decision without subjecting herself to their pitying concern.

She wondered if she might find a similar job in Garland, but she knew she was kidding herself. There was nothing like that here.

The main thing was to stay out of the house when Alls was home alone.

She knew what his footsteps sounded like, their particular creak. She knew his cough. She knew better than to be alone with him. They could never speak of what had happened. She had to act as though it *hadn't* happened; she had to believe it herself.

There were signs, if someone had known to look for them. Grace and Alls seldom joked around with each other anymore, and when Grace tried to tease him in front of Riley, he no longer teased her back. He was too aloof, too serious around her—too much like someone hiding something, she thought. Riley remarked on it one night, and Grace said that Alls was probably a little unhappy about her moving in.

"I probably ruined the manly vibe," she said.

"It's not like you bought coasters or something."

True enough. Grace was a slob, and she left her dishes and empties around the house just as the boys did. "Maybe I'll surprise you," she said, anxious to stay with the joke. "Start a chore calendar."

"With geese in wheelbarrows on it," Riley said. "No, I think he's always had, you know, kind of a thing for you."

"What?" she said, heart thumping. "Really?"

"He's so weird about girls, and you're always around."

"I'm quite the femme fatale," she said. "Always being *around* and whatnot."

"Ah, shut it. You know. You're hot, you're not an idiot or a screecher, you hold your booze fine. You're probably the only girl he's not scared of."

"Thank you, husband. I'm tremendously flattered," she said. "He's had girlfriends."

"Never for long."

Grace knew she would never slip, but she worried that Alls would. She wished she knew what he was thinking, if his mind sloshed with the same cocktail of guilt and stinging desire that hers did. That night flickered in her mind, without permission, like the flashing lights of the vision test at the DMV: there, then there, there, there, persistent, peripheral. Some nights she lay in bed, unsleeping, knowing that he was in the room just below them, doing the same. Worst of all were nights when she was on top of Riley, looking down through him, through the bed, through the floor, and into Alls, and almost cried out his name instead. She hated him for this.

She took up jogging. She jogged all of Garland, looking for help-wanted signs, for any sign that she could use to change her life. She jogged until she knew he would be gone. Then she went home to the safely empty house to shower before heading out to T.J.Maxx.

She was jogging around the Wynne estate one morning and she stopped at the water spigot by the office for a drink. She stared at the four-columned white mansion surrounded by cottonwood trees while she caught her breath. She hadn't been inside the house in years. The Wynne House had been so normal, so boring to her as a child. Now she realized that the house was full of newly interesting antiques. She touched her forehead and sniffed under her arms. She was fine to go in. It was just Garland.

An old woman was sitting just inside the front door reading a large-print Thomas Friedman book. Grace startled her. "Oh, hello there!" the woman said. "Did you want to take the tour?"

"Yes," Grace said. "But I was just out running and I don't have any money—"

"It's a suggested donation," she said. "You can make it up next time you come."

"Thanks," Grace said. "I will do that."

The woman got to her feet. She came up only to Grace's chin. She wore dark blue polyester pants and a sweater with pears on it. "Well," she began, clasping her hands. "First I'd like to welcome you to the Josephus Wynne Historic Estate. Is this your first time here?"

Grace shook her head.

"Well, the estate was built in 1804 and renovated by the family in 1824 and 1868. It has been owned by the Wynne Trust since 1951, and in 1960 it was renovated slightly for public viewing. That's when the velvet ropes went up, et cetera. Josephus Wynne was one of the most important figures in Tennessee history, and *the* most important in the whole history of Garland. He was a judge, politician, and skilled orator, and he was a member of the Whig Par—" She began to cough. "Excuse me. He was a Whig."

She led Grace through the rooms, telling her about the Mexican-American War, nineteenth-century table manners, the Tariff of Abominations, and tuberculosis, but Grace's attention was on the stuff. The furniture was mostly American Empire and Sheraton style with some Hepplewhite mixed in, though she didn't know all that yet. She wanted information about what she saw, but the docent knew little about the pieces themselves. Grace asked her about the bird's-eye maple secretary, and the docent only nodded and said, "Yes, all the pieces are original to the period, though not necessarily to the family, except for the wax fruit."

Grace took in the mahogany pier table with acorn feet, the trumeau mirror with the carved wreath relief, the needlepoint footstool. The docent chattered on: Two thousand people came through the Wynne home each year, and the tours were entirely guided by community volunteers, and the estate housed one of the most important collections of nineteenth-century French porcelain clocks in the southeastern United States.

Two thousand people in a year? That was less than half of the people who entered MoMA in a day.

Even years later, when Grace looked back on that first visit to the Wynne House, she was sure she had meant no harm. But she went back three days later, with a camera.

There were four other people on the tour this time, a couple and their teenage children. They had stopped in Garland on their way to Memphis to see family, a visit they evidently wished to delay. Grace took pictures of every room from every angle, and the docent, this time a yellow-sweatered man in his seventies, was delighted by Grace's knowledgeable questions, and Grace was grateful for his reaction. She had learned a lot working for Donald. Looking through the photos that night, she felt excited for the first time since she'd come home. It would take her months to identify everything in the Wynne House.

"But why?" Riley asked her when she'd been at her research for three nights. "What are you going to do with this?"

Grace shrugged. "Show them a report, I guess." Maybe the Wynne people would give her a job. Maybe they wanted a researcher. Did they know, for instance, that the silver bowl that held the wax fruit was a John Wendt, probably from his early Boston years, and that Wendt identified himself as a "silver chaser," which sounded like a burglar but was actually a term for a metalsmith who used the techniques of repoussé and embossing? Did anyone *want* to know that? Or that even the wax fruit was kind of important, and not quite contemporary? That the apples' curly stems indicated that they'd come from Rayhorne Table-Effex, a decor manufacturer from the mid-1970s that supplied all the wax fruit for the Four Seasons hotels? And that the company dissolved in 1981 when the EPA discovered they had dumped tons and tons of DDE waste into a local river? And that the wax fruit, which had originally sold for eighty cents apiece, now brought more than thirty dollars per dingy banana?

Who would ever care?

For a few weeks after Anne Findlay cut his check, Riley had felt special, above the other art students. He was a local celebrity who wouldn't be local for much longer. But in January, Findlay had a new artist up in her gallery, and Riley was a student again. Grace, usually adept at consoling him, was too unmoored herself to hold his ego together. He had started a new piece, this one of the courthouse, to Grace's silent dismay. Yet, her recent convictions about the ideas and experiments of artwork seemed both hysterical and snobbish now. She looked at the watercolor portrait he had painted of her, delicately taped onto the wall of their bedroom, and felt impotent.

Riley puttered among his canvases the way he always had. He sat in the basement amid the party detritus and abandoned half-built bicycles with lamps aimed at him from four directions. He listened to Les Claypool and leaned forward in his chair, muttering to himself or to his canvas, carrying on a long, low-stakes conversation that always ended in agreement. Grace would sneak downstairs under the pretense of looking for something and watch him as he smoked and talked to himself. She watched him paint the highlights on a sunny patch of sidewalk and tried to believe.

She made him sandwiches.

She cleaned his brushes.

She repeated these exercises of love, desperate for a sign of divine clemency.

One evening in February, Grace drove home from T.J.Maxx, where she had stayed late cleaning up the sticky chocolate milk that a toddler had spilled in the handbag racks, and found a black Jaguar sitting in the drive-way. Riley had bought the car from a Knoxville dealer on a whim and Greg's you-only-live-once advice. The Jaguar was six years old and had 140,000 miles on it. She and Riley had had a dozen joking conversations about what he might buy with the Findlay money (a pontoon boat, a show dog), but she had not realized how susceptible to shitty ideas he really was.

Thus caught by surprise, that was unfortunately exactly how she put it to Riley.

"What, you think I won't let you drive it to T.J.Maxx?"

He had not paid in full for the car. He had spent all his remaining Findlay money on it and gotten a loan on the spot for the rest, around fifteen thousand dollars. He knew he'd made a mistake but wouldn't admit it. Grace was embarrassed for him. They'd become so unhappy, and the surface failures, small though they were, seemed rooted too deeply to express. Disappointment stuck in the back of their throats like pills swallowed sideways.

He sold the Volvo to a pregnant graduate student from Lexington and put the thirteen hundred toward the auto loan. Now Grace would have to drive the Jaguar to Pitchfield. She parked it far from the strip-mall storefront, not wanting her coworkers to see.

Not two weeks after Riley bought the car, Grace was driving home from work, doing a responsible fifty-five on the Dry Valley Parkway just after six o'clock, when she found herself seemingly suspended in air as she abruptly slowed to the speed of a bicycle. She shoved down the gas pedal and then yanked her foot right back, yelping, when she heard what sounded, impossibly, like an explosion. A wide white pickup rushed up on her from behind, horn screaming on the two-lane road, and Grace wrenched the steering wheel all the way to the right, drifting onto the shoulder like spreading molasses. The truck swerved into the oncoming lane, just missing her.

She didn't want to pop open the hood, because she knew a teenage girl alone on a country road at dusk with her hood up might attract uncharitable attention, to say the least. She locked the doors, smashed one of Riley's hats over her hair, and sank down in her seat to call him. She watched the thick ribbons of smoke coming from the hood and prayed that this was not her fault.

Riley got there forty minutes later with Alls, driving Greg's car. It was pitch-dark already and freezing.

"What happened?" Riley shouted.

"Nothing!" she said. "I didn't do anything! The engine light wasn't on. Everything was fine!"

"Jesus," he said. "You didn't even look at it?"

"I *can't*," she said. "I'm a *girl*." This didn't say at all what she'd meant. He snorted.

Alls was not watching them. He already had the hood up. "You smell that?" he said. "Look at that hole, man. You don't even want to know."

The car had thrown a rod. There was a hole in the block. Grace didn't know what any of this meant, but she could see the hole just fine. It was the size of a Coke can. Riley didn't believe Alls, even when he showed him, but Alls said that fixing it was beyond him anyway.

Pat, the mechanic the Grahams always went to, said they were looking at twenty-five hundred dollars minimum, and that was the friends-and-family price.

Riley bent forward, his hands on his knees, groaning and laughing at the same time.

"You still got the Volvo?" Pat asked.

Grace shook her head. Riley shook his head too, but at his shoes.

"Who'd you get this from, anyway?" Pat asked. "This comes when the oil ain't getting changed."

They had the car towed home, where it sat in the driveway like a big dead bug. He agreed to sell it, but there were no takers. And now she had no way to get to T.J.Maxx. She and Riley had each gotten something they'd wished for.

Shortly thereafter, Greg's father cut him off. Grace learned that Mr. Kimbrough had made this threat at the beginning of the semester: Greg was ruining his chances of getting into any law school, and if he didn't pull in a 3.0 that term, his parents would "withdraw their support." Grace subsequently learned the extent to which the Graham and Kimbrough parents had subsidized the rent and utilities on Orange Street, where she, Riley, and Alls each paid only $150 a month. Greg had not believed his parents were serious.

If those things had not happened just like that, right on top of each other, and if they had not all become so lost and unglued from their plans, they each might have struggled through. None of them could tell their families what had gone wrong. Their problems were all too juvenile, too embarrassing. Grace knew they had only themselves to blame—they had all been too comfortable in their seats. With the exception of Alls, whom she despised for different reasons, the boys had not realized how insulated they'd been by privilege. She too.

18

Research brought Grace her only satisfaction, and she could do it safely from their bedroom, avoiding Alls and also Greg, whose regular brattiness had curdled into unpredictable nastiness. He'd never been broke before. Riley wasn't mean, only muddled. He'd thought his optimism was a quality of his person, not a consequence of his upbringing. Without it, he was lost even to himself.

Three framed Audubon prints hung in the Wynne House, all of them songbirds, and so Grace made a careful table of Audubon values. Original paintings were of course the most valuable, then completed but unpainted drawings, then sketches, then limited-edition prints, and mass prints at the very bottom. Dr. Graham had a framed Audubon something—she wasn't sure if it was a print or a poster—in his study, some pheasants and quail. She'd ask him about it; he would like that.

She did hope, though she hated to admit it even to herself, that such research might help her spot treasures at yard sales and flea markets, like the people on *Antiques Roadshow* who found themselves millionaires after picking up a "pretty picture" for twenty dollars. Who didn't hope that would happen to them? Instead, her research led her to an old news story about some college boys in Lexington who had stolen rare books and original Audubon sketches from their school library and attempted to fence them at Christie's. She laughed, with both delight at their bravado and pity for their mistakes. If you were going to pull a stunt like that, you wouldn't steal *art*. To steal anything one of a kind would be to steal a tracking device. And they'd Tasered the librarian. The thieves had been caught in a matter of weeks.

The spoons she had rescued from the Upper East Side bachelorette estate—that was the kind of thing you should steal. They were rare enough to be worth something, but they would be easy to sell without raising any eyebrows. Without violence, resources, or experience, one could take only unguarded, underappreciated treasure. Silver. Small clocks. Prints that were signed but not numbered. One couldn't steal them from a museum, with its deep records and security guards, or even a library. Not from someone's house, where the missing family heirlooms would be wept over. Not from a store. You'd want to take them from somewhere like the Wynne House.

She looked for the flaw in her logic. There had to be one; otherwise the historic houses all across the country would be treated like ATMs. But she couldn't find the tangle. Her pulse quickened.

Grace could probably get a job cleaning the place and slip one thing into her pocket at a time. But when something went missing, people always accused the cleaning woman or the poor kid. She could hardly see setting herself up as both.

At three o'clock in the afternoon, Grace put on a flouncy skirt that had deep interior side pockets.

If she met one of the same docents, she would just take the tour again, pretend it was for school, and go.

She rode her bike there, propped it against a crabapple tree, and went up to the door. The old lady who opened it was a woman she recognized from the Grahams' church. Grace didn't know her name, and the woman didn't recognize her.

She followed the docent through the rooms, nodding and smiling, taking notes in her small field book. The library was easily the room most crowded with stuff. Returning to these rooms after she'd studied them in photographs was eerie, like going back to a place you had lived years ago. Everything looked both better and worse in three dimensions. On the desk sat a bronze inkwell in the shape of a lion. Grace imagined how it would feel in her pocket.

The docent gestured outside toward the peony garden. "They bloom in May and June," she said. "But it's been a warm winter this year, and I'm just worried it'll—" She then leaned forward, her nose almost touching the glass, and Grace's right hand darted from her body to the bronze inkwell, which was far heavier than she'd expected it to be. The docent turned around and smiled. "Sorry, I thought I saw a rabbit. They do terrible damage to the little spring shoots, and sometimes right in the middle of the day. Just brazen!"

The bronze was heavy on Grace's thigh, and she worried it would drag down the waistline of her skirt. She still had her notebook in her left hand. She crossed one arm over the other and told the docent that the rabbits in her parents' yard would practically eat out of your hand. Together, they shook their heads.

Outside, Grace mounted her bicycle and positioned the pocket of her dress to hang between her thighs instead of on the outside, and she rode home slowly, the cold, heavy weight swinging beneath her, her ears pounding with the thrill of what she'd just done.

Alls was home, eating cereal on the couch and watching a *Seinfeld* rerun.

"Hey," he said without looking up.

"Hi," Grace said, too brightly.

"What you got there?" He nodded at one side of her skirt, which hung a good three inches lower than the other. Next time, she'd need a better receptacle. She took out the inkwell. She felt better than she had in months—good enough, even, to look him in the eye.

"I got it at Lamb's," she said. "Sixty percent off." She set the inkwell down on the coffee table. The lion had an oversize head atop a tiny, cublike body on a square marble base. She lifted the lid, the top of the lion's mane, and looked into the bottle. "See, that's where you pour the ink."

"What ink?"

"*The* ink," she said. "I'll have to put something else in it."

"Weed," he said, chewing toward the TV screen. Whenever they found themselves alone together, he was resolutely stupid toward her.

The inkwell was sitting on an open bill. Grace reached for it. "You're never home right now," she said. It was Alls's car insurance bill.

"I need another job," he said.

"Are they cutting down your hours? Is that why you're home in the middle of the day?"

He nodded. "I need eighteen hours a week, and I can only get twelve with my practice schedule. They pay me sixteen an hour, though, and I'm not going to do better than that around here."

"Do you have time for a second job?"

"Fencing is thirty-six hours per week plus travel. Class is sixteen plus the actual work. It's true that I'm sleeping a luxurious forty-two hours per week. Maybe there's some fat to cut there." He rubbed his eyes.

"Why don't you just get a loan?" she asked him.

"Never going to owe anybody anything," he said.

"But you can't possibly—"

He rolled his eyes. "If it's all the same to you, ma'am, I'd rather not go through the particulars."

"Do you want to talk?"

"I just told you I didn't."

"I mean, about anything." This was idiotic, this hand patting. He would think that was what she was doing. But she felt generous and daring. *Look!* She wanted to whisper. *I just stole this from the Wynne House! Nothing is as bad as it seems!*

His eyes were blank with anger and blinking fast. "No, I don't. You're not my girlfriend, Grace."

"I know I'm not, but I am your friend, and—"

"No," he said, standing up. "Do me a favor, okay? Don't try to make me feel better. Don't even talk to me." Alls then gave her a look of such withering disgust that she could not say a word.

He went into his bedroom and closed the door.

She told Riley that she'd paid only twelve dollars for the inkwell.

"I think it might be worth something," she said.

He wiped some dark, gunky dust from the lion's roaring mouth with his pinkie finger. Outside the historical context of the Wynne home, its value did seem dubious.

"If I'm wrong we can keep weed in it," Grace said. "But I don't think I'm wrong."

She would sell the inkwell and help him out, and then he would see that she had not given up. She had merely redirected her ambitions and reclaimed her smarts, her grit, her allure. She would be not diminished by her return home, but transformed.

But after trawling the Internet and the Garland College fine arts library for information, she couldn't value the inkwell. She found no identifying markings, and the materials didn't tell her anything. Even the nailheads in the base were inconclusive. What if she'd stolen something stupid? What if the Wynne docents had peeled off the gold made-in-China sticker before they'd plunked it on the desk? She'd never come up empty before.

She called Craig Furst. She couldn't call Donald; she'd have to explain too much. She knew Craig had a taste for "gentleman" things—desk blotters, shaving kits, valets, humidors.

"Grace!" he said. "How *are* you?"

"I'm well, thank you," she said. "And you?"

"Oh fine, fine. Going to Boston to do a huge estate tomorrow, probably take me three days just to take photos of it all. Massive collection. The off-grid aristocracy, if you know what I mean. They're so desperate to legitimize. What are you doing? Donald working you to the bone?" He chuckled.

"No, not really," she said, relieved that he didn't even know she had gone.

"Oh? Do you think he—and your school, of course—could spare you for a few days? You know I'd love an assistant with me."

"I'd love to," Grace said. "But I'm not in New York right now. I had a death in the family."

"I'm so sorry! No one close to you, I hope."

"My grandfather," she lied. "He'd been sick for a long time."

"Terribly sorry to hear that." He sounded as though he meant it.

"This is going to sound so crass, but that's sort of why I'm calling you. He left me a few things, and it's been a lot of fun, actually, finding out what they are and where he got them and tracking them down and all."

"Grace, are you appraising your inheritance?" He laughed conspiratorially. "It's an addiction, I know."

"Just for information," she said quickly. "I just want to know where—"

"Uh-huh," he said. No one ever admitted their desire to sell off the family heirlooms, not at first. There was a required series of dance steps to get to that point—mourning the dead, enjoying their memories, discovering their treasures, "learning about them," feigning surprise or masking disappointment, and then and only then, quietly selling it all off.

"What do you have?" he asked.

"An inkwell. Totally unmarked, no stamps or anything. A bronze lion with a marble base, about five inches high. The lion has glass eyes, and you lift the top of his mane to get to the well."

"A lion! How charming. Is the ink bottle glass or pottery?"

"Porcelain, I think. And very irregular—not by machine. I think it could be nineteenth century."

"Sounds like it. Could be Austrian, or maybe French. Can you send me a picture?"

She said she would, and he asked her to have coffee when she returned. And then, just after she'd thanked him again and just before she hung up, he asked her why she had not asked Donald.

Of course he would wonder that. She could have said that she *had* asked Donald and he hadn't known, but of course Craig would tease Donald about that.

"I asked him about another piece," Grace said. "I don't want to wear out my welcome asking for freebies."

"Ha! Fair enough," he said.

The lion was unmarked precisely because it was so special. Craig Furst said the inkwell was Austrian, 1860s; the porcelain interior was the give-away, and he'd never seen a piece quite like it. *Usually*, he wrote, *the "power" animal motifs in inkwells are standing, looking predatory and masculine, etc. But your lion, sitting down, looks . . . cute. The glass eyes are really wild. Was your grandfather a big softie? (And not that you asked, but I'd say $800–$1,100 retail.)*

Grace called an antiques store in Nashville, the first fancy-looking listing she found. She told them what she thought she had and asked if they were interested, and they were. Could she send a picture?

Sure, she almost said. But then she realized that she'd already screwed up, taking a picture of it for Craig. Now there was a trail, however short, going right into her e-mail.

"I can just bring it in," she said. "I'm in the area this weekend."

The next day, she took a Greyhound bus to Nashville and sold the lion inkwell for $655. She told Riley the good news when she got home, insisting he take the money for his car payment or repair, whatever he was prioritizing. "We're married," she said. "Your problems are my problems too."

If Grace could have relied on the docents' poor eyesight and consistent amnesia, she would have robbed the Wynne House every day, one little *objet* at a time. She felt sharp and in control. She'd helped Riley, and she'd hurt no one. But she had already been there three times. She couldn't go back again.

She hated that she'd lied to Riley about where she'd gotten the inkwell. How stupid and unnecessary—that lie chewed at her, another sin to atone for without his knowing. She never used to lie to him. There was *one* thing she would never tell him, but these little lies had to stop. She knew they made her lonelier, built the wall between her and Riley, or between what they had now and the love they used to have, a few bricks higher every time she told one. And Riley would have *loved* the idea of stealing desk accessories from the Wynne House. He would have eaten it up.

"I have to tell you something," she said in bed the next night. "Don't worry."

"Uh-oh," he said.

"I didn't buy that inkwell from Lamb's," she smirked, rolling to face him in the dark.

"You didn't?"

"I stole it," she said. He looked at her, waiting, sure he hadn't heard right. "I stole it from the Wynne House. I went on a tour—"

"Again? Another tour?"

"Another tour, and I took it. The docent wasn't looking, and I just—took it."

"Christ," he said. "Why?"

"So you could make your car payment. And to see if I could, I guess. To see what would happen." She tried to sound sassy, playful, but it sounded wrong. She'd said it all wrong.

He sat up and turned on the light.

"That stuff is all just sitting there, and nobody gives a shit about it, and—what? I thought you would—" she faltered. Would what? Congratulate her?

"Would what?"

"I don't know," she said. "I can't say it right."

"What's the matter with you?"

She swallowed. "What do you mean?"

"Lately, you're just—not yourself. Really weird, actually. Irresponsible."

"Sorry, Riley, but there's not much to be responsible for. I get up, have nothing to do, read, run, look at the jobs, wait for you—"

"I mean, I figured you were depressed about school, but you won't tell me what went so wrong up there—"

"I flunked out," she said angrily. "I failed three of my four classes and the fourth gave me a B, but I have no idea why." She shut her eyes.

"Oh my God," he said. "Why didn't you tell me?"

"What the fuck would I say? There's no good reason. There's no excuse. It just happened. I got that job, and I got way too involved, and I forgot that school was, you know." She shrugged, awkwardly, since she was still lying down. "The reason I was there." The truth was even more humiliating once she said it out loud. She had loved her job's proximity to precious objects—being trusted with them, in a way. For as long as she could remember, she'd studied how she appeared to others, but to become the appraiser? To wield the power of evaluation, approval, dismissal? Knocking an old chair down a few hundred dollars had given her pleasure. All for Donald, at thirteen dollars an hour, ostensibly to help her pay for a college that was costing her $302 each day, many of which she had skipped to work.

She started to cry and tried to keep talking through her seizing throat. "I couldn't tell anyone. It's just too pathetic."

"Christ." He pulled her toward him and she wept on his chest. "You should have told me."

"I didn't want to disappoint you."

"It would have explained a lot. I thought you were unhappy with me."

"No," she blubbered. "I could never be unhappy with you."

He sighed and stroked her head, and there they lay in repair, the forgiver and the forgiven.

19

No one wanted Riley's car. He'd felt so flush when he bought it, he admitted; he couldn't imagine not having *more* money. He thought he'd sell a painting every month, that the commissions would come rolling in. But he'd satisfied Garland's needs better than he'd meant to.

They tacitly agreed to revise their memories of the inkwell argument for a tonal adjustment. Riley was determined to laugh—at the inkwell, at himself. He pointed to the objects in Grace's photos from the Wynne House, playing a version of *The Price Is Right*. "How much for that one? Three grand? Four? Too bad you couldn't fit that in your pocket."

She knew now how she'd screwed up. *He* had always been the rascal. She was supposed to play the goody-goody, Pollyanna looking over her shoulder for parents, teachers, and cops. Taking something from the Wynne House should have been his idea. If Riley had been on the tour with her that day, Grace could have cocked an eyebrow and he would have put the lion in *his* pocket, and later, he would have gloated as she pretended to scold him. That was how they worked; she knew their roles, and yet she hadn't really seen their limits until now. She vowed to do better. Every couple hit a rough patch from time to time. She would pull them through.

On a Tuesday night in late February, Grace was eating vanilla ice cream in the Grahams' living room after dinner with Riley, his brother Colin, and Dr. and Mrs. Graham. They were all talking about basketball, or they had been, and Grace had gotten lost imagining her teeth in Alls's shoulder, the nakedness of his stare, and (God, how unfair to remember this so well) the way he'd nuzzled down her belly, down between her thighs to tease them apart.

"Gracie and I are bored," Mrs. Graham said, startling Grace out of her daydream. "We'll see y'all later." She crooked a finger at Grace for her to follow.

Mrs. Graham led Grace upstairs into the master bedroom and shut the door behind her.

"They do go on, don't they?" she said, going to her closet. "Gracie, tell me, how are you *doing*?"

"Fine." Grace swallowed. "Relieved. To be home." Since she'd come home, she'd avoided being alone with Mrs. Graham, fearing that Riley's mother would somehow *know*, that she would look at Grace and see exactly what she was hiding.

"I know you two must have missed each other something awful," Mrs. Graham said. "You've never had to be apart before."

So this would be that conversation. "Yeah," Grace said. "I thought I could imagine it, but I just couldn't do it. I mean, I didn't want to."

"You know, Dan and I didn't go to college together," she said. "He was at Garland, but my parents sent me to Sweet Briar, you know. He'd drive up for any long weekend, but it was so hard. Well, you know."

"I know it's supposed to be hard and I'm supposed to do it anyway," Grace said. "But I don't think I can. Maybe because of where I went— maybe it would have been different if I'd gone to Vanderbilt or Sewanee. I just couldn't find my . . ." She gave up. *I had sex with Alls*, she imagined saying. *I had sex with Alls, and I married your son.*

Grace had thought Mrs. Graham had gone to her closet to get a sweater, or to show Grace something she had bought, but Grace now saw that Mrs. Graham was only straightening a row of shirts on their hangers, looking into their collars instead of at Grace.

"And it was too expensive," Grace said quietly.

Mrs. Graham turned around holding a pale green blouse. Her first name was Joanna, but Grace had never called her that, and even though she secretly thought of Mrs. Graham as her real mother, she couldn't imagine calling her anything but Mrs. Graham.

Mrs. Graham fingered the blouse's collar. "Don't I know it," she said absently. She smiled. "Honey, remember at Thanksgiving, when Dan gave you some money to give to Riley?"

Grace's hands were under her thighs. She dug her nails into her jeans. "What money?"

"He gave you an envelope, with money inside," she said carefully. "For Riley's supplies."

It had been three hundred dollars in cash, crisp fifties. Grace had meant to give it to Riley, but she hadn't. She'd used it for his Christmas present and some other things; she could hardly remember now.

"I don't remember," Grace said, growing hot at her temples. "He did?"

"Yes, about three hundred dollars." She didn't seem to know what to say then, and neither did Grace. "I told him not to do cash, in case it got lost or something. But he didn't want Riley to have to go to the bank, since he was working all hours for his show." She went back to her closet and hung up the blouse.

"I didn't open it," Grace said, groping for time. "It's probably still in my coat pocket." She'd given over her last paycheck to Riley. She had no way to come up with that money until she found another job, but if she could just hold off—

"Oh, your winter coat? Downstairs?" Mrs. Graham's shoulders collapsed in relief.

"Yes," Grace said with false hope that quickly became real. Maybe the envelope would be there; maybe she *hadn't* spent the money. She held on to this prayer as she stepped downstairs, Mrs. Graham right behind her, to check her pockets. But of course there was no envelope. There were drugstore receipts and a ChapStick, a few crumpled straw wrappers.

"Oh dear," Mrs. Graham said. "What could have happened to it? Do you think you put the envelope somewhere? I'm sorry, honey, but three hundred dollars is a lot of money, and Dan was in such a piss that Riley never thanked him, and I wondered if—well, let's just try to find that envelope."

But three hundred dollars wasn't that much money, not to the Grahams. Grace's sudden flare of anger only made her more scared and more ashamed.

"I don't remember taking it out," she said. "It could have fallen out at the airport? Or I guess someone could have taken it? Oh no, I had this dry-cleaned."

"Well," Mrs. Graham said, biting her lip. "That's certainly possible."

"This is awful," Grace said. "Let me pay you back. I'm so sorry I lost it."

She expected Mrs. Graham to say that it was okay, that everyone lost things now and then, and let's go downstairs and get some ice cream. That would be the Mrs. Graham–like thing.

But Riley's mother smiled grimly and took Grace's clammy hand in hers. "Honey, I'm saying this out of love. You know that."

The heat shot up Grace's neck and wrapped around her skull in a second. Mrs. Graham's face floated before her like a too-bright light.

"It's not the first time something like this has happened, right?"

Grace shut her eyes.

"When you took one of the little silver spoons, I—I was even a little touched. And a scarf once, and some earrings, remember?"

Mrs. Graham was talking as if Grace had stolen the spoon, the scarf, the earrings. You couldn't steal your mother's earrings, not if you were her daughter. Grace had just wanted to have them as a piece of—

You couldn't *steal* from your own household—that was the point. Riley took his brothers' old things and his dad's pocket change all the time. That wasn't stealing. That wasn't wrong. It was family.

"But this is different," Mrs. Graham went on. "This is another kind of thing." She swallowed. "And we love you, and we just want to take care of you and make sure you have what you need. You need to talk about this with someone, okay?"

Grace wanted to die and she wanted her hand out of Mrs. Graham's, so she pulled it back.

"Gracie, it's okay. We're going to get you some help. Maybe we should talk to your mom?"

Grace lurched forward in a silent sob.

Mrs. Graham put her arm around her. "I'm just glad it was us, instead of—you're here with us and it's going to be okay." She rubbed Grace's back. "Oh, sweetie, I didn't mean for you to—I'm used to yelling at boys! Come here, honey. We didn't tell Riley, okay? Is that what you're worried about?"

How had they not told Riley? Curled like a bean on their bed back in their room on Orange Street, Grace pled menstrual cramps as she clutched at her stomach. That was what this misery felt like, her insides being carved out of her.

Whether she had meant to steal from the Grahams was an impossible question. Of course she hadn't meant to *steal* from them—or rather, she hadn't meant for *stealing* to be the right word for keeping the money. It had been something else, the answer to a split-second series of emotional calculations, not quite conscious and immediately suppressed. She had wanted to be the beloved daughter but had tunneled in as a wife. Community property applied to wives, even secret wives. What was Riley's was hers; the money was a gift to her. But she knew that she had kept the money to feel like a daughter, not like a wife.

Riley was on one of his rare picking-up sprees, shaking the dust bunnies out of their clothes and stuffing them back into drawers. Grace's pile grew up from her suitcase, which she still had not put away, and now it seemed too symbolic, as if her time were up and now she would have to go.

She didn't know how she could find out what they had told him without dragging everything up to the surface.

She tried hard to imagine the scene: Mrs. Graham would have asked Riley about the money, to remind him to thank his father. Riley wouldn't know what she was talking about. *But he gave it to Gracie,* she might have started. Riley would have asked if she was sure, and Mrs. Graham would have had to think then. *Maybe not,* she would have had to say. *I'll ask him. It's probably buried in his desk or something.*

"Sorry, what?" she asked Riley. He was holding up a pair of black tights.

"Shouldn't you *wash* these?"

Mrs. Graham must have thought quickly, to say those things, to protect her. Grace had always known that Riley's mother loved her; she had never doubted it. That was why she and Riley couldn't tell anyone they'd married, because Mrs. Graham would be crushed to have been left out of the wedding. Her daughter's wedding. But no, Grace was not her daughter. Mrs. Graham had made that clear. *Why* had she and Riley gotten married? Why hadn't they gotten engaged? That, they could have told everyone. Marriage had seemed bigger, more romantic and risky, she guessed.

No, she realized. They'd married because marriage had seemed final, as though it would protect her, protect them.

Dr. Graham knew about the money too, of course. Oh, it was worse than if Riley knew, so much worse.

"Are you *sure* you're okay?" he asked her, his hand on her calf. "They're not usually this bad, are they?"

She shook her head. "No, not like this. I feel horrible." She began to cry, her throat burning, and Riley went downstairs for her bag, where there was ibuprofen. He came back upstairs clutching her purse from the side, and he looked so young—his face pale and pink and childish, his green eyes big and worried. He'd poured her a glass of Coke.

When you'd known someone this long, she had often thought before, you could rarely see what they looked like at any present moment. Riley's face was a composite of every face it had been since she had met him. Only every now and then did his face become singular. Now it shocked her, how young he looked. Like a little boy. She felt desperate to fall back in time with him, to go back, back, back, and sickened that she couldn't.

2 O

A week later, Grace was eating a mealy apple, dumbly clicking through auction records, and staring at her phone, both desperate for and dreading a call from Mrs. Graham asking them to come to dinner, when Riley burst in the kitchen, flushed with panic.

"My dad says I have to pay *taxes* on my painting money."

"Oh," Grace said, looking up from a listing on Mdina pottery. "I hadn't thought about that. All the jobs I've had, they were just taken out."

"Obviously, I hadn't thought about it either," he said, blowing up at his hair. "This is fucked up."

It wasn't that she *had* thought about his taxes, but more his look of indignation, as though someone else were at fault. She wanted to smack him.

"Well," she said, looking back at her reading, "maybe you should rob the Wynne House."

She was surprised when he laughed. He sank down the wall and sat on the floor, his hands over his face, his laughter muffled.

"Just put on some nice ski masks," he said. "Just get some flashlights and clean the place out."

"Strip it," Grace said, biting a side out of her apple. The cold hurt her teeth. "Lock old Dorothea in the powder room, throw it all in the back of a pickup, and drive to New York City."

"What do we tell the people who buy the stuff?"

"That your grandfather died. Great-aunt. Great-something."

"Grandpa Dwight promised me his guns," he said. "At the home, right before he died, when my mom was out of the room. He also said, 'The ass is the lass.' Didn't elaborate."

"He died when you were, what, thirteen? Did you get the guns?"

"Nope, he gave them to Nate and Colin. He mixed us up a lot." He stared at the ceiling. "Maybe we should just move into the Wynne House. Then we wouldn't have to pay rent."

Grace got up from the table and joined him on the dirty floor. "We could sleep in the tiny bed together," she said. "All snuggled up."

"I will be the statesman and you can be the . . . the—"

"They didn't have stateswomen," Grace said. "I get something crappy. The charwoman."

"No, you just don't have a job. You're the lady of the house, just like now."

She swatted him and he laughed into her hair.

"No," she said. "We should sell it and move to Canada or someplace, never to be seen again." She imagined never seeing Alls again, never seeing the Grahams again, and felt momentarily peaceful, as though someone had turned on a white-noise machine.

"Canada? You want to rob the Wynne House so we can move to Canada?"

"Anywhere," she said. "Belize. Peru. Rome. Anywhere with you."

Alls got a second job as a cashier at the drugstore, so he bought the groceries. Grace had applied for the drugstore too, but they had not called her, and of course she couldn't take a job there now. Riley had called the wedding photographer he worked for in the summers, but it wasn't wedding season yet. So far, he had refused to take less than he owed on the car, but no such offer was forthcoming. Somehow, it had not yet occurred to Greg that he would have to find a job. He ate the pizza Alls brought home as if it had long been his due. If they'd lived in Memphis or Nashville, getting jobs would have been less of a problem, but Garland was too small to employ them, and now Riley and Grace were without a car.

Grace's heist fantasy became her and Riley's private joke, increasingly elaborate. At night, eating saltines, they "debated" the pros and cons of single-item theft versus all-out looting. Grace drew "maps" of the site, including floor plans of the interior. They walked by the house sometimes, wondering about the locks on the doors and the windows, noting the curtains and shades, which ones were drawn and when. But these conversations all fell disappointingly within the bounds of their standard what-ifs, no different, really, from folding a four-pointed fortune-teller. Grace wished the robbery were not a joke to him. Each time he made a crack about shoplifting from the Wynne House, he was laughing on the edge of the idea, and Grace waited for him to step over. The real idea would have to be his, she knew.

Even if their Wynne joke stayed a joke, she was grateful for the shared diversion, which gave them something that had been missing: a game, a secret that, unlike their secret marriage, let her imagine them somewhere other than where they were. They read together about the unsolved 1990 robbery of the Isabella Stewart Gardner Museum, in Boston, where two men dressed as police entered the museum late at night, tied up the guards in the basement, and stole five hundred million dollars in Rembrandt, Degas, and Vermeer. They read about the thieves who rented a storefront across the street from the National Fine Arts Museum, in Paraguay, dug a tunnel ten feet underground into the museum, and stole five paintings. Never caught.

Riley had been utterly charmed by the San Juan Surfer, later rechristened the Surfer Bandit, who robbed ten banks in Southern California before he was caught, always wearing "casual surfer attire" and escaping on a maroon 1983 Honda motorcycle. Riley had shaken his head in wonder at the published security camera photos; the man bore an uncanny resemblance to Greg. Grace preferred Blane Nordahl, a cat burglar who'd stolen *only* hallmarked antique silver from wealthy Americans along the East Coast for decades. He chose his marks from *Architectural Digest* and *Town & Country*, where people eagerly displayed their most portable capital in situ. To get in, Nordahl would painstakingly cut through a single pane of window glass, so as not to provoke the security system by raising the window. He was at large again. Grace thought of her Dianakopf spoons and felt the glow of camaraderie. She knew which silver to take.

In 2008, four men in drag stormed into a Paris Harry Winston with guns and grenades. They bashed in display cases and swept the diamonds within into suitcases while the employees and shoppers trembled in a corner. All told, they got away with $108 million, never recovered. Grace loved the audacity of it—broad daylight, broken glass, one of the most famous jewelers in the world. She caught her knee bobbing as she read.

The Wynne House had no security guards, no security system beyond locks on the doors. All they would have to do was show up.

Grace, Riley, and Greg were sitting at the kitchen table eating cereal one night when Riley read the local police blotter out loud from the *Record*. The complaints of Garland's citizens were always ripe for mockery.

"'A resident of the three hundred block of Lowery Avenue called police Friday afternoon at four to complain of two youths, estimated twelve to fourteen, cutting through her yard and disrupting her garden. The youths' parents have been notified.'"

"When I'm an old lady, I will collect dead birds to throw at the youths," Grace said.

"'A Garland citizen,'" Riley continued, "'found a lewd drawing on a napkin near the Lions Club picnic.'"

Greg snorted.

"Here's one: 'The Josephus Wynne Historic Estate reported the theft of an antique desk accessory from its premises.'"

Grace stared at him. What was he playing at?

"They don't even know when," Riley said, avoiding Grace's eyes. "Because who would notice a missing desk accessory?"

"I'm surprised people don't steal shit from them constantly," Greg said. "All that old shit no one cares about."

"I bet it's all crap," Riley said. "What do they call it?" He looked at Grace. "When they make new stuff that looks like antiques?"

"Shabby chic," Greg said with authority.

"Reproduction," Grace said, seething at Riley's indiscretion.

"No, they probably don't allow that," Riley said. "Against the rules or something."

"Some people go in for the dumbest shit," Greg said. His family's house was full of crystal decanters and silver napkin rings, but maybe he had never noticed them amid the rubble. The Kimbroughs were more into biannual kitchen renovations than they were into heirlooms.

Riley shrugged. "I'd rather have George Washington's spittoon than a home theater."

"No you wouldn't," Greg said. "You'd be like, how many Xboxes can I get for this? You're just saying that because of *her*." He got up and dropped his bowl in the sink. "They should just liquidate the Wynne House and build a water park."

"We're doing it. Raiding the Wynne House," Riley said, clasping his hands behind his head. "Me and *her*."

"Hot damn, I want in." Greg laughed and leaned against the counter. "Then what? Yard sale?"

"Then we drive the loot to Atlanta or whatever and sell it off. All our grandpas died."

"Come on," Grace said, getting up. "We need to get to Walgreens before they close." Grace needed to pick up her birth control, but Riley didn't need to walk with her, and he knew that.

"Why do you hate me?" Greg asked her. He'd said it as if he was kidding, but he wasn't. He smirked at her, daring her to answer. She rolled her eyes.

"No, you really do," he said. "Like, it's painful for you that I'm laughing at one of your jokes."

"Christ, man," Riley said. "Will you chill?"

Grace was getting tired of Riley's *Christ*, which seemed to stand in for his brain so he wouldn't have to think of anything to say.

"You don't have any money anymore," she said to Greg. "What are you going to do?"

Greg shrugged. "They'll give in. They're not going to let me starve."

"Doesn't it bother you, though, that it's up to them?"

Riley was clearly nervous. In the six years they had known each other, Grace and Greg had never had any real discussion, and she certainly had never flaunted her contempt for him.

"It bothers you more than it does me," he said, surprising her.

"We need to hurry," Riley said. "They close at nine."

They closed at ten, but Grace followed him out.

"What the hell was that?" he demanded on the sidewalk.

"What the hell was *that*? You tell him everything we talk about?"

"It's a *joke*," he said. "I didn't realize that was such sensitive information."

"I feel like we have no privacy here," she said. She could not tell him what she had meant to say without looking like a fool. "I feel like we have less privacy now than we ever used to."

He looked at her then as if she were crazy. "What is this about?"

"Riley, how are we going to pay the rent, huh? And buy food? By selling your stupid car?"

"Look, I know you're worried, but something will change. Worse comes to worst, we move back home for a while. We're not *adults*."

"I can't *go* back home," she spat. "Don't you get that?"

"Calm down. My mom *made* you a room, for chrissakes."

They walked the rest of the way in silence. It was only a matter of time until Riley found out *something*, she knew. If the Grahams told him about the money, she knew that Riley would want to believe that his father had made a mistake, that he had not given her the envelope. Or that he had, but she had not opened the envelope, that she had simply lost it. She didn't know which was better to say.

She wished she could take something else from the Wynne House, just so she could sell it and pay the Grahams back. They could all pretend she had simply misplaced the envelope. Everything could be the way it was before, or at least the Grahams would think it was.

The horrible shame of knowing Dr. and Mrs. Graham thought— *knew*—she had stolen the money seemed like it couldn't possibly get any worse until she imagined the further conversations: Riley telling them they were wrong, that *of course* he believed her. Mrs. Graham knowing that Grace had lied to her son, and so effectively. Grace wouldn't be a girl with a little problem of borrowing and not giving back, their girl who just needed some sessions with a counselor. They would never really trust her, or even look at her like *her* again, *their* Gracie.

But that had already happened, she knew. Mrs. Graham had been clear. Grace was not their daughter, not all the time.

Grace and Riley had not been to his parents' since Mrs. Graham had confronted Grace. She had dreaded Riley's questions about why she didn't want to go, but he barely noticed. Grace had been the one pushing for those weekly dinner visits, and she and Mrs. Graham had always arranged them. Two weeks had passed since Mrs. Graham had taken her up to the bedroom, and she had not called Grace about dinner. About anything.

This was what happened when your heart wanted two things it could not have together: You lost them both. Everyone knew that.

But she still had Riley, the only person who still thought she was a good girl, and she could not let him change his mind. She knew this even as she fought to ignore the inexplicable, grotesque rage she felt hissing deep within—at Dr. and Mrs. Graham, for treating her as their daughter and then humiliating her like a stray who'd forgotten her place; at Donald and at Bethany; at Lana and Kendall; at Craig Furst, wanting to know if she *enjoyed* Miami; at her parents and at the twins for revealing them to her; at Greg, who coasted through the days in an Xbox fugue state, blank-eyed and gassy. At Alls, who had picked her like a lock. At Riley, for being so loved and so smug, even now, and in love with her. At herself, more than anyone, for not smacking her own hand back when it wanted, so often, what was not hers. She looked at her husband and saw a ticking clock. She had to take him away, and she had to take him before she ran out of time.

The next morning, Grace and Riley were lying in bed when Grace heard a door slam in the driveway. She turned over and covered her head with her pillow, trying to stay asleep.

"RILEY!" Greg bellowed from downstairs. "YOUR CAR'S GET-TING TOWED!"

She heard the front door swing open and shut, Greg shouting at some-one. She elbowed Riley, her eyes squeezed shut.

"Wake up," she said, her throat dry. "Greg is yelling."

What had Greg said? The car?

She pulled a T-shirt over her head as she stumbled to the window. "Riley," she said sharply. "There's a tow truck in the driveway."

He rubbed his eyes. "It's our driveway," he said. "I can park in my own driveway."

"I think you better wake up," she hissed, raking through the pile of clothes for a pair of jeans.

All at once he sprang up and sprinted downstairs. Grace followed him. Alls was already outside, demanding to see the man's papers, and Riley ran out into the March frost in only his shorts, shouting at the man to stop.

"What are you doing?"

"Repossessing your car," the man said. "You want to give me the keys?"

"What? *Why?*"

"Are you sure you have the right car?" Alls asked the man. "You check the VIN?"

Greg turned away and shambled up the porch steps. He stood next to Grace in his sweatpants. "I've never seen a repo man in real life," he said.

Later, draped across the couch, Greg said it was fucked up that they could just come take your car like that, and he wanted to call his lawyer dad but Riley stopped him. He hadn't made his last payment, he said, and the one before had been late. But he hadn't realized they could just take the car back. Alls told Riley he was relatively lucky, that when his father's car had been repoed, the repo man had followed him to work, at Hawkes' Sports, and taken it from the parking lot without his dad knowing, and then he was stranded out there, and Alls didn't have a car yet and couldn't go get him, so he'd had to spend the night in the camping department. Riley's was a pretty okay repo guy, as far as these things went. He'd even let Riley get his stuff out of the car.

"We should rob the Wynne House," Riley said. "I'm serious."

"I'm ninety-nine-point-nine that there's *no* security," Greg said, as if he'd given it real thought. "Not even a camera."

"Your dad's going to cave, right?" Riley asked Greg. "He always does."

"Fuck him. I don't want to go to fucking law school. Alls is poor as shit and bagging tampons. You don't even have your ghetto Volvo anymore. And she flunked out of school."

Grace felt Alls looking at her. She couldn't believe Riley had told them.

"What a freaky morning," Greg said. "But for real? It'd be awesome."

Alls groaned and looked down into the pipe they were handing back and forth, his thumb on his lighter.

"Think about it," Riley said. "There is a house that belongs to no one. It is full of very, very valuable antiques. They belonged to someone who died a century ago. There is only one person in this uninhabited house at a time, someone with trifocals, hearing aids, and an absolute *absence* of suspicion. We could go in there and take whatever we wanted, and it would have no effect whatsoever on *anyone*."

"But it's stealing," Grace said.

Greg dropped his head back on the couch, gaping.

"Is it still stealing," asked Riley, "when the things don't belong to anyone?"

"Is the stuff even worth that much?" Alls asked.

"If only we knew someone who could help us with that," Riley said.
"You are *not* using my research like that," Grace said prissily.
"Sure, it was a joke," he said to Grace. "But maybe it shouldn't be."
"Oh, man." Alls laughed now. "Man oh man oh man."
"We'd be millionaires," Riley said.
"No one would ever suspect us," Greg said. "Not in a million years."

21

It took Grace thirty-four days in all to track down every interesting item smaller than a breadbox from the snapshots she had taken of the Wynne House. She'd also observed the house itself: who the docents were and how able they seemed, what days and times it was visited least, and which windows were visible from the office and the parking lot.

One person would take the tour, and once the docent had led the visitor upstairs, the others would enter and quietly fill up the shopping bags. They would rob the Wynne House in broad daylight, early summer: leaves on the trees for cover, the office windows shut and the air conditioners running full blast, and no school groups to interfere. Alls listened to Greg and Riley's plans absently, as if they were telling him unbelievable stories about someone he didn't know. Grace let Greg spin his wheels. When the time came, the plan would be hers, even if she had to feed it to the others through Riley. She hated that Greg and Alls were involved at all, but she would work with what she had.

She and Riley pored over the photos at night, his eyes racing over Grace's careful, typed notes. They knew they couldn't take everything, not without five hours and a moving truck. They prioritized portable items of exceptional value. The maple highboy with shell-carved apron and birdlike ankles—a similar example had fetched twenty-two thousand dollars at Sotheby's last year—would have to stay behind. The brass-bound oak cider jug, however, while worth only thirty-four hundred, was smaller than a loaf of bread. Grace evaluated each room for its value-to-risk ratio. Some rooms they would not even bother with.

They would take nothing that appeared to be one of a kind or even close. If Grace couldn't find at least two comps for something, she crossed the item off the list. She narrowed each room down to ten to twelve pieces, which they marked carefully on their maps with a number, a highly simplified checklist at the side:

Front Parlor

1. cider jug
2. flat-face doll
3. copper bucket
4. red bowl with white inside
5. three blue vases
6. andirons
7. horse weather vane ($26K!)
8. eagle wall sconce
9. green needlepoint pillow
10. porcelain clock

Only Grace knew what these crude nicknames really meant. The three blue vases were Mdina, the pillow made from a seventeenth-century Flemish verdure tapestry. With everything she had learned about the riches within the Wynne House, she became convinced that she almost had a right to them. There was so much, after all, that they *wouldn't* take. The highboy. The chandeliers. The tall clock. The Wynne House wouldn't disappear. The occasional tours could continue, unchanged.

Greg didn't want her to get a full cut. "Like hell," he said one day. "If you're not going in with us, you're not taking on the same risk as we are."

"I can't go in," Grace reminded him, "because I've already been in too much."

"Look, we can cut you in for ten percent," he said.

"Who is this 'we'? You don't even know what this stuff is worth."

"That's why I'm willing to pay you a finder's fee. For all the reading and clicking."

Greg had always seemed so silly to her, relentlessly stupid. She had asked Riley once how he could even stand Greg, and he had replied, shrugging, that Greg was "fun." But since she had come home, she had grown to truly loathe him. She was about to tell him exactly how much of this plan she was responsible for, but his arrogance stopped her. If they failed, their failure would be Greg's fault, most likely. His condescension made her queasy. He was going to fuck it up.

That night, she and Riley walked to the playground of their old elementary school. He sat on a swing and she sat in his lap. She tried to tell him her concerns about Greg, but Riley was distracted by the news that Ginny's Ice Cream was going out of business for unpaid back taxes.

"Too many people," Grace said. "I don't trust *him*."

"It's fine," he said. "It's perfect. You trust me, right? And I trust them. I've known them even longer than I've known you." He squeezed her sides.

This was not comforting in the least.

"I'm going to save Ginny's," he said. "All the same flavors. We'll be local heroes."

Grace had imagined that she and Riley would leave together, as soon as they had liquidated their new assets. That was the whole point, to shoot out of Garland with no option to ever return. Now she realized he meant to stay there, with his friends, forever, idly drawing on a secret checking account.

The plan was doomed unless Riley gave something up. He would have to choose: her or them. If he didn't choose now, he would later, when Grace fell off the wagon again, as she surely would if she was made to stay around Alls. Next year or in a decade, in the house on Orange Street or at a birthday party for their future children. She would always want him.

"Hey," Riley said, nudging her with his shoulder. "Where'd you go?"

She tried to shake off the fear that this wouldn't be an easy choice for him. She knew she was the stray cat. He had a life without her, but she had never made one without him.

"I'm just surprised," she said. "I thought we were making our big move. Together, away from here."

"We can't, Grace. We won't be able to leave right away, maybe not for a long time. It would be too obvious. I mean, think about it—"

"I have thought about it," she snapped, still, absurdly, on his lap. "So what's the point, then? So you can make your car payments?"

"I didn't know you—"

"No, you didn't. You want your life to be just like it is now, but with nicer beer. You don't want anything different." He didn't even know *how* to want something different. But she still wanted him, so maybe she didn't either. Without his mother's love, Grace's love for Riley was wearing thin, but it was all she had to wear.

Grace and Riley began to argue, at first about what seemed like only safe, little things: whose turn it was to pay for groceries, her getting tired of his tired jokes, he smoked too much, she drank too much. *Of course I didn't mean it*, they reassured each other at night. She hated herself for fighting with Riley, but she couldn't seem to stop.

Greg had always been oblivious to Grace and Riley as a couple, the way he behaved toward his parents. Now he left the room when one of them began to pick on the other. In the past, he would have laughed lazily, perhaps even taken sides. *You* do *do that*, he might say. Not anymore.

One afternoon when Riley was at school, Alls asked her if everything was okay with her and Riley. He was worried.

"Sure, I guess," Grace said, reddening as if he'd discovered some secret. "We're just—we're going through some stuff. It happens."

"So it's not serious," he said. "I mean, you're not thinking of—"

She was. She was thinking of him all the time.

"No," she said. "We'll be fine."

"You can't tell him," he said. "Even if you ever leave him, you can't tell him."

He didn't feel what she did and probably never had. Instead, they shared mutually assured destruction—a refusal to lose Riley. That was how she knew their secret was safe.

"I will never tell him, ever," she said. "Even if he leaves me."

"He'll never leave you," Alls said.

Grace was rooting through their closet looking for missing socks when she came across Riley's "Future Lens," the deadly earnest series of drawings of them he had made at sixteen that he later insisted was a joke. They had always taken the long view, picking out houses, naming children. They'd gone through Seamus and Tigerlily as kids, Vincent and Aurora by high school, later Casper and Annette. Annette would be quiet and clever, well bred and well tended. Casper would be adored and popular, but more elusive and subtle than people thought him.

Grace pulled out the first sketch. She hadn't seen the drawings in years, and the sight of this one startled her, both with its technical skill and with its eerie accuracy. He'd drawn them in their early twenties, and the Grace in the drawing looked like Grace now. Riley hadn't aged himself as accurately. He probably wouldn't look like the drawing for a few years yet—with a jaw that had lost its baby fat and shoulders that were broad and square. She knew the wedding drawing was after this one; guiltily, she skipped it. In the drawing after, Grace held an infant wrapped in a blanket. She remembered the first time she'd seen it.

"I'm fat?" she'd said, peering at her lumpy stomach, her blocky hips.

"You just had a baby," he'd said. "You'll bounce back."

There were two more. In the last, their children were the ages they'd been when he'd made the drawings. Grace and Riley themselves looked sexless and decayed. Grace had asked him not to do any more. She didn't want to see his vision of them in wheelchairs, tubes taped to their noses, waiting for the children to visit.

She sat down on the bed, staring at her husband's too-perfect vision of their future. She had lost her faith in him, true, and she blamed herself for that. But maybe her faith had been misplaced all along. Her husband had an impeccable eye for detail and a rare gift for translating it—no, reflecting it—onto the page. He could probably copy anyone, anything. He had no imagination. Admitting it, finally, made her feel a little bit free. She felt as though she'd been staring at a beloved family heirloom for hours, struggling to evaluate it, and suddenly, she understood its worth.

Grace hadn't researched the paintings hanging in the Wynne House. Selling a stolen antique was no different from selling one she'd come by honestly, but she didn't know how to sell a stolen painting. Now she found herself returning to a photograph she had taken of the study. Among the many boring portraits and landscapes hung the possible exception to her rule: the most boring, forgettable painting imaginable, a funereal still life of flowers and a bowl in shades of flax and mauve. There were Styrofoam peanuts with more character.

Naturally, these qualities made the painting difficult to identify. The style, milky-eyed botanical photo-realism, suggested that the still life was very old and probably northern European. She zoomed in on the image until she could just make out the initials AB, or AH, or AS. She told herself this was innocent curiosity, but she didn't believe herself for a moment. She narrowed down the style to Dutch Golden Age. The only painter of note who matched these criteria was Ambrosius Bosschaert the Elder, Antwerp, 1573–1621.

A yawning cornucopia of Bosschaert fruit had fetched $2.3 million at Christie's three years before.

Two million dollars was enough to make up any kind of life they wanted. The four hundred thousand she'd estimated they could pull with the best decorative arts in the Wynne House now seemed insufficient. Riley was right: Split four ways, or even three as Greg wished, was *staying* money. Grace wanted enough money to leave forever.

Riley would paint a fake Bosschaert. He would take the guided tour and they would swap it out, put it right into the original frame. They would go to Paris or Barcelona. She could see the scene in black and white—she and Riley zipping around Monte Carlo in a convertible, her stupid mistakes all left across an ocean—and felt light-headed at the romance of this future. Not only would she never have to see Alls again; Riley couldn't either. His friends would never forgive him for leaving, and neither would his family. They would be gone, all the way gone, forever.

She went into the basement the next time he was painting. He had hardly painted at all since they had begun their plan, and now she found him listlessly dabbing at the courthouse lawn. She showed him the photograph of the Bosschaert she had just printed out.

"What is that?" he asked, wrinkling his nose.

"Two million dollars," she said.

She knelt on the floor in front of him.

"It's in the study, at the back of the house, surrounded by other paintings, all of them more interesting and noticeable."

"Christ," he said. "I've never copied anything."

She felt the briefest impulse to argue that point. All of his paintings were copies, in a sense: of the buildings themselves, of all the paintings he had painted before.

"You could paint this," she said. "You could paint this better than he did."

"Who is it?"

She told him what she knew. He was listening carefully. When he asked about selling the painting, she paused. She needed to get this perfectly, exactly right.

"I can sell it," she said, "the same way I could sell a clock or a pitcher. This painting isn't famous. There are no images of it online, or in any of the Wynne House's brochures, or on their website. I doubt they know what it is."

He nodded.

"The idea would be to replace the original with a copy so good, they would never notice anything different—ever. The painting would be on no lists, no stolen art databases. But we still shouldn't *sell* it here. In America." She held his knees in her hands. "We'd go to Europe together, and after that, we could go anywhere. We could have any kind of life."

"We could come back," he said. "After we sold it."

"Riley, I have to get out of here. I'm suffocating. I came back because I can't stand to be without you, but there's nothing for me here. At least, not now. I feel like we might as well be thirty already, and I don't want to feel like that. I mean, are *you* happy?"

"What about the other stuff? The plan, Greg—"

"Greg is going to fuck it up. I'm positive."

"I can't just cut him out," Riley said.

"If we both pull out, what's he going to do? Go in there alone?"

"Alls."

"He's not going to do it," she said, growing frustrated. "But if you think they can pull it off without you, then what's the worry? They get to split the proceeds fifty-fifty. They're *happy*. But if we stay here, something is going to happen to us. I know it. I can feel it."

He took her hands in his. "What do you want, Gracie? I just want to give you what you want. It's all I've ever wanted, for you to be happy with just me—"

She looked at the piece of paper in his lap. "You can paint this, Riley. I know you can."

The next day, Riley made his first visit to the Wynne House since his

own school field trips. When he came home, he disappeared into the basement, and Grace collapsed on the couch with relief.

The painting was not difficult for him. The first day he stretched the linen
canvas, nailing it onto its temporary frame instead of stapling it. They
discussed aging the fabric with tea, coffee, or dirt, but decided that aging
didn't matter. The goal was for the painting to look good enough in its
frame to never be noticed. They called it "Still Life with Money and Tulips." He applied the sizing and began the underpainting. Every night, he
hid the canvas behind the courthouse painting.

Riley had asked her to let him tell Greg that he—they—were out, but
he was slow to do so. The next week, Greg sold the sound system from his
car to buy getaway cars. He had decided they needed two. Riley continued
to nod in agreement when Greg debated the best place to steal license
plates. Grace had been so careful lately, not wanting to create any doubt
or disturbance, but finally, she pressed him.

He knew Greg was going to be disappointed, he said.

"Disappointed."

"Yeah," Riley said. "Disappointed."

He was a coward, she thought, too addicted to positive attention to risk
any other kind. His parents had loved him too much. The accusations
coiled up inside her, rearing back to strike, but she felt the change in pressure and fled. She ran upstairs and yanked on her sports bra and laced up
her running shoes. She was out the door and sprinting down the block
before she had time to answer him.

He was a good person, she chanted in time with her stride. A good
person. She was a very lucky girl to have him. She was a very lucky girl. A
very lucky girl. A very lucky girl.

She hadn't brought any water, so when she got too thirsty to go on, she
went into the drugstore to use the fountain. Alls had been home when she
left. She never went there when he was working. Gasping for breath,
Grace went down the makeup aisle toward the pharmacy, eyes down at her
knees, pink from the cold, and almost walked into the two women standing at the end of the aisle, waiting to pick up their prescriptions and quietly talking with each other.

"Gracie," Mrs. Graham said, smiling apprehensively.

The other woman turned toward her. It was her mother.

Grace stumbled back. They didn't look a thing alike, but at that moment, their two faces appeared as a nightmarish replication. "Excuse me," she said.

She turned around and ran home.

Riley's father lent him the money to pay his taxes, and Riley used it to buy Grace an open-ended plane ticket and admission to an eight-week summer study abroad program in Prague. He didn't want them leaving Garland at the same time, he said. He wanted it to look like he was going to visit his girlfriend during her summer study abroad, and when the program was over, they would travel around together for a while. She was wholly relieved to see him focusing, cautiously, on these details of presentation. He was thinking like her, finally. To account for the windfall that would later allow him to go to Europe, he told his parents he had sold three dog portraits on commission, payment upon delivery, to an out-of-towner who had seen his work at Anne Findlay when she passed through over the holidays visiting family. Grace regretted only that he'd lied so self-deprecatingly. He needed to hang on to some of his arrogance to get them through this.

He was just as cautious about the forgery taking shape in the basement. She wished he would pick up the pace a little bit. It was almost May—she was leaving in just six weeks, and she didn't want them to rush the switch. They needed to choose their day carefully. Riley would take the Wynne tour alone, as Grace had, and once he was upstairs with the docent, Grace would come in behind him with her big purse containing Riley's painting, stretched around a thin frame; the quiet pneumatic staple gun she would use to secure the canvas; and a knife to cut out the Bosschaert.

At night, she and Riley lay in bed facing each other, talking quietly about the secret life that awaited them. "I can't believe we're doing this," they said again and again, as if they were having an affair. The dull pink roses and rust-tipped tulips blooming in the basement had begun to look very sweet and beautiful to her, and Grace felt a greater potential for happiness, or for the relief she had decided was happiness, than she had in a very long time.

22

Three weeks before she was supposed to leave Garland forever, Grace was spending the day in the public library looking at back issues of *Architectural Digest*, compiling a list of European dealers from the adver- tisements. Riley had gone to his parents' for dinner.

His mother had called him to arrange it, after leaving a tentative mes- sage on Grace's phone and receiving no response. When Riley called her, Grace said she had too much of a headache from reading to talk to anyone tonight, but to please give everyone a hug for her.

"You haven't been over there in months," Riley had realized then.

"I know," Grace had said. "I don't know how it happened."

"We should go next week. In case it's a while before we see them again."

Now she worried what they were saying at the Grahams' house without her there.

Riley texted her at eight. "You need to be gone when I get home," the message said. "I'll meet you at the arboretum as soon as I can, but please wait for me there. Will explain."

Her fears leapt: Something had gone horrifically wrong. The Grahams were having her arrested. Her mother had told them that Grace was not to be trusted and now—what? Riley had let something slip. Lana's video of her sobbing meltdown had gone viral.

She sat shivering in the arboretum. She and Riley used to sneak in at night for fun and debauchery. Her thighs were cold and wet from the deep damp of the concrete benches. She stared at the outlines of the bushes against the sky until it was too dark to make anything out.

Riley came at ten. He kissed her, and she was relieved. Whatever the catastrophe was, it was not that.

"Your lips are freezing," he said.

"I've been here since the library closed. What *is* it?"

"So, this afternoon, I told Greg I was out of the plan. Really out, totally out. The plan is nuts, he's nuts to do it, too much risk for not enough money, all that. And, you know, he wasn't pleased."

"Okay," Grace said.

"But I thought it was settled, and I went downstairs to paint."

She swallowed.

"And he came downstairs about an hour later to argue with me. I heard him coming, and I moved the courthouse in front of the painting. But as he was talking, he was looking at the paint."

"The paint."

"The pink fucking paint on my palette. He saw it, Grace. He saw the paint, saw the courthouse, saw that it was bone dry, and pulled it forward and saw the other thing."

"What did you tell him?"

"Tell him? I didn't have to tell him anything. He knew. He knew I'd never painted any bowls of flowers before. He knew it didn't look like my stuff at all. He just knew."

"Exactly what *did* you tell him?"

"He told *me* that I was copying something from the Wynne House, and he knew—guessed—that it was your idea."

Greg. She wanted to choke him with his own hubris, just ball it up and shove it into his throat.

Riley swallowed. "So I told him we broke up. Are breaking up."

"*What?*"

"He said he's never trusted you, and that you had brainwashed me, and I can't just fuck everyone else over, and I—I told him the painting was my idea, that I'd been working on it, and then I showed it to you and you freaked out, and we had a big fight, and we'd been having a lot of problems anyway, and this just made it clear that we weren't—that you were moving out."

"What the fuck, Riley? Why would you say that?"

"He caught me off guard. I said the first thing that—"

"That was the first thing?"

"You've never made up something stupid when you got cornered?

Look, I fucked up. I shouldn't have been working when they were home. I should have had something to say in case this happened. But it's going to be fine, okay? We just have to pretend we broke up. It's three weeks, Grace. Three weeks. Then the rest of our lives."

"Why can't we just switch the paintings now and get out of here?"

"I'm not finished yet," he said. "Jesus, it's not a coloring book."

"You're the worst liar," she said, and then she realized he might be lying to her. He never had before, but then, how would she know?

"Yeah," Riley said. "But Greg believed me."

Grace could not bear to ask her parents if she could come back home, or even to tell them. She sneaked into her childhood bedroom to sleep that night. "Riley and I are going through some stuff," she told her mother the next morning, after she'd clutched her chest and yelped in fright at the sight of Grace coming out of the bathroom. "It's just a few weeks, until I go to Prague."

The next day, she went back to collect her things. Riley was at school. Greg leered at her on the stairs, and she swore she saw in his eyes some perverse triumph. Grace's disgust with Riley made her role as his bitter ex easier to play.

The storm door slammed on her ankles as she shoved her big wheeled suitcase out the front door. She could almost feel the neighbors watching. When she was nearly to the corner, the suitcase lurching over the fat cracks in the sidewalk, she heard the door slam again. Alls ran up behind her.

"We broke up," she spat. "Ask him." She yanked her suitcase forward.

Riley called her that night and she didn't answer. His messages pleaded with her to talk to him and promised that everything could still work out. But that was impossible. She'd collapsed every possibility except the one in which she and Riley ran away alone, and now she and Riley could not run away. They could never rely on Greg to keep the painting a secret. She thought of the plan as she had made it, as they had made it just between the two of them, and how simple and clean it had been, and theirs alone. And then he had passed it around—twice!—to his friends, and now it was ruined, a soggy, dirty blunt that she wouldn't touch with anything but a bleach rag. They could have it.

She had never thought about splitting up, but he had, obviously. Why else would that have been the first story to leap to his mind?

By the end of the second day, her voice mail was full and he couldn't leave her any more messages. He showed up at her parents' house and banged on the door, first demanding, then pleading, and then demanding again. She sat in her desk chair with her arms crossed and let him talk. Her mother knocked on the door and asked them to keep it down; the boys were trying to go to bed. She said that was fine, Riley was just leaving.

She had come to despise his arrogant halo. He was a youngest child, accustomed to forgiveness. In the face of Grace's doubt, he did not reassure; he condescended, as if her agreement was something he owned outright.

Grace's twin brothers, now ten, regarded her suspiciously, like a cousin visiting from the branch of the family with a different religion. Aiden accidentally kicked a ball into her room and retrieved it as if he'd kicked it into the neighbor's yard and Grace were the Doberman on the chain. Her mother offered her a stack of clean towels with a tight smile that seemed to say she had predicted this. Grace's mother probably thought Riley had dumped her. Grace hadn't known she could feel so livid and so limp with defeat at the same time.

That afternoon, after she had run and showered, she was eating yogurt alone at her parents' kitchen table, doing the newspaper crossword and watching her wet hair drip on the comics, when Alls drove up in his old blue Buick. The weather was warm enough now to have the windows open, and she heard the sound of the motor idling at the curb, and then the engine shutting off.

He'd never been to her parents' house. She met him at the front door.

"Hey," he said. "A minute?"

"Hi, yeah." Her voice was off pitch. She didn't want to let him in, but he stood there, waiting. She stepped back and he came in and stood with his hands in his front pockets.

"How are you?" he asked, too casually, and then he looked at the floor. "I just meant how are you, how's it going, you know."

"It's hard," she said flatly. She wanted him with her whole self, from the prickly hot soles of her feet up to her temples.

"You'll be fine. I know it. He knows it."

"How is he?" she asked.

"Depends on who you ask," he said. "He acts like he's been born again."

"Ah," she said, vaguely stung.

"I mean that in the lunatic sense," he added quickly. "He's like a hyper kid, tearing around, can't slow down."

"That doesn't sound like him."

"He's in shock. He's headed for a crash." Alls chewed his lip and stared down at the potted shrub in front of him. "That's why I'm here, to talk to you about that. This Wynne bullshit."

No one was home. "You want anything to drink?"

"Water."

She led him into the kitchen, pushing aside the tent the twins had pitched on the carpet to catch their soccer balls when it was raining outside. She poured him a glass of water and sat down behind her yogurt and newspaper.

"You weren't really going to do it," he said.

"No," she said.

"I didn't think it would go this far," he said, and for a lost moment, Grace forgot that he was talking about the Wynne House.

"Greg always does the dumbest shit he can think of," he went on, "and we all laugh about it. But Riley's usually smarter."

She shook her head. "I don't know what's going on in his head."

"He thinks this is going to work. He thinks he had a perfect idea. Stealing paperweights and selling them for millions of dollars."

The fork in the road: Play dumb or don't. She hadn't thought Alls would come to her. She'd thought they had both chosen Riley, his good opinion.

"He said it would be a good project for me," she said. "Identifying them, since I was so bored. I thought he was just trying to get me out of his hair."

"And then he said you guys should rob the place? The both of you?"

"Well, I thought he was joking at first," she said. "We all did."

"Right."

"But then, this painting thing." She shook her head. "I mean, he's really doing it."

Her parents' cuckoo clock whistled. "Excuse me a sec."

Grace went into the bathroom and turned the water on. She put her hands on her hips. She just needed to get away from him for a moment and think. Her chest felt like it was going to crack open. He was here, in her house, alone with her. She had to get him out of there. She'd promise to talk Riley out of the forgery, and tonight, she would. That was all there was to do.

She came out and sat down across from him again. "He thinks he can get away with anything, just because he always has."

"Is this really why you left him?"

Grace swallowed. Did he *want* her to have left Riley?

"Would it make a difference?" she asked. She looked at him, sitting in the sticky oak Windsor chair, elbows on his knees. Her hand slipped down the condensation on her water glass and she wiped it on her bare leg.

"What are you saying?" he asked quietly, watching her hand.

She saw then the narrowest chance that she had misread him, that he might be as torn up as she was, that he wanted her as much as she wanted him. "I thought you—I thought—"

But she didn't want to say what she had thought. She wanted to have been wrong.

Grace knew that she couldn't be both the good girl and the bad one anymore, but she was less and less sure which was which, and she had failed at good already, and she desperately wanted to fail at good again.

"I can't be what he needs me to be," she said. "Or I don't want to anymore."

"You'll get back together. You'll see." He wasn't trying to comfort her.

"The reason he shouldn't rob the Wynne House," she said, "is that it isn't worth the risk. The antiques money wouldn't last longer than a few years, not split like that. I tried to tell him, but he doesn't do the math."

"I bet he thinks he's going to win you back or something. He thinks that way, you know."

"I know."

They hadn't hurt Riley yet, she thought. She and Alls were just miserable, alone.

"What I didn't tell him," she said then, "is that his fake painting is a great idea, only there's no way he can pull it off. He can paint well enough,

I have no doubt." She swallowed. "But Greg is going to fuck up and get them both caught."

He nodded, intent on a plate of crumbs leftover from breakfast.

"The original is in the back, in the study. Reframed, easy to cut out and roll up. I can promise you that no one has looked at that painting since the day it went up. No one would ever notice, unless they hired a Dutch Masters scholar to do the dusting. But Riley and Greg, together—" She paused. "They don't know how to keep a secret. Not like we do."

Alls tapped his fingers on the table for what felt like hours. Did he know what she had meant to say? Would she have to say it more, worse, louder?

"I always knew you weren't who they thought you were," he said, finally raising his eyes. "But I guess I don't know either."

What *they* did he mean? It didn't matter. "Join the club," she said.

"He trusts you, even now." He stood up.

She'd overplayed her hand. He didn't want her as badly as she wanted him. She tried to think of something to say to undo it, to be just kidding.

He hesitated, standing behind her. She could feel him, but she didn't move.

"Don't tell him—" she started.

Don't tell him what? She didn't know how to finish.

He let the door slam behind him. She listened, but she didn't hear his car engine turn. She went to the window and saw him sitting in his car, his head back. Finally, the engine turned, and he left.

How had she been so sure in that moment that he was hers for the taking? He had come to her as a friend—to *Riley*. She'd thought he'd known how wrong a person she was, hiding behind all that nice-girl hair that Kendall and Lana had dismissed so easily, under all those pastel sweaters Mrs. Graham had dressed her in, but she had been wrong. He'd thought she was a good person who'd made one awful mistake, the way he was a good person who'd made one awful mistake. But now he knew. She had told him herself.

23

That night, Riley begged her to meet him at the playground.

"Gracie, my painting is *good*," he protested. "No one is ever going to guess that *I* did this." He looked at her as if he were on the verge of laughter. "Look at me, baby. Look at me." He pointed to his face. His curls were aglow from the street lamp behind them. "No one—*no one*—in Tennessee is ever going to suspect that Riley Sullivan Graham would do something like this."

A wave of nausea drowned her guilt for a moment. She wanted to kill him. "Don't," she pleaded. "Just forget the whole thing. This was supposed to be a game, right? A game."

He tried to kiss her and she pulled away. "What is this? We didn't break up. *That's* the game."

"No more games."

"You want out? Fine, you're out! You're too sensitive for this anyway. You worry too much."

"Riley," she warned him.

"You'll see."

Alls called her the next morning. "We agreed that we would never tell him," he said, "and we're going to stick with that."

She held her breath.

"But I know what I want," he said. "And I can't help that."

She slid down the wall until she was on the floor. "Yes," she said.

"We can't let him rob the Wynne House," he said. "It's suicide."

"Yes," she said. "You told him you're out?"

"He doesn't care."

"I've created a monster," she said.

"How do we steal a painting?"

She had not expected that. She marveled at the *we*, which sounded now like a word she had never heard before.

"We—we have to replace it with a fake," she said. "We could buy a fake online, a print of some crappy still life in the same colors, and we put an old frame around it, and we switch them."

"No sweat," he said doubtfully.

"It's not a great idea," she said. "And besides—he could still try to steal the original, not knowing. And then it would be very clear to him what we'd done."

"So we can't do that."

"No."

"We need to save him from himself," he said.

"Yes," she said, disbelieving. "How close is he to finishing the painting?"

"I don't know how to tell. I can send you a picture."

"Yes. He'll tell me, though, when he's done. He won't be able to help it."

"Oh, you guys are talking?"

"It's like you thought," she said. "He thinks this is his grand gesture."

"And then?"

"Then you take his painting. When he's in class, probably. And then you take the tour," she said. "Once you're upstairs, I come in and make the switch. You have to ask questions, upstairs, to give me time. We couldn't sell it in America. That would be stupid."

"Where are we going?"

"I go to Prague in two weeks," she said.

"Me, too," he said.

She laughed, a short burst that startled them both. "We don't have any money," she said.

"Riley's going to pay you back for the rent," he said. "He called it 'priority uno.'"

How easily they slipped into mocking him, this person they were so determined to protect.

He did pay her back, and then some. Anne Findlay had gotten a call requesting one unsold painting.

"With interest," he said, eyes gleaming. It was as if he were taunting her with his autonomy now. The *we* was gone. Her husband now showed off how easily he could act without her input. Riley seemed determined to prove that he could do whatever he wanted without losing her. But prove it to whom? If Riley wanted to show Grace that he held her under the thumb of his love, he had grossly miscalculated. Grace had been gone longer than even she had known.

"You are not a criminal," she pleaded. "I won't let you do it. I'll set off the car alarms across the street. I'll pretend I'm having a heart attack on the office's steps. I'll call in a bomb threat. I'm not going to leave you here when you're like this."

"Like what?" he said, gently biting her ear.

"Manic. Delusional. Like *this*."

"Well, when I whisk you off to Paris, I won't be like this anymore. I'll be cured. I'll be cured and I'll be rich."

For a moment, she hoped he *would* do it and get caught, once she was long gone. His family couldn't save him then. And Greg, well—she longed to see him regret *anything*. But this was not in her best interest.

"I won't be party to this," she said stuffily. "It's dangerous and it's wrong and I won't be associated with something like this."

"We both know that's not true," he said.

The snag appeared when, just ten days before Grace was supposed to leave for Prague, Riley had still not finished his fake. Of course, he saw no hurry, since he believed he was meeting her there later. He bragged to her about his glazes, his shadows, his brushwork, the *luminescence*, until she gave him a warning look. "I don't want to hear about it," she said.

"I'm almost done," he said. "Shame you won't get to see the finished product."

If Riley did not finish the painting in time, she and Alls would be sunk. The two of them had to switch the painting together, one upstairs, occupying the docent, while the other made the switch.

But, Grace thought, if Riley didn't finish his fake in time, they would still have to steal the original. To protect Riley, so there would be no painting for him to steal. His heist would be ruined, and he would be safe in his little Garland life, and she and Alls would be gone, forever. Alls agreed.

Again and again, they spoke of saving Riley from his own happy arrogance, from Greg's caper-movie logic, from trying to win Grace back when she could no longer be won. She was not a prize.

"I'll buy the fake," she told Alls. "I'm sure I can find something close enough."

He stood across the aisle from her, three feet between them. They had not been any closer than this since New York. Alls had called her on the phone with this condition: They had done something terrible and they were planning something worse, but until they were finished, alone together and away from Garland, away from Riley, there could be no physical contact. Alls wanted to hang on, he said, to some scrap of—of—

"Honor?" Grace had said, disbelieving. His was a *very* relative, *very* negotiated kind of honor. But she had agreed, more because she feared losing control. If she so much as touched his hand, her mind would leave her. She had to focus.

Now she knew it hadn't mattered. A toddler was wailing for Pepsi in the aisle behind them, and Alls, backed by bright plastic vacuum cleaners, looked sallow and sleepless under the fluorescent lights, but Grace didn't feel at all in control.

"Just for a few days," he agreed. "Until I can swap in the better one." *The better one* meant *Riley's forgery*, which neither of them liked to say.

"How would you do that alone?"

"I'd have to follow another tour in," he said.

She bit her lip. This was a rush play, sloppy and desperate, exactly the kind of talk that had made her sure that Riley had no business trying to pull off something like this himself.

"Or we could just leave it. No one would ever notice except Riley."

"No, we have to get his forgery into Wynne House," Alls said, swallowing, "so that he can't rat us out."

She nodded. She wished he hadn't said it. She preferred the narrative that they were protecting Riley to the one in which she and Alls were only ensuring their escape.

"I can do it," he said. "I could go at night, pick the lock."

She nodded: They weren't making sense anymore. They wanted it to work too badly.

Buying a fake painting was easy. There was an entire industry devoted to printing images cheaply on canvas of any size and then swabbing clear "brushwork" over the top, nonsensically, to approximate artistry. Grace's fake Bosschaert wasn't even a Bosschaert—his work was neither famous nor fun enough for hanging over couches—but a Willem van Aelst, who had worked in roughly the same time, place, and style. The *Bouquet of Flowers* she bought was identical in size, similar in composition and color palette. She opted not to purchase the fake brushwork, which looked like wrinkled plastic wrap and would attract more attention than the painting itself ever had. Her van Aelst cost $149 plus rush shipping and arrived in five days. Grace pulled the canvas from its bubble wrap and sucked in her breath. They were really going to do it.

She went to the Wynne House on Tuesday morning with her hair pulled back severely, wearing dark lipstick and glasses. She borrowed clothes from her mother's closet. She took the tour grimly, as if she were a serious historian. Dorothea, the ancient docent who had first toured Grace months ago, didn't recognize her. Grace was not charming; she was not herself.

While they were upstairs, Alls slipped in downstairs with the fake, which they had cut from its frame. They had, Grace had estimated, ten to twelve minutes while Grace and Dorothea were upstairs. If it wasn't easy to get the painting from its frame, they agreed, he would walk right back out. But it was; it was *so* easy. He popped the frame's back off with the screwdriver tip of a Leatherman, cut the painting out in four clean cuts, and stapled the fake in its place. He rolled up the painting, put it in his backpack, and walked home to Orange Street. By the time Grace and Dorothea came down the stairs, he was gone.

When Alls called her on the phone that night and told her he'd slid the painting above the panels of the drop ceiling in his bedroom, Grace was lightheaded with joy. She was in love and was very close to getting to keep it, forever. Alls didn't want to save Ginny's Ice Cream, and when he'd found out that Grace was not quite the sundress sweetheart she had tried to be, he had loved her anyway. She felt newly honest and exhilarated, as though she were skinny-dipping at night in a dark lake.

Grace thought she should take the painting with her to Prague but Alls disagreed.

"You would proposition your ex-boyfriend's best friend to steal a two-million-dollar painting with you," he said. "There is a limit to how stupid you make me."

Not her ex-boyfriend, but her current husband. She never told him. She had limits too.

Grace was leaving for Prague in just three more days. She took deep breaths and tried to keep the strands of her relationships untangled, though she herself was unraveling. She had read about men who had whole secret families in other states or countries. The distance was key. You could not sustain something like this when the two men you were planning futures with lived in the same house. Worse than managing this duplicity was navigating the relationships—plural—she was having with each of them. There was the relationship Riley thought they had, the one Alls thought she and Riley had, and the one she and Riley actually had, whatever the hell that was. And there was what she had found with Alls, which was real.

The night before she left, Riley showed up with a surprise. He propped it up on Grace's childhood desk, against the bulletin board of all their prom photos.

"What do you think?" he asked her proudly.

The painting seemed to glow. Without thinking, she reached out to touch it, and Riley grabbed her hand. "Christ, it's not dry yet."

"Don't do it, Riley. You are such a good painter. You don't need to do this."

"Painter," he said. "You know, you used to say I was a good artist."

"If you do this, I'm going to leave you. I'm serious."

"The fuck you will," he said. "Just try. You can't." She recoiled, and his face became pitiful. "I'm not asking you for help, just some faith in me. When have I let you down?"

If she told Riley that she didn't love him anymore, he would certainly rob the Wynne House, just to show her what he could do, like a little boy having a tantrum with a real knife. Had this Riley always been there? How much of him had she created? Telling him the truth would make him crazy, she told herself. It would only destabilize him further.

Also, she didn't want him to cancel her plane ticket.

Alls would follow her as soon as he could switch the paintings. He said it was best that they weren't leaving at the same time. "Leaving a few days apart is the kindest thing to do," he said, calling her on his cigarette break at the drugstore. "He can choose not to put it together this way, and he will. You know him. He only ever sees what he wants to."

"You will come," she pressed. "How do I know you'll come?"

"I'm coming," he said. "I promise."

That was what Riley said too.

If only she had believed! Instead she felt a seed of distrust that she couldn't ignore: that Greg could still fuck it all up somehow or that Riley would, even that Alls was setting her up.

It was nine o'clock. She knew that Riley was with Greg now—he had said they were going to Target with strange, ominous vagueness—and that Alls was at work.

Grace slipped on her backpack and went over to the house on Orange Street, letting herself in the back door. She stood on Alls's bed to lift the ceiling tile and pulled out the painting. The canvas was so slight in her hands—it might have been a vinyl place mat. She just couldn't take any chances.

Riley borrowed Greg's car to drive her to the airport, mistaking Grace's worry for a different kind. He didn't know that he would never see her again. He thought he was comforting her, and that was intolerable.

"I'll be there soon," he said. "So soon!"

"*How* soon?" she asked.

"You're going to love it! Old buildings, cheap liquor, that one poet you love. Sites of historic terror! What are you crying for?"

"I can't believe you did this for me."

"Well, I can," he said. "I'm almost insulted that you would say that."

"Please don't do it," she said. "Just forget it."

"Do what?"

"Rob the Wynne House!"

"Oh," he said. "Okay, I won't."

She knew, of course, that he didn't mean it. She had lost her control over him. Whatever he did now was for an idea of her. For that, she could not be responsible.

Grace spent her first day in Prague searching, lost and sweaty, for an Ethernet cord to plug in to her computer. The Communist-era dorms didn't have wireless and she was anxious to talk to Alls. When she finally saw his face flicker at her on her laptop screen, she thought she might pass out from relief. She had shut herself in the tiny WC for privacy and was sitting on the toilet. The long blue Ethernet cord stretched under the door and back to her desk.

"You made it," he said, almost shy.

"I made it," she said.

Her roommate was doing the same thing on the other side of the door, and for a moment Grace felt that they were the same, just two girls lovesick and homesick and talking to their boyfriends on the Internet.

But her joy at seeing him was short-lived. Greg and Riley's plan, Alls told her, was now in motion. Riley had just been waiting for her to leave.

"Wait, why are they still doing the antiques?" Grace asked when Alls told her. "That's insane, if he has the painting."

"Yeah, I know," Alls said. He was sitting in his car in the parking lot of the Whitwell Starbucks. They had Wi-Fi there and no one from Garland would see him. "It's Greg, I think. I'm trying to derail the whole thing, since I can't exactly tell them to focus on the painting."

Greg had told his parents that they were going to spend a few days at the house on Norris Lake. It was only an hour and ten minutes away. They would drive up in the afternoon and be seen: eating ribs at Hale's, buying beer and whiskey at the liquor store, filling up the gas tank. They needed Alls to come with them, Riley said, even if he was going to puss out on the rest. At the end of the evening, they would park Greg's car in the garage next to their second car, untitled and anonymous, already there waiting for them.

The next day, they would drive together in the second car to the Walmart in Pitchfield, where their third car, also untitled and anonymous, waited in the parking lot. Greg had been moving it between Walmarts every three to four days. They would switch cars and drive to Garland, arriving at the Wynne House at nine in the morning. If there were no unexpected cars in the lot, Riley would go in for the tour. When they got upstairs, he would lock the docent in the windowless study, and then meet Greg and Alls—Riley was sure Alls would come around—downstairs.

"*Lock* her?" Grace was incredulous. "She's an old woman. She'll have a heart attack."

When the boys were done, they would calmly walk out with their sacks to their car. They would drive together back to the Walmart, where they would switch cars again, transferring their Walmart bags of Confederate antiquities, and return to the lake house. They'd spend the evening goofing off at the lake, shouting over the water to annoy the neighbors. The next morning, Riley would head to New York, leaving Greg at the lake for appearances. In New York, Riley would liquidate everything over the next week, using a list of vendors he had compiled.

"It's my list," Grace told Alls mournfully. "I made that fucking list."

"Just come," she said. "Just leave the other one and come. Get *out* of there."

"It's almost dry, I heard him say it. They need longer than that to tie up their loose ends. I bought a ticket for Saturday, okay? He says next Thursday is the day. But by then, his painting will be gone, and he won't be able to do a goddamn thing about it. Their whole machine will fall apart, and I will be with you."

The summer study program itself was just an excuse for rich college kids to drink beer that was cheaper than water and get school credit for it. Grace went to the classes without knowing why—for show, she supposed. Her roommate was a whiny communications major from Connecticut, the kind of girl Kendall and Lana would have eaten alive. She found herself missing them. God, what would they think of her now?

After a few false starts, the other students gave up on talking to her. She saw in their reactions that she was giving off something both scared and scary, as if she were contaminated. Not that it mattered. The dorm was just a place to stay until Alls came. She could hardly imagine. When she started to—the sight of him, in the lobby downstairs, or the sunlight through the window on his bare back—she tried to wipe away the picture, suddenly superstitious. She waited through the next three days half present in a sort of anxious purgatory, waiting for him, for her real life to begin. The past year had been just a bad dream.

Once a day, she e-mailed with Riley. He didn't mention the plan and she didn't ask. She told him her webcam was broken so she wouldn't have to see him, but she otherwise went through the motions. Now that she was away forever, she could afford to be what he wanted again, for just a few more days. She'd learned how to speak the truth, or part of it, to the wrong person, so that it didn't even feel wrong, just misplaced. When she told Riley she loved him, she was talking to Alls.

When she saw Alls on her screen, a thrill ran through her like ice water, bracing and aching. The universe would give you whatever you wanted if you twisted its arm hard enough.

She knew she needed to tell him she had the painting. It wouldn't change anything; it shouldn't, as long as she told him before he stood on his bed to make a cursory check in the ceiling tiles and found out himself. If she'd had the painting all along, she would have checked it every day, probably twice a day. Her mother probably would have seen and thought she was hiding drugs or something. Alls had been right to keep it with him.

She needed to tell him that night.

"Where are you?" Grace asked him that night. His face floated fuzzily against a gray wall. "Are you at *home?*"

"There's no one here," he said. "Listen, they're going to the lake tomorrow."

"You said—"

"Greg's parents want the cabin then, so he and Riley are going up early." Alls had clenched his jaw and kept looking toward the window. "He baked the painting to dry it faster. It was in the oven when I got home."

"Shit. Shit, shit, shit."

"I think I have to break in tonight," he said.

"No," she said. "No way."

"I can pick the lock," he said. "It's an old one, shouldn't be too bad." He raked his hand through his hair. "There is no good way out of this anymore."

"Listen, I have the Bosschaert," she said. "I took it. Cut Riley's up and throw it in the Dumpster and come."

She watched him absorbing what she had said. She saw the moment it registered in his eyes: stunned, disbelieving.

"I'm sorry," she said. "I was too worried about Greg—"

The window where his face had been went black. And of course, he never came.

The next day, Riley, Greg, and Alls robbed the Wynne House. Riley locked Dorothea in the upstairs bedroom so they could ransack the rooms of all Grace's little red dots. Then the groundskeeper, who Grace herself knew was not supposed to be there that day, walked in and saw them and collapsed.

The plan fell apart. Grace imagined that Riley, awakened to the reality of the crumpling old man and himself as the one who'd hurt him, would not go to New York. He and Alls left the lake house and returned to the house on Orange Street, where they were arrested on Greg's information four days later. The groundskeeper went home from the hospital, and the boys went to prison. All of the stolen antiques were recovered from Greg's car at the lake house before investigators had completed their inventory of what was missing.

No one noticed the missing painting. Grace watched and waited from four thousand miles away as her fate sputtered out in two-hundred-word updates on the *Albemarle Record*. But no one ever said her name.

VII

Paris

24

It was dark now outside the studio's high windows. Grace had helped Hanna finish beading the snow onto the branches of the winter trees, but they had set down their tools now.

"Where is the painting?" Hanna asked.

Grace shrugged sadly. "I sold it to a collector in Berlin. Some creep. I was too scared to go to a dealer or an auction house—scared that I wouldn't be able to keep my name out of it. And I wanted cash."

In Prague, Grace had not looked at the painting, which was the size of a wrapping paper roll and hidden, even from her, along the inside edge of her suitcase, until the trial had concluded in August. She tried to will it into invisibility. When the summer program ended, she moved to a hostel for two days, where her laptop and raincoat were stolen from her luggage, but not the painting tucked beneath her suitcase's lining. She went back to the dorm. The desk matron agreed to a price of $210 per month for a single on the fourth floor. The room was the size of a car and hadn't been repainted in decades, but Grace flipped off the buzzing overhead light and sank down onto the cool floor, relieved to be alone.

She bought a used laptop and then had little money left. She found work tutoring easily at first, then less so. She hard-boiled eggs in the lobby's microwave and ate them with bread and pickles in the beginning, without pickles later on, as she trolled the European auction records for sales of paintings with questionable or nonexistent papers. They were easy to spot; these were the "discoveries" people had made in sheds and attics. The laptop died after three weeks, and she moved to the college's computer lab. Her swipe card still worked. She hated using those machines, leaving traces of her plans on them, but there was no longer any other choice.

In the second week of September, after several weeks of dead ends and hang-ups, Grace tracked down the original owner of a dubious Corot and inquired if he collected Dutch Golden Age. He'd given her the phone number for a woman, Katrin, who'd in turn sent her to Wyss.

Wyss had given her a date and an address in East Berlin. She had lived in New York, she told herself—she could do this. She packed up what little she had and went, via bus. People had romantic ideas about European trains, but the bus was cheaper, and this trip was not at all romantic. She didn't *want* to sell the painting anymore, but what else could she do?

When the bus dropped Grace at Schönefeld, she badly wanted to scrap her directions and take a taxi. What if she screwed up now and missed the meeting? But she had enough for a night in a hostel and a return bus ticket, with little margin for error. She followed the crowd out of the bus station to the train. She had to make only one transfer, at Ostkreuz, and when she got off at Alexanderplatz she could not believe that this part, at least, had been easy, that she was not lost. She walked up the street until she found a place calling itself an Irish pub, and there she waited until four, when she walked outside to watch to see how someone hailed a taxi in Berlin, and then she did it herself. When the driver pulled up to the address, she gave him twenty euros and asked him to wait half an hour. She didn't know if he would, but there was no one around for him to pick up instead.

She never knew whether she had met Wyss or not. There were two men. The one Grace would remember was the one who was waiting when she pulled her rolling suitcase up to the building, the last concrete block in a tight row of ten-story concrete blocks the same color as the sky. He'd shown her to the elevator, and she had noticed the grime that arced beneath his gums. In the elevator he was closer to her, and when he smiled, she was startled to realize that it was not dirt under his gums, but shadow. His gums were loose, hanging over his teeth.

He had shown her to a bright, empty office, big water stains on the carpet but no desks or chairs. She'd unrolled the painting on the floor, where a second man, stout and spectacled, looked closely at it, but only for a few minutes. He asked her where she'd gotten it. "My grandfather," she said, knowing it didn't matter. He sent the first man away. Grace didn't understand the German. When the man returned, he opened Grace's suitcase and emptied a garbage bag of cash into it.

"How much did you get?" Hanna asked her now.

"Seven hundred thousand euros," Grace said, and Hanna gasped. "Maybe. I didn't have time to count it. He had me followed, and the next morning, I heard a key in the lock, and I thought it was the hotel maid, and I shouted that I didn't need anything." Without thinking, she reached to run her fingers over the rough patch on her crown where the hair was still sparse. She wore her hair back now, to cover it. "But it was not the hotel maid," she said. She tried to laugh, but she still couldn't manage it.

She would not tell Hanna everything.

Grace had quickly decided against the hostel. She'd been robbed once already and now she had a rolling suitcase full of cash. She hadn't made any reservations, suddenly superstitious about jinxing the sale. Living without a laptop, and traveling especially, was like going back in time. She didn't know how to do *anything* without a computer. She got back into the cab and had no idea where to go. A folded tourist magazine was jammed in the crack of the seat, and on the back cover was an ad for the Hotel Reiniger. Grace showed the driver the ad and told him to take her there.

She had enough cash on her for the cab, but she had to unzip the suitcase in the hotel lobby restroom to peel off the money to pay for two nights. The sight of the money—not neat bricks, but a messy pile with grimy bands—sickened her. Those dirty stacks were so damning and yet looked so insubstantial, like kindling.

She'd planned to open a bank account, but now the idea seemed impossible and cartoonish—showing up with wads of cash, like a drug moll from the movies. She couldn't take the money anywhere but obviously she couldn't just leave it either. She rolled the suitcase under the bed and waited to know what to do. She wished she had someone to talk to. She wished Alls had come, and when regret crept up to remind her *why* he had not come, she shoved it down as best she could.

She wished she could call Mrs. Graham and ask to come home.

For the next seventeen hours, Grace didn't leave her hotel room. At six in the morning, she called for room service and ordered some proud German specialty that sounded like French toast. She clicked dumbly through the TV stations, stopping at a performance of what appeared to be quintuplets in vinyl catsuits. It was Eurovision, the multicountry singing contest. She and the boys used to watch clips of it online, baked and howling with laughter.

She had gotten what she wanted now, hadn't she? She was rich and away from Garland. But it was like one of those three-wishes fables: She'd duped herself. Yes, she was on a down comforter in a Berlin hotel with gilded mirrors, but at home in Garland, Mrs. Graham wished Grace had never met her son. Alls likely wished her dead.

She jumped at the knock on the door.

"Room service," a girl's voice said.

Grace undid the chain and gestured her inside, embarrassed to be alone in this fancy hotel room. The girl was probably Grace's age, and Grace wished she could offer some explanation. But she was rich now, and rich girls could go to hotels alone without any explanation.

"Danke," Grace said. She didn't think you tipped for room service in Germany, but she wasn't sure. A fifty-euro note was the smallest bill she had, change from check-in, and she handed it to the girl, whose eyes flickered briefly in surprise. When the girl had gone, Grace peeled off a five-hundred-euro note and put it in her nightstand drawer. She needed to be brave enough, at least, to get some change.

She was eating, ravenous but surprised that she could eat at all, when she heard another knock at the door. She stopped chewing and looked to make sure she had chained the door again. She had. "No thank you!" she called, her voice unexpectedly quavering. She fumbled for the German. "Nein!" she called. "Nein danke!" The do-not-disturb sign should have been hanging on the knob. She had checked it when the room service girl left.

She muted the television and listened for whoever it was to go away, to apologize for disturbing someone who wasn't to be disturbed. Instead there was quick, slick sound, a soft click. The swipe of a key card. And then her door was open a crack.

"Excuse me?" she accused like some hysterical mother who'd just been cut in the checkout line. "Stop!" she shouted. "Halt!"

She jumped up from the bed and ran to the end of the room, her back to the wall, which didn't make any sense, but when you heard a frightening noise you ran away from it; you couldn't help it. She watched the crack, the chain tight across it, and then a pair of bolt cutters clunked up the gap and quickly, neatly cut the chain in two.

The man in the door was the man who had taken her up the elevator yesterday to Wyss. The man with the slack gums.

This cannot be the end, she thought. *Not this.*

"Okay," he said, shutting the door behind him. "Give it to me. Give me the money." His voice was teasing, almost amused.

"I don't have it," she said as he came toward her. "I don't." She should have gone to the phone, she realized now, not the window.

"Oh?" His mouth stretched wide. He had stopped just before his body touched hers and now he loomed over her. She could see the dark shadows where his teeth disappeared. He nodded toward her half-eaten breakfast. "How will you pay for your *Kaiserschmarrn?*"

She knew that he would look under the bed first, maybe in the closet, behind the curtains, in the bathtub—

"This won't be like the films," he said. "I won't ask you again and again." He threw the bolt cutters onto the bed and grabbed Grace's shoulders, hurling her onto the bed as if she were a bag of laundry. Grace kicked at him furiously, but her legs seemed to fall through the air. All her self-defense training had come from Mrs. Graham, who'd taught her to dig her thumbs into a man's eye sockets, or, failing that, to knee him in the groin, or, failing that, to bite hard, anywhere. She could do none of these things. And she was supposed to be screaming. He planted his knee on her shin, pinning her down. Her bone was going to snap. Then he opened the bolt cutters and brought them up under her Achilles tendon.

"If you were a professional, I would cut you here," he said. "But you are no professional."

She would have told him where the money was then, if she could have spoken. This was that nightmare in which she needed to scream and couldn't, her voice trapped in sleep, and she woke up at the sound of her own frail whimper, lungs gasping.

"It's okay, *Liebchen*," he said. "I will help you grow up."

He stood up and yanked her ankle, flipping her onto her stomach, and she heard her sob of terror before she felt it. She shut her eyes. Her head was yanked back. He had grabbed her ponytail. The first hairs to break were the ones on the outside, growing from her face and behind her ears. But as he twisted her ponytail in the bolt cutters, she felt instead all the hairs that wouldn't break, that wouldn't release, dense inside her ponytail. Her scalp was coming apart. The grinding snap of breaking hair gave way all at once and her head fell forward, her face crashing into the pillow.

He tossed the ponytail onto the pillow next to her and she heaved, sobbing. Then he looked for the suitcase. She could hear him. The curtains, the bathroom, the mini-fridge. When he came back and looked under the bed, he laughed.

He pulled out the carry-on, and there was the money, nearly untouched, just as he had put it there. He zipped it back up and extended the telescoping handle.

"Okay, bye," he said. "Enjoy the rest of your trip."

Grace lay weeping, dry-throated, at the pain until she opened her eyes and saw the blood on her pillow, the blossom spreading as it dripped down her scalp. She pushed herself up. In the bathroom, she ran the water until it was lukewarm, and with a sharp breath, she pushed her head under the sink faucet.

She gasped through the stinging and blinked the water out of her eyes. Blood ran in trails down her arms and neck. The sink was stained pink with it. Most of the blood seemed to be coming from her crown, which she couldn't see and couldn't bear to touch. She groped in her plastic toiletry bag for a compact and held it up at an angle, turning away from the sink mirror, terrified of what she would see. A patch of skin, perhaps the size of poker chip, had been torn away with the hair.

She grabbed a hand towel and, too gingerly at first, dabbed at the wound. She cried out at the pain and pressed the towel harder to her head. She was going to pass out, she knew—already there were dark flashes wherever she looked—and then she would bleed to death. She leaned against the bathroom wall and lowered herself all the way to the floor, back flat. She braced her legs against the vanity and pushed back until her head was against the tiled wall, the balled up towel smashed between them.

Later, she went back into the bedroom and picked up the ponytail by its tip, trying not to look at the root. She wrapped the ponytail in toilet paper, the better part of the roll, until she couldn't see any part of it, and then she dropped it in the wastebasket.

What hair was left hung around her face in jagged shards. Her hands shaking, she found her scissors, little pointy things for hangnails and loose threads. She held the ragged ends of her hair gently and cut the rest of it off.

Hanna was watching her. "I got a little roughed up," Grace said, shrugging. "But I'm here."

"My God," Hanna said.

"They could still turn me in," Grace said. "One word, you know? Everything would come unglued."

"It's already unglued," Hanna said.

They looked up at the sound of the studio door. Jacqueline started at the sight of them sitting together at the worktable.

"What are you two doing working so late?" Her voice was overly friendly as she recovered herself. "I can't pay overtime on that thing," she said, nodding toward the centerpiece.

"We know," Grace said. Hanna said nothing.

Jacqueline paused at her office door. "Julie, a moment."

Grace followed her.

Jacqueline smiled nervously. "Good," she said, as if Grace had answered some question.

She opened the black velvet box before her to reveal another ring, this one an Edwardian engagement ring. Grace thought it was beautiful. The ring's setting was empty around the center solitaire. The four sockets were darkened with age. Jacqueline handed her a packet of four stones, emerald cut, probably from her bag of zircons.

"Do it here," Jacqueline said.

"In your office?"

"Yes, now."

When Grace went to fetch her tools, Hanna was staring distractedly at the centerpiece.

Grace sat down in Jacqueline's chair and took up a loupe. She saw the sharp, bright track marks in the sockets where someone had crudely plucked out the stones. She nestled the first stone in its square socket while Jacqueline, sitting on a file box of papers, watched her. Grace glanced up and saw her boss's mouth set tightly, a white rim around her lips.

Grace set the first two stones on either side of the solitaire. When she sat back and looked at the ring under the light, she nearly laughed at how bad it looked. The center solitaire was an antique, old mine cut. It glowed softly and looked almost buttery in the light. Jacqueline's blowsy zircons looked like cheap sequins next to it.

Jacqueline was biting her lip, and Grace waited for her to say it, that the ring looked bad, that it would never pass, but Jacqueline nodded. She couldn't tell.

Grace set the remaining two stones, feeling sorry for the ring's owner. Jacqueline had gotten sloppy, making these lousy substitutions that she didn't have the eyes to understand. She was going to get caught. But if Grace told Jacqueline that she knew, she'd be gone in ten seconds.

And then what? Back to being a chambermaid? An "English tutor"?

"It's good to have something to fall back on," that man had told her three years ago, zipping up his fly before he paid her at his door. "For when times get tough."

What wouldn't she do with no one watching? Grace remembered thinking then. What wouldn't she do, now that she didn't know who she was anymore? Her sense of self had quickly turned to vapor. Whom was goodness for, when you were all alone?

Grace handed the finished ring back to Jacqueline and left, closing the door behind her. Hanna had left.

25

For the next two days, Grace and Hanna worked in near-silence on the centerpiece. Grace glued woolen snow to the winter ground. Hanna curled the string hair of the new shepherdess beneath her bonnet to match the old shepherdess. They spoke only about the materials in their hands. When Hanna stood up each day to go aboveground for lunch, it was clear that she did not want Grace's company.

On the third day, Hanna cleared her throat, startling Grace, who was edging the fall quarter with piles of painted paper leaves.

"The quiet ones always surprise you," Hanna began. "I was the fourth in a family of five daughters. Everything was always filthy, and we all looked at our mother and swore we'd rather die than have a life like hers. Klaudia, my second-eldest sister, was the one who waited on her when she was sick or pregnant, took care of the babies, cooked. Never made a fuss.

"When Klaudia was sixteen, she told my parents she was leaving the next day to go to Austria with a man who'd come to town to bury his mother. He was twenty years older than she was—she had met him at our father's grocery, working there. My parents said no, of course, and then Klaudia told them she was pregnant. That was that." Hanna perched the shepherdess on a metal spike and gently adjusted her arms. "We never saw her again."

Grace grimaced.

"I was thinking about her, because, like you, Klaudia didn't really like the man. She got pregnant on purpose, to get away from us and never be able to come back. I don't know what or who she thought she'd find when she left."

"I loved him, Hanna. I was young and very stupid, but I did love him."

"No," Hanna said. "I don't think you know what love is, not the kind that makes you forget yourself. You were always out for *you*."

"I didn't want them to rob the Wynne House," Grace said, knowing how feeble it sounded. "I told them not to."

"Because you wanted the painting. How kind. I don't think you're sorry. You're just pissed you couldn't pull it off."

Grace crossed her arms over her chest.

"It's the way you kept lying to them—over such a long time! My ex did that. She would grow a lie and tend it like a houseplant. But you've never stopped, have you? You're probably lying to me right now, but I'll never know, so what's the point of even wondering? It's not like I would ever *trust* you."

How could she explain lying to someone who didn't know it already, through and through, deep in her bones? Lies charged compound interest. You tried to fix what you had broken before you were found out, making little payments as you could afford to, just enough to keep the whole weight of it at bay. But the lie kept growing and growing. You could never pay it off, not without losing everything. The cost was total.

"You want me to judge you, Julie. You're hungry for it. You don't judge yourself harshly enough and you know it."

When Grace had first arrived in Paris, she'd thought about confessing. Mrs. Graham went to confession every week, and when she came back she always looked less harried, relieved. And once, when her husband had teased her about it, Mrs. Graham had said, "I don't get spa days, dear, and Father Tilton has a pay-what-you-wish program." Grace had thought it would feel good to confess to a stranger, someone professionally obligated to forgive. Like throwing up, or taking out the trash.

"He could have picked up his life right where he left it when he got out," Grace said. "He could have had the life he wanted, finally. He could paint the Wynne House! People would love it. He's so *forgiven*, Hanna. He always has been. Prison probably would have been good for his career." His art would seem more interesting, even if it hadn't changed at all. "Now he's gone and ruined his chances to do anything."

She meant Riley, of course. She couldn't blame Alls for running, but Riley was only hurting himself.

Hanna gaped at her. "You are *unbelievable*. Prison was *good* for him?"

Grace pushed her chair back. "I have to go to the bathroom."

Hanna shot her leg under the table and hooked Grace's chair leg with her ankle, trapping her there. "You don't pick up where you left off. You can't. You're changed."

"Well, he could more than *some* people—"

"Let me tell you a little about what prison is like," Hanna said. "Since you obviously don't know."

"Hanna." Grace pushed the table, trying to move her chair, but Hanna had her locked in.

"Imagine a hospital. Now bust out half the lights, and make the rest buzz, incessantly, like insect traps. Now tip over all the jars of alcohol and formaldehyde. Because that's what prison smells like, all the time." She grabbed a bottle of rubbing alcohol from her supply rack and poured a thin stream of it into a puddle on Grace's table.

Grace grabbed for a rag to mop it up. She didn't know the woman who was speaking to her now. "Hanna, stop. I didn't mean that how it sounded."

"Prison smells that way because you're always cleaning it, all day every day. It smells like shit and vomit anyway, from three hundred open toilets. Someone is *always* shitting right next to you. And if your boy wasn't on any drugs, he is now. Because you have to make the time go somewhere. Time loses all meaning; a day feels like a year, and a year becomes a day. Those first months, all you can think about is what the people on the outside are doing without you. What they are laughing at on TV, what they are whining about in their days. What they are eating. Who's in bed with them. And you think, why *not* try heroin to ease the transition to absolutely *nothing*? Tetanus gets you a week in the infirmary, and they have magazines in there. Someone is always watching you, getting ready to steal from you, spit on you. The officers, the others on your block. People will claw your eyes out because they're *bored*, because the boredom drives you *insane*. And yes, that's in Poland. But that's also in a *women's* prison."

Jacqueline's office door creaked open. Grace's heart was pounding. Hanna had never spoken to her like that. Rattled, Grace tried to undo what Hanna had said somehow, to generalize it or pretend that her anger had been unfocused, impersonal. Instead, Grace could only think of Alls, and the hard, committed patience of his stare, as though for the entire time she'd known him, he'd been watching a clock, awaiting his release.

Prison would have destroyed Riley. She tried hard not to think so, but she knew. She imagined him laughing at someone, so used to being liked, and getting punched in the gut. She saw him in brief loops, flip-books, in which he collapsed like a pool float, again and again.

Hanna unhooked her ankle and leaned back. "You don't know them anymore," she said. "And I bet they never knew *you* at all."

Jacqueline clacked over to their table. "What is that, alcohol? Wipe that up, the smell is horrid. Julie, come with me."

The job was another ring, a hulking emerald with trillion-cut diamonds the size of Grace's eyeteeth on either side. Jacqueline looked right at Grace and told her to replace the diamonds with something less valuable. The owner, she said, wanted to give the diamonds to her son's new wife.

"What a lovely mother-in-law," Grace said.

"Use moissanite," Jacqueline said. "It's warmer." She hurried to open a second box and then stopped, patted the lid back down, and closed her hand over it. "One thing at a time," she said. "You'll need to go to Fassi."

Grace had been to Fassi only twice before, for rhinestones. Then, she had taken the pieces with her so she could match the replacements. "Just don't get mugged," Jacqueline had said when Grace left with an art deco jeweled hand mirror in her purse. For a thief, Jacqueline was awfully trusting of others—or perhaps just arrogant. She probably thought Grace lacked the nerve to steal from her.

"We'll need to measure them here," Jacqueline said. "Obviously, you can't take this out."

Obviously. Grace went back to her desk for a ruler and a loupe. Perhaps Jacqueline did not trust her quite as much as she'd thought. When she returned, Jacqueline was on her knees, opening the safe. Grace sat down in her boss's chair and switched on the desk lamp. She held the ring against the ruler. The stones were nine millimeters on each side and six millimeters deep at the point. She peered through the loupe, looking at the way they sparkled.

"Nine on each side, six deep." Grace noticed a minute speck near the bottom tip of one of the diamonds. An inclusion. These diamonds were very real indeed.

Jacqueline leaned back on her heels and held out her palm for the ring. She restacked the boxes deep in the safe and clanked the door shut.

"A friend of mine since we were teenagers—her husband has a little jewelry shop." Jacqueline paused to frown. "Monsieur had a heart attack and she has been at loose ends, trying to keep up while he's recovering. They still have orders that came in before his accident. They have small children, and it's just chaos for her."

Grace knew the trap of trying to explain your answers before anyone asked a question. She smiled and nodded. "You're a good friend."

On the bus, bouncing toward Fassi in Montmartre, Grace sat next to a girl just a few years younger than she was. The girl held her gray leather purse in her lap and balanced a book on it. She was reading Huysmans, *À Rebours*. The copy was new, its pages bright and flat, no dog-earing or wavy expansion from reading in the tub. Her fingernails were smooth ovals, unpolished and startling in their pink health.

"I love that book," Grace said, scarcely aware that she was speaking.

"It's for school," the girl said, her French flat and closed-throated.

"You're American?"

She blushed and smiled grimly. "Yes, sorry, my accent is not very good."

Grace shook her head. "No, it's good! You're studying abroad? What's the course?"

"Literature of the Belle Époque."

"Oh, are you reading *Bel-Ami*?"

The girl nodded vigorously. "I love that novel! It is very scandalous!"

Grace almost laughed. To be scandalized by the mustachioed gigolos of the 1880s! Her chest cramped with regret. This girl's was the life Grace would have had—should have had—if she hadn't done so many stupid things trying to get it. The bus was not at Grace's stop yet, but she rose to get off.

"Enjoy your trip," she said in English, smiling at the girl, whose eyes lit up at Grace's American accent. Grace had delighted her.

She pushed toward the front and hurried off the bus.

How much time did she have left? Telling Hanna the truth—*the truth*, out and gulping for breath, squalling for attention—had left Grace exposed. It didn't matter whom you told: A secret always sought its own life. Someone would find her now, or Jacqueline would get shut down, maybe arrested, or Grace would. She needed to leave. It was time to start over again, somewhere bigger this time, or more difficult.

How different from her that girl had looked. Those fingernails, like a living doll's.

Grace stopped under an awning, next to a wire carousel of black-and-white postcards, and waited for her light-headedness to pass.

Fassi was two blocks farther. The gall of Jacqueline, lying to her so obviously—she could have at least taken out the stones first and told Grace they'd fallen out. That would have been considerate, to spare the underpaid, immigrant help the burden of knowing.

She pushed the buzzer outside Fassi's building. "Julie, for Jacqueline Zanuso," she shouted into the static of the ancient intercom. She climbed the stairs to the third floor and wound around the cracked marble corridor to Fassi's door.

He pushed the door open just a crack—she knew to catch the knob before it fell shut again—and returned to his post behind the glass case.

"Vous-desirez?" His grumble was half phlegm, half resentment. "I'm having lunch soon."

She pulled out her crumpled slips. He shuffled to the long row of card catalogs and map chests that lined the back wall. He flipped through file cards, returning with three brown paper envelopes, each in use for many years, old tape clinging to their edges. Grace pulled a velveteen mat in front of her and they each grabbed a loupe.

"How many?"

"Two, a matched pair."

He muttered as he sorted and measured the trillions. They easily found a pair in the right size, but Fassi discarded one after looking at it through his loupe. He set it aside and ran his stubby finger through the pile, looking for another.

"What's wrong with that one?" she asked him.

"Not perfect." He shrugged. "A little ribbon near the bottom."

"An inclusion? In moissanite?" She picked up the stone. He was right. The white needle, like a crack in ice, was so tiny she had to squint to see it even with a loupe.

Fassi set two more stones with the first trillion. "You choose," he said. "These are all good."

She paid with the blank check Jacqueline had sent with her, made out to Fassi, and he handed her the taped paper parcel, no bigger than a saltine cracker.

Grace hadn't known that moissanite had inclusions. Of course it did; moissanite was natural, flawed like any precious stone.

She fished out her crumpled note again, making a sour face.

"Wait," she said. "I was supposed to get *two* pairs. Four of them." She frowned in annoyance. "I'll have to take the one with the inclusion. And I already gave you that check." She rummaged in her purse for her wallet. "How much for the bad stone?"

"Eh, you can take it for two twenty-five."

He was ripping her off. "And two fifty for the other. Here's four seventy-five." She made a neat stack of notes on the counter. Her rent money. He raised his eyebrows.

"She better reimburse me quickly," Grace said.

It was possible Jacqueline had noticed the small inclusion in the diamond trillion, but Grace was certain she would not have inspected it closely enough to register its exact size and shape. Still, her palms grew damp. The only thing she was sure of was the flaw's placement. Even if Jacqueline hadn't thoroughly examined the inclusion, the ring's owner might have. It would be a month's rent and nowhere to go if she were caught.

No. This ring wasn't owned by a gemologist. Someone had been sloppy enough to trust Jacqueline, whose fingers were too stiff to repair fine work but plenty sticky enough to steal it. Even to a jeweler, an inclusion didn't warrant truly investigative attention, only enough to dock the stone's value accordingly.

When Grace returned to the workshop, she showed the pair of perfect trillions to Jacqueline, who looked them over next to the ring and nodded. "I'll bring the ring out to you in a moment."

Grace went back to her desk. Hanna was there, biting her lip as she clipped the loose ends from wire loops. Grace took the imperfect trillions out of her purse and began to work them over with a damp cloth.

Jacqueline came out with the ring and pulled up a chair. She was going to sit there and watch as Grace removed the diamonds.

"I'm going to put them right back in the safe," Jacqueline said. "We can't have diamonds floating around the piles of sawdust and glue guns."

There was no sawdust. There were no glue guns. Their workshop was spotless.

"Of course," Grace said, carefully setting the wad of cloth, trillions deep inside, on the table. Damp, the cloth stayed together. "I don't think they'll be hard to remove."

The ring was old, the gold soft, and Grace's prong lifter easily pulled apart the weak jaws of the jewels' settings. She lifted out one trillion, and then the other. There was a rim of grayish gunk around the perimeter, decades of dirt, hand lotion, and flaking skin cells.

"Let me clean them up," she said.

Jacqueline stared at the diamonds in Grace's left palm as though they might jump up on their own. Grace took the balled cleaning cloth in her right hand and let the stones fall into a fold. She massaged one through the cloth, and then the other, feeling for the other stones, deeper in the fabric. When she found them, she reached into that fold and plucked them out. She dropped the two moissanite trillions into Jacqueline's waiting hand, one of them featuring a small inclusion.

"Perfect, thanks," Jacqueline said, standing up. She hurried back to her office, leaving Grace alone with diamonds and disbelief.

"She's got you on the leash now," Hanna said.

She had not seen.

"Stop pretending you wouldn't do it, if you had nowhere else to go," Grace said. "I can't say no. You're almost finished with the centerpiece and there's nothing else."

Satisfied surprise flickered across Hanna's eyes.

"I'm only worth what someone will pay me," Grace said.

Hanna had nearly finished the centerpiece, earlier than she had expected, but she had been interrupted by no other jobs. Grace felt a peculiar envy as she looked at the centerpiece. She wanted something beautiful to work on, something with some substance and worth and history. It was impossible to hang on to any ideals in the current atmosphere. What beauty was there to aspire to?

Grace cleanly set the pair of perfect moissanite trillions in the ring, next to the solitaire. She looked at the prongs through her loupe. They were gently closed and clinging tightly to the stones. Perfect.

She took the ring to Jacqueline, who uncrossed her legs to lean forward and admire it in the light of her desk lamp. "You really can't tell," Jacqueline said. "Moissanite. It's a shame the name is so ugly."

It was right to steal the diamonds because Jacqueline was a thief herself, and because she had used Grace to help her steal. She hadn't given Grace any choice *but* to steal. And the high, the *high* that raced up and down her, was electric, filling her head with champagne fizz, causing curls to spring up in her hair at her temples, making her forget, for moment, everything else.

26

Parolees Still Missing

August 21

Cy Helmers

The Tennessee Department of Corrections continues to search for two missing parolees. While it was initially believed that the men may have absconded together, law enforcement officials now believe the men may be acting or traveling independently.

Riley Sullivan Graham, 23, was last seen Saturday at Swiftway Dry Cleaning in Garland, where he had been employed since his release from the Federal Correctional Complex in Lacombe.

Allston Javier Hughes, 23, is believed to have disappeared as early as Thursday night from his place of residence, 441 Jewett Road in Garland. After Hughes missed a scheduled meeting, his parole officer contacted Hughes's father, employer, and known associates, including Graham and his family.

Graham and Hughes were paroled on August 10 after serving 36 months for robbing the Josephus Wynne Historic Estate in June 2009.

The Department of Corrections has issued warrants for both men's arrests.

She didn't know what to make of it.

Freindametz had gone out but left the TV on. A French game show cackled and screamed from her bedroom and Grace went in to switch it off. She wished she weren't alone in the house. She poured herself a glass of the Scotch she kept far back on a high shelf above the stove and sat down on the stairs.

If they'd headed for different places, they were after different things. Alls would start over, finally. Better to be a nobody headed nowhere than to be a convict in Garland, surrounded by Kimbroughs and people like them.

But Grace was not going to sit and wait for Riley to find her. Whatever he wanted from her, he would have to find somewhere else. She trudged up the stairs and set her sweating glass down on her nightstand. She fumbled in her bag for the brown paper envelope and unwrapped the trillions, adding them to the scattering of diamonds that was already sparkling there on the desk. God, how they gleamed, even in the dark. She turned on her bedside lamp and sat there on the edge of her single mattress, staring at the big stones, like two bright eyes, looking at her and everything else.

"Your problem," Riley had shouted during one of their fights, "is that you want everyone to think you're so goddamn special, but *you* don't even think you're that special. No one is!"

"I'm not special," she'd protested. "Please, I don't think that at *all.*"

"EXACTLY!" he'd roared.

Grace sipped her drink.

She had just been looking for the most love, that was all. Like anything you believed to be scarce, you had to take it for yourself wherever you found it.

Lachaille would buy the trillions. Maxine Lachaille knew her well enough now; she might even take them for cash, though not for nearly as much as if Grace had had enough time to set them in something. Selling a naked diamond was nearly impossible, but Grace would have to try tomorrow and leave Paris straight after. It didn't matter that Jacqueline knew Mme Lachaille, as long as Grace left right away. That was a guarantee, Grace decided, that she would really go.

She pulled down her suitcase and began to fill it. Her books would have to stay. Just clothes. She pulled her skirts and dresses off their hangers and dropped them in. She'd buy a train pass and start moving; that was the main thing. She listened to a woman outside chattering at her baby as she pushed a stroller along the bumpy sidewalk. It was dark. In the apartment across the street, the teenage boys were smoking pot and listening to drum solos.

Because of the drumming, she didn't hear the knocking right away. But when the drums quieted, the knocking kept on.

Someone was knocking at the front door.

She looked out the window to the street below but saw no car. She tried to see around the awning over the front door, but she could see nothing.

No one ever knocked on the door. Freindametz's daughter just barged in.

Riley. She had known it would happen just this way.

Grace sat on her bed and waited—for what, she didn't know. If she went downstairs and opened the door, there he would be, her cheated husband who never broke a promise.

The knocking stopped.

Grace stood next to the window, looking out from where she couldn't be seen. No one.

Then she heard the door open. The hinge squeaked and the sound hung there. Shoes. Slow, pausing, stopping, looking around.

On the stairs now.

It could be Hanna, or some disgruntled boyfriend of Freindametz's daughter, looking for her. Was she sure Freindametz didn't have a son? A husband. A handyman. Any man she did not know. The footsteps, though soft, were a man's.

On her little writing desk was a cup of pens, some scissors, a sterling letter opener. She reached for the letter opener and shut it in her fist. She should have turned around but she was scared to.

In the hall.

He cleared his throat behind her and she knew, she knew, she knew.

"Grace," he said. "Long time no see."

27

Alls was taller than Grace remembered, and broader. His chest was deep and upright, not crouched and hollow like it used to be. She couldn't yet stand to look at his face.

"It's you," he said. "I knew I would find you, but I still can't believe I did."

Grace stepped backward, but there was only wall behind her. Alls shut the door.

He took her hand in his and looked over her nails, her hot palms. She stared at his fingers, his knuckles, his wrist, the cuff of his sleeve. She couldn't stand him touching her. She held tight to the letter opener in her other hand. She knew he'd seen it.

He dropped her hand and sat down on her bed. "You look exactly the same," he said.

He flicked his eyes up at her impatiently. She sat down next to him, nearer her pillow, enough space for another person between them.

He took out a cigarette and offered it to her first. Grace shook her head and smoothed her skirt over her thighs. His were already splayed out care-lessly. He rooted for a lighter in his jacket pocket. The weight on her narrow, lumpy mattress shifted and her body pitched toward him. She reached out to steady herself, trying not to touch him. She crossed her legs and pulled at the hem of her dress, like some schoolgirl at a babysitting interview, and he laughed, though exactly how he was laughing she couldn't tell. He was a stranger.

"You didn't think I would come," he said.

"No," she said. "Or, not alone."

She saw the twitch of surprise in his neck.

"This isn't what I thought Paris would look like," he said.

"It's only Paris in the municipal sense."

"This room is very similar to the last bedroom we sat in together." He patted the blanket on either side of him. "Little bed against the wall. One window to the street. Little desk, little chair."

Grace felt like Alice, already little herself and shrinking to a crumb.

"A dorm room," he said. "You came all the way over here to live in the same goddamn dorm room?" He nodded toward the window. "Cobblestones, I guess."

He had lines around his eyes already, as if he had been squinting into the sun for years. But the sadness she used to see there was gone. She didn't know what she saw instead. She had imagined this moment, a hundred variations on the wrong theme, for years, and now Alls had broken into her house and she didn't think it was her place to ask why.

"How did you find me?" she asked him.

"It's always *how* with you. Never why."

"I can't ask you that," she said. "I don't think I want to know."

He stood up and went to her bookshelf, stooping to look over the titles. He went to her desk and picked up one of the trillions, rolling it between his thumb and forefinger. "Still a magpie," he said quietly. He turned toward her and she flinched.

"You think I came all this way to *hurt* you?"

"I'm sorry, I didn't—"

"You don't know me anymore. I get that." He shrugged and nodded toward her desk, toward the loose diamonds and piles of books under the poster of Petit Trianon that hung over her desk. "Is it possible you haven't changed? That as different as I am, you've just been sitting up here in your little room, changing your hair but staying the same?"

She shook her head. "I'm not the same."

"What," he said, looking toward the diamonds again. "You steal those yourself?"

But stealing alone was a real difference, wasn't it? She had grown up, if sideways. She raised her eyes to meet his. "I did."

He raised his eyebrows.

"I know what you must think of me," she started.

"You can't imagine," he said.

"Where's Riley?"

"No," he said. "I'm not taking questions just yet."

"Please tell me," she begged him. "You don't know what I—"

"I don't?" he shook his head. He reached for her drink and when he saw that it was empty, he asked for his own. "Scotch?" he said in disbelief. "Benedict Arnold."

"When in Rome, you'll take any whiskey," she said evenly. "Did you want a cup of tea?"

She needed him out of her room. He followed her downstairs to the kitchen table, where she poured them both a finger of Scotch.

"How was your day?" he said, as though they sat there often.

"Not my best," she said.

"Why, what happened? Get caught with your hand in the till?"

"Christ," she said. "What is this?"

"That's his word, not yours." He crossed one of his legs over the other. "I thought this was how it was supposed to be. We'd run off together and live happily ever after, and at the end of the day we'd have a drink and talk about our days. I'm just trying it out. Seeing what might have been."

"The good life? Alls, you can't know how sorry—"

"Hush," he said. "You had a long time to speak up, and that moment has passed." He paused. "Where is it?"

The painting. "I don't have it," she said. "I sold it, and then the money was stolen from me."

"Nobody likes to be lied to."

"I'm not lying," she said. "I was rich for sixteen hours."

"How much did you get for it?"

"Seven hundred thousand euros. Just shy of a million dollars."

He whistled. "You said you'd get two million."

"I was wrong. Cash-only limits your market."

"Well," he said, "guess I'll be heading home, then."

She didn't say anything.

"You could have told me," he said, and then he laughed. "You could have told me a lot of things." He pulled his glass across the table, watching the trail of condensation.

"What did you want me to say?"

"That you'd married him. That you were still together, actually."

"Would it have mattered to you?"

"Doubt it. I'd lost my mind."

She couldn't look him in the eye for very long before her own eyes began to burn. She kept looking away, just behind him or beside him, but still she could feel his eyes.

"I can't believe it's really you," he said.

She wasn't sure it was, really. She had undergone too many transformations to know. She had been a tutor, a prostitute, a chambermaid, and Julie from California. She had been twice robbed and partly scalped. Now she was an antiques restorer and a part-time jewel thief. She swallowed. "How did you find me?"

He smiled now, but she didn't know what his smile meant.

He had imagined she had stayed in Europe, he said. He knew that she had not come back to Garland after the arrest. He imagined she'd sold the painting, that either she was back in antiques or jewelry or art, or she was a kept woman.

"Thanks a lot," she said.

"The beauty-for-profit sector, I figured that much. And in a major city: London, Paris, Tokyo. Probably Paris. I mean, you speak the language."

"You didn't come all the way here because I took French in high school."

He ignored her. "I was going to be locked up for close to three years, if I was real good and real lucky." He leaned back in his chair. "I feel like I should talk slow to make sure you get a sense of the time. Do you understand the kind of time we're talking about here? Days are just gravel underfoot. Do you have any idea what I'm talking about?"

"I might," she said carefully. Beneath her fear, she felt an ache of longing that she knew couldn't be returned.

"And at first, I'll admit, I just wanted to find you to win. I wanted to scare you." He swallowed tightly. "I couldn't *believe* you married him. Then. I think I get it now." He paused. "You know, I used to imagine what my life would be like if I were Riley. All the time. He had everything and everyone I wanted. Less often, and this is pathetic, I'd even settle for Greg's life. But I'd never thought about what it might be like to be you."

Grace reddened. "We wanted the same thing," she said.

"I always thought of myself as Riley's worse half, if you were his better."

She smiled grimly.

He leaned forward and his chair legs hit the floor. "Anyway, hundreds of magazines came in every month. Mostly shit, but we *treasured* them. A paper scrap of the outside world, a piece of personal property you don't have to guard. A magazine! And when guys are done with them, if they're in good shape and not ripped up or covered with piss and whatnot, they go to the library. I spent a *lot* of time in the library, my last year. I didn't get library privileges until then."

He looked excited, as though he were about to explain a card trick. "*Architectural Digest*, May 2011. You've seen it?"

"I don't read it."

He cocked an eyebrow. "You used to."

"It's too Hollywood," she said. "You read that in *prison?*"

Alls rolled his eyes. "I apologize—what magazines do you think are convict appropriate? What books? My cellmate wrote dirty poems by circling single letters in *The Purpose-Driven Life.* Another guy stuck his eyelashes and eyebrow hairs to the wall with his own spit, made little drawings with them. There were eighty-three books in the prison library, and I read every one of them. I read anything—*Rolling Stone*, *Maxim*, fucking *Country Weekly*, cover to cover. But I guess we're all supposed to act like the convicts we are, right?"

"I'm sorry," she said. "I wasn't thinking."

"A thick stack of *Architectural Digests* showed up in the library when somebody got released and left them behind."

He looked at her, his eyes fixed just below hers, on her nose or her chin or her neck. He was disappointed, and she wanted to explain that she had been thinking of them, all the time. She'd thought of them so much that she'd fixed a narrow vision in her mind and populated it with details that were now irrelevant.

He pulled out his wallet and from it unfolded a worn page, white at the creases.

"There," he said.

"Americans in Paris," the article was titled. "Emile Eustace and Heather Franks indulge in Americana elegance in their Triangle d'Or loft." A reedy, bespectacled man in a black western-wear shirt stood behind a tan blond woman in a Federal Bentwood armchair. Surrounding the text were photographs of the couple's prized possessions: a wrought-iron cane rack, a Chippendale tall-case clock, a birchbark canoe that they had mounted high on the wall, and a bracelet of horse cameos. Grace's bracelet.

She gasped.

"You can take the girl out of Tennessee," Alls said.

"*Equestrian Cameo Charm Bracelet, c. 1880,*" the caption read. "*'We found this treasure at a little jewelry shop in Saint Germain des Prés.'*"

Mme Lachaille had only given her four hundred for it, the weasel.

How little it mattered that Grace had hidden, changed her name, changed herself inside and out. Riley's family heirloom had tracked her across an ocean.

"I couldn't believe it either," he said. "I thought it would take me *years.*" He brushed imagined dust from the picture with his thumb in what appeared to be a habit. "But you were in the goddamn library."

"I could have moved," she said, her voice catching. "I sold that thing years ago."

"Yeah, I know. I checked with Cy when I got out to be sure."

"*Cy?* Helmers?"

"How many people do you think read the *Albemarle Record* outside the state, even the county? You should have seen the map, Gracie. He pulled it up in two minutes. You're this red dot that never quits blinking."

Grace was speechless. Of course. She spent her days nursing the artifacts of centuries past, but she couldn't escape the year she lived in.

"There are only eight little jewelry shops in the Saint whatever. I took my picture and asked around—but for the bracelet. I told her I collected cameos."

"She didn't *believe* that," Grace protested.

"You're the one who told me collectors were snotty creeps. You called them 'dollhouse fetishists,' remember?" He shrugged. "It's not a real complex persona."

"I didn't think you did personas."

"I've learned that it pays to be flexible."

"She told you where I worked," Grace said. She had left America and made Paris into a town as small as Garland.

"Yes, *Julie*, she did. It's easy to find what you want, if you pretend you're looking for something else."

Greg had given Riley and Alls ten thousand dollars each in cash—guilt money, start-fresh money—upon their release. He had gone to work in his mother's wine shop—he could never become a lawyer now—and saved for his friends' release. He had brought Alls care packages—requested books, candy, better socks—every month. Greg, Alls said, would be ashamed for the rest of his life. He was castrated with it.

Alls left town with his magazine clipping. He'd procured the necessary travel documents with the assistance of a friend of a friend he had met in the prison library, "reading *National Review*," he added.

"You have a fake passport?" Her own false identity was so flimsy in comparison.

"I couldn't have left otherwise, and now I can't go back."

"Why would you do that, violate your parole? Risk *more* jail time?"

"There's nothing there for me, Grace. My parole is contingent on me living with my father. In Garland. Some people can do that, but I can't."

"I know," she said quietly. "I couldn't."

He was silent for too long and she hurried to fill the space. "When did you get here?"

"Two days ago," he said. "Today, I followed you home, rode behind the bus on a bicycle."

"And what—what were you planning to do, once you found me?" The real question, the one she wanted to ask but could not bear to, scratched in her throat like a struggling cough.

He shrugged. "That depended on who I found."

He wanted to know everything she did at Zanuso et Filles. She told him she restored antiques. Her boss gave her broken things, and her job was to unbreak them. What kinds of things, he asked. All kinds, she said. Furniture, lamps, china, weird old art projects. She told him she filled gouges, melted enamel, puzzled together shattered porcelain, cleaned dirt from unseen crevices, found duplicate handles, bases, hinges, and pulls when the originals had been lost—

"You love it," he said.

"I do," she admitted.

He looked around. "They don't pay you much."

"It's not that. I really like the things. I don't have to talk to the owners, who I'd probably hate. I just make repairs, and take my pleasure in the beauty of the thing itself." She tried to explain to him how the work— repetitive, probing, apologetic, minute—felt like a service. Not to people, but to the objects.

"A penance," he said. "You're doing penance."

"In a way."

"For what we stole, not who we stole it from, and not to me, not to Riley."

"No one made you rob the Wynne House," she said.

"Where does stealing diamonds fall within this belief system of yours?"

"My crooked boss had me stealing for her, replacing diamonds with fakes."

"So you're skimming a little off the top. That's beautiful." He stretched, wrenching his back from side to side. He reached down into his pants pocket and then spread her trillions and her little stones on the table. She had not seen him take them. He turned a trillion to catch the light and studied the bright spots that floated on the ceiling.

"Gracie," he said. "You know you owe me."

28

So she'd learned about jewelry, he said. Not much, she protested. She didn't know *about* jewelry, only the simple mechanics. Jewelry repair was a skill accidentally acquired.

"Like you and the locks," she said. "You had perfectly fine reasons for picking locks."

"Perfectly fine," he said wryly. "Almost like we couldn't help it, what happened after."

"Where is he?" she begged.

He smiled. "Show me your office. I'd like to see where you work."

"I don't have a key," she lied.

He shrugged: a minor inconvenience.

It was after two o'clock in the morning. No metro. He told her to call a taxi.

"Tell him to pick us up at your stop and drop us off at—what's the nearest landmark building to you?" When he saw that she would not help him, he rolled his eyes. "I have the address. I've already been there. Just save me the step, okay?"

"Sacré Coeur," she said.

They walked to Gallieni in the balmy night haze, passing no one on the street but a group of teenage boys who heard Alls's English from up the block and began making lewd comments in approving tones. They were excited, Grace could tell. Tourists never came to their neighborhood.

"Put it in her ass tonight, man? Put it in her ear?" The boy couldn't have been eighteen. "I bet she sucks it good."

"Mange de la merde," she said, passing them by.

In the cab, Alls chattered loudly about how excited he was to be here with her, and how sorry he was that they had to stay in such a crappy hostel, but if she could just see past that for a sec she'd see that they were finally in the most romantic city in the world, headed toward Sacray Core late at night, and did she bring the camera, and baby please don't pout, I promise I'll bring you back in ten years and we'll do it up in style. Grace was mute with anxiety, the color gone from her face and her lips dry, but when the driver glanced at her in his rearview mirror, her grim pallor only added to Alls's charade.

The walk from the cathedral to Zanuso was just over a kilometer.

Grace had so many questions for Alls that she was scared to ask because of all the questions he could ask her in return. The small, impossible hope she had felt that he was here because he still loved her was drying up, a persistent drip from a faucet finally wrenched closed.

"I don't know what you think I can give you," she said. "I have nothing."

"And isn't that why you're taking me to your work? Because when you have nothing to give, you take from someone else?"

"You can have the diamonds," she said.

"I already have the diamonds," he snapped. "How much you reckon those are worth?"

"The little ones aren't much, maybe four hundred each, but those trillions are special. At least five thousand each, as much as ten. Euros. I'm far from expert but you could take those and get on the Eurail and sell them in Madrid next week for fifteen thousand dollars, probably."

"Bullshit," he said. He put his hands in his pockets. "But is that what you think the last three years of my life are worth? Five thousand dollars a year?"

"No," she said quietly. "But I'm not going to help you. I'm not going to steal anything."

"Anything else," he said.

"Anything else," she sighed.

"If only I believed you," he said. "But it's not like I found you working in an orphanage, healing the sick or disfigured. I see great potential here."

Grace was worn out with fear and now she was exasperated. "Just tell me what you want from me."

"I want from you what you wanted from me."

"I wanted you," she said.

"Too little, too late."

They were quiet for a minute, listening to the echo of their footsteps on the sidewalk. Grace wondered what would happen if she ran.

"I was bringing the bags from the study to the living room," he finally said. "Riley was loading up his own bags. The front door opened, and the old groundskeeper was standing there."

She listened.

"And Riley ran at him."

That hadn't been in the papers.

When Alls saw the groundskeeper, his first thought was to turn around, to hide his face. And so he saw Riley, in the doorway behind him, his face monstrous with fright, run at the groundskeeper holding an andiron over his head. The groundskeeper, clutching his trash bag, fell against the doorway, hitting his head on the jamb, and dropped to the floor. The andiron swept through the empty air at the end of Riley's arm.

"If that andiron had hit him, that man would have died right then," Alls said. "But no one knows Riley swung it except for me and Riley. Not even the groundskeeper. He couldn't even pick Riley out of the lineup."

Alls called for Greg, who came crashing down the hall with his bags and kicked the door open. He ran out to the car, jumping over the old man on the floor. Riley stood over the groundskeeper, staring at his slackened face, until Alls shouted at him to get moving. They drove to the Walmart and switched cars, but Riley was a wreck. He stayed glued to the TV at the lake house, certain that they were missing crucial details because their crime was only regional news at Norris Lake, not local news. He wouldn't go to New York and he was in no shape to anyway. He had sorely overestimated his own nerve.

"When you left with the painting," Alls said, "you left me with him."

"You could have made the switch that night," she said. "Or shredded his copy and left it all behind."

"How was I supposed to believe in you at all, huh? You have me tear out the painting for you, you have Riley fake a copy for you. I'm sure there's a real deep record of things you *didn't* do."

"I wanted you to come. I was just worried something else would go wrong—"

"And it did."

Riley insisted on returning to Garland; he said it was less suspicious for him to be there, like everything was normal, even though he himself wasn't normal at all. The groundskeeper didn't improve and Riley started threatening to turn himself in. He listened to the people on the news describe the thugs who'd locked a frail volunteer in an airless room and couldn't believe they meant *him*. He wouldn't leave the house, and for three days he neither showered nor slept. He had glued himself to the TV and seemed to be praying to it, for the groundskeeper to pull through, for himself to wake up from a bad dream.

"And you were worried about the painting," Grace said. She'd played out the scenarios in her mind thousands of times: They discovered the painting was missing and blamed the culprits of the second crime for the earlier one; or Alls was found out and then so was she.

"No," he said. "Not that."

"You weren't?"

"You were so focused on the painting," he said. "The days before you left—like you didn't trust me with it. And I started to wonder if you really wanted me at all." He stopped and looked at her. "I really wasn't sure. And then you took it."

I wanted you, she wished she could say.

They had reached Zanuso. "Stand here," he said. He nodded to the brick wall, under the awning. "Watch," he said, nodding first toward the street and then up at the building's windows. He seemed comfortable; he knew where he was.

There was not a soul in sight. Alls got to his knees. When he moved his feet, his shoes made no scuffing sound against the pavement, as though he were barefoot. He reached under his shirttail and took from just inside the waistband of his jeans a leather case. He silently unzipped it and pulled out a small tension wrench and a steel pick. He wriggled the short end of the wrench into the keyhole and then slid the pick in next to it. She couldn't tell him she had a key now. He pushed gently on the wrench, bobbing it clockwise, as he pushed and pulled the pick with his other hand, raking the inside of the lock. He frowned, and Grace looked nervously up and down the block. Still silent. Alls pulled the pick and wrench from the lock and slid the pick back into his case. He chose a small hooked one now, and, shifting his crouch to get even closer to the lock, he slipped the hook inside the keyhole and began to probe, pushing down on the handle, then pulling the pick out a bit and pushing down again.

She heard something inside the building and touched his shoulder, but he had already heard it. His tools were out of sight and he was on his feet, hustling her toward the corner. They made it just around when she heard the door burst open, a man muttering to himself as he hurried up the sidewalk in the other direction, the door falling shut behind him. She could hear Alls's heartbeat against her, or maybe she could feel it through his clothes and his skin.

He worked on the lock for what felt like a very long time, but when Grace looked at her watch, only ten minutes had passed. She heard a car, probably two blocks away but getting closer. Alls pulled the pick from the lock and made one quick tug upward on the wrench. The lock clicked. He turned the doorknob and nodded for her to enter.

She let him close the door behind her. He was almost silent, and in the dark, with only her yellow dress as light, it seemed impossible that she was not alone. But she heard his voice behind her. "Go on," he whispered.

She reached out for the wall to steady herself, and she followed it to the stairwell. She groped for the rail and stepped down, one two three, feeling the wall for the turn, and then the nine steps to the bottom. And then there was another door, and another lock.

This time, he used a flashlight. He had it open in two minutes.

Grace had spent hundreds of hours alone in the studio late at night, lights blazing. But now she was scared to touch the light switch.

"You know what they say," he joked, his voice overwhelming the dark. "Weakest part of a lock is the keyhole."

She felt him in the room, moving silently about. She stood still. In a moment he had turned on her desk lamp.

He looked over her table, the tools neatly grouped by form and by function in glass jars, the stack of folded cloths.

"You should pick locks," he said, more to himself than to her. "You'd be great at it."

He walked around to the Czech centerpiece. "What is this fairyland here?"

She took a deep breath. "You can't take that. You'd never find a buyer for it."

"I just asked what the hell it *is*," he said. "It's as big as a doghouse anyway."

She toured the centerpiece for him, the silk cornstalks and beaded trees, the muslin shepherdesses and wax peaches. Hanna had done such beautiful work.

"The peaches are mine," she said. "And these acorns, this beading."

"What about the jewelry?" he asked. "Where is that?"

"In her office," Grace said, glancing at Jacqueline's doorway.

She followed him in.

"In here?" he asked, pulling open her desk.

"No, in there." She pointed to the stack of magazines sitting in front of the safe.

He took a quick breath and flexed his hands.

"You're kidding," she said.

"You going to try to stop me?"

"Could I?"

"I haven't done this much," he said. "Could take a while." He lay down on the floor, on his belly. His legs bent at the knee and his feet stuck up, shoes dangling. He didn't fit on the floor.

Grace watched for a while as he spun the dial back and forth. "Are you listening to it?" she asked him.

"No," he said. "I wish. These wheels are too light to click."

"What are you doing, then?"

"Not your problem, remember? Any guesses on the combination? Birth date, phone number, weird superstitions?"

"I'm not going to help you," she said.

"Yeah, I got it. You would never."

He asked for scrap paper and a pen, and Grace brought him the supplies from her desk. He began to try combinations and mark them down. What he was doing looked like a joke. Cracking a safe couldn't possibly work this way and he couldn't possibly believe it would.

"You can't try every combination," she said.

"You know, in some ways, you seem really different. Right off the bat. For one thing, you're not trying to get everybody to fall in love with you all the time. Laughing and covering your mouth, telling little stories about how clumsy you are. But you're still a know-it-all."

"If I was so transparent," she started, but he interrupted her.

"To answer your question, I don't think I'll need to try every number." He'd clenched his teeth in concentration. "The wheel was parked at thirteen, so we'll start with that as the last one. And there's a little forgiveness for the shaky handed. Multiples of five should do it."

She didn't know what to do. She sat down in Hanna's chair and flipped through her notes on the centerpiece. *Vendredi, 24 août*, the top page read. Tomorrow. *Nous ratisserons la pelouse et finirons la caisse.* Comb the lawn and finish the case.

Ratisserons, finirons. We will comb, *we* will finish. Hanna had accepted her help more fully than Grace had realized.

At five thirty, he came to her table with three sheets of paper marked up with numbers. "Let's go," he said. "You need to change your clothes."

"I'm not coming to work," she said. She hadn't told him that she'd meant to leave Paris today. "Not if you robbed my boss."

"Yes, you are," he said. "Unless you want her to think you did it."

"Jesus Christ, have you learned nothing?"

"More than you have, apparently. But I didn't get the safe open. Not yet."

"Yet? You think I'm coming back here with you tonight?"

"Yes," he said. "You're going to sit there like a cherub and watch me crack your boss's safe. Because you haven't changed at all, right?"

"You think I get off on this," she said in disbelief.

"I know you do."

They rode home on the first train of the day. She had sometimes gone to work this early, but she couldn't remember ever coming home so late. When they got there, Freindametz was still gone, and Grace found herself relieved. She didn't know what was happening, but at least she didn't have to explain it.

When Grace got out of the shower, Alls was asleep on her bed, on top of the blanket, stretched out straight on his back. Her wet hair dripped down her chest as she watched him. She quietly pulled a skirt and shirt from her closet and took them back into the bathroom to change.

He could have been hers, if she had done it right. But that was an Alls from a long time ago. She didn't know this one at all.

When Grace got to work, only two and half hours after she'd left it, Hanna was checking her measurements for the carrying case. Grace had no work of her own. She watched as Hanna jotted a series of tidy check marks in her notebook. Her vision was distorted with fatigue, every shape over-sharp and indistinct. When she reminded herself that Alls was at home, asleep in her bed, she found herself doubting that it was true. She might have hallucinated it—him, what he would say to her. He might have been a dream. But then, staring at Hanna's table, she saw Hanna's notebook, the familiar printing, and she knew that all of this was very real.

"Hanna," Grace whispered. "He's here. Alls is here."

"This is a great day," Hanna said proudly. "Last tasks. On Monday I send this carnival packing."

Grace stared, and Hanna blinked gaily at her as if she had not heard.

"He broke into my house last night," Grace said.

Jacqueline stepped out of her office and curled her finger toward Grace.

At her desk, Jacqueline took the lid from a cardboard box. Coiled inside was a pearl necklace. "It's filthy," Jacqueline said, lifting it out. Hanging between the pearls were six gold disks with impressions of concentric circles, and in the middle of each disc was a ruby cabochon, each one like a lozenge of melted sugar. They reminded Grace of the cookies Riley used to have in his packed lunches, the ones with a blob of cherry filling.

"Take these stones out and replace them with something semipre-cious," Jacqueline said. "Take out just one to match at Fassi and leave the necklace with me."

This time, she didn't even offer an explanation.

At her table, Grace extracted the first ruby cabochon from its gold doughnut.

"Do you need anything from Fassi?" she asked Hanna, as if she were going out for a sandwich. But Hanna didn't respond, not even a nod, a twitch, a flicker of recognition. It was as though Grace had not spoken at all.

In his shop, Fassi laid out rhodonite, rhodolite garnets, rubellite, red spinel, and lab rubies. He and Grace held each stone up to the light. The lab ruby was closest. The bill for all six was only twenty-two euros. Fassi dropped them in a sack like jelly beans, not even wrapped.

"Hanna," Grace said just before six. "Please talk to me."

"It's too convenient, don't you think?" Hanna was sealing the plywood's edges with polyurethane.

"What?" Grace asked, startled that Hanna had finally responded to her.

"That you tell me this story you've been holding back for years, and now you tell me he's here? A little too neat." She tapped her pencil on the table. "Shit," she grumbled. "I'm going to have to come in tomorrow."

"Why?" Grace asked. "And that's why I told you. Because I was sure they were coming."

"The poly has to cure overnight, and then the glue has to cure before I apply it, and then it takes twenty-four hours to set completely. A messy calendar."

Distrust and then disregard—that was all Hanna would give her. Fine. "Can't you pick it up Monday?" she asked.

"I'm getting a Biedermeier on Monday."

"You are? When did that happen?"

"While you were at Fassi. Jacqueline says it's a beauty, a chaise longue! I've been promised loose gimp and scratched arms." She seemed as pleased as she seemed far away. "I can hardly wait."

Grace's hand was cramped. The sixth ruby popped out, plinking like a tiddlywink on the table. "I'm telling you the truth," she said, nestling the imposter into the gold. "I have no reason not to."

"That's a real problem for you, isn't it? That you need a reason." Hanna pulled off her rubber gloves and dropped them in the trash.

Hanna was packing up her things quickly and Grace hurried to follow her. She returned the necklace and all its parts to Jacqueline without a word and raced up the stairs after Hanna.

"See you Monday," Hanna sang out in the echoing vestibule. She pushed open the front door.

Alls was there waiting, leaning against the building and smoking a cigarette. He didn't look at Grace, giving her the chance to ignore him in front of her coworker, but Grace realized that a beat too late. When Hanna turned to give her a cool wave, Grace's face had already betrayed her.

Hanna noticed the man standing there, the man Grace was trying not to look at. She looked from Alls to Grace and back again

Alls smiled casually. "Hey," he said to Hanna.

"I didn't believe you," Hanna said. She turned and pushed between the people walking too slowly and raced down the sidewalk, her shoulders stiff with being watched.

"You should sleep," Alls said. "Did you sleep at all last night?"

"You know I didn't," she said. "How could I sleep?"

The ease and intimacy with which they were discussing her sleep irritated her. He had come here to claim the painting or what money she had gotten from it. She knew that. Still, desire curled upward, a wisp of smoke. His ease was almost mocking, as though with every casual aside and every unfinished thought, he was reminding her what might have been.

At home she climbed the steps to her room and kicked off her shoes. She lay down on her bed and the scent startled her. Her sheets smelled like a man. She buried her face in her pillow.

He woke her up at midnight. "Got to wake up now, Gracie. We're going to be late for the party."

She blinked. He stood over her, blocking the light that streamed from the hallway. He reached to flick on the overhead light. "Back to work."

That night, Alls filled another three pages with numbers. Grace sat on the floor just outside the office, keeping her eyes open as she had been asked to. She wasn't worried about him cracking the safe, not really. She was leaving anyway. He would get what he wanted and they would part ways, again.

"I hope you're not disappointed when you get in," she said. "There's a very good chance you're going to find nothing but fakes." She thought about the real rubies she had effortlessly returned to Jacqueline that afternoon. She hadn't even *thought* about keeping them, she realized with pride. "I'm almost sure of it."

"Well, we'll see." His voice floated from behind her.

"Why this safe? I can tell you a dozen places more promising."

"Because this is the closest thing I know of to *your* safe. Do you have a safe deposit box you want to tell me about?"

"The stuff on my desk is all I have."

"*Stuff,*" he said. "Too bad for you, then."

"There are other things I can do," Grace said. "Sometimes I fix things up to sell them. I've probably made eight or nine hundred euros this year that way."

"Inkwells," he said. "Weekend projects."

"It helps."

"I can't believe you're not rich yet," he said. "That is what really surprises me. I was sure you'd find a way."

"I'm not qualified for much, you know."

"Look, I'm self-taught too. It's nothing to be ashamed of. A bachelor's degree just isn't for everyone. But I thought you'd be with some asshole, someone really sleazy, like a banker or someone always about to make a movie."

"Lovely," she said. "That's not really my thing anymore."

"What isn't?"

"Hitch your wagon to a star. It turns out I can't stick to the trail."

She heard him scratching his pen at the paper, coaxing out more ink.

"When did you find out we were married?"

"The day after the robbery. He was in a sorry state, telling all his secrets. I had no idea you were such a nasty piece of work, Gracie. That you put him up to the forgery, that it was pretty much an ultimatum—I mean *really.*" He sighed dramatically, sarcastically.

She swallowed. "And when did you tell him—"

"About us?" he asked.

"Yes."

"Never."

"What?"

"I never told him. He doesn't know."

"He doesn't know *what?*"

"Anything. Everything. I told him nothing."

"But what happened when he saw the painting wasn't there?"

"He didn't. I made the switch, I had to. And then he freaked out so bad afterward he didn't want to look at any of the stuff anyway, wouldn't touch the bags. I cut our SkyMall fake into pieces and flushed it down the toilet. I didn't want him to know either, Grace. Not after you'd left me high and dry. You forget that."

It couldn't be.

"I told them I'd hidden the painting in the boat shed," Alls continued. "We'd all agreed that if anything happened, there was no painting, never was. Later, I told Greg I'd destroyed it, and he was relieved. But Riley never said another word about it, not even to me."

But Grace wasn't thinking about the painting. She was thinking about what Riley didn't know about her. He might have sensed *something* about Grace and Alls but never let on, not even to Alls. He had that much pride. It was impossible to think now that Riley didn't know, when for so long she had been sure he did. That his parents didn't know either. Her heart heaved.

"I can't believe you didn't tell him," she said. "Even after you were arrested."

"Why would I? To punish you? To beg for his forgiveness? Grace, he was still talking about you all the time. How disappointed you would be, how he had let you down, how he could tell that you weren't really feeling it anymore but he thought he could get you back."

She had been wrong about everything. She had been carried away on loop after loop, thinking Riley knew everything she had done, that he had thrown open every deception. Now it seemed worse that he didn't know. It meant that she had gotten away with it. She had fixated on so many fears, but that had never been one of them. Grace felt guiltier than she had ever felt before.

"So he still doesn't know," she said dumbly.

"What, you want to go back to him? Is that it?" She heard him push himself up. "Is that what you're telling me?"

"No," she said. He was standing in the doorway. "No, not at all. I just can't believe that all this time I thought—I thought you would—"

"I was in love with you! Do you understand that? Did you *ever* understand that? Maybe you think you bamboozled me or something, that you made me do what I did for you. Well, you didn't." He slid down the doorframe until he was sitting on the floor.

"I did everything I did because I *loved* you," he said. "I fell in love with you when I was sixteen, as stupid as a person ever is, and I couldn't let it go. I stayed in Garland because of *you*. I used to read your books, you know that? I used to go around the house when you weren't home and pick up the books you left splayed open, and I would read the page you'd just read. I never knew what the hell was happening, but that seemed right, in a way, since I never knew what the hell was going on with you. I would read these pages that you'd just read and try to catch some glimpse of you, some clue. No, they weren't pages of your thoughts, but they were as close as I could get, like I was sitting in the seat behind you on a train, seeing every tree the moment after you did. And that is a stupid way to try to know someone, but how *else* can you know someone who refuses to be known?

"When you came home from New York," he continued, "I thought you came home for *me*. I felt horrible about what we did, but when you came home you were going to leave him. I was sure of it. But the looks you gave me that first week, Grace, goddamn. You turned on your fucking flood-light so bright I couldn't see to walk in front of me."

He squinted, watching her closely. "I half expect you to do it right now, but you can't anymore, can you?"

"I don't know what you mean," she said, wishing it were true.

"When I don't want to be looked at, I look *down*, close up, and shut up. But not you. I watched you do it for years—the second anybody crept too close, your motion sensor would trip, and you'd *laugh*, you'd smile, you'd nice up so fast and so bright that you'd bleach out every shadow, every detail. You'd have everyone in the room staring at you and they couldn't see a goddamn thing. You came back and *blinded* me. And I fell for it again and again, just standing there blinking in the dark, because I couldn't stop staring, trying to see."

"I'm so sorry," she said.

"Why? I knew better. You didn't fool me, Grace. I only fooled myself."

"I loved you," she said.

"It doesn't matter now."

29

When they went back to Bagnolet in the morning, Freindametz was making tea in the kitchen, still in her raincoat over her nurse's uniform. She had just returned from the hospital. Usually, she had a cup of tea and then went to bed.

She must have been exhausted from her night of work, because it took her a moment to register the presence of a strange man in her kitchen. She tightened her raincoat as if it were a bathrobe and turned a bitter eye on Grace.

"Qui est-ce?" she asked. "Qui est cet homme?"

"C'est mon cousin, en visite," Grace said. "David, this is Madame Freindametz, my roommate."

"Bonjour," he said badly, extending his hand.

"Where is he sleeping?" Freindametz asked.

"In my room. I'm sleeping on the couch."

"A gentleman," Freindametz sniffed, not believing Grace for a moment. But she took her mug and trundled off to her room, and Grace refilled the kettle.

They slept for a few hours, Freindametz in her room, Alls in Grace's, and Grace on the couch as she had promised. Grace woke up at noon and made coffee. Freindametz stayed asleep and Grace and Alls sat at opposite ends of the couch, drinking coffee, an illustration of something more normal. She did not know what to say to him. Alls flipped through one of Grace's books, looking up now and then to ask her about repoussé or bas-relief. Grace was pretending to read too, but she couldn't. She felt as if she were in a play, and at any minute, a curtain would fall and she would run away, escape through a back door to the alley behind the theater, relieved and devastated with disappointment.

Alls snapped the book shut and asked her what she would usually do, what her day would be like if he were not here. He sounded friendly but cagey, a performance that made her cringe at how she wished for the real thing. Fine, she could do that too. She told him she would probably go to the grocery and then see the traveling exhibition at the Musée des Arts Décoratifs. This month there was a show of trompe l'oeil and pastiches.

He marveled at how boring she was, how consistent in her habits.

"What if I really were just here visiting?"

"How?"

"If you'd gone off to Europe to find yourself, and liked it here and stayed, and left us at home to our own devices, and no one had ever set foot in the Wynne House again. And then I came to Paris to visit my old friend Grace."

He unfolded his crisp tourist map and spread it on the coffee table.

"I can't imagine that," Grace said. "I can't even begin to imagine that life." She stood up. He was at the other end of the sofa, but he seemed to take up all the space in the room. "For either of us. How can you stand it?"

"Don't ask me to comfort you, because I won't."

"I would never."

"And how about if it had gone like it was supposed to?"

"You'd come to Prague with a rolled-up still life and we'd sold it for millions of dollars?"

"And now we lived in Paris together, in the shitty rented room upstairs, poor and hungry and run out of money, but we'd really done it."

No one could have imagined such a life. There was no script for it. It wasn't like being fifteen and imagining yourself in a wedding dress that looked like a wadded-up tissue. It wasn't like attending an art auction and wishing you could transform into someone comfortable, in every sense of the word, like the people standing around you. They had planned a heist, and heist dreams always ended in a firework, the blaze of triumph, nothing of the mess but the smoke that hung over the ground. That was the point. You never dreamed of bickering, whining, trouble banking, stolen luggage, bleeding head wounds, the man you love in prison, and running out of money. You never had to deal with the wreck of yourself, whatever had gone so wrong in your wiring that *this*, this scheme with its fakes and maps and comps and fickle timetables and reliance on old Dorothea Franey's ruined hearing, seemed like the best way out of the life you couldn't live any longer. No. In the dream you only got as far as the sale, the hotel room, the suitcase full of cash, and then what? *What?* She had gotten that far alone, and then she'd learned, grotesquely, that Greg wasn't the only idiot who'd confused real life with the movies.

"I can't imagine that either," she said to Alls.

"Well, let's pretend," he said. "I won't be satisfied with your diamonds, and I'm not going home. So let's just take a Saturday together and pretend we're who we wanted to be." He stood up and got close to her. "Can you do that?"

First they went to the grocery, where Grace nervously chose some plums and Alls marveled over the vast selection of yogurt. She showed him the things that had been unbelievable when she'd first arrived, the minor luxuries that made life here seem more precious, as though you could fill your grocery basket with enough to satiate your whole life's hunger. Fatty yogurt in tiny blue ceramic pitchers, spotty cheese, duck confit in a can, butter wrapped in gingham foil, plums and apricots. On their way back she pointed up to the balconies in the buildings they passed and told him about the old woman who came out to water her hanging baskets in her red nightgown, the kid on the third floor who dropped sacks of something along a cord to waiting children on lower balconies, the set of sliding glass doors that had been painted over in mostly opaque purple streaks.

They walked through the mall at Gallieni and she watched him wonder at how dark and mundane it was, just as she once had, how crass and dumpy. She noticed his peculiar satisfaction in how disappointing Paris could be. They could have been in the Albe-mall, in Pitchfield. She pointed out the Boulevard Périphérique and the man who sold incense under it, the same smell in any country.

When Alls clasped his hands together on the bus, looking around almost shyly, she began to relax, just a little. She wondered if he wanted to prove something, to show her what they could have been, if she'd just stuck with the plan. He didn't know that he already had.

Maybe this fake coziness was another way to shame her. But she would try to believe in it, or look like she did anyway, just for one day.

Lunch was surreal, a blind date in which they knew all the worst of the other person but little else. They ate buttery galettes and drank

Coca-Cola. They laughed at a one-legged crow hopping around the sidewalk, tenacious and accusatory, cawing at the people eating at tables above him. The sight of Alls's teeth when he laughed made her almost dizzy. She wanted to leap across the table and kiss them, to kiss his teeth and his lips and under his jaw. She wanted to hold his head in her hands and feel the weight of it resting on her lap. She wanted to pick the sleep from the corners of his eyes. She wanted to hit him on the chest to feel how real he was, how really *there* he was.

A man at the next table argued on his cell phone. He took off his sunglasses with his other hand and banged them against his table to punctuate his sentences. The man was telling the person on the phone that their offer was too low, that they should offer twice as much to even be in the running. He hung up abruptly and nearly smacked his phone on the table. He ran his hand down his face and then stood up to go inside, probably to the toilet. Alls took the man's sunglasses from the table and tucked them into his pants pocket. No, Grace said softly, almost a whisper.

He raised a corner of his lips.

Because we're being good today, she wanted to say. *Because we're being what we meant to be.*

But good wasn't what they had ever meant to be.

He shrugged, defying her to object further.

And this was what it would have been like, really. Poor and unspeaking, committing petty theft at sidewalk cafés, maybe pawning pricey sunglasses to cover the lunch they'd just bought. Fighting without speaking. Now she could see it.

"This is where you wanted to go?" he asked her as they passed the Musée des Arts Décoratifs.

She shook her head. "It would bore you."

He insisted. Inside, she paid and they walked through the trompe l'oeil exhibit, where whole rooms were rendered in paint, flat on the wall, as though you could step into them. A violin hung from a ribbon on a heavy wooden door. *You see a violin on a door*, the placard read. *There is no violin, and there is no door.* She had read about the painting before. The wording of the placard struck her as particularly French.

Alls's favorite was a painting of a painting: The inner painting was of

Venus, rising naked from the sea, in an ornate frame; the outer painting was of a white cloth draped over the frame to conceal her nudity. The white cloth looked ten times as real as the woman behind it. Grace tried not to read anything into his appreciation of it.

She remembered the grandfather clock Riley had drawn with permanent marker on the wall of their living room on Orange Street.

"Do you remember the clock—"

"Yeah," he said.

There wasn't anything else to say after that, and after a diminished show of appreciation for the next few pieces rendered along the wall, they drifted toward the door. But then Alls caught sight of the sign for the fourth floor, for the traveling Van Cleef & Arpels exhibition. She saw the glint reappear in his eyes.

"It'll be totally clogged with old American women," she said.

"I want to see you see it," he said, making looking at bracelets sound like something dirty.

Grace had been right: In the first room, it was hard to see anything for the women in bright cardigans bent over the glass cases. In the next room, the jewels were mounted behind glass bubbles set into the wall, like in a public aquarium, with a wide round tank on a pedestal in the center. She and Alls slipped into the ring of people.

Much of the jewelry looked like animals. In one brooch, a peacock's tail fanned out into a half dozen individual feathers, scalloped and lined like madeleines. The peacock held a citrine teardrop in its open beak; an emerald carved into a plume arced from its golden head. The lace wings of a wooden butterfly brooch were inlaid gold droplets. An onyx bangle became a panther's carved head on one side and its tail on the other. The tail was inset with oval wreaths of diamonds inset with emeralds carved into tufted pillows. Even the ugly things impressed her; she felt humbled by the detail. She had always found jewelry very boring when it was stripped of sentiment. The shiny rocks, the little claws that held them—the formulas seemed so simple and so limited. But here was a jeweled flower that appeared to be soaked completely red: There were no visible settings, no telltale golden prongs, only an undulating grid of ruby cubes packed shoulder-to-shoulder.

Grace felt the familiar glimmer of envy. These pieces were so far beyond her. She had never made anything from scratch. She could cobble together the picture, but only if it were already broken into jigsaw pieces.

She showed Alls a ring of pavé diamonds surrounding a spray of topaz and pink tourmalines. The design was a bird of paradise, the gem petals' sharp ends tucked safely into gold bezels.

He leaned over the case. "How do you make something like that?"

"I'm not a jeweler," she said, shrugging. These pieces had been made by bench jewelers, niche experts in an assembly line. "I don't know how to dance, just follow."

"Come on," he pressed. "Say that pink one came loose, what would you do?"

"It wouldn't come loose," she said. "It's bezel set, see? You'd have to pry the bezel open all the way around to take the stone out. You cast a cup for the stone out of metal, make the rim too high, and then once the stone is in you have to file the edges down so there's just a shallow lip, and then you push the edges down tight around it. Then you have to burnish them until they're flush and smooth." She shook her head. "Now those little diamonds, the pavé, those are just held in with claws. But it's like a jigsaw puzzle. It's hard to get just one piece out if all the others are in tight. You have to really sneak down under the stone and pop it."

She pointed to a fly brooch with a yellow diamond body and bezel-set lapis eyes. "Now, in that one, the most precious stone is the big yellow one, and it's held in with nothing but a few fingers."

The women next to them were staring. Alls nudged her to move along.

"What do you want from me?" she asked him once they were back on the street.

"Are you going to ask me that every day?"

"How many days are there?"

"I don't know," he said. "I'm collecting on a debt."

"The safe where I work. Will that be enough?"

"I don't know what's in it."

"And you think I'll just go in there Monday morning like everything is fine," she said.

"It will be, for you. You can keep your job."

"Like she won't know," Grace said emptily. She would have to keep going to work now.

"But she won't know, will she? What'll she do, call the police? She's a crook. You said it yourself."

"And you'll rob somewhere else? You think they won't catch you?"

"I don't think they will identify and apprehend me, no."

"Where will you go?"

"You think you're the only girl who works in a jewelry shop?" he said. "I have to think long term."

"You'll leave me when you've emptied it," she said. "You'll leave me alone then."

"Why wouldn't I?"

She had known it was coming, so why did it sting so badly? Not today, she wanted to tell him. Today, they were pretending.

Because it was Saturday night, Alls didn't want to pick the lock before three a.m. He would take as many nights as he needed, he said. It could be forty. He wouldn't rush and risk making a mistake with the safe, skipping a number.

He went to sleep at eleven and set his watch alarm for two. "I suggest you do the same," he said, lying in her bed.

She hadn't his gift for rational sleep execution. She curled up on the couch downstairs and half-watched *Qui Sera le Meilleur Ce Soir?* on TV, pulling at strands of her hair. Tonight Christophe Dechavanne, the diminutive host, presented an array of child performers vying for prize money. A fifteen-year-old boy juggled fruit from a grocery cart. A girl of twelve entwined herself in a length of rope descending from the ceiling to perform proto-sexual acrobatics, her ribs gleaming under her shimmery leotard. Victoria Silvstedt, the towering Swede and retired Playmate who assisted Dechavanne, nodded and clapped squarely and evenly for every performance. The juggler won.

One morning, Hanna would be nursing her Biedermeier and Grace would be leeching diamonds out of a Mickey Mouse brooch or something when Jacqueline discovered the empty safe. Alls would be gone.

Hanna hadn't believed her.

She'd been too caught up in Alls to think about Hanna until now. "I didn't believe you," she had said when she saw Alls. But now she did. When Alls robbed the safe, Hanna would think it was Grace. Why wouldn't she?

Grace was drinking cheap Beaujolais out of a jelly jar when she heard the bed creak and the sound of his feet hitting the floor. He came downstairs with his shoes on. In the kitchen, he plucked an apple from the colander on the countertop and chomped into it. He didn't look the least bit nervous.

"I don't want to come," she said.

"You don't have a choice."

"I don't see what difference it makes. You know what you want and you either get it or don't, and you go. If anything, I'm a liability."

"That's what you said last time," he said. "You never want to help anyone, Grace. You want all the help. But you're coming with me, and you're going to sit there and watch."

30

That night, he picked each lock in less than a minute. He was on his belly before the safe in no time at all. Grace sat down at her desk and slumped with her head in her hands. A strange cocktail, dread cut with impatience. She tapped a pencil against her desk and stared dully at Hanna's table in front of her. The carrying case was where she had left it, in pieces, stained but unassembled.

Grace lightly touched a piece of the particleboard propped in the vise. It was dry. The jar of epoxy Hanna had left overnight was dry too. Grace picked up the jar and jiggled it. A hard crust had formed over the rest, which rolled in a thick goop. It was unusable. Hanna must not have come back today.

But Hanna was supposed to have come back today. She had said that she would. Not only had she said it; she had set up this glue. Hanna would have come back wrapped in coats if she had pneumonia, propped on crutches if she'd broken an ankle. At first Grace didn't even recognize her worry for what it was. Something had happened to Hanna.

She picked up her cell phone and put it back down. She couldn't call Hanna without telling her why she thought something was wrong—that Grace was in the studio at three in the morning. It wasn't unheard of, but she wouldn't *arrive* at three—that was crazy—and besides, Hanna had seen Alls. She would have to call from some other phone. Grace rushed into Jacqueline's office. "I have to step out for a minute."

Alls shot upright and grabbed her wrist. "The hell you do."

"Hanna didn't come in today," she said. "I think something happened to her."

"You're not using this phone. She's going to have to wait until Monday."

"I could go to a pay phone," she said. "But I can't wait. It's not like her."

He looked hard at her, wondering, no doubt, what kind of scheme this was.

"I can even hang up if she answers. I just want to know she's okay."

He shook his head. "It's almost four," he said. "She's not going to answer."

"She's my only friend."

He pulled a flip phone from his front pocket. "I haven't used it yet. Hang up as soon as she answers. If I hear you say even a word, the phone's on the ground."

Grace dialed Hanna's number and it went to straight to voice mail. Dead.

"I would like to call the hospitals," she said.

"Absolutely not."

"I won't identify myself," she said. "If she's there, I'll hang up."

Alls looked up at her as if she'd just entered the first stages of dementia, putting her shoes in the oven or trying to put the trash can inside the trash bag, but he didn't try to stop her. She called the closest hospital, and then another. "Je téléphone pour une patiente, Hanna Dunaj? Est-elle là?" She spelled Hanna's name. "Oui, je suis sa soeur."

Alls gave her a warning look.

She turned to face the wall. They didn't have a Hanna Dunaj, the man said. Grace hung up and called Hanna's phone number again. Dead.

She began to riffle through the contents of her boss's desk, looking for a list of employee phone numbers and emergency contacts, anything. She found it inside Jacqueline's ledger, in the left-hand drawer, a small moleskin notebook. On the inside cover, Amaury's name was scribbled first. The next four names were lined through and scratched out. Grace and Hanna were near the bottom, separated by a few more of the rejected or departed, but there were no other numbers for any of them, no emergency contacts. Jacqueline had never asked Grace for one, but maybe this was another thing they all had in common. Grace felt a knot of worry rising in her throat.

"Enough," Alls said.

"She was upset when she saw you," Grace said. "She thought I was making you up."

"She knew who I was?"

"She knows everything," she said without apology. "I told you, she's my only friend."

"Jesus, Grace, I hope something *did* happen to her. Are you insane?"

I didn't believe you, Hanna had said. Grace couldn't get it out of her head. Why hadn't Hanna believed her? Because she'd lied before, of course. But Hanna had believed enough to be disgusted with Grace, instead of amused or annoyed at the ravings of a harmless lunatic. What she had not believed was that Alls—or anyone, probably—would show up.

How did you ever get anyone to love you like that? Hanna had asked her. Nina, Grace realized.

I was helpless to her, Hanna had said. *I could never get enough.*

It had to be. Grace turned on the computer. She had read about Hanna's past life in the *Copenhagen Post* only weeks ago. This time she searched not for Hanna, but for Antonia Houbraken.

Copenhagen police arrested a woman lurking outside the home of FC Copenhagen player Jakob Houbraken this morning. Antonia Houbraken reported that at around three thirty a.m., she heard someone knocking repeatedly on the door and then trying to get into the house. From her third-story window, Houbraken argued with the intruder, an unnamed woman in her thirties. Police took the intruder into custody. Houbraken was unharmed.

Hanna must have left right from work, right after she saw her with Alls. She wasn't allowed back in Denmark, but at the sight of Alls, she had gone to Nina. Grace tried to understand.

How did you ever get anyone to love you like that?

A real liar never came clean, Grace knew. A real liar only scrubbed away a patch here and there, just enough to clear herself for a few minutes, days, or weeks at a time. Hanna, Grace saw now, was a real liar. She had divided Nina and Antonia into two women, one who had loved her and one who had only used her. One had hurt her; the other she had hurt. Grace's heart ached for her friend and what she must have thought was love. But who was Grace to say? She hadn't really known Hanna at all.

She stepped quietly into the office and sat down at Jacqueline's desk, watching Alls turn the dial back and forth. He was most of the way down his second page for the night.

"Do you want anything? A glass of water?"

"No, I'm fine."

If Alls hadn't been held back by an ocean and the threat of more jail time, why should Hanna? The sudden, impossible appearance of Alls must have looked heroic to Hanna, must have helped her to believe that Nina, deep in her heart, wanted Hanna to come back.

Alls had come for what he was owed, or, barring that, a sense of vengeance, and perhaps Hanna had gone after Nina for the same reason. But now Grace looked down at Alls and hoped, with quiet desperation, that Hanna had seen something in his sudden, fearless appearance that Grace herself had not dared to.

She turned back to the wall and began to page through the ledger, trying not to watch him. Amaury and Hanna were paid the same, twenty-eight hundred euros per month. Jacqueline paid herself three thousand. Infuriating. Jacqueline had charged sixty euros for the cabbage teapot the last time Grace had repaired it. The birdcage job had been billed for six hundred. There was an entry for "Centerpiece Deposit" for two thousand. She turned the page, looking for Amaury's jobs. He had been busy before he'd left: In the past month, he'd had more than four thousand euros in billings. Grace hadn't realized his work was so much more lucrative than hers, and she felt momentarily defensive. But the jewelry that Grace had worked on was not in the ledger, not that she was surprised. There were several small payments to Hanna on this page that she didn't recognize, thirty euros on five occasions, maybe reimbursements for supplies or something. But Hanna had only gone out for supplies once recently; she had everything she needed ordered in. Grace stared at the tiny amounts. All were from the past week. They hadn't been doing anything except the centerpiece and jewelry.

The dates: thirty euros twice on August 17, thirty on the nineteenth, thirty on the twenty-third. Every time Grace completed a piece of jewelry.

Had Hanna been making a finder's fee on her? Getting a cut while Grace scraped by on a thousand per month?

"You all right?" Alls asked her.

"Fine," she said. She closed the ledger and slipped it back into the drawer.

She could almost hear Hanna's voice, so generous she was nearly singing. *I'll talk to Jacqueline*, she had said. *I'll make sure she knows how valuable you are.*

Grace heard a soft click. Alls had opened the safe.

He began to pull on a pair of Grace's cotton gloves, too small for him.

"Wait," she said.

"Nothing you can do, Gracie."

She took his gloved hands in hers and began to pull the gloves off by their fingertips. She slid them onto her own hands. Gloved, her hands looked more like her own than they did naked.

"I want to do it," she said. "Myself."

He sat back. Grace reached into the safe. The first box was the pearl and ruby necklace, the rubies just sitting in the box with it, like extras. The second box was a bracelet she'd never seen. The third was the ring, the pretty one. There were four more boxes. In the last box was a brooch, an orchid in enamel with pink and green tourmaline spilling out at the throat. The column was tipped with a natural pearl. She carefully put the lid back on.

"Not this one," she said.

He'd been watching her but giving her room. Now he became skeptical. He thought she was getting sentimental.

"It might be one of a kind," she said. "We don't want to mess around with that again."

She stacked the remaining boxes in her lap and picked them up as a tower, one hand below and the other above. She stood up and Alls followed her to her desk. He held open her bag and she nestled the tower along the bottom.

"Hanna has been arrested in Denmark," she told him. He didn't understand, not yet. "She lied to me."

It was ten after five. Together they returned to Jacqueline's office. She pushed the safe closed with her gloved fingertip.

"Should I turn the dial?"

"Be my guest."

Everything in its place. He put on his jacket.

"Just a minute," she said. This time, he did not object.

Still gloved, she returned to her table and packed up her very best tools for small work from her station: tweezers straight and curved, her set of needle files, cutters, two pliers. A starter kit. Then she moved Hanna's tools in their place. Jacqueline would never know the difference.

Her eyes fell on Hanna's notebook. *Lundi,* the top page read. *J'emballerai le cadeau et le livrerai!!!* Wrap the present and deliver, ecstatically. Grace fixed a shepherdess's dress, the hem askew, and smoothed down the little corn stalks. The green leaves, bent backward and down over the ears, shouldn't have been quite as jagged and uneven as in real life. She put Hanna's notebook in her purse.

Jacqueline could no sooner call the police than a drug dealer could when his stash was stolen. And Hanna had already been arrested; it hardly mattered what anyone accused her of now.

They emerged from their return taxi just before dawn. The rush was still with her, the suspense more powerful with each step away from Jacqueline's safe. They walked silently to her door and crept up the stairs. Alls waited by the window while Grace locked her bedroom door. She took the cardboard boxes from her bag and opened them one by one, setting them in a row across her desk.

She had reached in and taken them with her own hands. Her conscience felt resplendently clean. She felt whole, even. He had watched her do it.

Two selves, collapsed.

Alls had been quiet. He was leaning against the windowsill and watching her, she realized, the way he used to, without looking right at her, as though she might vanish if he looked too hard. She swept her hand through the air over the jewelry.

"These are for you," she said.

"I know," he said. He sat down on her bed.

A delivery truck rumbled down the street. She sat next to him, just inches away, but it felt as if there were a glass wall between them. It was almost seven o'clock in the morning, and the dawn sun was glowing on its way up, covering her room in velvety golden light.

"I'll miss her," she said to Alls. "Hanna might have been my only friend."

"You just threw her under the bus," he said.

"She threw herself," Grace said. "And she threw me first."

"A match made in heaven," Alls said. "First love?"

Grace shook her head. "Asshole." And then, newly brave, she asked him, "Do you think I never loved you?"

"I don't know," he said.

She had loved him—still did, a punishment—but hers was love mixed with harder metals. It hadn't been enough to run away from the Grahams' house back then; she had wanted to drop a match on the lawn as she left. She'd felt no transcendence, no generosity. Love was supposed to make you better, to fill in all the mean little holes in your being. Instead, it had opened up new ones.

"You need one person who knows you," she said. "Just one person you can't fool, even when you fool yourself."

"One didn't used to be enough for you," he said.

"Don't you see?" Grace implored him. "It wasn't about Riley. It was *her.*" She looked at him, waiting for him to understand.

He didn't make her say it.

"We both wanted to be one of them," he said. "But you'd really made it."

She shook her head. "I can't talk about that. Anything but that."

He took a deep breath. "Well, you'll never fool me again."

His voice seemed to make the room vibrate. She felt the buzzing, the shivering, in her fingers and in her teeth.

"You liked reaching into that safe," he said.

She wanted to squeeze him between her thighs and never let him go.

"Admit it," he said.

"I liked it."

"Listen," he said, leaning back. "I'll need to be going. Sunday's a good day to travel."

It was like waking up alone when she didn't expect to. "Where will you go?"

He picked at a scab on his forearm. "Probably better for you not to know, right?"

She stared at the wall as the light climbed over it, moving queer, sourceless shadows.

"You should get some sleep," he said.

"I can't," she said. The insides of her thighs were damp, and she felt a trickle of sweat behind her knee.

"I can't believe you came all the way here just for that," she said.

He laughed, though with bitterness or regret, she could not tell. He didn't want her. He just wanted money and a new life, away from the place he'd always lived and the people who thought they knew him.

"Not this time," he said. "I don't do *accidents* anymore."

She nodded.

He licked his lips. "You have to say it." He looked at her mouth. "I'm going to make you tell me what you want."

Last time, no lights had been on, no words spoken. Now she could see the sweat on his upper lip, the sun catching his stubble.

"I want you," she said.

"You want me," he said, looking at the wall over her desk.

"I want you," she said again, and this time she stood up, nudging his knees apart to stand between them. She gently pushed a thigh forward to his groin and felt that he was growing hard, and she put her hands around his neck, trailed her fingers through the short hairs there. She ran her thumb across his lower lip, holding his chin still in her hand. She wanted all of him for herself. His hands were still, beside him on the bed.

"You are not smarter," she said. "You are very, very stupid if you still want me. But I want you now, and I wanted you then. And I am so sorry, but I still want what I want."

She bent to brush her lips to his damp temple and then under the corner of his jaw. She would touch him everywhere; she would wear him down. She lingered there until she felt his hands on her waist, clear and sure, pulling her down with him.

She woke up tightly fitted into him in the bed, her bed, his arm holding her close. She hadn't slept next to anyone in years.

She lay there awake and blinking for a long time, their bodies growing sweaty where they were pressed together. She didn't want to wake him up. She knew better than anyone that the night brain consented to thoughts that the day brain wouldn't.

He stirred behind her and she held very still, wishing him back to sleep, but he pulled his arm back. She watched its shadow on the wall, stretching upward, and then it dropped back down, returning to her.

Freindametz gave her a nasty look when they came downstairs. They quickly left the house.

They walked to the cemetery and shuffled between the shady patches. She showed him where Delacroix was buried, and then Jacques–Louis David, Jim Morrison, Oscar Wilde, and Gertrude Stein. Each grave had its own little crowd of pilgrims. Grace and Alls toured the tourists. Walking by the Americans and hearing their accents, she felt a rush of daring, as though a flicker of recognition on her face might give her away to these strangers. She and Alls kept going, wandering away from the people, and she felt the warmth of being with him, the invisible tether that kept them moving in the same direction, despite the crowds of strangers. Together, alone.

At one point, he took her hand in his, and she was so shocked at the feel of his skin that she stumbled forward, half-witted with lust and disbelief.

Neither of them spoke of his leaving, and when they got home and he went to the bathroom, she thought this was it, that now he would pack up and leave to make the last Sunday train. But he did not go and instead ran his hands up the backs of her thighs, under her skirt. He pressed his nose into her belly and slid his fingers behind her underwear, moaning when he felt how slick she was. *I have been waiting for you,* she wanted to tell him, *knowing you would never come.* She pushed him down on the ancient flowered couch and told him that she didn't want him to leave, she never wanted him to leave, every way she knew how to.

You still haven't learned any other way to get what you want, she thought, but she pushed the thought away. All she wanted was him, and all she could do was give—show him how badly she loved him and hope to make him want her even half as much in return.

Afterward they sat at the table, radiant and profane, and Grace fed him greengage plums and buttered toast and wine. Alls didn't talk and so neither did she. She didn't want to disrupt whatever fragile balance was keeping him in the chair across from her.

"Someone will search your house," he said.

She pushed the crumbs on her plate into a line. "She can't call the police."

"Then someone else, someone worse. It won't be nice."

"She's going to think it was Hanna," she said.

"I don't know your boss, I don't know what kind of people she's with, but you can't stay here." He rubbed his eyes. "I thought I'd leave your life in shambles," he said. "I planned on it. But not like this. Where can you go?"

She shrugged, trying to swallow her dismay. "Anywhere," she said. "Anywhere I haven't been yet."

"This isn't how I thought it would be," he said.

She waited. She didn't know what he meant yet.

"I thought you would have figured it all out now," he said. "I thought you'd be telling redneck jokes for Europeans at dinner parties. I thought you'd be a well-dressed alcoholic. I thought you'd have just what you wanted and then I'd come and take it from you." He laughed sadly. "I thought you'd be the collateral damage—some revenge on the side—on my way to get what *I* wanted."

"What do you want?"

"Fuck if I know. I never did."

"I knew," she said. "I wanted you."

"I wish I believed you."

No, she'd misheard him. *I wish I'd believed you*, he'd said.

"Then," she said, making sure.

He nodded.

"I do too," she said.

"You haven't destroyed anything," she said. "I needed to leave here anyway. This isn't any life I wanted either, and I think you know that now, right?"

He sighed, almost imperceptibly, and she felt an opening.

"Let's go together," she said. "This time. I know you can't love me, not like you did. I can do jewelry, swap out the stones, I can—"

He was shaking his head. "No fakes. We'd be caught in a week."

"Precious for precious," she said. He was listening. "Nothing fake. But if you switch amethysts for emeralds and put in a diamond where there used to be a topaz—everything would check out with any jeweler. We could steal and sell for years and years, and nothing could be traced, as long as I changed enough. I could do that," she told him. "I'd be good."

He laid his head on the table.

"We'll sell the trillions to get started," she said. "To buy stones for these pieces from the safe. And then we'll use the stones I pull from these in the next pieces. Not all at once, there are sizes and shapes and all that to consider, but we could move them a little at a time, as much or as little as we needed. The rocks from bracelet A into necklace B into brooch C into ring D. Nothing would be recognizable, as long as we only use mass jewelry. Nothing one of a kind. Gold, platinum. We'll go everywhere. I'll get a job as coat-check girl when we run out, or a maid, and you can sneak in and open their safes. There's jewelry everywhere," she said, running out of breath. "The harvest would be endless."

"You've been wrong before."

"I'm not wrong this time."

He had closed his eyes hard, shutting her out. Now he lifted his head. "Where is Riley?" he asked.

She hadn't checked since Alls had come.

31

The story was two days old. NY AUTHORITIES FIND MISSING PAROLEE, the headline read.

> U.S. marshals say they have found a Garland man who left Tennessee while on parole as part of a robbery sentence.
>
> A parole warrant was issued on August 19 for 23-year-old Riley Sullivan Graham, who went missing from his place of employment the day before. Graham was arrested for drunk and disorderly conduct in a Queens, New York, bar on Tuesday. Upon his arrest, the U.S. Marshals Fugitive Task Force ordered him returned to Tennessee, where he will reappear before the court for sentencing.
>
> Graham had served nearly three years for the robbery of the Josephus Wynne Historic Estate in Garland in 2009.

He had been looking for her. She saw that Alls was reading the page again and then again. She sat down on the bed and crossed her arms tightly. Her throat began to seize.

Everything she touched, she thought.

"I should have told him," he finally said. "I should have made him hate us both."

Grace closed her eyes. She couldn't look at him. "Where did you think he'd gone?"

"I thought he needed to start over as someone else, away from his family." He shook his head. "I didn't care what he did."

She dug her palms into her eyes. "He was looking for me. I knew he would."

"I thought he was over you. I was the one who wasn't."

The air between them was thick and human. She felt drugged. "Don't you see? I ruined *everyone*. One bad apple. This will never end."

"Who's the fucking apple? Don't *you* see?" he said. "This *is* the end." He pulled her hands from her eyes. "We have to leave him behind. He has people to take care of him."

"You don't get it," she said. "I'm poor. I mean, I'm poor like this"—she looked around the kitchen—"but I'm *poor*, here." She thumped her open palm on her chest. "I'm a vacuum, just sucking up everything I can."

"Take it," he said. "Give me what you've got, and I'll give you what I've got, and that will have to be enough for us."

They needed cash to travel. Alls had some left from Greg but Grace wanted to pull her own weight. Jacqueline had not paid her regular wages on Friday and she didn't know what that meant. Alls had been hoping there would be some money in the safe but there had been only jewelry. Grace could have told him that Jacqueline didn't have any money.

On Monday morning, she put on her best white sheath and a black cardigan over it for work. First she went to Lachaille with the trillions. She didn't need to be at work right at nine. Jacqueline didn't even know she had a key—Grace had copied Hanna's without asking their boss—and this would be a poor time for Jacqueline to realize that she did. Jacqueline wouldn't come in until ten, and Amaury and Hanna had keys to get in before then, but they were gone. Grace would get there just early enough to wait outside for her boss.

Lachaille's steel grate was still down, despite that the sign said they opened at nine. Grace walked around the block. If Lachaille didn't open soon, the day was already shot.

At 9:20 the grate flew up. Grace was watching from the café across the street.

"We don't buy loose diamonds," Mme Lachaille said, shaking her head. "And no certificates? No, we don't do that."

Grace spread out Alls's torn page from *Architectural Digest* and pointed to her bracelet. "How much did you get for this? Five times what you paid me?"

The older woman pursed her dark lips. "It was a fair price."

Grace folded her arms and waited. "I've sold you some really beautiful things," she said. "I didn't expect that I was—"

"These are not my business. I sell antique jewelry. These need antique jewelry behind them. You're not going to get a good price anywhere." She shook her head quickly. "Put some clothes on them," she hissed.

Grace had expected a lowball offer that the magazine clip would improve; she had not expected to be turned down entirely.

"I can make a call for you," Mme Lachaille said. "That's it."

"Please."

Mme Lachaille rooted through her address book, grumbling, and then put up a finger. "I have to ask my husband," she said. "One minute."

Grace wouldn't sell the trillions today—an early blow. She'd never sold jewelry anywhere else, and she didn't have time to try, not if she was going to make it to work before Jacqueline, which she had to because she always did, and this day could not look any different. She needed to be there when Jacqueline discovered she had been robbed so that her accusations would fall on Hanna. And who would Lachaille send her to, anyway? She had no idea. No, it was too risky to improvise.

But Madame had left her address book splayed open on the glass counter, and under it, her blank pad of carbon paper receipts. An invitation. Grace knew her stoned-heiress-abroad act might not work everywhere. She had no certifications, no little slips of paper to legitimize her. Her charm had definite limits. She slipped the pad into her purse and then reached for the address book too. She might need to make some new friends soon.

She left quickly and quietly, stilling the bells that hung from the door in her hand.

On the sidewalk, she flipped open Alls's phone. He had not called yet, but it was early. He was to go out this morning to buy another phone, and he had given her his to take. He said he would call her as soon as he had it so she could call him when Jacqueline discovered the safe had been emptied. "Just call the number back," he said. "I won't answer." They needed to be ready to go, in case Jacqueline or her superiors went for Grace and her apartment instead of Hanna and hers.

Grace feared the call would not come and she would be left holding the bag. That was what she had done to him. But there was nothing to do except wait and see.

At work she pressed the buzzer as she always did, going through the motions but expecting silence. No one answered. Good. She leaned against the brick wall to wait. But then there was a crackle on the intercom, then a buzz, and the front lock clicked open. Damn.

The studio door was propped. Grace didn't like this, any of it. She pushed open the door and saw Amaury standing there, baggy-eyed and grimacing, as if it were he who had been caught at something.

"My God," she said. "I didn't think you were coming back."

He shook his head slowly, as if he couldn't believe it himself. "And yet, here I am again. How are things?"

"Fine," Grace said. "Slow. Very slow." She dropped her bag on her chair and scratched her ankle. "Hanna's almost finished with the centerpiece."

"I saw," he said. "It looks very nice."

They stood together, admiring it. Grace had expected the project to take much longer, but Hanna had worked on nothing else. Grace blew into the air and watched the corn stalks flutter. She and Amaury laughed.

"I like the corn," he said. "And the peaches, the little pits."

"I did those," Grace said, knowing he knew that. Carving fruit seemed like ages ago.

Grace squinted toward Hanna's station.

"What is it?"

"She said she was going to finish the case on Saturday," she told him. "She mixed some glue before she left on Friday."

He frowned, but not as if he cared. Grace went to inspect Hanna's unfinished work.

"And what have you been doing?" he asked. "More jewelry?"

"Just a few things, cleaning and resetting," she said. "These rich people, knocking their jewelry around and breaking it. I guess if you have a lot of it, it's less precious." Too much, she thought. She should have said half that.

He nodded absently.

"It's really strange that Hanna didn't come in," Grace said. "I hope she's okay."

Jacqueline came in at 10:20, looking as if she'd spent the weekend drinking on a boat. "Hanna's not here," Grace tattled. "And she didn't finish the case."

"Well, what are you waiting for? It's due there at noon!"

The work was well below Hanna's code, but Grace hustled together the last pieces of the case with a staple gun and twine. She carefully slid the centerpiece into its wide wooden box with Amaury's help. It was heavy, maybe thirty pounds, and of what? Wool, wire, glass beads, and scraps of fabric.

She knocked on the door to Jacqueline's office. "Pardon," she said. "Are you going to pay us today?"

"Yeah," her boss said absently. "This afternoon."

"Because my rent is due and—"

"I said today."

Grace called a taxi, and Amaury helped her get the centerpiece up the stairs. They declined the driver's help.

"I should go with you," Amaury said. "To get it out again."

"Not necessary," Grace said. "But I should take the gurney. Wait here?"

In the stairwell she opened the phone. Alls still had not called.

Grace let the driver help her slide the box onto the folding cart, and she rolled it into the lobby of the collector's marble-floored building. She went up in the freight elevator, light-headed with nerves. She would unveil the centerpiece and show it off, and then she would return to work and the spectacle of horrors that would unfold there.

The collector, a man who otherwise looked disappointingly average in a starched white button-up, wore compass cufflinks, their arrows spinning indiscriminately. He breathed deeply, as if he were in the habit of meditating, but crossed and recrossed his arms as she pushed the gurney across the floor. He wanted the centerpiece in a small sitting room behind his library; he said he displayed his folk art there. The centerpiece was hardly folk art, but perhaps the man meant all his funny art, or all his miscellaneous art. She obliged, hearing him suck in his breath as she wheeled around corners. His walls were crowded with oils and tapestries, mostly religious scenes. She told him she would need assistance to move it off the gurney, and he doubled back to murmur into an intercom.

The room was furnished in bizarre simplicity with a single bed, a shabby dining table with one chair, and a child's writing desk. The bedspread was threadbare. Grace thought of her attic bedroom at the Grahams' and quickly shook off the memory.

"Here," he said, pointing to the table.

"Here?" Grace repeated. The man had been far too passionate about the restoration to have Grace drop it on a rickety table.

"It's bolted to the floor," he said, kicking gently at a table leg.

Another man had appeared, a secretary, perhaps, and the three of them together slid the centerpiece out onto the table. The collector sat down in the chair and stared, his hand over his mouth.

"It's like going back in time," he said finally.

Grace hadn't realized she'd been holding her breath. He was pleased.

"Yes," she said.

"Your work," he said, "is exquisite."

"Thank you."

He stood and backed up to the wall, never taking his eyes off the centerpiece. He pushed a button on the wall, just under a small crude oil painting of a pair of goats. She heard it before she saw it: A clear acrylic lid, a bottomless box, was descending from the ceiling on steel wires. The collector and his secretary switched places wordlessly and the collector hurried to the centerpiece. He motioned with his hands for the lid to drop, to pause, to drop a little more, as if he were helping someone park on the street. They stopped when the lid hovered just over the tops of the trees, and they waited until it was completely still in the air and they were sure the centerpiece was correctly positioned under it. Then the secretary pushed the button once more, and the lid settled around the centerpiece with a soft clunk.

The collector relaxed his shoulders and clapped his hands. "I love it!" he squawked. He put his hands on his hips and bent over his new prize.

"Did you see the peaches?" She pointed toward the orchard. "They're my special favorite."

He laughed when he saw the bite marks. "However did you do it?" he said. "You must have such steady hands. Me, I can't even thread a needle."

When she left, he tried to write her a check, she supposed as a tip. Grace couldn't take checks; she had no way to cash them. "I couldn't," she demurred. "No, please. You paid for our services. That is the arrangement."

"Please, please," he said. "You have made me so happy." He tried again to hand her a check. She saw that he had written it to Hanna Dunaj. Jacqueline must have told him—he might even have e-mailed with Hanna, or spoken to her. Grace had never had such intimate contact with a client.

"Really, I can't," she said.

His face changed; he was used to giving people money and used to them wanting it. "Ah," he said with a thin smile. He withdrew a clip of bills from his pocket and peeled off several of them. He handed her the rest. "You have given me so much joy—you can't be compensated fairly for that."

"Thank you, you're very generous. Would you like a copy of the notes?" she asked him. "You might enjoy reading our notes on the restoration."

He looked positively aroused. "I would love that," he said. "Oh do send *all* the notes, please."

On the sidewalk, she looked down at her phone. There, a missed call. She thought she might capsize in the wave of relief; the number on the screen was like a hand reaching out for her.

She couldn't fuck up now.

Outside Zanuso et Filles she pressed the buzzer.

"Who is it?"

Jacqueline never asked who it was. Grace knew she had opened the safe.

"Julie," she said, calling Alls at the same time. When the phone rang twice, she hung up. She tromped down the stairs, making up for her wobbly-legged anxiety by landing hard on her feet.

Jacqueline was at the door, dry-lipped and wild-eyed. She motioned Grace in and shut the door behind her. "We've been robbed," she said.

"What? When?"

"Over the weekend. The safe is empty."

"My God," Grace said. "What was in it?"

Jacqueline pushed her hands through her hair. "Where is she?" she demanded. "Where is Hanna?"

Grace shook her head. "I don't know."

"Yes, you do," Jacqueline said through her clenched jaw. "You two talk all the damn day. Tell me where she is."

"We're just work friends," Grace said limply. "I don't even know where she lives."

"*She* has a key, and *he* has a key."

"Jacqui," Amaury warned her from across the room.

"You've called the police?" Grace asked.

"Ha," Amaury said.

"We have to call the police," Grace said, stepping toward Jacqueline's office.

"No! I already called the police. They've already been here." She looked at Amaury, threatening him into believing it, but he was slumped over at his desk, arms crossed, looking at his lap.

"I knew this day would come," he said.

Jacqueline was almost gasping for breath. "I knew she was a thief," she said.

"Are you sure it was her?" Grace asked. "She might just be sick."

Jacqueline rolled her eyes. "You don't know her," she said. "Look, her things are gone too."

Amaury sighed.

"Go home," she snapped at Grace. "There is nothing to do."

"I need to be paid," Grace said. "You said you'd pay me on Friday."

"Get out!" Jacqueline shouted. "If you ever want to work again, just get out!"

Amaury groaned and stood up. Grace followed him out the door. She had almost a thousand euros in her purse from the collector. She reached in and fingered the bills.

"What will she do?" she asked Amaury outside the building.

He shrugged his soft, hilly shoulders. "What will *we* do, you mean." He looked at her tiredly. "The job is gone," he said, gently breaking the news. "You don't need to come back." She threw her arms around him, and he stumbled back in surprise. He gently patted her back, unsure and uncomfortable.

The ship had been going down anyway; he'd known it and so had she. She released him and slipped a hundred euros into his pants pocket. He was far too discombobulated to notice.

"I guess I won't see you for a while," she said to him.

"No," he said.

She had almost a thousand in her pocket but had planned to end the day with ten, and Alls was not expecting her for five more hours. She could have called him and said she was early; they had certainly allowed for the possibility that Jacqueline would close up shop immediately. But Grace had not sold the trillions, and while the money in her pocket was a nice surprise, it was not nearly *enough* surprise. Maybe she had the time, after all, to try again.

No one would give her a good price for loose diamonds. She had the ring she had taken the diamonds from; she could pop them right back in. But that wasn't the case she had made to Alls; she had promised him that she could set diamonds stolen from the Joneses into jewelry stolen from the Smiths.

Grace went to the third arrondissement to look for earrings. Her requirements were specific, and she knew she might come up empty. She needed a pair in eighteen- or twenty-two-karat gold with simple, three-prong settings and only semiprecious stones, so she wouldn't have to go too deep into her pockets to pay for them. Such earrings weren't fashionable here; she would have had better luck at the Albe-mall.

The small shops had nothing for her. She vowed to give up after two hours, but it didn't take nearly that long. She found them in Galeries Lafayette for two hundred, white gold with aquamarines. She paid in cash and threw the receipt in the can on the way out. Switching these stones at home would be easy for her, child's play. She was excited: This wasn't exactly the plan, but maybe it was better. She would show him. She would show him that he needed her.

Alls was not at home. The jewelry boxes were gone from her desk. He had left her. So tidily, hadn't even left a mess. Grace leaned back against the wall.

His duffel bag was still there.

She pawed through it, her mind sparking in a dozen panicked directions. No jewels. She yanked open her drawers, a burglar in her own home, searching desperately for evidence that he had not gone without her. And what if he had? She had half-expected it, hadn't she?

The Mont box. She had shown it to him last night, every varnished layer and every babied hinge. Now she threw it open. She groped in the slip until her nails hit metal. They were there. He had hidden them away. Yes. Of course.

When Alls came in an hour later, Grace had shoved the earring posts into the bottom of a plain wax candle that she held upturned between her knees. She sat by the window, hunched over. She would have to buy a new headlamp, a new magnifier, since she was freelancing now. She would eventually need a portable soldering apparatus like the one at work. But today, she had only to open the prongs and close them around a pair of diamonds as big as unopened sunflower seeds. She allowed herself a sigh of relief when she heard him come in.

He wanted to know everything that had happened so far. She gave it to him in detail, keeping her eyes on her work. He seemed more interested in what she was doing than disappointed that she hadn't sold the trillions, and that was how she knew. She felt like a plane touching down, finally on safe, hard ground.

She'd wrapped the aquamarines in a tissue. "We should save those," she said. "They might come in handy sometime."

He stood behind her as she clamped the last prongs closed.

"Hand me that cloth," she said, pulling the earrings from the wax. The diamonds were nearly naked, barely held. Only a woman with more money than she could ever spend would wear something so valuable and so vulnerable.

"Put them on," he said.

She wiggled the posts into her ears. He followed her into the bathroom, and they looked together at her reflection in the mirror.

"They don't look real," he said. "They're too big to look real."

"Diamonds only look real if you already look rich," she said.

He laughed.

"We could still sell them today," she said. "I can do it. Come with me. You'll see."

He shook his head. "These are probably easier to hide than the cash would be," he said. "Safer to travel with." He reached up and took her earlobe between his fingers, and she turned and pulled him closer.

Alls watched her pack with curiosity: Another Grace was emerging. The cardigans would be left behind with Petit Trianon and her books. When she tucked her black boots along the side of the suitcase, he remembered them. He'd taken a picture that day in New York, he said, of Grace smiling in Union Square on their way to the auction. She'd never seen the photograph, but she could imagine: At eighteen, she'd looked corn-fed, a babe in the woods but for another girl's dress and the stiletto boots and all that they implied. She had been so eager to change.

Now the boots suited her perfectly.

At dusk, they stepped off the bus at Gallieni. He had their bags, his small duffel and her larger rolling suitcase. They crossed the street to where the tour buses were idling, sweaty travelers embarking and disembarking.

"Tickets?" the stubbly driver asked, looking at his clipboard.

"We need to buy them now," Alls said, handing the driver the money.

He waved them onto the bus, and they turned to mount the metal stairs.

"No, no!" the man called after her, and Grace whipped around in the sudden grip of alarm.

"You have to put your big bag down here," he said, pointing under the bus. "Only small bags up there." He held out his hand, ready to assist her.

She looked to Alls, but he was already on the bus. Inside her suitcase were the Mont Box and all the secrets it held, her tools, precious metals, and a fortune in gemstones.

Grace smiled and let the driver take the handle. "Thank you," she said.

Alls had found them two seats together near the back. In front of them, a young mother nursed a fretful infant. Three backpackers, separated by four rows of people, debated what they'd heard about the Madrid hostels.

Alls took her hand as if they were any young couple traveling Europe on a shoestring, looking out the grimy windows, wondering at the smells of other people's food. The driver climbed into his seat, and the bus lurched away from the curb, where a small crowd of strangers waved them good-bye.

Epilogue

G race turned twenty-five outside Brussels, at the wedding reception of a
rich Belgian girl she'd befriended at a daytime watercolor class six months
before. Three hundred people were now crowded onto the brick terrace at the
girl's parents' house, and when the bride's father, silver-haired and American,
raised his flute to toast the happiness of his only daughter, Alls raised his glass
an extra centimeter for Grace. They would celebrate her birthday later, alone.
The crowd applauded the young couple and then began to spread across the
garden in clusters, waiters streaming between them with platters of canapés.
Alls set his champagne flute on a white-dressed table and disappeared inside
to find a bathroom. Grace plucked a tartlet from a passing tray.

"Galette de pigeon," the waiter said.

When Alls came out of the house thirty minutes later, he found Grace
chatting about Byzantine art with someone's uncle, who laughed uproariously
at her colorful jokes about Justinian. Grace fed Alls a bite of her lobster salad
and wiped the sauce from the corner of his mouth with her pinkie, and *l'oncle*
sidled away, beckoned by his wife to talk to an older couple. Alls had finished
inside, and Grace could tell from his languid gestures and the softness of his
forearm around her waist that his job had been an easy one, but they would
have to stay through dinner anyway, mostly to charm but also to commit
small, strategic offenses that would travel back to the bride and her family
tomorrow and over the next weeks: a dirty joke shared sotto voce during the
mother's tearful toast, an ungenerous comparison of the groom to his brother,
some uncovered yawning and unladylike postures. They had to kill any
friendships to ensure an easy exit from the lives of their marks. She'd long
since given up on others' kind opinions of her; she had to shed these as easily
as she shed her names. To offend someone swiftly, efficiently, even, as you left

forever was kinder by far than to slowly withdraw, to confuse and disappoint. You didn't want them to miss you. Anger was simple, self-sustaining as a cactus. You couldn't look too closely at it, lest the spines get you in the eye.

The people they had left behind were lucky to be done with them. Grace and Alls didn't have the luxury of forgetting anyone. Always, she listened for the ticking. Only Jacqueline had vanished without leaving a trace. Greg was selling time-shares in Florida. Riley had not gone back to jail after all, but to a private psychiatric facility for one year instead. When he was released, he and Colin opened an ice cream shop, just as he'd always wanted. Grace hoped he was happy. She chose to believe that he was.

But he still hadn't divorced her. He wouldn't need her consent if he couldn't find her, and she'd long since cut her last tie to Garland, just an e-mail address after all. The Tennessee courts would ask Riley only to make the appropriate gestures, the "good faith effort": calling old numbers, asking the post office for a forwarding address. Then the *Record* would run a legal notice, divorce by publication. But the *Record* had run no such thing.

She didn't know why, and when the question woke her up at night, she would go into the bathroom, face the mirror, and turn the lights out, a simple homemade spell for believing she had disappeared.

The Belgian wedding cake was American in style, tiered and fondant encased with gum-paste lilies of the valley, each no larger than a molar. Grace bent to admire the petals' ruffled edges. Miniatures always reminded her of Hanna, who worked for a frame shop in Warsaw now. The owner was named Dunaj; Grace assumed that Hanna had been given a family job. She hated to imagine Hanna glassing in impressionism posters and college degrees, wasting her talent. She'd be very good, Grace thought, at decorating wedding cakes. So would she, if she ever had to reform.

But even in her split-second daydream, *cake decorator* was another costume, a cover.

After cake, Grace found the bride and groom and paid her delighted respects, flirting a bit obnoxiously with the groom. The bride would not call her again.

That night, Grace sprawled gratefully on their downy hotel bed, still in her wedding clothes, and watched Alls undress. He was a careful dresser, and he neatly hung his jacket, his tie, his shirt, and his pants as he took them off. Grace sometimes thought that heaven, whatever that was, would be a small and potent happiness looped forever. Her heaven would be lying down on a soft bed and watching Alls undress.

He undid the five straps that bound his hidden pockets to his thighs. When he dropped the pouches onto the bed, the comforter puffed up around them. He knelt on the bed and slipped his hand through the slit in Grace's dress. Her own pocket snaked around to her inner thigh. Whenever she pushed something into it, something small and heavy, she would lean forward slightly, to laugh or take a bite, as the small lump traveled down the narrow tunnel to the soft purse fastened between her legs. She and Alls never put anything in plain pockets anymore, because of the inkwell problem: The weight made clothes hang wrong. Alls retrieved her spoils and dropped them across the comforter, puff-puff-puff.

He lay down next to her and she rolled onto her belly to examine their gifts. From the safe, Alls had taken a heavy tangle of jewelry containing at least twenty carats of diamonds and a smattering of other precious stones. In addition, Grace had picked up *l'oncle*'s Russian diamond tie pin and some his-and-hers gold card cases that Grace happened to know were in the forest green–wrapped box in the wedding gift pile in the guest room next to the powder room.

She opened and shut one of the card cases, enjoying the heavy, satisfying click. "These are revolting. The bride would have hated them anyway," she said.

He laughed. "You're a liar."

"Well, she *should* hate them." She bent her head to his and touched her nose to his nose. "I'm surprised there wasn't any cash. Or gold bricks, not that we could have fit them. They seemed like gold brick people."

"They've got more than one safe," he said. "Smart."

"Lucky me, then, that we got the jewelry."

Alls loved opening safes, picking locks and pockets. He didn't care whose or how; he craved the breach itself. Grace didn't, not especially. Working parties and weddings was only the necessary means of stocking her supplies. What thrilled her was the transformation: An audacious cocktail ring became a modest brooch; a bracelet studded with chartreuse peridots was renovated with stolen diamonds that made it 150 times as valuable but far less memorable to the eye. No one could remember a thing about their diamonds except the sparkle. They *all* sparkled.

She, too, was reborn in stunning ambiguity.

Turning her hands to herself, Grace could raise and lower her eyebrows, thin her lips into a patrician dash or blow them up into pillowy distractions. She could pin her hair across her forehead, a louche and slouchy party girl, or shave her hairline back to be the perpetually disappointed stepdaughter of a foreign diplomat. That was easy. She could starve a few weeks to deepen the hollows beneath her cheekbones and the wells above her collarbones, or fatten on bread and cheese until she puffed back into rosy-sweet baby fat. She could aerate her voice, make it low and soft as fog, or she could be Hanna, crisp angles and impatient expertise. When she scrubbed off her makeup at night, a naked canvas blinked back at her in the mirror.

When you stopped trying to be one perfect person, you could be many. Grace had been a dozen girls in the past three years, every one a sylph.

Alls pulled her on top of him and traced an imaginary necklace along her chest. "Do you wish we were having a liver-toast wedding?" he teased.

"A pigeon-pie wedding?"

"You can walk down the aisle right here," he said. "Start from the bathroom door and pass the TV—"

"We've got rings," she said. "Several to choose from."

Alls began to sing the wedding march as if he were the tuba in a brass band and he'd been told the song was a battle cry. Grace imagined toddlers throwing rose petals and broke into laughter, shaking against his chest.

"You know I'd marry you if I could," she said when she could stop.

"Who needs to get married? We're more than married."

They rolled onto their sides, nose-to-nose and knee-to-knee, and she knew it in her very bones: This was the only life for them. Here was her only anchor. She risked for him and he risked for her. She'd sinned for him and he'd sinned for her. For richer or poorer, in sickness and in health, and everyone else was a stranger, either a mark or a liar. This was their happiness and they would not let it go.

"Happy birthday, Gracie," Alls said. "I love you."

But that was the least of it. He knew the worst of her, and that was better.

On a cloudy evening about two weeks later, Grace sat down to work on the floor in front of the cracked laminate coffee table facing the TV, the best feature of the flat she and Alls had rented in Odense. She'd found a channel that played American movies, and lately she'd been turning them on for background while she worked alone. Alls had been out working on a job for the past six nights, and Grace had been uneasy without him. The life they'd chosen was riddled with chance, and with every triumph, she feared they'd finally tilted the odds against them. She always worried that Alls would be caught or worse until the moment she heard him clear his throat on the stairs. He did, every time, just to let her know that he was alone, intact, and that they'd made it another day.

Three Makeup Princess fashion dolls, the reviled plastic *modepoppen*, sat on top of the television, smiling at her from their cardboard cases. Grace poured half an inch of ethyl acetate into two bowls and mixed into each a stream of bright nail polish, one magenta and one turquoise. She would paint this solution on their loose diamonds and other pale gems, turning them into garish plastic fakes that she would use to bedazzle the dolls' lamé headbands and plastic necklaces, which were ideal for concealing gems in plain sight. She could have hot-glued the Hope Diamond to one of those dolls and no one would see it. On the off chance she and Alls were checked at customs, their savings should be safe in these toys Grace had supposedly bought for her nieces back home. Alls would have preferred to tape the stones into suitcase linings than fool around with bulky toys, but Grace was a better actress when she had nothing to hide. Then she could really *believe*.

They hadn't bothered about customs until now, traveling around the EU unchecked for the past few years, but they had never traveled with quite so much. As soon as he finished the safe he was working now, they would leave for London. It was a shame they couldn't sell this lot in Antwerp, but they never sold a piece in the same country where they'd picked it up, even after Grace had reset all the stones. They would stay in London only long enough to sell. They hadn't decided where to go after. Alls was tired of Europe and Grace wanted a break from jewelry, parties, laughing at other people's jokes. They had been moving so precisely, so purposefully—dancing, really—and neither could imagine what it would feel like to slow to a stop. "You don't think we'll get bored?" she'd asked him, really asking him if he would. Those too-quiet moments of doubt were perhaps the same in any kind of marriage: *How much do you love me, and what other choice do you have?* But he said he wanted to get bored, just enough to sleep through the night.

Sometimes she missed loving someone who she knew would always love her more.

They had three secondhand safes, each no larger than a microwave, in their apartment right now; Grace reset their combinations periodically so Alls could train for speed. Now she fetched the loose stones and spread them out on the newsprint. She began to dab at the first one with hot pink, holding it down with a toothpick as she moved her brush over the facets.

The commercial ended and the movie came back on. The voices were immediately familiar. Grace looked up to see a mink-clad woman, middle-aged, stubbing her cigarette out in a fried egg. Mrs. Graham had loved this part, hissing when the cigarette hit the yolk.

Ah, no. Not this. Not tonight.

To Catch a Thief. Grace had not thought about the movie in years. She watched, stock-still, as Grace Kelly swept into the frame in a yellow flowered day dress. She knelt on a damask couch, crossed her golden arms daintily over the back, and arched, smiling and preening. "You know, you might look a little like her," Mrs. Graham had said, and Grace had soaked in that compliment, though she was not so golden, her jaw not so haughtily square. But now she recognized herself in the preening smile, the balletic gestures of the other Grace, the one she'd meant to become. She watched the other Grace throw her shoulders around, tilt her face to the sun, spill her silvery voice like coins falling into a pile. Grace had loved that voice's faux-frank arrogance. The other Grace was all surfaces, as if she'd somehow rid herself of herself.

Grace remembered herself in the mirror, trying on Mrs. Graham's lipstick when she was a girl. Crushed Rose, wasn't it? If only she could laugh. Instead the ache of longing rushed up in her too fast for her to stop it. She set down her brush, the polish already dried hard on the bristles. She wished

Alls were home. She could have told him she was having a magnolia spell—
a euphemism for this sudden anguish—and he would have helped her
through it. He was not immune to such difficulties himself. But he was out,
alone, on his belly in black on some cold floor, and she was home alone.

I don't think you know what love is, Hanna had said.

Grace turned off the TV and sat in the quiet apartment full of fumes. She
opened her computer and typed *429 Heathcliff* into the search bar. *Garland
Tennessee USA*. She didn't allow herself a moment to recognize the mistake
she was making. She needed to see the house, the front door, the hemlock tree
they had climbed, the roof they used to lie on. First was the map, the dumb
green arrow pointing to the location of another Grace, left behind.

But under the map was a photograph, too nice for satellite.

Poplar Realty Featured Properties: 429 Heathcliff Ave.

The Grahams were selling their house.

She clicked.

Wonderful family home, the listing began. Grace pored over the photographs, every lamp and every rug an unreadable sign of life: the needlepoint pillow of sunflowers, the pie safe with punched-tin doors, the brass
tripod floor lamp they'd bought when the boys had knocked over their
third lamp in a year. In the dining room, Grace saw her, a ghost in white
lace with a high neck, her sandy hair swept up into a shell, her hands hidden by dark glossy leaves and open white blooms. Grace couldn't see the
details in the photograph, but she knew them by heart.

Grace knew what love was.

She hurried toward the bathrooms and stairwell, trying to get away,
but then she was in the bedrooms, first the brothers' and then Riley's.
Grace didn't recognize his room at first—gone was the striped blue bedspread, the cork board crowded with the detritus of their childhood. Now
the walls were painted pale lilac, the furniture white wicker. A guest room.
But there was a stuffed rabbit on the twin bed, long ears strewn across the
pillow. Then she recognized the toile-shaded lamp, and then her old quilt,
folded across the back of a white rocking chair. She clicked through the
rest of the rooms, all unchanged. Her attic was not pictured. It was probably used for storage now. Grace did not recognize that bunny on the bed.
It was not Mrs. Graham's.

She went back into the dining room. On the wall with Mrs. Graham, on the other side of the shot of the boys in the leaf pile, was a family photograph—new, or new to her.

Grace zoomed in until the photograph filled her screen, hopelessly blurred. The Grahams were shadowy silhouettes whose details she could not sharpen. They were standing together, water behind them. A lake or a beach somewhere. All four brothers, but she couldn't make out their faces, and two women Grace did not recognize, one with a blond ponytail and a white tank top, another with dark curls. Dr. Graham and Mrs. Graham stood in the center. It was Riley, she thought, standing next to his mother. If only they had been lined up better, she would know the boys by height. Grace leaned in toward the screen, desperate to see it clearly, but she couldn't. She could only see the baby girl, a fat infant in a red sundress, whom Mrs. Graham held in her arms.

Who'd had a child? Mrs. Graham was fifty-four now. But they could have adopted. Grace heard the refrain as if Riley were singing it to her: *always wanted a daughter.* Or a grandchild. Jim was the oldest, and Nate had had a serious girlfriend, Ashley, but was that her? Who were those women? *Wives?* Whose? Could *Riley* be a father now? Whose baby was Mrs. Graham holding? Who was she? Grace screwed her eyes onto that blurry little girl but she could not tell a thing.

The bedroom must be for her, Grace realized.

It didn't matter whose baby it was. Mrs. Graham had got her girl.

Grace had thought that she'd left a piece of herself behind in that house, some earlier girl who haunted the attic, a sweet and sorry ghost. But she was the haunted one, and here was the evidence. All signs of her were gone, replaced now with someone real. She had not left herself behind. There was no such thing. You couldn't leave yourself. No matter how far you went, you were always there.

Alls wouldn't be home for hours still. Grace took a deep breath and dipped a cotton ball in acetone and began to work the hardened paint from her brush. She picked up a three-carat square-cut diamond with her tweezers and dipped it into the paint solution, deep-end blue. The *modepoppen* stared from behind their plastic windows, flat eyes fixed ahead. Grace tried not to watch the door, waiting, as she coated another gem in plastic. She knew about love. She knew all the angles.

Acknowledgments

To conduct my research, I relied on the work of many others: Erich Steingräber, Oppi Untracht, Janice Berkson, Stephen Maine, Todd Merrill's work on James Mont, and Gregory Cerio's Mont piece in *The Magazine Antiques*. Several real heists are mentioned in this novel using information from news coverage. I'm indebted to the legend of Russian jewel thief Sonya Golden Hand, who might have found Grace a bit soft.

Thank you first to Susan Golomb and Carole DeSanti; Krista Ingebretson, Soumeya Bendimerad, Christopher Russell, Kym Surridge, Clare Ferarro, Nancy Sheppard, Carolyn Coleburn, and everyone at Viking. To the Helen Zell Writers Program at the University of Michigan and the many writers who've supported me there: Nick Delbanco, Michael Byers, Doug Trevor, and especially Eileen Pollack, Peter Ho Davies, and V. V. Ganeshananthan, tireless champion. To the Hopwood Program, which gave me a boost when I most needed it. To my fellow students: Let us raise a glass in an empty Skeeps. Others encouraged me more than they know: Charlie Baxter, Julia Fierro, Valerie Laken, and Jess Row.

Love and thanks to the friends who lent their gimlet eyes to these pages over the years: Anna Brenner, Tessa Brown, Nania Lee, Anna Sheaffer, Maya West, and extra (infinite!) gratitude to Katie Lennard. Thanks to Sharon Pomerantz, Jeremiah Chamberlin, Aline Rogg, and Molly Kleinman, whose doors were always open, and to Gina Balibrera. To my family, who made me this way, especially my grandmother Joan, who watched *Antiques Roadshow* with bated breath. To every single one of my friends: you are the truest hearts, the wildest minds. To my husband, the whole valley of love.